THE DEFENDER SERIES

SERA
DEFENDER OF FIRE

One Hero…One Destiny…One Great Adventure

AMANDA GRAINGER

Mapseeker Publishing

First published 2014

Copyright © Amanda Grainger, 2014

All rights reserved. No part of this book may be reprinted or reproduced or utilised in any form or by any electronic, mechanical or other means, now known or hereafter invented, including photocopying and recording, or in any information storage or retrieval system, without the permission in writing from the publishers and copyright owners.

Published by Mapseeker Archive Publishing Ltd,
Mapseeker Studio, 30 High Street, Aldridge, Walsall, WS9 8LZ
Tel: +44 (0)1922 288111 / +44 (0)1922 458288

Printed by Berforts Information Press Ltd
23-25 Gunnels Wood Park, Gunnels Wood Road, Stevenage, Herts SG1 2BH
Tel: 01438 312777

The moral right of the author has been asserted
British Library Cataloguing in Publication Data.
A catalogue record for this book is available from the British Library.

ISBN 978-1-84491-841-6

Artwork created by John Robinson and Stephen Moran
Typesetting by Adrian Baggett

Dedications

I would like to dedicate this book to my husband Paul, my parents, Janette and Paul and my sister Angela.

Acknowledgements

You know who you are... without you it would not have been possible.

PROLOGUE

MAURA

Her dark cloak billowed out behind her as she walked across the crumbling stone floor. The castle was icy and formidable, just like her cold, cruel heart.

It stood on a remote strip of desolate wasteland, surrounded by Lake Geneva, in Switzerland. Once a place of beauty and tranquillity, renowned for its magical properties. But not now. Not in her rule.

The castle itself was vast and spacious. It was once imploringly beautiful. The magnificent towers stood so tall it would make you dizzy to stand and gaze upon them. They were rounded and perfectly balanced with two slightly smaller buildings at either side. Both were round with cone-shaped roofs and two long, thin windows at the front. The towers were now crumbling from the years of neglect and the once white marble now greys with time and small amounts of moss creep by the sides from the years of standing by the brutal lake.

Behind these three magnificent towers sat a group of smaller buildings, all different in size, each with different purposes. They were once the houses for the servants and merchants that once thrived in this kingdom. They were surrounded by an enormous courtyard which sat out front.

This space was once peaceful, filled with rose bushes, colorful flower beds and fountains that made the air around the castle smell sweet. Now it was littered with decaying bushes, deserted patches of ground and rubble. No plant life could survive here.

A huge wall, half as high as the towers themselves emerged from the lake and surrounded the palace and courtyard. It travelled around, encasing the two watch towers and met at the Iron Gate with the draw bridge at the front. One watch tower had crumbled away from years of neglect whilst the other remained intact, heavily guarded by the Spirit Slaves.

These poor souls are fallen Defenders, mortals murdered by Maura's hand to remain trapped in her service until she is defeated. Forced to do Maura's bidding against their wishes, they are unable to fight the power she has over them.

The Iron Gate was the only entrance and exit that led directly into the palace grounds, unless you decided to climb the outside walls which would be suicide. The grounds were separated from the mainland by a narrow, long stone bridge that went directly over the lake. This kept the castle isolated and made it very hard for anyone unknown to cross its boarders.

People would once travel for days to gaze upon its beauty or rub the once lucky statue in the middle of the courtyard. The magnificent statue of a king slaying a roaring lion, now stood abandoned, choked by vines, with debris scattered around it. It was placed in the middle of the courtyard over three hundred years ago by the people of this land as a symbol of luck - erected after the ruler at that time, King Kar, had defeated the lion in a deadly battle.

It had attacked his kingdom, killing many, until Kar had slain it. The statue became the kingdom's most magical and, most believed, lucky symbol. It was well looked after, cleaned every day before Maura took control of the kingdom. Now it stood neglected, a symbol of danger and dark times as it crumbled away with each passing year.

Everything that had once made the kingdom great had gone. The castle's once white marble walls stood gray and weather beaten, an aura of decay lingering around them. The main tower's cone shaped roof slanted down to the one side, and it was infested with gargoyles, harpies and vultures.

These dark creatures were under the power of Maura Lilith, who was known as 'The Dark Spirit of the Night'.Rumours of her cruel punishments and ability to control the spirit world had circled the lands. Legend says that she was once a beautiful and caring tribal leader. Her people prospered under her rule until greed for power and evil corrupted her heart.

Her castle was now a place of constant misery and gloom. No one,except the brave and daring, tried to venture over the boundaries into the castle grounds. Those that did never returned.

High up in the main tower of the castle, Maura paced around an ominously glowing dark stone basin known as the Scrying Font, wringing her hands in frustration.

The circular, dimly lit room occupied the entire top floor of the tower. There was only one long, thin window, which let in a small sliver of light. The rest of the room was lit by tall pillar candles mounted upon the walls.

In the centre of the room lay The Scrying Font. It was a large, hexagon shaped basin, raised on a platform standing a rich, red velvet rug. It was deep, filled with a strange oil-like liquid and had extraordinary rune-like symbols inscribed along its top edges. It held amazing powers that she, the world's most powerful ruler, was only just beginning to uncover.

She had taken it from the Wizard prophet Mojo, who was said to be one of the greatest wizards of all time. Of course, Maura knew better, he was nothing more than a drunken misfit with only two talents: prophecy and that of realm travel. These powers were minor compared to her own.

She had sought him out four years ago when she had travelled to the Wizard's Town in Belgium to enlist the help of this so-called 'world's greatest wizard'. Yet she had met nothing but disappointment, as he had refused to help her take control over the realms. She punished him for his refusal by taking his family away from him. She had also taken the Scrying Font for good measure, knowing that his powers would dwindle into nothing without it.

He, of course, had tried to save his wife and daughter from her wrath but failed in the attempt. She demanded once more for his help and when he refused again she had his wife and daughter killed before him, leaving him to live with his guilt.

She now stared into the Font and the green liquid inside swirled beneath her powerful gaze. Three of the symbols of time, prophecy and power,glowed on top of the basin. An image began to form. This, Maura knew, was of the one who was destined to either join her or destroy her. She was only a baby, by the look of her maybe a month old and not yet a threat. But she soon would be.

The Fates had told her only days before of the girl's existence. At first, she was in a rage from hearing the news. She was not going to lose control and power over what she had. Initially she was scared by the words the Fates had spoken because she knew of their power to foresee the future.

The Fates were the most outstandingly beautiful women imaginable, which made them even more dangerous and deadly. Maura knew from experience the more beautiful something was the more deadly it could become.

The first Fate, Octavia, was the tallest and the smartest, being the fate of the past she had experience in what not to do. She had long silky blonde hair that floated around her slim body and seemed to flutter as if moved by a constant breeze. Her skin was copper brown and smooth. Of all the Fates she was the deadliest, having all the knowledge of the past.

The second Fate, Dara, had curly caramel hair that she had pinned up into an elegant twist with tendrils loosely draped around her shoulders. She had a sweet and gentle face, like an understanding mother, and she was deemed the kindest of the three. She was the Fate of the present.

The third, Alexandra, was the most valuable to Maura for she was the Fate of the future. She was curvy but taught and easily the dimmest of the three. She had the most amazingly bright green eyes. Her choppy black hair swung wildly at the sides of her chin and her skin was pale, like milk, but her cheeks were pink and rosy.

The Fates were perfectly balanced and bound to the earth. The threads of destiny spun themselves on an ancient wooden spindle connected the earth's core, the most magical connection to Mother Nature. The Fates, having been blessed by her, were given the power to spin the threads and see the future. They could not be biased or tilt the destiny of the world in any one direction. They alone could see the destiny of each thread, but could not change it in any way.

Having discovered the key to their location from one of her trapped souls, Maura visited the Fates and asked them about her destiny. Only those who are chosen, or in her case take the key to their Realm, obtain the knowledge of their location.

Before Maura had the chance to ask, Alexandra spoke.

"I have seen the beginnings of a new prophecy…" Instantly she began to recite like she had no control, "By the next planetary alignment a choice shall be made".

As if in response the middle Fate, Dara, instantly became rigid and a strangled voice seeped from her lips."The rise of the light by the sun or the fall of night into complete darkness, to aid or end the reign of the spirit of the night".

"Shush now!" Octavia reprimanded, hitting Dara over the head with a clenched fist, "We're not supposed to tell!"

Maura knew all prophecies recited would be written upon a scroll and sent to the Prophecy Keeper. Only he had the power to choose who was worthy of hearing them. It made her angry. Not hearing it in full meant she would now have to find the Prophecy Keeper.

"I demand you tell me!" Maura bellowed angrily at the Fates refusal, "I am the true ruler of the earth and you will bow to my will!" She slashed her hand through the air, causing a deep gash on Octavia's cheek.

"We are our own masters! Leave now before your destiny is turned upside down," she hissed back in anger.

Maura immediately changed her tactics. Taking a step back from the tallest Fate, she softened her face into a small smile, her eyes glazed as if she was about to cry, and she tilted her head to one side. She gazed pleadingly up through her lashes like a shy and innocent young girl, raised her hands as if in prayer and looked directly at the most valuable Fate, Alexandra.

"A name is all I ask of you, my dear, sweet, powerful Fates. I will leave here if you will be so merciful as to just give me a name" she said sweetly smiling. She just had to know the name of the one who would be making the choice, the rest she could find out herself.

"A name has not yet been given to her," Octavia said. Maura sank into a deep, void of despair. How could she find her?

"The Scrying Font will help you," Alexandra laughed wildly before being hit over the head by Octavia.

"Shut up!" The other two Fates shouted, bewildered by the stupidity of their sister.

Maura had returned to her castle, dejected and slightly frightened by this news, and had spent months figuring out how to make the Scrying Font show her the one she needed to see.

Finally, after numerous attempts at deciphering the runes around the Font, she had managed to see the image of the baby girl destined to join or destroy her.

The planetary alignment was due to happen in twenty one years and the Fates had not told her the choice that would be made. This girl had to be destroyed. Maura couldn't risk leaving her alive. But first she had to find her.

Maura frowned at the girl's image in the liquid, pondering her identity. She hadn't yet figured out how to use the full powers of the Font. It had taken her three months since seeing the Fates just to figure out how to get it to show her the image.

"Mojo!" She screamed in frustration and outrage.

He would know exactly how to find this girl! If only he would help her! How could she make him help? She had already taken his family and magical items, what else could be done? Who else did he care for?

She glanced down at the glittering garnet ring on her middle finger and smiled eerily. She fingered the magical jewel, deep in thought, then waved her hand out towards to floor.

Out from the shadows cast upon the floor, rose a head, followed by shoulders, and then the full body of a Dark Elf.

The Elf was at least three feet taller than an average man, with a face that would make the toughest of soldiers cower. The bright gaze of his piercing red eyes would haunt anyone's dreams for weeks. These were the creatures that nightmares were made of and they were completely under Maura's control.

The Elf took a step forward and stooped down to kneel. His filthy blue cloak fluttered around him as his spiritual energy converged into a solid form and he bent so low at Maura's feet, that his pointed nose touched the ground.

"What is your wish my Highness?" The Elf asked in a rough voice that would make the hairs on anyone's neck stand on end.

"Rise!" she bellowed. "Go to the Wizard's Town and bring me

Mojo. Do not fail me!" She clapped her hands in dismissal and turned back to the Scrying Font.

The Font began to glow a bright red color, bringing a new image immediately to her attention. The new scene was of a young couple sneaking past the open drawbridge and running for cover across the open courtyard. They were carrying backpacks and looked like they had been travelling for a few days. She looked closely and saw that the woman glowed faintly with the aura of a Defender!

Maura had fought for three hundred years against The Defenders of the Elements, and she was growing tired of them. They tried to overthrow her every few years but so far had yet to prevail.

She wasn't worried about these two, however. Defenders were all the same, young, new to the world of power and unwise. The woman's aura of power was weak for a Defender and her companion was hot-headed. He would be their downfall.

The Fates had already decreed the one who could overthrow her. These two were like a pair of flies that simply needed swatting. She watched them with interest as they ran through the castle grounds,stopping and crouching behind a dragon shaped rock to catch their breath. They were arrogant, thrilled and triumphant at having not been seen by the dark creatures on the castle roof above.

Maura snapped her fingers and summoned the spirits of tormented souls. These were easy for her to control and a single touch from them was deadly to mortals. She continued to watch as the two Defenders squatted beside one another, blissfully unaware that they had already been detected. Their fate was sealed.

LOSS

KENT

I passed my water bottle to Talia and touched her dirty face. She was breath-taking. So beautiful, even now after a week of constant monster attacks and sleeping rough. We'd been travelling for the past two weeks on our mission to reach the tower and retrieve the stolen Scrying Font and somehow she still looked like a Goddess.

I prayed to any of the Gods to survive what we were about to do. I love my wife dearly; we have been married for three years now, and I would do anything to keep her safe. She smiled sweetly at me and took the bottle. I watched as she took a big swig and poured some on to her hands.

I shifted my weight onto my back leg and peered over a dragon shaped rock to see if we were still safe and had not been spotted by the foul creatures that littered the roof.

I could see the main tower from this spot. It seemed to loom ominously, as if it was leaning over, searching for us, an omen of the doom that was surely to come. I squinted up towards the towers roof. The evil creatures were sleeping so we had not yet been detected.

I took another long look around the vast courtyard for a way in when I spotted the lucky statue lying on its side, covered with dying vines. I remembered my mother, Ruby, telling me the story of King Kar and the Lion and when I was younger.

We had spent most of the day crouching low behind decaying bushes and crumbling rocks trying to reach the castle grounds without being seen. We were dirty, cold and tired. It had been a dangerous journey and so far we had been lucky not to have been spotted by Maura's slaves. I knew that any one of her ghastly creatures could be watching and preparing to attack but the Slaves were the most dangerous of them all.

Now we had finally reached the border, my heart felt heavy with doubt and despair. What if I couldn't get my wife to safety? What would happen to my family then? Talia turned to look at me, and in that brief moment when our eyes met, she seemed to guess what I was thinking.

"Don't worry, my love. We were born to do this. We'll survive and we *will* prevail. You heard the prophecy for yourself. We're destined to end this!" Pride burst forth with every word she spoke.

I had always admired her optimism; I kissed her lightly on the forehead and then buried my worried face in her silky hair.

"We didn't hear all of the prophecy though," I mumbled, looking at her.

"You worry too much," she giggled, still amazingly full of hope.

I didn't want to worry her nor let her to see the doubt that I felt. It's not that I doubted my friend Mojo's powers, we had simply not heard the whole prophecy as the Wizard's Town was under attack when we had arrived, and he could not complete the reading. This worried me a lot. I knew that prophecies always had double meanings and were full of riddles. What is said is not necessarily what is meant.

"We need to move on now," Talia said as she knelt up to gaze over the rock.

"Wait!" I hissed back.

I rose once more onto the balls of my feet as I pushed her back towards the ground. I peered over the rock and jumped back in alarm. Grabbing hold of Talia, I pulled her back and onto her feet.

"Run!" I screamed as two pairs of ghostly white hands made a grab for us straight through the rock.

A yelp escaped from Talia as she stumbled to her feet. Holding hands, we ran straight towards the castle as fast as our legs would allow us.

I glanced behind me to see where the ghosts were and tripped over a dead shrub that sprung up from the ground. It began wrapping long, thin, decaying vines around my ankle. I tugged at the shrub and reached for my weapon, which I always kept in my jacket pocket close to my chest.

I looked up just in time to see Talia stop in alarm, her chest heaving and watching in horror as I hit the floor. She reached out her hands towards me and her face became calm and focused with concentration.

I knew she was searching within herself to summon all her power. A wave of concentrated water shot straight out from her outstretched hand, hitting the vines that were pulling at my leg. They instantly recoiled and sank back into the now muddy earth.

I jumped to my feet and ran towards her. We had miss-understood the prophecy and felt now more than ever that we were going to die here. I was determined not to let that happen.

The eerie looking ghosts circled around us like a pack of wild dogs going in for a kill. We were now trapped. I searched around wildly looking for a way to escape, for my powers were not yet as strong as Talia's. I couldn't even summon my element properly yet! I held on tightly to Talia with one hand and held up my weapon to chest height. Hopefully they would back off at the sight of it, after all, my mother once owned this!

"Get back!" I shouted, swinging my weapon wildly. "I will use this!" I shouted with all the confidence I could muster.

The ghostly creatures threw back their heads and laughed cruelly at me. This was not a reassuring sight! One of the creatures glided forward, she seemed to be looking directly at me through big empty black holes where her eyes had once been.

"You fool!" She laughed. "We cannot be defeated by a mere stick!"

These creatures were undoubtedly the most terrifying things I had ever seen. I wanted to recoil and hide behind something, but I couldn't. Talia needed me. I drew my weapon higher feeling Talia at my side clearly raising hers, a sword that was given to her by the mermaids of Magical Lagoon. She was ready to strike.

The ghosts advanced on us in one swift swoop, darting down faster than I thought possible. The air around us became thinner. Puffs of condensation escaped our mouths as the air became icy cold.

I slashed with all the might and strength I could as my fingers began to freeze around the hilt of my weapon. I managed to hit one of the ghosts straight through its middle and it instantly evaporated into mist, letting in a wave of warm air. One of the ghosts stopped still with shock. I slashed again and again, like a madman, until I heard a blood curdling scream. Fear shot straight into my heart. It didn't belong to any of the ghosts. It was Talia!

I turned just in time to see her clutching her chest. One of the ghosts had reached her and its hand was sticking straight through her body, directly over her heart. A cruel smile spread across its face, and I lashed out with all the strength I had, immediately evaporating the cursed thing.

Talia glanced over at me, with a knowing expression of what had just happened, as she crashed to the ground. Rage shot through my entire body as I ran towards the rest of the ghosts, slashing and ripping my weapon through the air until every last one had turned into a misty vapour. The air around us became breathable and warm once more.

I knelt down at Talia's side, holding her body close to mine, and whistled loudly between my two free fingers.

"Hold on Talia, hold on! You'll be okay!" Oh no! Please don't let her leave me! I sobbed as I scooped Talia up from the floor and into my arms.

Tears were rolling down my cheeks thick and fast, making it hard for me to see as I looked up towards the castle.

The tall figures of the Dark Elves emerged from its main double doors. They held huge black bows with quivers of, what I knew to be, poisoned arrows. I paced backwards clinging onto Talia, my heart pounding in my chest. I should not have let her talk me into coming here! I should have made her stay behind until we knew more! My face was burning with the effort of holding her up, and the sight of these creatures shot terror straight through me.

I had fought these before and they were not as easy to kill. The figures were advancing too quickly. I was going to die and so was the love of my life. If she went then my life would no longer be worth living.

Then I heard the flapping of enormous wings; the sound of hope. Peanut! I looked up as a magnificent chocolate brown winged horse landed with a soft thud on the ground in front of us.

I pushed Talia onto its back and jumped up behind, just as a poisoned arrow flew straight past my left arm missing me by mere inches.

Peanut flapped his enormous wings, ready to spring into the air. The Dark Elves were getting closer and I slashed the air with my weapon one last time, hitting three of the advancing creatures. They stumbled backwards hitting the ground as Peanut shot off into the air with outstanding speed.

I took a final look back at the castle and watched its outline fade into the distance as I clung to my wife's fading body.

MAURA LILITH

I watched as the couple flew away and laughed violently. Stupid people always think they can come here and defeat me! I swirled the pool's light away and moved away from the Font.

The woman's spirit would be mine in less than an hour; her life force was fading quickly. Her soul had been critically injured by one of my Spirit Slaves and would soon die. The Defender will become a prisoner of mine to be held in the spirit world, just like so many other Defenders before her, until I have no more use for her.

The man would be taken care of by my Dark Elves they wouldn't dare fail me again! I began to pace slowly around the cold, darkened room, thinking about the more important issue at hand: the one who may over-throw me!

"Tormitus!" I shouted in a shrill voice that would frighten the bravest of warriors.

I heard the flapping of wings as the bird-like creature approached me. I watched with disdain as it settled itself on the carved stone table. He raised his old, human head and looked at me with beady eyes. His hair was grey and wiry looking. He was a creature that had always saddened me.

He looked up at me, squawking in answer,and then buried his head back into his feathery wings. I watched him clawing nervously at the table with his bird like feet as a new plan formed in my mind.

"Stop that….. I have a job for you," I smirked wickedly.

SIXTEEN YEARS LATER

SERAPHINA

The flame was rising higher and higher, spiralling upwards the more I watched it. The open fire pit in the middle of the living room was lit and I was staring at it in an increasing panic. I had to regain control of my emotions; I could not afford to have another accident.

I was agitated with myself as I was about to disobey Grandma yet again! She had told me not to leave the house without her permission. I wasn't sure it was the right thing to do, but I had been left with no choice. I'm not a bad person, but try being eighteen and treated like you're still seven. If you knew Grandma you'd understand. In fact I don't think there's a teenager on the planet who doesn't have to put up with an over protective guardian or parent.

Conflicted feelings just made my ability worse. You see, I'd discovered when I was younger that I have a strange talent to influence fire. From making a candle flame dance to producing it upon my palms. I know what you've thinking: What a freak! Believe me, I feel the same.

At first I thought it was pretty amazing, until I accidentally set fire to Grandma's rug, which of course I then had to replace before she found out. It scared me more than anything else has or, I'm sure, ever could! The way it had burnt so fast absolutely terrified me. One thing was for sure, I had learned to respect the dangerous power of fire.

I hadn't dared tell anyone about it. I mean seriously, white coats and padded cells come to mind! No one would believe me anyway. This was also the time when I realised I had absolutely no control over my ability.

I had experimented a little bit, trying to figure out how I did it and how I could control it, but had come up with nothing. No explanation what-so-ever. Which was infuriating! Watching the flame rising in the fire pit, I realized I still couldn't control it, and putting it out wouldn't work either. It would only relight itself again! I was sure sometimes that I had an evil spirit who enjoyed tormenting me by relighting things.

The only option was to leave the house or meditate to calm myself down. Not an easy thing for me to do. Grandma always said I was too hot-headed and emotional for my own good. Sometimes she's right, but of course I would never tell her that. Don't get me wrong, I love Grandma. I just had a *tiny* problem with authority.

I gazed up at the small mahogany clock on the wall. I started to panic at the time and the flame beside me danced with glee. If I was going to go, I needed to leave in five minutes

"Decisions, decisions," I said to the empty room.

My heart started to race and the flame next to me shot so high I stumbled backwards,losing my balance and landing on my back. I propped myself up onto my elbows,wincing slightly,and watched the flames from my spot on the floor in fear. I needed to leave before I ended up setting Grandma's house on fire.

With that thought in mind I jumped to my feet, grabbed my mini leather jacket and headed for the door, pausing briefly in the hallway to check my reflection in the mirror.

My tan immediately caught my eye. It was looking good thanks to my job, especially with this top. I was wearing my favorite white cotton, long sleeved blouse, which rested just below my hip line and down my back in a V shape.

This was,my best friend Tiffany's, favorite top too and she had been trying for the last two years to get her hands on it. I twisted in the mirror so I could see the back, where my auburn hair hung in a long wave.

It was my best asset and it had a gloriously satisfying habit of curling around at the ends. Combined with my white top, the tan on my face glowed even more. It's hard being auburn and being teased at school by the other girls with bright blonde locks, but I actually like my hair color. It makes my chestnut colored eyes stand out more. My father always said I had my mother's eyes.

I pulled my jacket over my arms and chuckled at the memory of Grandma's face when she first saw it. Its soft leather had that glorious new smell and it was embellished with silver studs and buckles. Grandma had a huge fit over it, commenting on how I looked like a 'dangerous thug'. It matched my skinny black jeans fabulously, although they were starting to fade slightly. Hmmm... maybe I should go shopping.

I stared at my reflection, pondering what I was doing, absent-mindedly fingering the pendant on my necklace. This was a routine whenever I got upset or knew I was going to upset Grandma. I just didn't like upsetting her!

She had given it me on my tenth birthday and I have treasured it since. It was one of the most beautiful things anyone had ever given to me. It was made from white gold and rose quartz, circular in shape with an engraved pentagram in the middle. My favorite part of it was the six tiny symbols etched around the outside of a five sided star. Three of these I knew to be earth, fire and water, but I never really understood what the other three meant.

It always made me feel better somehow, maybe because

Grandma had told me it had protective and healing powers. The thought of her made me wince once more as the flame from the fire pit spiralled dangerously, threatening to spill over the hearth. Without thinking I bolted out of the door and up the driveway before guilt could trap me there.

I walked up the drive debating with myself whether I should go back or not. I pulled my jacket closer round my chest to fend off the bite of the night's chilly air. This, however, was mainly due to the wind over the lake that ran past our log house and I knew it would warm up as soon as I got past it.

I strolled casually beside the lake, watching the calm ripples moving slowly, almost lazily, before heading for the nearby forest when I heard a noise. I stopped still, the crack of a branch behind me set my heart pounding. I turned around slowly.

"Who's there?" No answer.

It must have been an animal. The forest has all kinds of them roaming around. Even so, I quickened my pace and clutched my jacket more firmly around me. It didn't take too long before I found myself on the long main road that snaked down to the town of Copalis Crossing, where Tiffany lives. Tiffany's really lucky as she owns her own apartment, a graduation gift from her parents. She had asked me to share with her, but Grandma refused, using the old gilt trip of being on her own. Ha! Like she would ever need my protection. Everyone in Town loves her.

After forty minutes I was only a mile or so away but couldn't help glancing back over my shoulder. I had the strangest feeling someone or something was watching me. Maybe I was being paranoid from all the sneaking around I was doing. After twenty more nervous minutes I finally reached my destination and, with a sigh of relief, pushed the front door wide open.

I was glad I'd disobeyed Grandma in some ways because this party was rocking. It was *amazing!* Loads of people were there. I probably sound like a bad granddaughter, leaving to go to the party, but I'm not really. I have a great amount of respect for my grandma. She has, after all, raised me single handed for the past several years! She has given me everything I could possibly need. It's just that sometimes her tendency to protect me ends up holding me back socially. She just didn't understand how important things like this are to me.

The party was the hottest event of the month and I couldn't have missed it! To be really honest I don't actually like parties, but in a small town like this social standing is everything. I promised myself that I wouldn't stay long anyway as I really didn't want to upset Grandma or feel her wrath if she discovered the truth.

Besides, the music and chatter of happy people was so loud it was hurting my ears. It actually made me feel a bit disoriented. Too much noise in such a small place wasn't very good. I have always struggled with things like that, loud noise and busy enclosed places. I've often wondered if I'm claustrophobic.

I did know, however, that I had to be careful. Any kind of slip in my emotions, good or bad, and I could have lost what little control I had over my ability. That would've been bad. Any flames near me would have just spiralled out of control. That wouldn't have been good in a room full of people, and especially not when I was standing next to my very best friend Tiffany who liked to wear a lot of hairspray.

Tiffany and I had met on our first day of kindergarten. We sat at the same table. I asked her if I could use her red crayon, and we had been inseparable ever since. She is calmer than me and very shy, maybe that's why we get on so well. She has also kept me from doing some pretty embarrassing things in the past. I'm immensely grateful to have her as a friend.

We were tucked into the corner of a small, dimly lit room. I felt agitated now! I was wishing that she would get a move on and ask the guy she was flirting with out on a date so we could go and dance and get out into an open space.

I gazed nervously at the flame of a candle that sat close by and started to sulk. The flame began to sway, as if dancing to the music. I concentrated on it next to me, trying to vent some of my annoyance through it. It responded by flickering,then slowly rose by an extra couple of centimetres. I jumped nervously as I realized how dangerous that was!

The sound of Tiffany's laughter broke my concentration and I looked over at her. I hadn't even told Tiff about what I could do. She was throwing her head back in laughter, flicking her long dark hair flirtatiously and holding onto the guy's arms.

I glanced back at the flame as it flickered and died down. I turned toward Tiff, making sure the candle was behind me. I watched her trying to think about something else. I needed to control myself. I thought about how we had been inseparable since we were six and the stuff we used to do. Like the time we painted my cat, Hiccup, blue and when we made mud pies with Grandma's best china. I chuckled at the memories and instantly felt calmer. We had helped and supported each other for years. In high school, Tiff used to help me get through science and in return,I helped her get through Math. I still to this day don't know how we made it to our graduation!

We even work together at the beach now. Being life guards was the perfect job for us. Who wouldn't want to save people's lives and get a great tan at the same time? We were going to have so much fun, although reality kicked in after a few weeks of work and Tiffany changed her mind and preferred the less glamorous-side of the job. She became the administrator in the life guard's beach hut instead, leaving me to get that perfect tan on my own. I think that was the first time ever that we'd done something separately!

However, we did still manage to work it so we had lunch together every day. I loved her to bits but sometimes, like now, she was really annoying and I would end up losing my patience with her. The thing is, I have quite a short temper, which usually gets me into a lot of trouble. Thankfully Tiff knew and understood that.

I'd stood there for almost half an hour just watching her chat to someone she'd had a huge crush on for years. Unfortunately for her it didn't look like it was going too well. She had become nervous and had started to babble.

After ten minutes, Tiffany finally grasped that she was failing miserably with her attempt at flirting and returned to me sullen faced. She handed me a large glass of coke and smiled sheepishly at me.

"Here, you look like you need this," she smiled and I took the glass from her gratefully and gulped it down.

"I can see you're uncomfortable. Do you want to go home?" She asked frowning slightly.

"Yeah, I feel awful. Grandma would be so upset with me if she found out I was here," I said.

"Wow! Did you see that?" she squealed. "That flame just jumped!"

I turned toward the candle letting out a derisive giggle, "It must be a sparkling candle. They sell those at Martin's," I said nervously. "Come on let's go dance."

Tiff looked momentarily stunned by my abrupt change of mind but shrugged it off as I pull her over to the opposite side of the room, away from the candle and the naked flame.

"You're strange sometimes, do you know that?" She smiled playfully.

"Why'd you say that?"

"I've noticed you're nervous around open flames. Are you afraid of fire?"

I shrugged nonchalantly, "I guess so, a little. Who wouldn't be?" I said avoiding her gaze.

She eyed me skeptically for a moment and I prayed for a distraction. I spotted the buffet table just as my prayer was answered in the form of a high shrill female voice.

"Tiff!" The voice rang.

We both turned to see Catrina, a friendly girl from the main office in The Hut. I smiled at her and pointed at the buffet, to display where I was heading, as she pushed her way through the crowded room to join Tiff. I hurried off, determined to escape, glancing behind me to see them hugging and giggling together.

I reached the table and grabbed the first thing I saw, a sandwich. It was hard and felt like it had been there all day. I sniffed it then took a brave bite. Big mistake. It was revolting! I made a dash for the nearest trash can and threw it in just as someone tapped me lightly on the shoulder.

"Hey you. I'm surprised to see you here."

I turned round to see our good friend Dean. He went to school with Tiff and me but left in our last year to attend a trendy art school in England. I smiled sweetly at him, taking in his torn, paint-splattered jeans and faded black shirt. He hadn't changed - even his hair was still longer than mine and jet black. He held a scruffy-looking note pad and there was a pencil perched behind his ear.

"Dean!" I squealed, hugging him hard. "When did you get back?"

"About an hour ago I called your gran's but there was no answer." He shrugged and took my hand firmly, "Then I bumped into Mrs McGee from the post office and she said you might be here."

Another annoyance of living in a small town - everyone knew everything. I started wondering if Mrs McGee would tell Grandma I was here!

"Well here I am," I laughed as he pulled me down onto the sofa next to the buffet table.

"Where's Tiff?" He asked, looking around the room and grabbing a sandwich from the pile.

"Oh she's here somewhere and I wouldn't eat that if I were you."

He smiled widely and took an enormous bite from the sandwich anyway. *Boys!* I looked around the room still giggling at his now appalled face. Where had she gone? She was here a moment ago.

"Oh!" I exclaimed, "She's over there." I pointed over to the garden patio where Tiff was sat at a table with a disheartened expression. I felt a twinge of sadness deep in my stomach as I watched her. What was wrong with her? She was fine a moment ago.

"She doesn't look too happy." Dean frowned slightly.

"She was fine a minute ago. She was talking to Catrina," I said feeling a wave of protectiveness.

"I'm guessing she upset her then?"

"I don't know," I replied. I looked down at my feet. I could feel his eyes on me for a few seconds. Then he pulled me up to stand.

"Come on, let's go find out and see if we can cheer her up," he said, smiling sweetly. He really was a good friend to both of us.

I made my way through the crowd holding onto Dean's hand when the edge of a chair caught my foot and sent me flying towards the floor. The crowd around me started to cheer and laugh. My face burned with embarrassment. I jumped up and gave Dean a quick dig in the ribs for laughing at me.

I reached for his hand to pull him outside, clasping it firmly so he couldn't let go, and felt a large ring on his middle finger. It made me stop and take a closer look.

"Wow! That's really nice. Where did you get it?"

It was plain and made from white gold, like my necklace, but sparkled as if it was made of diamond. In the centre of the ring was a small symbol that resembled three swirls that intertwined onto each other. It was mesmerising to look at.

He chuckled a little nervously and withdrew his hand from mine quickly. "It's from a friend," he said glancing to the floor.

"Come on let's get Tiff.

Tiff spotted us then, and like me, she squealed and ran over to him. I smiled at them and continued to look around me. I was looking for that one person I was really hoping was here.

Then I spotted him and my heart skipped a beat! The glorious eyes of Joey Parkinson were fixed on me and me alone!

THE INTERVIEW

SERAPHINA

Joey was my boss, my mentor, my good friend and everything I could ever hope to be. He was the manager of The Hut, which wasn't surprising really as his family owned it, and I was utterly and uncontrollably in love with him head over heels.

Ever since I had first seen him my heart had beat twice as fast. I'd become flushed with excitement every time I clapped eyes on him. I'm not joking or being super soppy! I seriously felt like this, each and every time I saw him. People would laugh and say "young love" or "schoolgirl crush", but everyone was in love with him really. They just didn't admit it.

I remember the day I had gone for my interview. I was, in truth, not just nervous but completely terrified. First job and dream job! It meant everything. My skills, experience and age could have all gone against me. Most life-guards are put through training before they're given a chance, but I was really hoping my many years of swimming lessons and voluntary hours at the local pool were enough to get me through.

Things would only go my way if I worked hard enough. Grandma always drilled that into me: work hard at school, know what it is you want to be and know it inside and out. Only then will you succeed. She's right, of course, and thanks to her encouragement I have built up a lot of experience and knowledge. Although being prepared doesn't mean your nerves are under control, which for me could cause very big problems!

Although I was nervous I had a grim determination. I wanted to get the job because I was good at it and because I had the right skills. I had been training very hard every day since I was eight years old, hoping that one day I would become a life-guard. I had wanted to save lives for as long as I could remember. It was all I have ever wanted to do. I knew why, of course.

When I was younger I lost my mother. Dad had told me once that she had drowned in the lake, and that was why I wasn't supposed to go near it. I was too young to remember the day she died, but I'm sure that's why I felt such a pull towards the lake, almost as if she's calling out to me. That is why I trained myself to become a strong swimmer, so I could help others from suffering the fate my mom had, and not to suffer the same one.

I had felt confident and okay until I got to the interview and had seen everyone else waiting. Then, just like always, self-doubt started to kick in. It coursed through my mind, incapacitating every inch of me. I started to go clammy and hot with fear.

I knew I needed to calm down before my usual habit of hyperventilating and I would end up passing out. I had a habit of doing this whenever I got too wound up or when I lost control of my ability. Of course, I would always end up burning something back then. Thankfully every time I had lost control it was always something small that had got burnt, like Grandma's rug and, thankfully she was not around to see it.

I remembered asking Grandma if there was something wrong with me - epilepsy or something - because I always seemed to black out or faint.

Of course, this was before I had discovered my special ability. Grandma wasn't particularly helpful whenever I did ask her. All she would say was that I had a condition passed down from my Dad and that one day, when I was old enough, I would understand. For years I had thought my blackouts had something to do with getting older and because I was a Basco. It makes you laugh, when you think about all the rubbish grown-ups tell you! Anyway, by now I had learnt some moderate control over it, as well as how to hide it from people. I'd found that if I got too wound up, all I needed to do was control my breathing before my body temperature shot up and I ended up setting something on fire!

So before the interview started I went outside to call Grandma. The air was cool, crisp and felt wonderful on my overheated skin. I took a deep breath, smiling at the familiar smell of sea salt and sand. To be honest, I needed a tiny bit of reassurance which, surprisingly, she was actually really good at, but before I had pulled out my phone I had seen *him* for the very first time!

He was walking toward the main door. A certain aura of strength and importance emanated from him like a glow of warm light. Maybe it was the sun glare from behind him, but you get the picture.

His hair was dark blonde, wavy and hung down to his shoulders. His skin was pale and as he approached me I noticed his eyes were a dazzlingly bright blue and his smile was glorious.

"Hi, you must be Miss Basco. I'm Joey Parkinson." He held out his hand for me to shake, beaming at me.

"Hi," I mumbled, taking his hand and feeling an electric shock travel up my arm.

We stood for what seemed like hours just staring at each other and shaking hands. His eyes were so bright and his frame so muscular and strong. I smiled at him sheepishly then dropped my eyes to the floor. Although the summer air around me was cool, my face burned with overwhelming embarrassment. I was suddenly more aware of the small tea stain on my shirt from that morning.

"Please, come in," he said, waving his hand towards the door of the office. "Unless you were planning on leaving?" He chuckled, arching an eyebrow, obviously referring to the fact I was outside.

"Oh… no, I was just…err never mind," I said, slightly flustered.

I followed him inside where he nodded politely to his receptionist, Catrina, and continued towards his office door. He opened it and gestured for me to go inside. I skirted nervously past him, taking in a deep breath and trying to concentrate on the speech I had prepared.

His office was small but still seemed spacious, with a single solid pine desk in the middle, over loaded with paper work. A black leather chair sat on one side and a smaller, pale blue one on the other. Evidently this had been brought in from the reception just for the interview. I glanced around the small room and noticed the massive double bay window doors that led right out onto the beach front. I watched for a split second as a small boy in red shorts ran by pulling a kite through the sand, covering a nearby woman as he passed. I heard the door click shut behind me and stiffened as Joey squeezed past me.

"Please, have a seat" He walked around his desk and sat gracefully in his seat""Would you like anything to drink?

"No, I'm fine thank you." I sat not-so-gracefully in the seat opposite him.

He chuckled under his breath at my attempt to look elegant and I felt my face burn with embarrassment. I was messing it up before I had even started.

"Are you alright?" he asked smiling. Oh man, his smile was distracting.

"Err… Yes thanks," I said, straightening myself up in the chair and trying to claw back some self-control.

He gazed at me intently. I placed my hands in my lap and twirled my fingers round each other as my mind raced. What do

I say? What do I do? I should have practiced some more interview techniques with Tiff when I had the chance. I looked back up at him as he cleared his throat with a low rumble of a cough.

"So then Miss Basco, or can I call you Seraphina?" He asked, shuffling his papers round his desk.

"Yes. Seraphina or Sera," I said, trying to sound confident.

"So can you please tell me about yourself? What training and experience do you have?" A pen was poised in his hand, hovering over a notepad.

Oh man, I struggled to remember my experience! I started to panic at the first question and felt my face flush again.

"Well…err… I don't really have any experience on a beach front, but I've been volunteering at the local pool for the last two years whilst I was at high school. I mean, I've just finished high school. I graduated top in physical fitness and I am a very strong swimmer. I can swim 400 meters in seven minutes." I blurted it all out.

"Wow! That's impressive Seraphina," he smiled, writing something down on his notepad. I straighten back up, my heart pounding in my chest. My palms had become sweaty with nerves and I tried to wipe them on my trousers.

"Okay," he smiled, "relax, you're doing fine. So, tell me. What are some of your interests and hobbies?"

I laughed out loud in relief at being asked a normal question. He raised an eyebrow at me and I shuffled in my seat.

"Sorry, I was surprised you asked that after that last question."

"Well we do like to know we can get along with future colleagues."

"Oh of course, yes. Well I like to read, mainly science." I stopped at his expression.

"That's interesting." He smiled as he wrote something down.

"I would have thought you were mainly fantasy based considering your *abilities* and mind set," he stated boldly as he crossed his fingers and almost glared at me.

I started to squirm at his almost unfriendly gaze. What did he mean by that? My palms sweated once more under his glare. How could he possibly know what I can do? No one knew that!

"There's no need to look so worried, I merely meant your list of hobbies on your résumé quite intriguing. I thought you would like myth and legend books. I know I do!" He shrugged impassively, looking back down at his clip board.

I squirmed once more with embarrassment. Of course that's what he meant. Way to panic Sera! I *really* needed to stop worrying!

"Why do you believe you would make an excellent lifeguard?" He tried to break the now lengthening silence.

I swallowed hard and took a deep breath."Well, I am devoted to saving lives," I said. It suddenly sounded lame. He raised an eyebrow once more and sighing, wrote something else down. I panicked and blurted out, "I lost my mother to water and I will not let anyone else grow up without a mother or a father if I can help it." I was breathing heavily.

He stopped writing and looked up at me, concern showing in his eyes.

"I'm very sorry to hear that." He placed his hand on mine. A shiver ran up my arm. I blushed and moved my hand away to brush a lose strand of hair out my face and behind my ear.

After this question the interview proceeded with a lot of questions to which I had no real answers which drew a lot of nervous giggles from me. I was losing hope in my dream job. It didn't look like I was going to be offered it. I was about to suggest I leave when he beamed at me with *that* smile.

"Well, from what I've seen here today I'm very confident you'll fit in well here."

I glanced up at him, my mouth hanging open comically, and whooped with joy.

"Really? Oh man.... I don't know what to say," I spluttered, jumping to my feet.

He chuckled. "Well, you can start with 'Thank you and when do I start?'"

I bounced up and down with joy then flung myself at him, hugging him tightly and knocking him back onto his chair. Oh man, why did I do that?! I jumped up quickly and smiled sheepishly.

"I'm sorry... I'll just... err... go now," I stumbled, grabbing my jacket, and headed for the door, still pink faced.

"Miss Basco," he said. My heart sank.

I turned on my heel slowly, regretting my rash behaviour. He was about to rescind his offer.

"Yes, Mr Parkinson?" I whispered.

"You start first thing Monday morning, eight thirty sharp." He sat back down in his chair with an amused smile.

"Err yes, I mean... yes sir, Monday eight thirty." I bounced out of his office and ran out of the building.

I managed to make my way back home in a complete and utter daze. I felt beguiled and bewitched by him. This was a dangerous feeling! When I finally got home I couldn't stop smiling. I told Grandma all about him and the interview and I told her about how he had made me feel - all warm and fuzzy - and how much I liked him. To my dismay she went mad, shouting and stomping around the house, blabbering on about how I had to 'stay professional' and how 'I was not to go throwing myself at him.'- This made no sense to me at all. I wasn't doing that! He was my *boss* now! I tried to calm her down and said that I was nothing but professional and my interest in him was nothing more than professional admiration, to which she replied that I should try to get another job at the local pool! Seriously! What was with *her*?

This was the first of many fights concerning my career. It turned out she didn't want me near the ocean. She was probably just being over-protective like parents and guardians often are… or was it because of my mother?

Over the next few weeks, after accepting the job we actually become great friends and enjoyed each other's company a lot. Unfortunately though, every time we had come close to anything *more* than a professional relationship, Grandma would always seem to pop up out of nowhere and interfere. It's like she had an inbuilt radar or something. In fact, I remember when I was five she told me she had eyes everywhere, including the back of her head. It's only recently that I'd be forgiven for thinking that she actually has. Nothing goes unnoticed by her. Or unpunished.

I had complained to Tiffany, one afternoon over coffee, about how over-protective she was and how she always seemed to appear out of thin air. I always bored her with my complaints about Grandma, and I'm sure she was getting fed up of hearing about it all the time.

However, now I doubted my actions. She was bound to find out that I had disobeyed her and come to this party. Then I'd be in major trouble. I knew Grandma wouldn't be back for hours yet as she was visiting her friend in Olympia but I still started to worry. Maybe I should go home now.

I had called her earlier to reassure her and now I felt guilty about lying. I had promised her that I was just reading and getting an early night and that I wouldn't be going out anywhere. I know it was wrong and I felt awful about it now. A rush of regret hit me. Would I be home before she got back?

WORRIES AND WOES

RUBY

I watched as one squirrel chased another up a tree. Happy, funny little things they are, completely unaware of the dangers around them. They stay nice and safe in their trees, hunt for food when they are hungry, and sleep when they are tired. For a moment I actually found myself envying them. I had to stop thinking like this! Life is life, and some have a harder time than others. It's how you deal with it that makes you who you are. They also wouldn't be here now if it weren't for people like me. People who were actually spending most of their lives protecting forests such as this one.

I actually stood in a small and remote clearing deep in the Olympic National Forest, the home and magical dwelling place of the Woodwives,one of the vital reasons to protect it.

The Woodwives were well hidden and impossible for non-magical folk to find, thanks to ancient protective magic. It was darker and colder now, which made it both the best and worst time for meetings such as the one I was about to have. Best because no one would be wandering around the forest alone this late at night so couldn't stumble across us, and worst because it was the perfect time for the creatures under Maura's control to come out.

A twig snapped from somewhere behind me. I spun around to

see that the squirrel was back again. We stood motionless, watching each other for a moment, before he scurried off, happy with his new find of ripe berries. I glanced down at my watch – eight fifteen. They were late!

I hated it when they were late. It meant I would be away from Seraphina even longer, which, I might add, was not a good thing. That girl caused trouble in her sleep and I hated to think what she could do when I'm not there. I had actually made the mistake of leaving her on her own once before, came back to a different rug and found the old one in the trash, burnt!

I paced up and down, becoming increasingly frustrated the longer I thought about what my granddaughter could be up to. I sighed and took the small silver cellphone out of my back pocket and dialled.

Ring, ring...

Ring, ring...

"*Hello Grandma,*" she answered, her tone indignant.

'Seraphina, what are you doing? It took you ages to pick up."

"I'm fine Gran. I was in the shower. I'm...," she paused, "I'm getting ready to go to bed."

I didn't believe a word she was saying, she didn't go to bed early, at least not *willingly*. I usually had to nag at her for ages before she turned her light off. That's the problem with teenagers - they think they're all grown up!

"Okay..." I replied slowly, "You don't normally go to bed this early."

"I'm not going to bed now! I have some stuff to do first. I'll probably still be awake when you get back...what time you will be back?"

It was my turn to pause and think. I knew she was up to something. I could tell by her voice, but I couldn't leave until I'd seen Dana. I decided on the truth, but with an edge of a warning.

"My friend's running a tad late, so I'm not sure when I'll be home," I said firmly.

She should have been able to tell that I wasn't in any kind of mood for games that night.

"Okay Gran. Don't worry about me. Take your time. I have lots of studying to do anyway," she said cheerfully.

That was the last piece of evidence I needed. She never studied! The only time she ever has was for her precious interview, and that was over.

"Right, Seraphina. You best behave yourself whilst I'm gone. Nothing stupid please," I say vehemently.

"Grandma! Why do you always do this? I'm fine, and I'm not doing anything I shouldn't be doing," she snapped.

I let it go. I couldn't argue with her - it was too dangerous for her to get fired up. She was such a danger to herself. I wondered if I should tell her before it was too late.

"Okay. I trust you. Bed by ten Seraphina! Goodnight," I said softly.

"Goodnight, Grandma."

I stared at the cell for a moment then sighed. I would know if she was doing anything silly anyway as Filbert was watching her.

I continued to wait, growing increasingly restless. I looked back at my watch. Twenty to nine. I hope they haven't gotten into any kind of trouble.

"Ruby," a woman's voice called softly.

I turned to see Dana emerge from out of the trees. Her dark cloak hung around her tall, muscular frame. The hood hid her beautiful face and curly dark hair. As she stepped forward I looked past her through the rest of the trees, searching but finding nothing.

"Are you alone?" The sorrow was clear in my voice as she stepped out from the shadows into the clearing.

"Yes," she stared at me wide-eyed, then gestured for me to sit on a fallen log. "He's fine Ruby. He'll be here in a few days. We got separated on the way back from Argentina, but he's fine. He's been spotted not too far from here," she said as she settled herself down.

Tears of relief welled in my eyes. I hated these missions, unless it was me who was on them. Kent, my only son, had been going on them for years since he'd taken my place as Fire Defender. He had thrown himself into discovering the truth behind the prophecy ever since he'd lost Talia. He was determined to make Maura pay for his loss and keep us all safe.

"How did the mission go? Did you succeed?" I willed my voice becoming firm again. Dana shifted uncomfortably and I knew what she was about to say.

"No… We were ambushed on a gravel road in the valley of the Pinturas River. We were forced to retreat into the caves." Her eyes shifted from side to side, anxiously watching the trees.

We sat for a few minutes in silence, watching the forest around us. Where was he now? Was he safe? What would I tell Seraphina if he wasn't?

My thoughts wandered back to my grand-daughter. I had already been away for too long. It was growing increasingly difficult lately to keep her safe. She was showing more and more signs of the 'Pass Over' and soon it would be too late and she would have to leave. My blood began to boil the more I thought about it. Maura had to go! She couldn't keep destroying people's lives like this!

"What do we do now? Maura is growing stronger and so is Seraphina's power. It won't be much longer either before Maura finds her or before the Pass Over begins," I moaned, fear evident in my eyes.

Dana continued to stare into the dimness of the forest ahead before looking back at me, her expression one of concern.

"There's not much we can do at the moment, Ruby."

I sat in silence, helpless, for what seemed like a life time. There was so much I needed to know, but without the Scrying Font or

Mojo it was impossible.

Our forces had been constantly defeated by Maura since Mojo had... my thoughts trailed off. I tried to remind myself that it wasn't his fault. I couldn't stay angry with him. I had been where he was, and it if wasn't for Kent I would have been lost too.

Dana stood up swiftly and grabbed her bow from her shoulder, notching an arrow from her quiver, ready for release. I followed and grabbed the two small daggers from the sides of my legs.

"What is it Dana?" I scanned the trees around us with intense concentration. I knew she could sense any trouble here before me - that was part of her gifts as a Woodwife.

I waited in silence, the air around me turning sour, like week-old milk left to go bad. My stomach was churning, tying itself in knots. I wrinkled my nose in a poor attempt to block it out. I knew the scent well, I had smelt it a hundred times before.

It was the foul scent of a Troll.

Sure enough, moments later the heavy foot-fall of a Troll could be heard. It shook the ground and the trees began to sway, making squawking birds fly away.

My body tensed up, ready for action. Generally, Trolls travelled at night and alone, unless they had been forced together in groups by Maura.

The trees directly in front of us sprung to one side and the vulgar smell hit my nostrils and made my eyes water. He stood for a second, towering above us, looking more lost than threatening.

He was the biggest Troll I had ever seen, at least twenty feet tall and as wide as a school bus. His chest was bare except for the small amount of hair that covered his bulging belly, which was smattered with dirt and clumps of leaves. A long piece of rope with an assortment of random objects tied to it, hung from his neck. I could see a bicycle wheel, a rubber tyre from a car, and a smashed up shopping trolley, not surprising as Trolls like to collect shiny, round objects.

His dirty face was lumpish and badly bruised, probably from a fight with another Troll. They had a tendency to fight one another - they weren't the brightest of creatures. He took a step forward, lifting his giant sized foot up directly over us. Decayed tree branches and big clumps of moss were caught between his toes. The smell was unbelievable.

Dana watched, perfectly poised. That girl had no fear, ready to release her arrow at a moment's notice. We stood very still and watched as the absent-minded Troll strolled past us dragging a long metal rope attached to a pick-up truck. It reminded me of a small child pulling a toy car along behind them. He paid no attention to us at all, for which I was grateful. I don't like hurting creatures as small-minded as Trolls if I don't have too.

"He's no harm to us," Dana noted. I nodded.

"Where do you think he's going? He's quite far from his home."

Trolls usually stayed up high in the mountains. They hardly ever came down, unless called for. He might have been out for a stroll and gone too far, or he may have been summoned. A feeling of unease washed over me. Maybe we should have stopped him. Even if he wasn't on his way to find Maura he could still cause a lot of casualties if he goes too close to a town.

My thoughts strayed back to Seraphina. She had no idea this world even existed yet, nor of her powers and her cruel destiny which she was going to have to face soon. I had tried several times to tell her, but no time seemed quite right. To be honest I also didn't think she was strong enough yet to cope with it all.

"For now," Dana said, pulling me back from my thoughts, "we need to sit tight... at least until Kent returns." She tagged the second thought on after catching my expression.

"You're right," I sighed. Things will at least be that little bit easier when he returns.

My health had not been good lately - old age was catching up with me. I promised Kent I would look after Seraphina and prepare her for what was to come. After all, I did raise and prepare him, but Seraphina just seems considerably harder work than he ever was.

She was stubborn and far too selfish to understand that what I did was for her own good. This had been causing immense problems ever since her powers had begun to appear. I had watched her closely over the last two years and as her powers had begun tapping into her emotions, such a dangerous mix for a potential Defender. It is unusual for a Defender's powers to latch to emotions. It makes them unstable.

"I think you're needed," Dana said, interrupting my thoughts again.

She nodded her head in the direction of the trees behind us and relaxed her stance. Cubby, the gnome, ran out of the forest cover, panting and clutching at his sides as he gasped for breath.

He bent over holding onto a low branch for support and I went to his side. His childish face was pouring with sweat and his pale green dungarees were torn in several places, most likely from running through thorny bushes. His shirt, under his dungarees, was missing a sleeve and streaks of green ran across his chest. He looked terrible, as if he had taken quite a big stumble - not unusual for him.

I hovered over the young Gnome and smiled adoringly at him. I loved the Gnomes - they were always helpful and good natured, especially this one. He was exceptionally good hearted and eager to prove himself.

He was very young - only fifty two years, still a baby, in Gnome years. But his presence here could only mean one thing; Trouble!

"Mrs Basco, Filbert has sent me to you with a message and I fell down a big hill but I got back up and I am fine. I got here as fast as I could run," he said, his voice high-pitched and childlike voice. "My little legs are tired and hurting but I'm here." He beamed up at me, his cheeks burning red with exhaustion and pride at his achievement.

"Sit down and catch your breath, Cubby." I said warmly and slightly amused. Why didn't he time travel? Gnomes had the power to do that and could appear anywhere in time and space instantly.

I watched as Cubby scrambled over to the log and tried to climb onto it. It would have been quite funny if I wasn't so worried. The log was twice his size, and eventually he gave up and sat himself on the soft grass next to it. He was still young and had not yet gained full powers over the forest. He pulled of his blue boots and moaned, rubbing his feet before removing a small scroll from one of his boots. I suppressed a small laugh at the sight of his big toe sticking out of a hole in his sock.

"Filbert sent you a message," he said, holding out a small scroll and smiling proudly at his mission being accomplished.

I took the scroll from him and let him catch his breath. Dana had wandered towards the edge of the forest where the troll had disappeared and I unfurled the scroll, reading aloud so she could hear:

Dear Mrs Basco,

She has left your home and has made her way through the forest down to the main town. She is now at a party with the other girl. I will watch her until you arrive here.

P.S THAT BAD MAN IS HERE TOO!

Filbert

I look up at Dana, fear sprouting its ugly head at my discomfort.

"You need to go. If he is there alone with her you might already be too late. I'll inform Kent when he arrives," Dana said grabbing her bow from her side and slinging it over her shoulder.

I sprung to my feet, fatigue vanishing at the thought of my granddaughter in danger. I looked over at Cubby, then Dana. She nodded at me and I knew she would make sure Cubby got back home safely. I ran as fast as I could go to the forest edge where I had parked my car, jumped inside and sped off into the night.

JOEY PARKINSON

SERAPHINA

I looked down at my feet, trying to concentrate on controlling my rapid breathing, and peeped upwards through my hair to see Joey. I give him a small, sweet smile as he looked right back at me - his face lighting up. He returned the smile. He was… unbelievably gorgeous.

I had hardly taken a breath before he was manoeuvring around everyone else to get closer to me. I could feel Tiff's eyes on the back of my head and turned to hear Dean gasp.

"Who's that? He looks like trouble!" He spoke protectively. I shook my head at him in disbelief and turned back in Joey's direction.

I stared intently into his eyes and spotted something else - a strange glint I had never noticed before. Something was different about him. His eyes looked darker and I could see why Dean was worried. He made me nervous. I wasn't sure why, but I felt a sudden urge to move away from him. It must be the lighting in here.

Trying to be inconspicuous to those around me I made a quick dash for the door. Worry seemed to climb up my back and cling to my neck, cutting off my supply of oxygen. I felt dizzy as I moved and had the odd sense that I was being followed or watched again by others than those around me.

I stood in the golden glow of the patio lights and looked out over the calming ocean in the distance. I tried to control my breathing. The night's breeze was cool now as it skimmed off the sea, leaving a strong smell of salt in the air. I heard light footsteps behind me and the clink of pebbles being tossed to one side. My heart lurched and began to race.

I turned at the sound and was startled to see how close he was to me. The unease sank slowly back in as his eyes seemed to glow with a faint red color.

"Hi," he said brightly, which made his eyes look less frightening. I relaxed once more.

"Hi," I said weakly.

"You look beautiful," he breathed, and my heart leapt over itself in response.

"Thanks," I mumbled nervously.

"I like your hair this way," he said pulling it from my back and round my shoulder.

My skin tingled by this contact and I giggled nervously. I tried to respond, but before I could I was abruptly shoved to one side by a strong, tanned arm. It was Dean.

"Hi I'm Dean," he said, holding out one hand as the other protectively pushed me slightly behind him.

I glanced at Tiff, who shrugged.

"Hey, I'm Joey," he said slightly surprised, but shook Dean's hand happily.

I glanced at him sideways, apologetically, and his intense blue eyes stared at me.

This is our friend from High School," I said, glaring sideways at Dean who was beaming with satisfaction.

"Yeah, he's an artist," Tiff added in a lighter tone, trying to break the uncertain tension radiating off the two of them.

"Oh yeah, I've seen some of your work. It's good," Joey replied cheerfully, taking a sip of his drink. It was a dark brown liquid, brandy. Maybe whisky? I didn't know he actually drank that kind of stuff.

"Really?"Dean's eyes narrowed in mistrust, "Which one?"

"I think it's a painting of a young girl with black hair," his face narrowed in concentration. "Yeah… she's standing in a lake holding a sword!" Joey stated boldly.

Dean's eyes widened almost in concern at his words. Why did he look so shocked and worried?

Tiff came to stand beside me then, walking directly between the hostile pair. She giggled and took my hand.

"Come on, let's go dance," she said brightly, taking Dean's hand too.

The sudden sound of screeching tyres made us all jump in alarm. I turned with recognition to the sound of *that* car. Immediately, before I had even seen it, I knew who it belonged to. It was my Grandma.

I turned towards the sound, squinting against the glare of the bright headlights. Sure enough, there behind the wheel, sat my Grandma. She looked over at me with a face of pure thunder and gestured, none too kindly, for me to get in. I winced sheepishly, letting go of Tiff's hand, and trudged towards the open car door.

I paused for a second to glance back behind me at Joey with a small apologetic smile. He stared back, disappointment etched on his beautiful face. I turned and carried on walking.

He glowered against the bright glare of the headlights and for a brief moment I thought I saw that strange red glow again. It must have been the light reflecting back at me because it had disappeared as soon as I thought I saw it.

Dean looked positively relieved and waved happily at Grandma who, to my surprise, nodded and waved back.

I slammed the car door, annoyed at both of them. I was so mad at being treated like a kid who needed saving! Joey had already drifted away, moving back towards the party, leaving Tiff and Dean staring after me. I cursed under my breath and stared out of my window, avoiding Grandma's eye as she sped off down the road. It was all so embarrassing!

I sat, stewing in anger. All I could do was stare out of the window, holding back the tears, as we raced home. Grandma would have a raging fit at me in her own time I was sure. I was certainly not going to encourage it by talking to her first. To my utter surprise, she kept completely silent, her eyes fixed on the road ahead of us. Stubborn, just like me! This actually worried me more than if she had started to yell at me. After what seemed like a very long, silent and uncomfortable journey we pulled up outside the house.

Grandma's house was made partly from the old timber of Granddad's sailing boat. When he had married Grandma, he had dismantled his sailing boat, his pride and joy, and used it, alongside new timber, to make a family home. It's all we have left of him now. Over the years my own father helped build some small extensions, and I had been given the small garden inside the gate to look after. I think it was mainly to keep me out of the way as I had a fascination with the plants.

It stood high on the bank of a dark but tranquil lake. The lake has always frightened me, maybe because of my mother's death or maybe because of what was in it. It might sound crazy and superstitious, but I had always believed that something evil lurked in there.

I have a vague memory of being young and playing tea parties with my dolls by the lake. I'd had a profound sense of foreboding by the lake almost like something was watching me play and just waiting for me to get closer. It might have just been my imagination, but I was never brave enough to investigate further. Ever since that day I had always played on the other side of the house, away from the lake's edge. It's only really recently that I've been brave enough to walk past it, but still not too close to it.

The house itself was beautiful. Ivy and roses were intertwined up the sides and around the windows pale blue shutters. It was remarkable to look at, especially first thing in the morning when the sun was rising.

I remember when I came to live here permanently after my mother's death. It had looked so magical. I had spent most of the first day crying for my dad, so Grandma had taken me to the side of the house. Pointing to the ivy she had said,"Life is full of turmoil, loss and trouble, Seraphina. However, if you stay strong you'll prosper like this ivy and grow strong and graceful. You will only survive this world by being strong! Strong minded and strong hearted - that is how our family has managed to survive for so long. Now, you must pull yourself together and concentrate on the prospects of being in a new place. You can become whoever you want to be, for no one knows you here yet." I have never forgotten those words.

I have tended to the ivy and roses ever since, and dwell on this piece of advice whenever I do. I have to say that I have come to the conclusion that she is right. I won't allow myself to spend time crying over silly things like moving house and as a result I became the strong person I am now, although I'm sure Grandma thinks I have become a little too strong minded.

We walked into the warm and familiar house in silence. I was growing more anxious by the minute at the lack of communication. This was a whole new tactic by Grandma, and I had just started to realise how upset she was with my betrayal.

"Sit down!" She ordered.

I threw myself down on the cream sofa with an exaggerated humph and curled up into a tight ball. I locked my arms around my knees and kept my eyes fixed on the now dying flames of the open fire in front of me.

The flames started to dance and sneer at me menacingly. Just then my cat, Hiccup, jumped up beside me, interrupting my sulking. He started to purr loudly and I absent mindedly stroked his back of pure, white fur as he curled up onto my lap as I remembered when I first got him.

It was on my eighth birthday, and I was upset about something. I can't remember what it was *exactly,* all I know is that I had crawled under the small square kitchen table to hide. I only did that when I was really upset because I always felt safe there - maybe because it was a small, warm space, or maybe because the adults were too big to fit under there. Even then, at the age of eight, I had nightmares about fire, monsters and my mother.

I could see my dad's feet approaching from under the flowery table cloth and watched as he struggled to join me under the table. He could only get his head, arms and torso under, but he didn't complain. He just hugged me tightly and guided me out from under it.

When I came out I remember spotting a large red box on top of the table with a great big pink bow balanced carefully on top. My dad had gestured to it and said, "Go ahead sweetheart, it's for you."

When I opened it I had squealed with delight. There was a tiny, pure white, fluffy kitten with big blue eyes inside, and he was wearing a pink bow round his neck like a collar. I immediately fell in love with him. I felt so happy I had cried tears of pure joy.

My dad told me the kitten would grow up strong and powerful and would always protect me because he was a special cat. That's why he has the unfortunate name Hiccup. I *was* only eight when I named him! I remember my dad and Grandma had tried to talk me out of it, but at the time I was adamant he was to be named Hiccup. Looking back on it now I should have chosen something a little bit more sensible, but I was eight and hiccupping from the joy and tears, so it just made sense.

I giggled at my own stupidity and resumed carefully stroking Hiccup. I placed him securely on my lap and carried on waiting for Grandma to start ranting properly. Any minute now! It was coming, the big lecture about how spoilt I was and how my parents would be so ashamed if they could see me now. I sighed, thinking of my mother, and decided to break the uncomfortable silence.

"Look Grandma," I began, "I'm eighteen! When are you going to stop treating me like a child? *I* can make up my own mind and make my own decisions." I spoke in a rush, putting a lot of emphasis on the word I.

I peeped up at her, expecting to see a stern-looking face glaring back at me. What I saw instead, however, shocked me. She looked sad; her eyes glistening with tears, and her face looked worn and tired. I immediately felt guilt run through me. I could be so selfish, after all she *was* just trying to look out for me. I hung my head in shame, afraid to look into her saddened, disappointed eyes.

"I promised your father and your mother that I would take care of you and keep you safe. You're making that very difficult for me," she said.

Of course, I did know the promise she had made to my parents, and being reminded of it made me ashamed of my actions. I hung my head, deflated.

"Mother would have understood," I whispered faintly.

Her face looked shocked for a moment, then hardened. Well, my mother *would* have understood about my feelings for Joey, although I *think* she would. I hadn't really known her. My dad would never tell me much about her. He had only told me how she had died and I was too afraid to ask Gran about her, it always made her sad.

My eyes welled up with bitter tears as I thought about how differently life would be with her here now, with me.

I glanced back up at Grandma nervously. I could tell that something else was bothering her, but before I could ask what, she turned her back to me and heaved a sigh.

"Go to your room. I'll see you in the morning. I'll be sending a letter to your father about this. Now go to your room." She spoke with a trembling, tear-filled voice and my heart crumpled inside my chest.

I rose slowly, disturbing Hiccup from the sofa, hesitating as to whether or not I should apologize and hug her. I stretched out my hand to place it on her shoulder, but withdrew it self-consciously. I trudged off to my room, feeling a huge wash of guilt swell up and stick in the back of my throat as tears trickled down my cheek.

There was, of course, no point in arguing with her. Once she had said, "go to your room," the conversation was over. I had learnt that a very long time ago. Still, I thought that I had gotten off quite lightly considering how upset she looked. I was expecting her to shout and give me an hour long lecture about growing up and being a responsible young lady. After all, only two nights ago she lectured me for a whole twenty minutes after I accidently broke one of her favorite china mugs!

I pushed open my bedroom door, flicked on the light and sat down on my bed. What was I going to do now? I wasn't in the mood to sleep, I was too wound up for that. I needed to calm myself down because I was starting to feel hot and bothered. Never a good sign.

I got up lazily and grabbed my iPod from the chest of drawers. I flicked through the music, looking for one to distract me from my thoughts. I chose Lady Gaga, and put it into the docking station. I pressed play, turned the volume up and danced around my room to Bad Romance, picking up a few bits and pieces I had left lying around.

I looked at my still untidy room and frowned as I hadn't made much improvement to it. I picked up my clothes, getting them out from under the bed and placed them in a small white wicker basket by the side of my desk. I soon gave up on the tidying and turned to my dresser, grabbing my nail varnish case. Maybe that would help. I switched albums and turned the volume down until it was just background noise.

I sat myself down at my desk and still felt very unsettled. I thought about Grandma's threat and decide to beat her to it. I grabbed my writing set and pen and began to write my dad. This was the only way I could communicate with him as he never has internet access. At least this way he would pick up the letter as soon as he checked in at the museum. He was abroad somewhere in Argentina, on some kind of historical dig trying to find a rare stone for the museum's new geology section. I don't really know what he does, to be honest. I had stopped paying attention to what he was actually doing when I was about ten.

All I knew and cared about was the fact that it kept him away from me so much. After all, he had been gone for nearly eleven years now. It had been at least five months since he had last visited me. I always felt bitter whenever I thought about it, so I often tried not to although that was almost impossible.

I used to sneak off to my room, where Grandma couldn't see me, and cry myself to sleep when I was younger. I would always mope around the house for days after he visited because I wanted to go with him but he would always say that it was far too dangerous.

I scoffed thinking about it-he just didn't want me around! He did write me every month without fail though. It wasn't much, but at least he did that and now could do something productive for me and talk to Grandma. He owed me that much at least!

With this in mind I start writing about my week and tonight's events.

Dad,

I hope you are well and this letter finds you as such. Work has been slow these last few days although Tiffany is now working in the office as the receptionist. She's really excited and it's practically impossible to have a normal conversation with her now. So really nothing has changed there!

My driving lessons are going well. My instructor thinks I might be ready to take my test soon. Fingers crossed!

I need to ask you for something and I know you can't do much for me whilst you're in Argentina, but I need your help with Grandma. She's becoming impossible and more and more controlling every day. I can't take her anymore!

I have talked to her already about getting my own place and got the expected result. She said, and I quote, "No child, you will stay here with me until your dad says differently." So I'm writing you to ask you to write her. Please, I'm an adult now and I want to start living my own life. I promise I will stay close to her and help her whenever she needs me.

We argued for a full hour that night and it ended up with me going to my room without having dinner. She continues to treat me like a child and I won't take it anymore!

Grandma said she is going to write you tonight. I went out to a house party down in the bay and she went mad at me. Okay, I know, I did disobey her because she said I couldn't go, but she never lets me go out! Please write her soon and tell her to stop smothering me!

Love, your Sera x

I finished writing and placed the letter into an envelope, leaving it on my desk ready for the morning post, and started to paint my nails. I decided to go with an unusual deep red color, which wasn't really my thing, but it came free with my magazine. I stretched my fingers out in front of my face to admire the effect. It wasn't that bad - really quite effective, vibrant and fun. Grandma would *not* approve.

As I sat there blowing on my now red nails I thought about the night's events, most importantly about Joey. He had to feel the same way about me as I did him about him but self-doubt suddenly rose up in my stomach and I felt sick. Did he? Was I being too naïve? Maybe he just wanted to be friends. Even if he did like me, Gran would never allow us to be together.

Anger flooded through me, coming out of nowhere, which shocked me. It made my hands shake, beads of sweat popping up on my forehead. Why shouldn't I be with him? Why was Grandma being so difficult about me having a boyfriend? I couldn't stand it any longer! I was to see him tomorrow at work, so became determined to ask him out on a date. If I was lucky he would say yes.

Then I deliberated; what was I going to do about Grandma? I wouldn't be able to ask Joey out because she would put a stop to it, even if he did say yes. *Why* is life so complicated?

I stamped my foot in frustration and a bright white spark flew out from under it. I stumbled backwards in shock. What was that?

I trembled as I cautiously looked at the bottom of my shoe. Small wisps of smoke were rising from the sole and it had actually melted slightly. I looked at the floor and, seared there right into the wooden flooring, was a perfect imprint of the tip of my shoe. It was actually burned into the wood! How was that even possible?

I blinked rapidly in disbelief at the burnt spot, my heart pounding erratically, and I struggled to breathe for a second. I bent down and traced the outline with my finger. It was still warm and the smell of burning wood scorched through my nostrils, making me wince.

The door creaked open, making me jump, and Hiccup wandered in looking around cautiously. He eventually made his way over to where I was sitting and sniffed at the mark on the floor.

He peeped up at me and nudged my hand with his nose, rolling over onto his back and wanting to be tickled. I obliged, tickling his belly and feeling immediately better. After a while he rolled over onto his feet and strolled lazily to my bed. I watched him go, suppressing a giggle, when I remembered the floor. I looked back down at the spot I had been looking at and gasped in shock - the scorch mark had gone!

"I'm going crazy," I sighed, shaking my head, and scrambled onto the bed to join Hiccup.

MORNINGS

SERAPHINA

I was woken early from an extremely troubled sleep by the shrill shrieking of my alarm. I hated that alarm almost as much as I hated getting out of my warm bed.

I rolled over, groggily extending my arm out towards the alarm clock and hit it a few times until it stopped. I blinked my eyes, trying to focus on the flashing digital numbers. It was five a.m. My usual work day start time.

I closed my eyes again and struggled to recall the dream I was having. I remembered being in my room with Hiccup and standing at the foot of my bed. My feet were hot and stinging. I was screaming in pain, and was standing in a small fire. I had to move; I had to get away from the searing pain. As I ran, my feet left footprints burned into the wooden floor behind me.

My eyes flew open. I sat up and stared at the floor beside my bed. Nothing! There were no footprints. I shook my head in exasperation. It was a dream… just a dream. I was seriously losing a grip on reality if I thought I had actually done that!

I yawned loudly as I stretched and contemplated the day ahead. I stared around my room. It was still dark, with no hint of the sun from the outside. My curtains hung limp, a dark purple.

The sun wasn't up to turn them to their normal rosy pink color.

"I really hate mornings!"

The day hadn't warmed up yet either, and the thought of having to get out of my warm bed, into the cold, and get ready for work was making my head hurt.

I lay there, just watching the clock's digital numbers slowly progress. Five minutes had passed and the sun still hadn't reached my window. Ten minutes later, I finally give up and, pushing myself up straighter in the bed, yanked the thick duvet off. I did it quickly, like you would when ripping a band aid off.

The cool air hit the warm skin on my arms, making little goose bumps appear. I bravely made a dash for my red housecoat that was draped across the back of the desk chair. I really should put it at the side of my bed ready for the morning but I never think of these things until it's too late. I flung it around my shoulders and hastily shoved my arms inside. I tied the belt around my waist and managed to keep the warmth of my body trapped inside. There was nothing I hated more in the world than being cold and getting up early!

I made my way across the room still dazed and half asleep. Somehow I managed to bang my leg against the chest of drawers on my way to the door. I swore loudly, using a word Grandma would not approve of. That was going to leave a mark!

I growled at the chest of drawers in frustration and gave it a swift kick, hoping to relieve my anger. It did not. Now I had a bruised toe as well as a bruised leg.

I pushed my bedroom door open, switched on the landing light and hobbled out. The dazzling light made my eyes sting and scream in protest. I blinked them a few times and stood still, waiting for them to adjust. When they did I tried to quickly march along the corridor, but ended up moving with a funny sort of hop.

I walked into the bathroom, flicking that light on too. I walked across the room to the sink and found a pair of stockings soaking in the bottom. That's the only problem with living with someone else; I have to share a bathroom. I can't wait to get my own place. I pulled them out and hung them over the radiator to dry.

I finished up and turned on the shower, letting the steam warm up the cold room. I placed two towels ready on the side and turned towards the sink again. I began to brush my teeth whilst rubbing the steam from the small mirror above. I studied my reflection for a split second and gasped. I looked dishevelled, in serious need of a hairbrush, (which was normal for most mornings); my hair was sticking up in every direction you could think of. I tried to flatten it down with my fingers, my tooth brush hanging half out of my mouth, but I didn't have much success. I gave up on and finished brushing my teeth.

Eventually the steam from the shower had warmed up the room and I climbed in. The warmth of the water felt glorious as it unknotted my stressed muscles and relaxed my body. I squirted a small amount of cherry shampoo into my hand and massaged it into my long hair. The smell made me feel warm and fuzzy - it was my mother's favorite shampoo.

This always made me feel sad as I tried to recall my memories of her. All I could ever remember was sitting on her lap and sleepily inhaling the sweet smell of her hair.

Grandma told me that Cherry Blossom was her favorite flower and she loved anything with that smell in it. I had never washed my hair in any other shampoo since.

A sharp rapping on the bathroom door made me jump and Grandma's voice shrieked, "Hurry up in there!"

"Sorry Gran, I'll be finished in a minute," I shouted back in shaky voice.

I rinsed the remaining shampoo from my hair and washed the rest of my body. I leaned my head against the wall and had closed my eyes, again thinking about my mother, when Grandma rapt the door once more.

I rolled my eyes and reached for the shower's off switch. The water trickled to an end and I stepped out, wrapping the now warm towels around my body and hair. I picked up my bathroom stuff and opened the door expecting to see Grandma's stern face, but she wasn't there. She must have given up on waiting and gone back to her room. I tiptoed past her door and tried not to alert her to my presence.

I hurried back into my room and shut the door quietly. I went straight to my iPod docking station and hit the shuffle button to listen to whilst I continued to get ready. I walked over to my desk and pulled out my make-up bag, taking care to cover up the fatigue, which was now spreading itself round my eyes from lack of sleep.

I wouldn't go anywhere without applying makeup first. Who knew who I might end up meeting during the day? I mean, what if I meet Johnny Depp or Robert Pattinson and I looked like a train wreck? It's a disaster waiting to happen, and knowing my luck it *would* happen to me.

I was careful to apply just the right amount though, keeping the colors neutral and remembering to apply my waterproof mascara. Just in case! I am a life guard after all.

Last time I'd forgotten about this and ended up looking like a panda – we'd had a training day at work and I had to swim under water. Water and mascara just don't mix. I felt so foolish. I shuddered as I remembered the humiliation.

I hunted around my room for my bathing suit –which was complete with the company's motto 'Be smart! Be safe!'– and put it on. We try to spread this message as far and wide as we can.

I pulled on my favorite baggy black t-shirt over the top which would keep me warm until the sun graced us with its presence. My only pair of black jeans was lying on the floor by my bed where I had thrown them the previous day. Of course! I had forgotten to wash them last night. I picked them up and gave them a quick inspection. I couldn't wear them - there was a coffee stain right down the one leg from Tiffany's mishap yesterday with her mug. Now what was I going to wear?

I checked through my wardrobe, pulling out every pair of jeans I owned. Finally! I found a pair of dark green combats that didn't need ironing and pulled them on.

I grabbed my black and white trainers from the shoe box and laced them up tightly. I was going to walk and didn't want to give myself blisters or, worse, trip over my laces resulting in a black eye!

I managed to brush my long, wet hair up into a high ponytail, I didn't bother drying it the sun would do that for me. Besides, it was so much easier to deal with when it was wet because it didn't stick out at the sides. I sprayed it in place. It really annoyed me when my fringe fell into my eyes.

I took one final glance at myself in the full-length mirror and sighed. That would have to do. I headed for the door, picking up my black rucksack and grabbing my iPod from the docking station. Then I remembered the letter I had written to my dad last night,went back for it and stuffed it into my pocket.

Grandma was already sitting at the table in the kitchen by the time I came down. She was wearing her blue fluffy dressing gown. This was unusual; normally she would be dressed by now. She had a small china cup of tea in one hand and a slice of dry toast in the other. I didn't get why she always ate dry toast - I liked mine loaded with hot, melting butter. I smiled shyly and watched her from the corner of my eye as I passed the table. I felt a little guilty at how long I had spent in the shower. Maybe that was why she wasn't dressed yet! She didn't pay any attention to me as I walked into the room.

She was reading the morning paper and moaning loudly at the news, the same thing she did every morning! I don't know why she bothered reading it as it always made her angry and she would spend the rest of the morning moaning about how the world was crumbling and how we were responsible for destroying it.

Grandma had a passion for forests and wildlife. She had organised a lot of successful protests in her time. She's quite a rebel when she wants to be- maybe that's actually where I get it from. She used to drag me along to them until I was fourteen and that's when I threw a big tantrum, finally winning the right to sit in the car. I shook my head at her complaining and placed my bag on the chair next to her. I walked over to the ancient toaster next to the kettle and flicked it on.

"Good morning Grandma, did you sleep well?" I tried not to think of last night's fight and the letter that seemed to burn in my pocket.

"Yes, thank you. It would have been nice to have had a shower before my breakfast though," she chided, making me cringe with guilt. "What time are you working today? Do you need me to drive you?" she asked me hurriedly.

I blinked at the rapid change of topic and frowned. She was looking expectantly at me - obviously last night's fight was forgiven but not forgotten. I thought about my response quickly before answering.

"I'm on the early shift today. I can walk if you want, save you going out when you don't need to." She snorted loudly. She knew perfectly well that I didn't want a lift.

"That's good because there isn't enough time for me to shower before you have to leave now anyway." Great. That made me feel even worse! "Or maybe that's why you spent so long in the shower." she accused, her eyes thinning into a scowl, her eyebrows slightly raised. I was abashed by this and a tiny bit annoyed. Was she picking a fight or not? Tomorrow I would let her go first, but she was right; I *had* done it on purpose, but I certainly wasn't going to admit that. I don't want her driving me to work again because the last time she did she told Tiff off for wearing a skirt that went above her knees.

"Is that a skirt or a belt my dear? What is it with the fashion sense of young girls today anyway? Seraphina, don't let me see you wearing anything like that," she had said, pointing a dry, time-worn finger at Tiffany's skirt as she drove off.

I was so embarrassed. I couldn't stop apologizing to Tiff every time she pulled at the hem of her skirt. I shook my head at the memory.

"Can you blame me? After all, last time you upset Tiff," I said angrily, turning my back to her before she could say anything else.

I placed two slices of soft white bread into the toaster, thinking about my letter as they cooked. I could take it into the post office and have it sent urgently on my way to work without it being interfered with. That's the main reason I didn't want her driving me today. I turned towards the table and started spreading a generous helping of butter across my toast. Grandma paused with her toast midway to her mouth and gave me a stern look.

"Straight there Seraphina," she snapped, "No stops on the way. I'll pick you up when you've finished."

"Alright," I said, not wanting to fight, and walked over to the fridge.

It was easier to just agree with her. I would keep the peace instead of causing another argument. I grabbed the strawberry jam from the fridge and spread it across the steaming melted butter.

"What will you do today?" I asked her, genuinely interested, whilst I made a strong, sweet cup of coffee - spilling half of the milk in the process.

"I'll have to do some food shopping by the looks of that," she replied pointing, annoyed, at the spilt milk.

I sighed and mopped it up with the dish cloth from the side of the sink. I just can't do anything without a lecture.

RUBY BASCO

The sound of Seraphina swearing loudly had woken me from a deep sleep. I promised myself I'd give that girl a stern talking to about her language. If there's one thing I won't stand for, it's bad language.

I sat up on the end of my bed and placed my tired feet into my slippers. I was exhausted. Yesterday's trip had taken it out of me much more than they used to.

I'm not getting any younger, and despite what Seraphina thinks I am growing weaker. I had spent most of last night pondering what Dana had told me about Kent's safety. He is my only child and, at the moment, the only Fire Defender left - unless Seraphina can change that. That thought did not fill me with confidence. In fact, it terrified me. I knew that one day soon I would have to let my granddaughter go out into that world without me.

If Kent had failed in his mission then it would fall on Seraphina's shoulders instead. I had contemplated telling her last night after seeing her with that awful, Joey guy! Why can't he leave her alone?

Unfortunately, it's not a simple thing to do. It's not like I could just say, "Come on now, Seraphina. Stop wandering off on your own because there's an evil woman out in the world somewhere who is trying to kill us all. Oh, and by the way you're a Defender and have special powers." That would be a recipe for disaster.

I sighed as I heard Seraphina banging around, eventually making her way to the bathroom. I got up slowly and shakily as my old bones got used to my weight after the night's rest. My housecoat was draped over the end of my bed where I left it and it looked warm and inviting.

I made my way across my room slowly and flung the curtains open. The sun was still low in the sky not yet risen fully. It must have been about five thirty. The morning looked cold, always a bad sign for us Fire Defenders. We prefer the heat.

I took in the scenery outside and my eyes latched onto the black lake. I shuddered remembering the number of attacks we encountered when Tailia was with us. Especially when... well,I pushed the memories out of my mind.

I continued to look outside at the surrounding forest when Hiccup stalked into my room, turning my attention back inside.

"Ah, good morning. How was she last night? Trouble?" I asked the cat as I stroked his fur.

He purred loudly in response and I nod at him. After a few minutes I made my way to the bathroom and rapped sharply on the door. How long did that girl need in there? Sharing a bathroom was starting to become a real annoyance. Maybe it was time for a new extension.

I thought back to when Kent was her age and how he spent as much time in there. Adonis and I were always talking about building an extension, but we never got round to doing it and, before I knew, my husband was gone. A tear escaped my eye and rolled down my cheek. I quickly brushed it away. I would not cry over the past.

I tapped the door once more, "Hurry up in there," I called.

"Sorry Gran, I'll be finished in a minute," came a somewhat shaky voice. What was she doing in there?

I decided not to wait for her and made my way downstairs. I have to take my medication at six every day, and I'm usually up and showered before Seraphina. It was an old, deeply ingrained habit I had picked up when I had stayed and trained with the Woodwives. They're always up before dawn.

I flicked the light on in the kitchen and made my way to the kettle. I filled it, switched it on and placed an English Breakfast tea bag into the teapot. Another habit I picked up from Talia - English tea.

I grabbed the small silver key from the old vase on the window-sill and took a small wooden box from under the sink. I opened it and took out my pills - popping two out of the silver foil and placed them back into the box.

I heard soft music emanating from Seraphina's room and knew she'd finished in the shower.

I looked back at the picture taped to the inside lid of the box, fingering the beautiful tanned face of a dark haired and dark eyed, man.

"I'll be with you soon, my love," I said locking the box. I placed it back under the sink.

The kettle flicked up and I went about making breakfast. I have to have a dry slice of toast in the morning because of my medication. I'm sure Seraphina thinks I actually enjoy dry toast. I chuckled to myself, then straightened up as I heard her descending the stairs.

WORK

SERAPHINA

I stepped out of the front door onto the wooden decking, the morning sun instantly hitting my face. The cool morning breeze swept past me, revitalizing my mood. Today looked like it would be a good day after all.

The sunrise came through the trees and the sunbeams bounced off the calm lake, making it look less ominous. It really was a beautiful place to live. I especially loved the way the lake glistened and sparkled like some sort of precious gemstone.

I took one last glance at the lake and decide to walk the long way, hoping it would clear my head. I would go around the lake and through the surrounding forest, the same route I had taken last night. I shuddered at the memory of feeling like I was being followed.

As I walked I reminisced about when I was younger and how the lake and forest had scared me. Admittedly that might have been because of the stories Dad used to tell me about the trees that could transform into people. I would lie awake at night listening out for the 'tree people,' in case they came to get me. It's really silly, the stuff adults tell their children! As I've gotten older I've realised that he did it on purpose to keep me out of the woods after all, there are dangerous animals in there, which is less scary than 'tree people' when you're younger anyway.

However, nothing could spoil my mood today, not even my old fear of the trees. It really was so beautiful here in the morning. I felt amazingly happy and tranquil. All the stress from the previous night's argument seemed to disappear.

It didn't take me too long to wander through the trees and reach the main road which led straight down to the town. It might have had something to do with my trainers. Last night took me twice as long because my boots kept sinking into the mud or catching on tree roots. If I didn't know any better I would have sworn that the trees were actually trying to stop me going out. The idea made me shudder and I quickened my pace.

I finally emerged from the trees, blinking in the bright glare of the morning sun. It was darker in the forest and I hadn't noticed how high the sun had risen. The town was half awake when I arrived, with only the locals around. They were putting up the signs outside their stores before the tourists and holidaymakers turned up.

The small row of stores led straight down the road towards the beach. They were all crammed together in a messy array of color. There were several tourist stores that sold all kinds of cheap, tacky souvenirs - the type you can only get from a seaside town.

The biggest store of the stretch was 'Martin's Convenience Store,' which had everything you could possibly need, and a lot of stuff you never would, but felt compelled to buy anyway.

Next to Martin's was the post office, which was where I was headed. It wasn't *officially* open yet, but I had known the woman behind the counter since I was nine and would always serve me early.

I walked in setting off the little bell above the door in the process. A small, withered-looking woman was alerted and peeped up at me from behind a pile of forms.

"Seraphina," she beamed. "Good morning, angel. You're really early today. Is everything alright?"

She was short and plump, with curly greying hair. Her square spectacles were too big for her face and kept sliding down her nose, but that just added to her charm. I had always liked Mrs McGee and I used to go to school with her son Rupert.

"Morning Mrs McGee, I'm fine thanks. I just need to get this letter sent off before my shift starts. Is it okay to send it now?" She beamed a brilliant smile at me.

"Sure, come on down to the counter. How's your Grandma?" She asked whilst making her way around to the little plastic window.

"She's fine," I smile fondly, "Thanks for asking. How are your family and Rupert? I haven't seen him for a while. What's he up to?" I inwardly kicked myself.

That was really the wrong question to ask Mrs McGee. She immediately launched into a long rant about her husband's poor aching back and her ungrateful son wanting more money off her.

It turned out that Rupert had gone off to college and had fallen in love with some 'hare-brained' girl and they were now having a baby together. That shocked me as he was only my age, and the thought of being a mother at this age freaked me out. I wondered how Rupert felt about it.

"It's not a sensible thing to do, is it?" She asked, then carried on ranting before I could answer. I smiled and nodded accordingly as she went on to tell me about how they were moving in together but needed her help to pay for their house. I had to remind her several times that I needed to send an urgent letter. I eventually emerged from the post office twenty minutes later, and noticed that the town had woken up. It was now twice as busy as before.

The early tourists had already started to arrive and I was now late for work. Oh man!

I had to power walk as fast as I could for the rest of the way.

It took twice as long as normal though because I kept having to pause so I didn't bump into any of the tourists. I had to clutch my side from the stitch that had formed. That was not good. I made a mental note to take an extra trip to the gym.

I finally arrived at the beach hut panting heavily. I looked at my watch and sighed. I was five minutes late. That ended my good mood.

I pushed open the door and exhaled in relief. Luckily enough it was Tiff on signing in duty. I looked around to see my colleagues waiting to start shift. I gave her a small, desperate 'help me' wave and she immediately excused herself from the woman she was talking to. She bounded over to me with a beaming gleeful smile.

Her hair was short and spikey with purple streaks. I stared open-mouthed at her new look. When had she done that? After I left the party, maybe? I bet it was Dean's idea. I was about to comment on it when she gripped my arm tightly.

"What happened to you last night?" She demanded in an accusing tone.

"I was about to ask you the same question," I said, running my fingers through her outrageous new hair.

"Never mind that now!" she said, batting my hand away "I'll tell you later. What happened with your gran? Are you in trouble for sneaking out?"

Oh man. She was really concerned. Mind you, I would have been too if she had a gran like mine. Her parents were amazingly laid back. Then again she could have called me. My phone *was* on!

"She didn't really say anything," I replied, shrugging my shoulders and looking at who was around me.

"Ooh... Seraphina! You're such a liar! Tell me! Joey disappeared last night too straight after you," she said, nonchalantly.

He did? He must have gone straight home then instead of returning to the party. I suddenly felt like everyone's eyes around me were focusing in on me and their ears pricking up at our conversation so I shook my head mutely.

"Fine, don't tell me. I'm only your best friend," she groaned, pouting. She knew I didn't want to discuss Joey here.

"Alright!" I said, rolling my eyes, "I'll tell you, but not now…" I said, glancing over at a couple of my other work colleagues.

I didn't like talking about Gran at work either. I was already a source of gossip. After all, it was no big secret that I liked Joey and Gran didn't.

"What time is your break?" I asked, lowering my voice to a soft whisper.

"I've put us both on the one thirty slot," she said, shrugging her shoulders and glancing around the hut.

It was her turn to feel uncomfortable. "I'll meet you at your post. You'd better tell me every tiny detail," she ordered, pointing her finger at me again whilst walking back to her desk.

I smiled at her as she went. No doubt I would have to tell her every tiny detail at lunch, not that there was anything to tell. Maybe I would be lucky and we wouldn't have time to chat about it.

I arrived at my post on the beach, climbed up the tall watch tower and sat myself down in the little red chair at the top. There was something very satisfying about sitting up here. I took a quick look around to see only one family on the beach at, but knew it wouldn't take too long before it got full.

I sat quietly and watched the small family for a while as they settled nearby. They spread a big green and white stripy blanket on the sand and placed a massive yellow parasol beside it. What a strange combination of colors. It clashed magnificently. I guess it would be easier to find on a crowded beach.

I watched as the mother, I presumed, unpacked a very large picnic basket full of food and drink. This was way more than one small family really needed and I began to wonder why families did that when they went away. They always seemed to pack more food than they would need, more than what they would ever eat if they were at home.

I watched as the overly-fussy mother started covering her children from head to toe in sun-cream. I had to stifle a giggle when the smallest child, a young girl, told her off for missing a spot right on the end of her nose.

"Right there, mommy. It hasn't got cream on it," she said in a very British accent pointing to the tip of her nose.

The little girl was very pretty, with long, black, shiny hair dangling down her back. I watched as her mother twisted it into a long braid and placed a frilly pink bonnet on her head. I looked down and noticed she was wearing a little frilly pink costume that read,'I'm the cutest girl in the world' on the front and 'just like my mommy' on the back. I rolled my eyes at the statement.

I watched her curiously as she took a yellow bucket and spade over to her dad. I knew I was staring, but I couldn't help it. She was just so cute to watch, and for some strange reason I felt like I had seen her before. It was bizarre!

I giggled as she started to bury her dad's feet in the sand. She was sniggering wildly as she did so and it was infectious. The girl's dad laughed back as he scooped her up and whirled her around and around. He threw her into the air whilst she laughed madly. I don't know why, but this made me feel sad and uncomfortable. I hastily turned away at the sudden rush of emotion and grabbed my sunglasses from my rucksack. I put them on and looked out towards the horizon.

I scanned the ocean for a while to stop myself from watching the little girl again. There was a group of teenagers out in the water now. Three were trying to surf the smaller waves whilst the other two batted a bright red beach ball back and forth. I soon got bored with watching them and found myself drawn back to the little girl again. She was now screaming at her mother and demanding chocolate ice cream. Wow! What a sudden change: from angel to devil. I thought of Rupert and immediately felt sorry for him. He had all this to come!

At one o'clock, Tiffany rode down the beach towards my post. I burst out laughing - it was such a funny sight to see a girl of eighteen with black and purple spiky hair and wearing a red swim suit, driving a sand buggy down the beach whilst waving enthusiastically at me. She was getting quite a few funny glances, even some cat calls from the group of teenagers. I sniggered at her, feeling sorry for the timid looking girl sitting alongside her and started to descend the watch tower.

I signed off, swapping places with the other girl in the buggy and jumped in with Tiff. Instantly she stepped on the gas pedal and flew down the beach towards our favorite café. I laughed as my hair billowed out behind me from the passing wind. I felt free and at the moment, completely untroubled.

We sat outside Café Royale eating pineapple summer salads, which were a specialty here, and drinking large bottles of water. I don't like water much - it always seems to drain and tire me. I know you're thinking "don't be absurd," and "water's great for you", right? No! Honestly, it really makes me feel drained!

Anyway, Tiffany always insisted on drinking water whilst working in the heat. She was sensible like that. The day had brightened up considerably and in the last hour it had gotten unbelievably hot. I didn't mind the heat though, in fact I liked it when the day was hot and bright. It made me feel happy.

"So?" Tiffany said, placing her fork down on her plate and looking up at me. "What happened last night? Did you get to see Joey again after he left? He won't tell me a thing."

I gasped and choked on a small piece of pineapple.

"You asked Joey?" I said feeling slightly betrayed.

"Of course I did," she said, waving her hand like it was no big deal. "Come on tell me!"

I shuffled my fork around my plate, trying to stall my answer.

"Seraphina Talia Basco!" she snapped, "you tell me now or

else." She grabbed her water bottle as if to empty it on me.

"Okay, okay," I said, holding my hands up in defeat. "I didn't know he left. Gran took me straight home and I went straight to bed. Well, after I wrote to my dad."

"Really…You're playing the dad card?"

My head shot up and I felt my cheeks burn pink as my mouth fell open into a comical O shape.

"What Dad card? I think I have the right to leave home now and if Gran won't let me then my dad will!" I stabbed the lettuce with my fork.

"Okay, okay. Take a chill pill. Jeez, Sera you're not very happy today are you? Look, I'm sorry. I'm sure your dad will agree then you can move in with me," she said warmly.

"I hate feeling like this. I'm sure we would have kissed if it wasn't for Gran last night," I finished lamely as Tiff smiled and picked up her water bottle again.

"That explains why he's in a bad mood today then."

"What do you mean?"

"He's stomping around the office complaining at everyone and barking orders at us left, right and centre." She shrugged like it was nothing to worry about. "We thought it was because of the amount of tourists that have turned up today. You know what he's like when he gets too busy." She spoke in what was clearly supposed to be a reassuring manner, but it didn't make me feel good. In fact, I wished the earth would crack open and swallow me up. I was suddenly sure he was mad at me for leaving him standing there instead of staying at the party. He wasn't normally touchy and I'd never heard him raise his voice before. Even when he was busy he'd always been polite to me.

"Dean doesn't like Joey, you know." Tiff said, breaking my train of thought.

"What! Why?"

"He said he doesn't trust him." She shrugged like it was no

big deal.

This confused and surprised me. Why would he think that, and why would he care? He didn't even know Joey enough to make a statement that bold. Maybe it was just me being over-protective, or maybe it was him doing the same thing. We had been friends for years, so I guess that would make you look out for someone.

"Oh my god, Seraphina!" Tiff squealed and threw her water over the table, knocking my hand out the way.

I looked down in alarm as Tiff ran inside the café. In the middle of the table lay a half burnt napkin. Oh no! I sat in shocked silence, staring at the table. After a while the manager came hurrying out with Tiff. He stood apologizing to us over and over again:"I don't know what happened, it must have been the sun reflecting through your water bottle," he said, shaking his head, obviously not believing it himself.

Tiff was reassuring the manager that everything was fine as I left the table in a hurry and headed towards the exit. What had just happened? Had I done that?

I heard Tiff apologize once more,before she ran to catch up to me. The drive back to my post was long and I felt extremely tired and drained. I had so much stuff whirling around in my head I thought it would explode.

Tiff dropped me back at my post with a worried expression and promised to come back and get me at the end of my shift. I changed places with the other life guard and waved goodbye to Tiff, trying to show her that I was fine and that she didn't need to worry. I climbed back up the watch tower in a numb daze. What *had* happened? Was it really the sun, or was it me losing control?

I put my sunglasses back on to keep the day's glare out of my eyes and scanned the waves once more. The same group of teenagers from the morning were now in a small peddle boat. They were pushing one another off it and acting like jerks. One of them was bound to get hurt and that would cause me a heap of paperwork. I sighed. Well, at least someone was having fun this summer.

There were several more people in the water now, and a couple of guys were surfing the larger waves. A speed boat was whizzing by, pulling a pair of girls along behind them and a group of elderly women were swimming close to the beach.

I scanned the rest of the beach watching each family group. One was playing a game of volley-ball, one was building sandcastles and another was heading towards the sea.

I looked back to where the first family, the one with the yellow parasol, had been this morning and began to feel uneasy. The more I looked, the more unnerved I became. Why? Then it hit me. Where was the little girl?

The mother was asleep on the blanket and the dad was reading his paper. The other two children were building sand castles by the rocks, but I couldn't see the little girl in the pink frilly costume on the beach anywhere.

I grabbed my binoculars from the side of the chair and started to scan the waves. I just had a terrible feeling… and I was right.

My heart leapt into my mouth. The little girl was in the sea, being swept up by the waves and taken further and further away from the beach. Her head was bobbing up and down, in and out of the waves. Her tiny arms were waving frantically as she tried to fight the current. I jumped straight down from the watch tower, landing in a crouch, my body responding automatically to the adrenaline pulsing through me.

I grabbed the bright orange rescue device and sprinted towards the water. The crowds around the beach seemed to stop and watch the young girl. Some were already screaming and pointing. The surfers were trying to swim towards her but were finding it hard.

The girl's mother sat upright having been woken from her

sleep by the sudden commotion. As I ran past her, she noticed why and bolted after me, pointing and screaming at her daughter bobbing in the ocean. I sprinted into the waves and dived into the sea. I swam out towards her concentrating hard and becoming alert and stronger with every stroke. I drove on, the muscles in my arms accelerating towards her. Grabbing the girl around her waist, I threw her upwards onto the safety device, making sure her head and shoulders were clear of the water. She flailed around in panic, accidentally kicking me in the ribs and elbowing me in the face.

"It's alright, I've got you," I shouted over the waves. "Just hold on to this." I hit the device, "I won't let you go."

The girl sobbed back at me, petrified, and whimpered for her mother. She clung on to my neck so tightly it hurt.

"Hold here," I shouted again hitting the device. She seemed to focus more and finally managed to grab onto it. I kicked my legs rapidly and began to move towards the shore-line.

The waves were trying to drag us further out to sea - it was almost like an invisible force was pulling on my legs, trying to haul me backwards. I struggled against it, kicking as hard as I could, thinking of my mother the entire time. Finally I felt the current lift ever so slightly and immediately we made more progress. Somehow, I knew my mother was helping me.

I arrived back to the shore and scooped the girl into my arms. A massive round of applause and a frantic mother greeted us. I made sure she was okay and radioed for a medic.

THE MEETING

RUBY

"May I speak to Mr Parkinson please?"

"Of course, I'll put you right through. May I ask whose calling and what it's regarding?" The voice was high-pitched, almost sing-song like, I could only guess that it was Tiffany.

I knew she was asking more to do with being nosy then actually needing to and decided it was best for her not to know it was me. Seraphina and Tiffany were inseparable and told each other everything. I really needed to do this discreetly.

"I'm Helen Row, calling from Life Guard Supplies," I lied quickly,I sensed her hesitation. Maybe she could recognize my voice.

"Of course, I'll put you straight through. Please hold." The line switched to some mind-numbingly terrible music.

I'm sure it was a song Seraphina listened to a lot, some new star called Lady Goo Goo or something. It was all a lot of noise to me. I waited patiently, listening to this woman ramble on about some strange romance or something. It was quite difficult to tell.

"Good morning, Joey Parkinson speaking. Can I help you?" A deep voice boomed at me.

"Good morning, I am Ruby Basco," I paused in pleasure at his audible gasp of recognition.

"Good morning, err... how can I help you, Mrs Basco?" he stumbled.

"I'd like to talk to you about Seraphina." I paused again and let the silence stretch a little.

"I'd like to arrange for a time that we can do that please," I say in a pleasant but chilled voice.

"Err... of course. When would you like to do that?" he stumbled, clearly caught off guard.

"When is your receptionist Tiffany on her break?"

He seemed quite surprised at my question and paused for another moment.

"I'll just check that for you now, please hold the line a moment," he said, panic evident in his voice.

I thought that he didn't like the idea of being alone with me. I smiled at his discomfort. After another few minutes of that awful music he was back on the line.

"My receptionist is scheduled for lunch at twelve forty five," he said.

I paused to think this through. He wouldn't like me to be alone with him, so he would, of course, lie about the time.

"Okay, Mr Parkinson I will see you then. Goodbye." I ended the call before he could respond.

I looked up at the small clock on the wall. I had an hour before I had to leave. That would ensure I arrived in plenty of time for Tiffany to have left The Hut. I would walk too so Seraphina couldn't see my car.

I grabbed my wicker basket and gloves from the table and made my way out into the garden, plucking away at the ivy and roses that were creeping up the side of the house, clearing away the over-grown vines and placing the best of the flowers into my basket. It took a long time and my back hurt, but I eventually have a full basket and a clear house.

I paused for a moment and looked over at the lake. My nerves were not what they used to be, and the memory of that dreaded day still haunted me. We came so close to destruction on *that* day. I shook my head, trying to rid myself of negative thoughts and glanced down at my watch.

It was time to start walking into town. I left the gloves and secateurs behind on the step and made my way towards the forest path. The path was a dirt track that had now etched its way into the thick of the forest from years of usage.

On my way through it I steadily dropped the flowers behind me. It was an ancient method used by the natives of this forest to help the lost find their way home. My ancestors had used this method to attract their Spirit Guides. I had been trying to find mine for years, but had still not been able to.

Seraphina was lucky to have found hers so easily, not that she knew it. It was indeed a rare occurrence. Even my son, Kent, had not found *his* and he was without doubt the most powerful of our line so far. If only he would apply himself to realise his full ability, but his will and persistence seemed to have vanished when Talia did. This was his one and only fatal flaw: emotional connection.

I finally made my way through the forest and walked slowly down the main road. I still had fifteen minutes to go. I stopped off at Martin's and picked up some more milk after Seraphina had spilt half of it this morning. She was so clumsy at times! Maybe that was *her* fatal flaw.

I finally arrived and, thinking Tiffany had not left, I ducked inside a tourist shop on the other side of the road, hiding behind a rack of postcards.

I watched and waited for her to leave. Finally, at one o'clock, she emerged with another girl and raced off in a sand buggy. I would need to have a word with her about the speed in which she is driving and *what* was going on with her hair?

I dashed across the road and into the office. No one was on reception, so I walked straight to Joey's open door. He was sitting in his chair, staring at the beach front and checking his watch. I smirked and entered without knocking.

His office was nice really; white walls and a double-bay door that led straight out onto the beach. I'd never actually been in here before.

"Good afternoon," I said sweetly. "Sorry I'm late. I needed to get some milk," I held up the bottle and grinned as he jumped in surprise.

He turned so quickly in his chair that it toppled over and he landed on the floor at my feet. I smiled, amused at what an appropriate place that was for him to be. He got to his feet hastily, brushing the dirt and sand from his pants.

"Good afternoon, Mrs Basco. I'm sorry about that, my chairs broken," he stammered, holding out his hand for me to shake.

I took his hand and shook it vigorously, smiling as I did so.

"That's quite alright," I said and sat myself down in the chair he had just vacated.

He looked perplexed but didn't say anything, instead settling himself down in the other chair across from the main desk.

"What can I help you with, Mrs Basco?" he said, trying to gain back the authority I had taken from him.

"I want to talk about Seraphina and your intentions with her," I said solemnly. I felt elated as his face paled and he gulped.

"My intentions…" he said warily.

"Yes, need I remind you of last night," I held up my finger as he was about to interrupt me. "I know why you were at that party Mr Parkinson, so let's not play games." I glowered at him as he shook his head. He was beginning to blush.

"Now then," I said, folding my arms tightly across my chest, "I would like to remind you that you are her *boss* and *nothing* more."

He looked up at me with a fury, a strange red glow blazing in his eyes. This actually took me back for a moment until I reminded myself of who I am. That was something to be concerned about. I'd seen that glow before!

"I know what *I* am!" He snapped. "I do not need you to remind me of that!"

I paused for a second and surveyed him closely. That was an unexpected turn around: one minute he was obviously ashamed and the next he was fighting. I placed my finger on my chin, my thumb underneath it, and surveyed him cautiously.

"That's good. I take it from your outburst that I don't need to warn you about keeping it that way," I said flatly.

He studied me in turn for a moment, his eyes wary, and I glanced out of the window. I ducked slightly as Seraphina and Tiffany drove past,heading for the one and only place they ever ate: Café Royale. Luckily, Tiffany was going way too fast for her to look through the window. Maybe speed does have an advantage?

"If that's alright with you," Joey was saying, pulling me back into the room.

"Err... What? Sorry, what did you say? I didn't catch that. Hard of hearing you know," I said, waving a hand at my left ear. I can't let him know my *biggest* weakness... upsetting and hurting Seraphina.

He looked at me sceptically, unsure if I was mocking him or not.

"I said that Seraphina and I are just *friends,* and that *won't* change. I'm sure you'd be happy to hear. I have a lot of respect for her," he said again, looking saddened as he did so.

He started to fidget with his hands and hair, staring down at his feet. It seemed that the scared boy was back. This guy was so hard to figure out! I couldn't make sense of this change in mood or the fluctuations in his aura.

"Very well," I said and rose from his seat. "I'll be seeing you then." I headed for the door. "Thank you for your time Mr Parkinson," I said marching out.

I needed to talk to Dana about this guy. He was not as easy to read as all the others.

SERAPHINA BASCO

I was sitting in the office reception area waiting for the girl's family to come out. They'd been in there for an hour just talking to Joey.

I could see them through the small window on the office door. Joey was pacing up and down by his desk, running his fingers through his hair in a frustrated manner.

The mother was squeezing the girl tightly on her lap whilst the dad was talking very animatedly. My view was momentarily blocked by an Arnold-Schwarzenegger-wanna-be, so I turned my head in the other direction. I shuddered. I had had a shock when I first saw this guy. After I got the girl back to shore, several of these muscled types had materialized out of nowhere, ran over and pushed me away from her. They scooped her up and ran down the beach towards the office with the parents close on their heels, leaving me staring after them like an idiot. After a minuet's shock I had realised that the police had turned up.

The only thing I could do was make my way back to my watch-tower. Several tourists had watched the dramatic scene unfold, shaking their heads and talking loudly. Some were even taking photos of me!

After an exhausting hour of emotional stress and tiredness, someone finally came to relieve me of my duties. I descended the watch-tower and was escorted straight to the office by one of the surly looking Arnold guys.

After another hour the father finally emerged from the office. The mother was holding on to her now sleeping daughter. She saw me sitting outside the office door and smiled as she rose from her chair. She walked out of the office, anxious to leave, and got into a black shiny car. The dad, now dejected and pale, followed her out. He was worn and completely horror-struck from the events that had unfolded. Joey trailed out after them looking just as horrified as the parents.

"Please be reassured, you have our full cooperation and I'll give my staff a full briefing," he was saying.

"Thank you, it's much appreciated," the father replied as he shook Joey's hand.

"Have a safe journey back to your hotel Mr and Mrs Morgan," Joey called after them as they left.

The dad waved as he climbed into the shiny black stretch limo. Wow, whoever they were they were not short of cash. We both stood and stared after the limo as it sped round the corner and out of sight.

"Seraphina, can you join me in my office please?" I hadn't noticed Joey walk back to his office door, and I jumped in surprise as he spoke. He wasn't looking at me. That wasn't a good sign. He wasn't happy with me, but I had followed all the right procedures. What could I have done wrong?

I cautiously made my way over to him. Why did I feel like I was in some kind of trouble? *Had* I done something wrong? Did I use the wrong technique pulling her out the water? Or was it last night's mishap that made him look so down-hearted? Maybe it was okay after all - he wasn't looking angry with me now, just tired.

"Take a seat," he said, gesturing to the small chair opposite his desk. "Let's start with the girl. I know you're anxious, but she'll be fine," he said, staring at me. "She needs to be checked over at the hospital, but I'm sure she'll make a full recovery." He grinned at me and my heart leapt at his smile. I relaxed instantly.

"I'm glad she's fine," I mumbled quickly.

I bit the tremble of my lips back and tried swallow the lump in my throat which had risen so quickly, straightening myself up as I did so. I had finally saved a life. It felt amazing. Still, I would not cry!

"The family wants to give you a reward," Joey announced

whilst knotting his fingers together.

It turns out they *were* a famous family. The Morgans' were from England. I thought I had recognised the name and the girl's face. I remembered seeing a picture of her in the paper. Although I was still certain I had seen her somewhere else too. Maybe she had been here before on another vacation.

"They've invited you to the Fortune Hotel tomorrow night for dinner." Joey said, his smile becoming wider, then without warning I thought I saw a glimpse of... what? Sorrow? Regret? Something was in his eyes. It could have been embarrassment. That was strange, maybe I was over-reading him.

At the moment however, he looked unbelievably handsome. The way he was smiling at me made my heart flip with joy. I felt I should tell him how I felt before my grandma turned up and dragged me home again.

I glanced at the clock: almost five thirty. Grandma was *always* on time, which meant that I had exactly two minutes.

"Joey..." I started, not sure what it was exactly that I was going to say, "I want to explain about last night..."

He held up his hand to stop me, which took me by such surprise. I faltered and fell silent.

"There's no need to explain, Seraphina." His smile faded and he looked sad. "Your grandma has already been to see me this morning." His face was hard, his mouth set into a thin line. Oh, he was angry.

"What do you mean Grandma has been in to see you? When? Why? What did she say?" the questions spilled out of my mouth before I could stop myself. I was so mad!

I couldn't believe it. She had stopped me before I could even do anything this time! I saw red, I was so angry. How dare she interfere like this! Wasn't it bad enough that she had stopped me last night? What had she said? I fidgeted in my chair, unsure whether or not to get up. Unease and anger were overwhelming me.

"It's alright Seraphina," he said, taking my hand in his, speaking softly and slowly. An electric current shot through meat his touch.

However, my body temperature had started to rise with the mixture of desire and anger. My emotions were so confusing at times. Anger at Grandma, passion for Joey and left-over adrenaline from the young girl's survival was not a good mixture.

The more I thought about what she could have said to him the angrier I got and the more I saw the hurt on Joey's face the madder I became.

I was losing it again. I was so hot. I couldn't control my breathing. It started to get more and more difficult, making me feel dizzy. I could feel myself sliding off the chair and my vision started to go wobbly, moving back and forth. Finally everything went black.

RUBY BASCO

I pulled up quickly outside the Hut and put the handbrake on a little too sharply. The car lurched to a stop, causing me to fly forward in my seat. Ouch, I would pay for that later, or at least my shoulder would from where the belt dug in.

I had seen Seraphina saving a small child on the news and fear had flooded through me. Suddenly, being a careful and considerate driver was the last thing on my mind. So much could have happened to her when she was in the water. It all could have been a trap set by Maura.

Sera's memories were so fragile I couldn't risk her remembering everything just yet. She wasn't ready. *I* wasn't ready.

I opened the car door and paused as I looked through the window of the office. I could see her in the office with *him*, again! God, this guy was starting to irritate me. Didn't he understand my warning earlier, or was he just a moron?

I watched for a moment, undecided about what to do, half

perched on the seat of my car. They were talking animatedly, then Seraphina rose from her seat in what looked like anger.

I faltered for a second, my hand hovering over the door handle. Did he tell her? I didn't want an argument with her tonight. I couldn't handle it, and she most definitely wouldn't be able to. She was like a time bomb ticking down.

I watched as he grabbed hold of her hand preventing her from leaving. As she sank back down into her seat I could sense her confusion. This was not good. I needed to get her out of there and *quickly*!

I made to move from the seat but found I couldn't - I was too terrified of her reaction at seeing me. I sank back into my seat and leant across to the glove box.

I pulled out a solid silver flask full of Appleton Estate extra dark rum. It was my husband's favorite and one of the best Jamaican rums around. I opened it, inhaling the scent, and took a deep gulp. That did the trick. My nerves were now like steel and I felt I could take on anything. I bolted out of my seat, slammed the car door as hard as I could and turned towards the office. I saw everything then in slow motion.

Seraphina slumped into her chair as a faint red glow emanated from her body. He shot up onto his feet, shock clear on his face, as she slid off her chair and hit the floor. Her glow died down and disappeared as he ran around his desk to reach her.

I ran inside, the afternoon breeze waltzing in after me. He jumped in surprise and narrowed his eyes slightly, then regained his posture before moving aside.

"Mrs Basco. I don't know what happened. She just collapsed!" he stammered like a schoolboy.

"Yes, I can see that," I snapped, approaching Seraphina. Her body was limp and damp with sweat.

"Don't just stand there, hold the door open," I barked.

Her body was far too hot for him to carry without noticing

the unusual amount of heat emanating from her. I scooped her up into my arms and struggled to stand. I was definitely not as strong as I used to be. She was getting too heavy and the heat was starting to make me sweat. I've never known a Fire Defender to get so hot, not even Kent and he had had a bad temper at her age. Joey just stood there, his mouth hanging open.

"The door," I snapped again.

"Oh, yes. Of course," he mumbled as he clumsily opened the door, hitting himself with it. What an idiot! I marched past him, fighting against Seraphina's weight and heat. I almost dug my elbow into his chest as I passed but decided against it. I made straight for my car.

He stumbled out behind me, asking if he could help, and ran to open the back passenger door of my car. *Does it look like I need your help?* I thought irritably. I carefully laid her across the back seats, ignoring the pain shooting up my back. My arms were exhausted. I moved around to the driver's door and slid in. The door was shut, the key in the ignition and my foot stamped down hard on the gas pedal before he could even blink. I raced off down the road, leaving him staring after us just like last time. I realized I'd never tire of that sight in my rear view mirror.

CONFUSION AND MEMORIES

SERAPHINA

I woke up in a complete state of panic and alarm. I was back in my warm bed, confused. How had I gotten there? I remembered being in Joey's office and I... I had passed out. Grandma must have brought me home. It was the only explanation I could think of. I gasped at the thought. I then cringed at another, embarrassment flooding through me: had *Joey* brought me home? Oh man, I hoped not. The embarrassment would be too much to cope with.

I turned over in my bed, blinking rapidly, trying to rid the sleep build up in my eyes. I focused a little more and saw a tall glass of water on my small bedside table. The glass was ice cold and had little beads of condensation dripping down the sides. My mouth seemed to get drier and drier the longer I looked at it. That's when I noticed a burning ache in the back of my throat, like I had eaten sand paper.

I reached out and immediately felt exhausted and extremely thirsty. I couldn't understand it. What was wrong with me? I'd never felt like that before. Was it because of the rescue? Had I managed to drink some of the salt water? I couldn't remember doing that.

I sat up very shakily and moved as best as I could, managing to guzzle the whole glass without pausing for breath. I instantly felt revitalized. The water had quenched a burning fire that seemed to be present in my chest, reaching up to the back of my throat. How strange, usually water had the opposite effect on me!

"Feel better now?"

I jumped, alarmed, and nearly dropped the glass on the floor. I turned my head and saw grandma sitting on the chair by my desk, Hiccup on her lap. She was stroking his long, thick fur and was looking grim and tired. Hiccup seemed to be watching me intently, almost as if he knew that I wasn't well. His yellow eyes were fixed on my face, his gaze steady and you could almost see the concern on that adorable face of his.

"Yes, thank you." I answered. My voice was hoarse. I didn't sound like me."How did I get here? I was at work, talking to ..." I broke off, remembering what he had said. The angry rushed back and I immediately felt like screaming at her. I remembered why I had lost control in the first place."What did you say to him?" I demanded, feeling the fire starting to burn in my chest again.

Hiccup leapt off Grandma's lap and jumped up onto the bed with me, pushing my hand up and round his head and purring loudly. I brushed him away angrily. "Not now Hiccup," I hissed, still glaring at my grandma.

"That is of no importance at the moment. Don't treat Hiccup like that, you need to calm down."

"Calm down! It's *your* fault I'm like this," I shouted back. She flinched, as if I had slapped her across the face.

"No importance?" I huffed, "Of course it is Grandma! I know that you think you're protecting me but you really aren't!" I immediately wished I *hadn't* shouted and lost control. Hiccup jumped up and hissed at me, taking me by surprise. What was his problem?

"How would you know what is or isn't good for you? You're still so young!" She replied.

I had to actually bite hard on my tongue to stop myself from retaliating. I really didn't have the energy to argue. Why did I feel so drained? I hadn't felt this tired after I pulled the little girl from the water, which I would have thought would have tired me out even more. I had felt completely fine until I thought about Grandma going behind my back and talking to Joey. It was only then that I started feeling tired, drained and extremely angry. I was about to question her again when I thought better of it.

I would ring him myself, later and ask him what she had said. *What was I going to do*? I knew one thing for sure: I was going to take a stand against Grandma and this so-called 'protection' nonsense.

I was about to tell her as much when the cat butted my hand again. I felt guilty, so petted him until he had settled back down on my lap, all forgiven. I stared at Grandma, not entirely focussed, pondering how I was going to continue.

She just sat there staring blankly back at me. I thought about getting up and leaving, just packing my bag and walking out. I could go and stay with Tiff if I had to.

I glanced at my rucksack, which was now on the floor beside my wardrobe. Grandma followed my gaze, shook her head slowly and said, "Take it easy, Seraphina. Just rest for a while. You're going to need to get your strength up. Dinner will be done soon. Do you want me to bring it up to you, or are you going to come down-stairs?"

This startled me, and for some strange reason, also really annoyed me. Strength for what? Was she really offering me dinner, like nothing had happened, completely nonchalantly? I tried to sit up straighter but realized I couldn't-my entire body hurt and all my muscles felt weak, like I was bruised all over. I felt like I had gone ten rounds with Mike Tyson. Hiccup purred at me and tried to climb higher onto my chest.

I finally admitted defeat and sank back into my pillows. Before I knew it I had fallen back to sleep - I hadn't even answered Grandma. Although, I thought I had because I could still feel Hiccup on my chest, settled and purring loudly. I could even hear her, getting out of the chair and walking out of the room, shutting the door quietly behind her.

My feet were moving, pushing the rough sand in and out between my toes. It felt nice in a strange way; safe and familiar. I stood watching my toes bury themselves deeper and deeper in the sand whilst the sun burned my skin. I inhaled deeply, taking in the salty smell of the sea and gloried in the sun as it dazzled above, warm and bright.

I looked around me and saw my watch-tower. It was taller than normal, but it was definitely mine. The little girl I had saved from the water sat perched on my seat. She was beaming down at me, waving energetically. I waved back, bemused, and looked around the beach for her family. There were several groups of people around but as I glanced at them they vanished. I blinked rapidly. Was I seeing things?

I turned my attention back to the watch-tower and stared as the young girl descended gracefully. I waited as she walked slowly towards me. As she did I noticed she was glowing, almost as if there was a bright light emanating from within her. I stepped back in alarm. As she came closer I saw it wasn't a light but the girl herself. She was transparent, like a ghost, and shimmered with a brilliant, purple-white light.

She looked up at me and smiled a warm and loving smile. She reached out for my hand and I instantaneously withdrew, shrinking back. I didn't want to touch her hand. It was strange to be scared of this sweet, angelic-looking girl, but there was something ominous about her.

She tentatively reached her hand towards mine once more. I tried to move, but found I couldn't. Her hand touched mine and it astounded me - I had thought it would be cold and pass straight through mine, but it was warm and solid. My fingers closed themselves around her small, warm hand, I found myself relaxed and smiling back at her.

She turned and walked away, my hand grasped firmly around hers. She guided me across the beach and over to a massive pile of sand. It was huge and looked coarse, golden and sparkly, almost like golden glass.

"We must finish building this sand castle and you must try to remember me before we can begin our journey," she giggled.

Her voice was soft and sweet, the voice of an angel. She giggled again and gestured to an enormous castle that seemed to be made out of black, glistening sandstone, not the golden sand around us. This didn't make any sense - the castle was clearly dark, hard and solid, whereas the sand from the pile was not. I watched, fascinated, as the girl bent over the golden sand-pile and began to form a brick.

She turned and placed it onto the half-finished castle wall. As soon as it touched the wall the brick transformed from golden beach sand to hard black sandstone.

She turned back to me and grinned. It was a knowing kind of a smile, and I found myself grinning back stupidly.

"Once you have finished your task you'll be ready to save me from the one who holds me prisoner," she said sweetly.

I had no idea what the girl was on about. I wanted to protest and reassure her, but a million questions had sprung to the front of my mind. Who was she? What journey? Prisoner!? Where and who was holding her? How could they impression such a young girl?

Before I could ask she held up her hands, stopping me with a hard 'do not ask' look and for a moment she seemed a lot older than what she was. Then, from out of nowhere, I felt compelled to start digging in the sand, making bricks just like hers.

I knelt down next to her, tucking my feet underneath me, and started digging, forming the sandcastle bricks and placing them on the wall. Hours passed as the sun beat down on my back making my face stream with sweat. It seemed to take forever, then with one final brick it was finished the sand pile was depleted. My eyes were heavy with fatigue, my muscles screamed in protest after the physically hard work, but I smiled down at the young girl who had been sat at my side all the time watching and singing.

She sang a song about a star with five sides that turn to one. It was a strange song but beautiful and catchy.

"Now you are ready to begin the real work, Seraphina," she said. Her voice had changed - it was too grown up for a girl of her age. I frowned in confusion.

I wanted to ask her who she was and what we were doing, but before I could speak I froze in shock as I watched her walk towards the ocean. I wanted to call out and run after her, but I was struck dumb and my feet were locked in place by some invisible force.

I gazed down and tried to scream, but no sound would come out my open mouth. The sand was moving, clawing at my feet with long skeletal fingers, continuing to pull at me. I tried to struggle against them, but still I could not move. I wanted to reach out towards the young girl. I wanted to stop her.

The burning was back, bringing my senses and limbs back to life. The whole of my body was blazing, aching, and I couldn't move. I couldn't seem to find my voice to scream out to her. All I could do was stand and stare as the girl was picked up by the waves and carried out to sea screaming. I felt hotter and hotter as fear began to crawl through my body. The little girl was drowning, I was burning, and there was nothing I could do to save her or myself. I sank slowly into the sand struggling to breathe.

My eyes flew open. My heart was beating rapidly, and my skin was hot and clammy. The smell of melted cheese, bacon and chicken brought me to my senses. My stomach growling in response to the smell even though my throat burned. I threw back the bed covers. Sweat was running down my body, my cheeks burning with the heat of fear that the dream had left me with, and my hands were shaking uncontrollably.

I took a few deep breaths to calm myself down. I told myself it was only a dream as I wiped at the imaginary sand from my feet. But it had all felt so real. I winced at the memory of the burning sensation. I shuddered and tried to calm down; it was only a dream!

I got up from my bed and went over to the mirror. My face was bright red and looked sun-burnt, which was strange as I always applied sunscreen. I never burnt!

I pushed my hair out of my face and tied it up into a ponytail. Yep, I was definitely burnt - there was a thin line around my face where my hair had been. I traced it lightly with my finger and winced. *It stung!*

Is that why I felt so bad? I pulled my blue, silky housecoat on, it was thinner and cooler than my red one, and I practically ran to the door and down the stairs. I didn't want to be alone. I felt confused, sore, unbelievably hungry and extremely thirsty.

"Ah," Grandma said as I came into the kitchen, "I see you're feeling much better now."

I nodded at her and sat down. Was she asking about the incident earlier, or did she somehow know what I had just dreamt? I presumed she meant earlier today, so I let it go. After all, how could she possibly have known about my nightmare?

"Why do I feel so hungry?" I asked, confused.

Grandma didn't answer me. I would have pushed the question, but I had just spotted the kitchen table which was loaded with all my favorite foods. How strange! It was as if she knew.

I sat down on one of the wooden chairs and gazed at the feast. Freshly baked bread rolls, pasta with chicken, bacon and cheese, fresh summer salad, baked potatoes over-loaded with hot, melting butter and the biggest chocolate fudge cake I've ever seen!

"Wow, Grandma! This looks amazing!" I felt completely overwhelmed.

"Well don't just sit there child, dig in," she smiled at me and then sat herself down, placing a big jug of fresh orange juice in the middle of the table. I didn't waste any time; grabbing a bit of everything I dug right in.

We sat and ate in silence, although I noticed that Grandma was watching me, attentively. It made me feel uneasy, but it also gave me a lot of time to ponder the dream I had just had. It was strange - I didn't normally have dreams, especially ones like that. I just couldn't shake the feeling that I'd seen that girl somewhere before, and it was bugging me. At first I thought it was the little girl from the beach, but I soon realized it wasn't her, but someone else, someone I used to know.

The more I thought about it the more certain I became. I *had* seen this girl somewhere else before, but the question still remained: where? What was troubling me more than the whole sandcastle building thing was what the girl had said:

"You need to complete it and remember me before you can begin your journey," I sighed that scared me, and the agitation made me push my plate to one side.

"What's wrong child? You haven't finished."

She hated it when I wasted food, but I was starting to feel tired again.

"Here, drink this," she said, pushing a tall glass of orange towards me.

She seemed to notice I was restless as I took it and drained it, all without a pause. She cocked her head to one side. "What's wrong?"

I looked at the glass and started fiddling with it, deliberately not meeting her intense gaze.

"It's nothing really, just a dream I had. I think I forgot to put my sunscreen on earlier, because my mind is playing tricks on me." I laughed, trying in vain to break the tension.

I just didn't want her to worry. I looked up at her and wasn't surprised to see that she wasn't smiling back, but was instead looking concerned.

"What do you mean? What dream did you have?" She asked abruptly.

She looked confused now as well as drained. I frowned, surveying her. Had she always been this thin and tired-looking? I make a mental note to quiz her on that when I felt strong enough.

I sighed. "I had a strange dream about the girl I saved yesterday." I stopped as she whipped her head up and gazed at me.

"The girl from the beach?" Her frown deepened.

"Yes. We were at the beach and she asked me to help her build a sand castle." She continued to stare at me, not saying anything.

"We sat on the sand for ages building a huge castle, and then she said something about a journey we would take together."

Grandma inhaled deeply, and then started clearing away all the dirty dishes, deliberately avoiding my eyes whilst she worked.

"After we finished she…" I winced at the faint recollection of the water and the burning sensation, "She went into the ocean and…" I faltered again, swallowing the huge lump that had appeared in the back of my throat, "…and she drowned. There was nothing I could do to save her. I couldn't move… I was…I was trapped somehow," I finished lamely.

I could hear the desperation in my words, as if I was trying to justify why I couldn't move. I again reminded myself that it was only a dream.

"The strangest thing was I feel like I've met her before. I mean somewhere other than the beach." I glanced up, hoping for reassurance but trying not to give away how frightened I actually was.

Grandma was still doing the dishes and didn't respond. She hadn't interrupted me once, which was odd for her. She had just carried on busying herself with the dishes. I was sure she was avoiding my gaze. I changed tactics and decided to ask her a direct question so she had to answer.

"I can't think of any other reason for feeling so drained, tired and hungry. What do you think Grandma?"

She wiped her hands on a dish towel and made a fuss of putting her rings back on. Finally, she turned round to look at me, sighing heavily.

"Yes," she said hurriedly, "It was because of the sun." She said this very unconvincingly and I was certain she was hiding something. She knew what my dream had meant. Why wouldn't she tell me?

I didn't believe for one second that she thought it was the sun. For one thing, she never agreed with me on anything, even if it was true! It just wasn't right, and the way she kept looking around at everything apart from me was making me more suspicious. It made me feel wrong, like I was crazy or something.

I pulled a bread roll onto my lap and picked at it whilst singing the words the girl had spoken, "To complete the star, five over one, the rise of the light by the sun."

"Where did you hear that?" Gran asked me, suddenly grasping my hand so tightly it hurt.

I grimaced and pulled my hand away, "The girl in my dream sang it," I said alarmed by the look on her face.

"Grandma..." I began, but was interrupted by the doorbell.

We both stared at each other. We weren't expecting any visitors at this time of the night. I wanted to ignore it and carry on talking to her. Why did she look so frightened?

AN UNWELCOME VISITOR

RUBY

I padded across the floor towards the kitchen window cautiously. I wasn't expecting anyone at this hour. I knew I had to be careful - Seraphina was showing too many signs of her powers and it had already attracted Maura's attention. That dream was no coincidence. The Fates were involved now. I pulled back the netting and sighed with relief and annoyance.

Standing at the door, a determined look on his face, was Joey. He was proving to be a nuisance as well as being unwanted! I turned and walked slowly towards the door. How was I going to handle *this* situation? His timing was so bad! I couldn't risk upsetting Seraphina as she was already in such a delicate state.

I saw her out the corner of my eye mimicking my movements; she pulled back the netting and gasped in horror. I watched as she looked down at herself. She was wearing her purple PJ's, bunny slippers and that old blue housecoat.

"Wait!" She shouted at me. She ran towards the stairs, giving me an urgent pleading look before running up.

I decided I'd give her a minute, but only because she wasn't dressed decently and not because she wanted to get *pretty* for him. I waited until I heard her bedroom door close then opened the door.

"Good evening, Mr Parkinson."

"Oh, hi… I mean, good evening Mrs Basco," he said, looking uncomfortable under my enquiring stare.

"Come in Mr Parkinson. It's a bit late to be calling," I said in the kindest tone I could muster.

This guy really irritated me, but for Seraphina's sake I decided to be nice. She couldn't be pushed anymore or it definitely would have been too late.

"Thank you, Mrs Basco," he said, smiling at me whilst wiping his feet on the doormat.

I showed him into the lounge and watched as he settled himself down in *my* chair. Ha! He thinks he can play *that* game in *my* house?

"Can I get you a drink?" I smile to show I wasn't fazed.

"Yes please, if it's not too much trouble. I'll have a black coffee please. Is Seraphina here?" He was getting straight to the point.

"She'll be down in a minute. You took us by surprise she' wasn't decent enough to greet you," I stated, making it clear I wasn't happy about the fact that he had come without an invitation.

"Please forgive my intrusion, but I was worried," he said, looking at his feet.

"It's fine. I guess your phone's not working. I'll fetch some tea," I said ignoring the fact that he asked for black coffee.

I walked out of the room and entered the kitchen, pleased at his annoyed expression at my rudeness. I returned in record time; there was no way I was leaving him alone in my house for long enough to allow him to snoop around.

"Here we are," I said, placing the tea tray down on the coffee table.

"Thank you," he said. He looked at my old china teacups and screwed up his face. It was clearly a look of disgust.

He could sneer all he wanted at my cups but I was fond of them! They were a gift from some good friends in England. Both our heads looked up as Seraphina burst through the door, looking dishevelled. She had hastily thrown on a pair of jeans and a scruffy tank top, her hair thrown into a messy ponytail.

SERAPHINA BASCO

Joey and Grandma looked at me as I rushed through the lounge door with a thunderous bang. I stopped and stared at Joey who was sitting in Grandma's chair, looking completely out of place.

"Err... as I was saying Mrs Basco, I've only come to check on Seraphina. She gave me quite a scare," he said, staring at me with wide, beautiful eyes.

My heart leapt. He was worried about me! My insides lunged as my mind wandered off, acting out a scene with him sobbing over my unconscious body, declaring his secret and passionate love for me.

Grandma let out a huge fake cough, dragging me back to reality, and I smiled at Joey. She proceeded to hand him a cup of tea and I shuddered. She was using the oldest, most out-of-date china we had. The cups were white with blue rims and had small winged horses on the front. Typical! Grandma was always trying to make a statement.

"I'm fine Joey." I answered before Grandma could. "I think I had too much sun and with all the drama that happened today I just got a bit overwhelmed, that's all."

This was a lie, of course. I knew what was wrong with me, but I wasn't going to tell him. He'd think I was a freak and would run like hell in the other direction! I *couldn't* let that happen.

"Oh! Well I'm glad to see you're okay. I was... I mean to say we all were worried about you," he said, in a bit of an embarrassed blunder.

I watched as he stumbled over his words. He looked so cute

and worried, but he also looked so out of place. I had to giggle.

"What's so funny?" Grandma snapped. Obviously rudeness was still uncalled for even if she didn't like him. I was still expected to show our unwelcome visitor the manners we would expect to receive, so laughing at him was quite rude.

I shrugged. "Nothing," I replied and hung my head to look at my feet. Great, odd socks! Oh man… why had I rushed?

"Cookie?" Grandma offered a plate to Joey.

I quickly walked into the room and sat down on the floor. I tucked my feet underneath me so he couldn't see my socks. Joey took a cookie, dunked it in his cup and took a huge bite, dropping half of it down his beautiful tan sweater. He shoved his cup back on the tray and swore loudly making me blink in shock.

"Oh, I'm so sorry. Forgive my language," he mumbled, picking at soggy pieces of cookie with shaking fingers. He was really nervous! Why did he look so scared? Okay swearing in front of Grandma was a bit of a stupid thing to do, but she hadn't even reacted to it.

"Don't worry," Grandma said with a sweet tone, although her face contradicted her words. It was set like stone: stern and annoyed.

"These are very unusual mugs, Mrs Basco. Are they from England?" Joey gazed at the winged horse.

Gran looked alarmed for a moment, which did not go unnoticed by either of us. "No I got them from China."

I starred at her. Why was she lying? I knew she had been given them for Christmas when I was young by one of her English friends. Maybe she was just being sarcastic.

"So then, Mr Parkinson," she spoke before I could contradict her, "is there anything else I can help you with or did you just come round here to look at my china?"

What? I was so embarrassed by her rudeness that I could have died! One rule for me –again -and a different one for her!

"Err... well actually I've come to give you these," he said, looking directly into my eyes.

He smiled softly at me, then that strange red glow was back again. I concentrated hard on his eyes, trying to figure out what it was, when he suddenly blinked and turned away. Did he just have a natural reddish brown in his eyes? He pulled out two pieces of card from his pocket. He handed them to me slowly and gently brushed his fingers across the back of my hand as he did so.

My heart spluttered and a swarm of butterflies began to flutter deep in my stomach. Taking a huge breath, I opened the card with trembling fingers as I smiled at him. I had to calm down before I ended up passing out again, or worse, igniting the fire beside me. I read the writing on the card and smiled.

"They're tickets for dinner at The Fortune Hotel," I said, passing them over to Grandma, who was holding out her hand for them, that stern look still fixed on her face.

I looked into Joey's eyes again and took the strength I needed from them. I would ask him now whilst Grandma was otherwise occupied!

"There are two tickets," I blurted out, "I can bring a guest. I would like you to come with me," I babbled in a rush of excitement and fear.

Oh man... What had I just done? I looked at Joey's face and tried to read his expression. It was difficult. Was it surprised, shocked, saddened?

Joey and Grandma both gawked at me, their mouths hanging open in a perfect O shape. It would have been quite comical if I wasn't scared out of my wits at Grandma's reaction and Joey's rejection. All of a sudden I felt sick.

As I stared back at them my confidence faded rapidly. I was starting to regret saying anything as the uncomfortable silence stretched on. I stared down at my fingers, wishing someone would say something, anything! Please! This was a bad idea. To my surprise Joey spoke first.

"Wouldn't you prefer your Grandma's company?"

I felt a pang of hurt in my chest, like someone had rammed a red hot knife through it. I looked over at Grandma and felt even worse as even she looked hurt by it too.

"Well… yes, of course I would, but I would like to take you with me too. After all, I wouldn't be going if you hadn't given me the job in the first place." I turned my head to face Grandma and gave her a pleading look.

She sighed and replied "I guess that would be okay. But I won't have any misbehaving." She glared at Joey, "You're going to take really good care of her, and no funny business. If anything happens to her I'll hunt you down," she scolded.

"Grandma!" I whined in dismay. What on earth was she saying? Was she changing her mind now? Somehow I couldn't believe she was allowing it; there had to be a hidden agenda somewhere.

Joey looked positively alarmed by her warning. I felt bad for him, I knew what it was like to have her forcefulness shoved on you. It annoyed me, that she would be so forceful with him.

But I was just so happy that she had agreed to it that I could have hugged her there and then. I knew she wouldn't have approved of that though, so I held myself in check.

The night came to an end with me standing on the doorstep waving Joey goodbye and with Grandma sitting in her chair, sulking. I knew she would lecture me for that little stunt, but at that moment I really didn't care. I would deal with her later. I was just so excited I could have burst.

I turned back to Grandma, beaming at her, when I noticed the open fire was burning brighter than normal. Oh man! I really needed to get a grip on my emotions before she saw!

RUBY BASCO

I watched as Seraphina waved, idiotically, to *him*. She really needed to learn some self-control. She might not have noticed the fire blaze, but I certainly had. It was brighter than normal; she was definitely getting stronger and, unfortunately, her powers were starting to connect with her emotions. That was *not* good for a Fire Defender!

I stared into the hearth, dwelling on what he wanted with her and why he was so determined to be alone with my granddaughter. I would have thrown him out for that stunt, but Seraphina hadn't smiled like that for ages. I guess deep down I'm still just a grandma. *Was* it me? *Was* I just being over-protective, or was it something else? I wished Kent would hurry up and return - I needed him now more than ever. As did his daughter!

Seraphina closed the door quietly and turned to face me. I didn't want to argue with her now. I was just too *tired*. My energy was just non-existent.

Instead of speaking she darted past me, her eyes cast on the floor. Evidently I was not the only one who didn't want a fight. I continued to stare into the blaze of flames as she gathered up her belongings and left the room.

I needed to stop this so-called date tomorrow night, but how? I sat and pondered several different scenarios, but each resulted in Seraphina losing control. I couldn't risk that. I squinted at the clock on the wall, barely able to make it out. I flicked on the lamp. That was better, I could see more clearly now. It was two thirty. I had sat for at least three hours and had come up with nothing. I needed help!

I pulled myself up and out of my chair and grabbed my thick woolly jumper from the back. Putting it on, I headed to the kitchen. I took the milk from the fridge, pouring a glass, and advanced towards the back door. I'd put it away on my return. I edged out, trying not to make too much noise. Seraphina must have been asleep as there was no light in her bedroom window. I walked down the crooked garden path leading out into the flower garden, away from the lake and the view of the house. I made my way towards my goal, a giant chestnut tree.

My husband, Adonis, had planted it when he built me this house. It was his wedding gift to me. He had no idea then of the uses it would have over the years. I stepped towards it and placed my hand over a carved heart containing the initials R.B. and A.B, which we had carved on the first day we moved in. I rubbed the letters, then wiped away a tear that escaped the corner of my eye.

"Warriors do not cry," I scolded myself.

"They do if they need to," a small voice answered.

I looked down at the base of the tree and saw a small gnome chomping on a fallen chestnut. He looked up at me, his eyes big and round and his forehead creased with worry. He stood up, which didn't make much difference to his height. He was roughly the same size as a one year old. His baggy blue dungarees, red stripy shirt and red shiny boots gave him the same sort of charm. I smiled at him warmly.

"Good evening, Filbert. Thanks for your comfort, but it's not needed."

"Oh, but it is Madame. You are unhappy, and when you're unhappy we gnomes are unhappy," he answered.

"I'm fine, Filbert. How's your wife and Cubby?" I was trying to change the subject. Gnomes can be very fussy when they want to be.

"We're fine, thanks for asking. Cubby is happy he delivered his first message safely," he said, smiling fondly.

"Thank you for that. She doesn't know it yet, but you may have saved her life," I said, frowning up at Seraphina's window.

I sat myself down on the soft grass next to Filbert and looked out over the lake. For a moment I was content and happy with my surroundings. The moonlight was bouncing off the lake, the trees were humming as the wind blew through them and the sound of soft clicking from the insects. It was so magical, but then I remembered why I came here.

"Filbert, can you deliver another message for me please?" I pulled a paper scroll and pen from my pocket.

"Of course, Madame. I am here to help you and the Basco's," he replied, bowing low at me. I smiled at him and begin to write.

Dana,

We need your help! Seraphina has a date tomorrow night - well tonight - and I cannot stop it!

Yes, it's with HIM and I am certain it's not just a normal date. I'm convinced he is up to something but it's difficult for me to tell.

Meet me at 10a.m. so we can discuss protection for her.

Reply urgently needed.

Ruby

I rolled up the scroll and handed it to Filbert, who shoved it into his boot and which still stuck half way out and up his leg. He grinned at me and I grinned back. He bowed low to me again and turned running through the forest towards the Woodwives' home.

There was nothing left for me to do, but sit and wait for the reply. I lay my head back against the tree and glanced once more at the carved initials.

"Here, Rubes?" Adonis asks me, pointing to the base of our tiny tree.

I giggle at him. "That's not going to last if you carve it now," I reply in a teasing tone.

"Then we will re-carve it every day. As this tree grows so will our love and it will be a constant mark upon it." He speaks in a serious but playful tone as he grabs my hand and pulls me closer to him.

I giggle wildly at the joy of first love. He takes my hand in his and kisses the top of it.

"I am going to make you so happy, Rubes. Everything we have dreamt of will be ours. I promise," he stares into my eyes with such an intense force that I cry tears of sheer happiness.

"Miss, Miss... Wake up Miss Basco. Cuby is here with Dana's note." A small hand was shaking my foot, jolting me from my dream.

I jumped to my feet in shock. The soft morning light was breaking through the tree tops, hitting my face and warming my skin.

"Cuby!"

"Hello," he said, beaming at me and holding out a small scroll that looked like it had been dragged through a hedge backwards. Well, in Cubby's case it probably had.

"What happened to this?" I asked a little too briskly.

Cubby shifted his feet, looking nervous. He hung his head.

"I am sorry, Miss. I was running here as fast as I could but I saw a pretty flower for my mum and I dug it out to give to her." He held out a small, battered looking Daisy.

"I am not that good at digging up flowers yet," he said as the flowers petals fell to the ground. His shoulders slumped.

"It's okay Cubby, you'll learn soon. It's very tricky," I said, hoping to cheer him up. "I need to go. Thank your dad for me and give this to your mother" I handed him a miniature bottle of honeysuckle wine.

He took the bottle, stuffed it into his pocket and picked up a chestnut. I walked back to the house slowly holding onto the note. It was my lifeline.

QUESTIONS

SERAPHINA

I woke early next morning and jumped out of bed so fast I startled a sleepy cat in the process.

"Sorry Hic," I sniggered, giving him a quick fuss.

Hiccup didn't take too kindly to being knocked off the bed and ran out of the room.

"Suit yourself!" I called after him.

I watched him go and could have sworn he gave me a dirty look, if that was possible. I shrugged. He'd get over it.

I rubbed my eyes and shook myself awake properly. I grabbed my housecoat and skipped down the stairs feeling elated. I was finally getting what I wanted and it felt wonderful. So wonderful, in fact, that I was able to jump straight out of bed. Wow! That was a first. I felt like I was going to like these new mornings.

I bounded down the stairs into the kitchen and noticed that Gran had left the milk out. That was strange! She didn't normally do stuff like that. She must have been very upset last night. I frowned at the thought.

I opened the bottle and sniffed it. It was off, so I emptied it down the sink, making a mental note to get some more when I was out.

I stood at the sink thinking last night's events over. Joey looked amazed that Gran had agreed for him to go. He had genuinely looked pleased when I waved him goodbye. Grandma, on the other hand, hadn't. I felt bad about parting in an awkward silence, but there was nothing I could do about it now.

I sighed and, grabbing a plate, started to make my breakfast - an egg bagel smothered in cheese. I wanted to get out before Grandma could stop me.

I finished my breakfast in record time and did the dishes. I cleaned the surfaces for good measure and hung the dish towel up neatly. I wasn't going to give her any reason to stop me from going out tonight. I decided to behave impeccably no matter what!

When everything was done I went back up-stairs and took a quick shower. I didn't even wait for the water to warm up - there wasn't time for that! But as I stepped in I soon realized that was a big mistake. The cold water shocked my body and I shivered. I showered in a matter of minutes and was out and wrapped in a towel before I could blink. I wouldn't be doing that again!

Unfortunately, getting dressed took longer than it would normally. I couldn't find my favorite top – the loose fitting black one - it was great for getting on and off quickly, which, considering my plans,was most appropriate.

I had decided last night, as I lay awake, to go shopping to find a dress for the dinner. I had a small nest egg that I had managed to save from my wages. It wasn't much, but it would have to do. There was no way I could ask Grandma for money!

I stomped my foot in frustration. I couldn't find my purse and I wasn't going to get very far without that. I really needed a maid. I wasn't the cleanest person on the planet and Grandma had refused to clean up after me since I turned ten.

I looked for a whole hour and finally found it under my bed of all places! I emerged from underneath it, my hair tangled and matted, and pulled my iPhone out of my jeans pocket. I scrolled to Tiff's number and called her. I waited for her to answer. It took four rings.

"Hey... Do you know what time it is?" she asked in a sleepy voice.

"Early?" It was a vain attempted at humour. It wasn't that early, was it? I glanced down at my watch... oops! It was only eight!

"Oh! Tiff I'm sorry. I didn't realize. I'm just so excited," I said energetically.

"Why? What's happened?" She suddenly brightened.

"After yesterday..." I began.

"Oh yeah! Congrats on that by the way," she interrupted me.

"Thanks," I said slightly annoyed, "Anyway... Joey turned up last night..."

"What! Why?" another interruption! I rolled my eyes in exasperation.

"He said he was worried about me..."

"Why?" She asked urgently. Geez, didn't she know what had happened yesterday?

"Because I passed out in his office!" I was bewildered. To my surprise, she started to laugh at me.

"You're unbelievable. What happened? Did you pretend to faint and let him catch you?" She giggled like a school girl.

"No!" I snapped, "Do you want to hear this or not?" I pinched my nose with my fingers and screwed my eyes up in an effort to calm down.

"Sorry," she mumbled.

"It's okay. Anyway... he came round not just to check on me but to give me some tickets to The Fortune Hotel."

"No way! What for?" She actually squealed. Oh man, she gets excited so easily.

"They're tickets for dinner. They're from the family of the girl who I saved yesterday."

"Oh! Cool," she replied, instantly sounding bored.

"Yeah," I said quietly. "Joey is coming with me." I tagged it on the end, trying to sound nonchalant.

She squealed again, this time so loudly I had to pull the phone away from my ear. I waited until she had stopped screaming and placed it back to my ear. I could just see her jumping up and down in an excited rush. She was so crazy. I chuckled.

"Is it a date?"

"Yes!" I said, exasperated with her. She could be so slow sometimes.

"Wow! Seraphina, that's unbelievable! And your grandma never did anything about it?" She sounded flabbergasted.

I loved the way she was so in tune with me when it came to my grandma. She knew this would be my only problem.

"No. I thought she would, but she didn't seem to mind. Maybe it had something to do with the fact that he was there and she didn't want to seem rude or cause a scene in front of him." I was glancing at the door as I spoke, not wanting Grandma to hear me being so flippant about it. She still had time to put a stop to it.

"That doesn't seem plausible. Since when does your Gran care about rudeness? It's never bothered her before!"

I didn't like her making comments, but I couldn't argue with her. I wanted to say something, but I didn't want her to get mad at me. Not today. I needed her help.

"So are you going to come with me to find that perfect dress or what?" I said in a daring tone, trying to change the subject.

I knew Tiff couldn't resist a chance to shop and I really needed her help finding something right. It seemed to take twice as long when you have fewer shops to work with.

"I'm *so* there," she said dramatically. "We could go for lunch too! I want to try that new Chinese restaurant. Oh, and you'll need new shoes as well. What time do you want to meet?" Excitement rose with every word she spoke.

"I have to finish a few chores first," I said, determined to be a model granddaughter, "Then I'll head out. Meet you at the post office in one and a half hours?"

"That's great, I'll see you there. Call me when you've left. Bye." Tiffany hung up before I had a chance to reply.

I pressed the end button, laughing to myself. No doubt she had jumped out of bed and headed straight for the shower. She never wastes time.

I sat on the end of my bed and started to feel a little bit guilty. I didn't like it. The cat butted my hand with his head for attention, as if he could sense my discomfort. I hadn't noticed him come back in. It never took him long to forgive me. I absent mindedly stroked him and as he started to purr I instantly felt better.

After sitting still for a while I got up and started to clean my room. I picked up my dirty laundry, cleaned up my closet, put away my shoes and made my bed. I felt pleased with myself for cleaning up so fast and skipped back downstairs.

I grabbed my bag from the closet by the back door, and as I turned around I collided with Grandma. She didn't look too good tired and worn out as if she had been up all night. I took a step back and stared at her, taking in her appearance.

"Are you alright? You don't look well!"

"I'm fine, Seraphina. Where are you off to?" Her voice was a faint whisper.

I wasn't happy with the way she looked at all. I could see her eyes were bloodshot and puffy, with deep, purple circles forming around them. What had she done? Slept under a tree all night?

I smiled at her, trying to break the tension that was thick in the air. I inhaled deeply and caught the scent of chestnuts. It seemed to be coming from her.

"Why do you smell like chestnuts?" I looked down at her. It was only then that I noticed she was still wearing her clothes from last night. Had she even gone to bed?

"Grandma," I began noticing the mud on her trousers, "Did

you go to bed last night? Have you been out?"

She grimaced at me and shook her head, marching past me to get to the table.

"What kinds of questions are those? Of course I went to bed! I haven't been out! How silly," she snapped.

I stood still like a statue. Why was she lying to me?

"Seraphina, I'm not waiting all day for you to answer my question," she snapped again as I tried to recall what she had asked.

"Oh! Err... sorry, what was the question again?" All other conversations had melted from my mind.

"Where are you going?" she barked, rolling her eyes in exasperation.

"I'm going shopping with Tiff because I need a dress... for tonight." I said quietly, looking down at the floor.

I didn't want to upset her and I knew the guilt I felt at these words would overwhelm me if I tried to explain. I shifted uncomfortably under the weight of her intense stare. I shouldn't really be going out if Grandma wasn't well.

"I can stay here if you need me to," I said and felt my shoulders slump. I didn't really want to stay home, but I knew I should if she needed me to.

"No," she said abruptly, "it's fine. I have lots of stuff to do today."

Well that was odd. I really wasn't expecting that sort of a reaction - I thought she would jump at the opportunity I had just given her.

"I don't mind," I said making sure this wasn't her way of making me choose before guilt tripping me later for not choosing right.

"It's fine. Where are you and Tiff going?" She poured hot water into her teapot.

"I'm not sure, we haven't decided yet," I said, fiddling with my rucksack handle.

"I don't want you leaving town. Stay in Capalis, please." She frowned at me, concern spreading across her face.

"Okay, we were anyway," I said, looking at her with widened eyes. Why was she concerned about me leaving town?

"Good, well… yes… err… that's good then. I want you home before two please." She poured the tea from the pot into her china mug.

"Alright," I said cheerfully, trying to pick up the dull mood. I could come home by two if it made her happier - after all she was letting me go, which was a surprise. I thought she would be protesting and trying all sorts to make me stay home.

I hugged her and gave her a quick kiss on the cheek. She smiled at me, then returned to looking sullen. I returned her smile quickly before dashing for the door.

"See you later Grandma," I shouted as I dashed out the kitchen.

I grabbed my stuff from the cream sofa and shoved it into my bag. I glanced sideways at the hearth and was happy to see it wasn't lit. I smiled in triumph then grabbed my keys and proceeded to the front door. Today was going to be a good day.

SHOPPING

SERAPHINA

Tiffany and I headed straight for the town's best store for evening gowns. It was also the town's only store for evening gowns. There weren't many on the high street. That was the only problem with living in a small coastal town- you were very limited.

We had been looking around the store for what seemed like hours. I was disappointed with everything I had seen.

"What about this one?" Tiffany asked, holding out a very frilly dress.

I pulled a face. It was revolting: white and navy polka dots, long to the floor with frills following from the collar down the front of the dress. There was a navy blue sash that went round the middle and tied in a big bow in the back, like the sort of dress six year old girls wear. The sleeves were long too and cuffed around the wrist with yet more frills. It was the worst dress I had ever seen and the worst part of it was that it was made from a cheap, cottony material. Very tacky.

I laughed and, closing my eyes, made a gagging gesture. I opened them just in time to see the look on Tiff's face. Oh no! She was being serious.

"Oh…" I stammered, not sure what to say or do. I opted for

staring at my feet and avoided looking directly at her. It was quiet for a long time and I eventually plucked up the courage to look up at her again. She was holding that revolting dress and looking at me with her, 'why are you laughing at me?' face.

"Well I'm just not sure that would be right for the hotel," I finally managed to say. I could feel my cheeks turning pink with embarrassment.

I didn't want to hurt her feelings, but the dress was like something Barbie would wear.

"Yeah, you're right," she sighed, placing it back on the rail. "Meringues are best left for proms and not fancy hotels, right?" She cocked her eyebrow up at me before raising her hand to her mouth to stifle her hysterical giggle.

"I was only joking. Seriously, I wish I had a mirror so you could see your face!" She burst out laughing.

I smiled at her in relief, wanting to hug and punch her at the same time. I turned back to the rack and carried on searching for something extra special as Tiff tried to control her giggling fit.

I wanted something that said, "I'm worthy of your time" and, "I'd be perfect a perfect girlfriend."

I started to become frustrated as nothing like that really stood out to me. The only thing I managed to find was a rack of pale red coats. It wasn't what I was here for, but I thought one might make a nice present for Grandma.

They were gorgeous; waist length and pleated. The sleeves had four gold buttons running down the side. I was fumbling with one, trying to find a price tag, when Tiffany shouted over to me.

"Seraphina, I've found it! It's the world's most perfect dress!"

I grabbed the coat and ran over to her, bumping into another girl in my rush.

"Oh, I'm so sorry," I said as I bent down to grab the dress I'd made her drop.

"Leave it!" she snapped at me.

I stopped mid-scoop and straightened up to glare at her. I watched as she bent down and picked it up.

"Do you know what this is?" she snapped again, her face pure hostility.

I looked at it. It was blue and silky, just a dress. The girl was obviously not amused by my slowness and gave me a look of pure loathing.

"This is a Dior," she said, rolling her eyes at my lack of knowledge. A defensive anger rose in me at that. Who cared what it was?

"So?" I snapped, taking an immediate dislike to this snotty girl.

"I didn't think someone like you would know, looking at that trash you're holding," she said, flipping the sleeve of the red coat that hung over my arm.

"Watch it!" I snarled, surprising myself.

Normally I didn't rise to girls like her, but the coat was for my grandma.

"Oh, I'm so sorry, did I hurt your feelings?" she sneered mockingly.

Who the hell did she think she was? My face started to burn with anger as I snatched the blue dress from her and threw it to the floor.

"What are you doing?" she squealed, bending down to pick it up.

I just stood watching her. She picked the dress up off the floor and marched over to a small group of gossiping girls.

"You better watch yourself! You're not as *hot* as you think you are," she called back over her shoulder.

Oh man! Why had she emphasised the word hot? Was it just coincidence? What a group of idiots. I was so annoyed!

"Sera, come on! What are you doing?" Tiff shouted from the other side of the store, oblivious to what had just happened.

I started to walk towards her, glancing over my shoulder at the group of girls as I did. They were all laughing at me and making exaggerated mocking gestures of me. I was getting so angry with them. I just couldn't believe how childish some people were!

I watch as the girl who I bumped into started making a shooing gesture at me. I halted and turned fully to face them, about to shout an insult when they started to scream and run. They were all scrambling to get out of the store and as far as possible. Cowards!

I stuffed the coat back onto a random rail, no longer wanting it. I just wanted to leave. They had ruined my shopping trip. What a bunch of stupid girls! I took one last look at them and turned on my heel to find Tiffany.

"Seraphina! I'm over here! Come on," she complained loudly, rolling her eyes up at the ceiling and tapping her foot.

"What's wrong?" she asked as soon as I reached her. My face must have been showing my frustration.

"Nothing," I whispered, looking over my shoulder at the group of girls.

It looked like they were now complaining to a man in a suit. It must have been the manager! I hurriedly looked away, feeling slightly agitated, and then saw the dress Tiff was holding. Wow!

"So... what do you think?" I eyed the dress in awe.

I glanced again at the girls. They couldn't be complaining about me. I did say sorry, well the first time anyway. Oh man! They were still talking to the manager and I felt a twinge of unease spread through me.

"Sera!" Tiff barked and snapped her fingers in front of my face, bringing my attention back to the dress.

"It's perfect. It's gorgeous. It's exactly what I was looking for," I mumbled. Tiff rolled her eyes impatiently.

"Go try it on then," she said, her eyes glancing between me and the group of girls.

The manager was now searching the shop floor for someone. My heart sank. He was holding a pale red coat - the same one I had randomly shoved back onto the rack. Oh no! Was he searching for me? I ducked behind a rail and started to panic. I should have put it back in the right place. Peering through the clothes I saw the girls striding behind him looking smug! I had to do something, but what? Then, without thinking, I darted into the changing rooms, leaving a bewildered-looking Tiff behind. I turned and gave her the best apologetic smile I could as I whipped the curtains shut.

Once inside the changing room I started to feel drained, light headed and a little queasy. I sat on the plush purple chair and put my head between my knees. I tried to control my breathing, taking deep, slow breaths.

After a while the dizziness started to fade but my heart started to race as I heard the manager asking one of the clerks if she had seen a girl with auburn hair: Me!

I couldn't believe my ears - the manager *was* actually looking for me. I quickly stripped off my jeans and top and slipped the blue dress over my head, fumbling with the silky material. Time was of the essence if I was about to get kicked out I would leave knowing the dress actually fitted and looked good. I could always then get Tiff to buy it. It slithered straight down my body to the floor and felt unbelievable against my skin. It tied around the back of my neck, dropping into a plunge at the front. Grandma wouldn't like that! I attached the sash around my waist and tied it into a knot in the back.

I glanced into the dressing room's small, dingy mirror and frowned. I could barely see it! I stepped out onto the shop floor and twirled around in the full length mirror.

Wow! It looked amazing, clinging to my curvy figure and falling lightly to the floor. I felt like Cinderella. I *would* finally get to go to the ball and win the handsome prince.

As I twirled on the spot, day dreaming about my Prince

Charming Joey, the girl I had knocked over shouted and pointed, "That's her there! The one spinning around like an idiot." Oh no! I was so absorbed in the dress I had forgotten about them again.

The manager started to walk over to me, like a lion stalking its prey, followed by the smug-looking girls. I started to panic again, feeling the sudden rush of adrenaline swell up inside me.

"That's her. She did it right in front of us, after she pushed me over," the girl said wagging her finger in my direction.

"Excuse me," the manager said, 'These girls seem to think that you're responsible for this."

He handed me the pale red coat and pointed to the sleeve.

"What! I didn't..." I began and broke off with a dreadful thought. Had I?

The sleeve had five small burn holes seared into it. I looked back at the manager's stony face, horrified.

"I didn't do that." I replied nervously. He looked at me skeptically. Even I didn't believe my own voice. I wasn't sure, I couldn't have. Could I?

"Well, you were standing next to these coats a moment ago and these girls said they saw you do it," he said in a serious voice.

He was looking at me, his face very stern. "I'm sorry," he finally said, "But you'll have to pay for this."

"What? But...I didn't do it!" I spluttered.

I was close to tears and my hands wouldn't stop shaking. I just couldn't believe these girls were doing this. They didn't even know me! What had I ever done to them?

I couldn't pay for the coat because I wouldn't then have enough for the dress. After a long time arguing with the manager and threats being made of police being called, Tiffany finally managed to rescue me.

"Excuse me, but I saw that on the coat earlier and I told your sales assistant about it!" She said, her hands on her hips. "She said she was going to move it off the rack! It's not her fault your staff didn't move it before these girls looked at it." She stabbed a thin finger in their direction as she spoke.

I was so grateful. She really was a good friend. I had no idea what I would do without her. We paid for my dress, under the frowning gaze of the manager, and departed under dirty looks from the others. I returned their gazes with interest, then opened the door and ushered Tiff out before she flew at them.

"That girl has a serious attitude problem," Tiffany said, as we walked out. "What did you do to her?"

"All I did was bump into her. It was a complete accident," I replied, following her out the door. "Thanks for that, by the way. You saved me there."

"Oh it's okay," she replied, waving her hand vaguely, "What are best friends for? How did you do it though? Those marks looked like finger prints!" she laughed whole heartedly.

I stiffened, then laughed with her, although mine sounded hollow and forced. Deep down I was terrified. I was pretty sure I *had* done it.

I couldn't understand what had happened to the coat, but I was sure those marks weren't there when I had looked at it.

"Here, it looks so good," Tiff said, interrupting my thoughts.

We were standing outside a small noodle bar and the smell made my stomach rumble. I hadn't noticed how hungry I was!

"Do you want to eat here?" Tiff asked, picking up a menu from an outside table.

"Yeah, it looks good," I said, dropping down into a chair and placing my bags at the side of the table. Tiff followed my lead, not taking her eyes off the menu, and I noticed my hands were still shaking. Was it adrenaline from the row earlier, or fear at how much my ability seemed to be causing problems lately?

Tiff and I ordered the Thai green chicken noodles, which turned out to be amazingly good, and starting to plan where to go next. I stopped, fork mid-way to my mouth and gaped -the same girl from the store was watching me from across the street. Well, not watching as much as staring - her face of pure evil and full of loathing.

"I think we should go to the salon and get our hair and nails done. You're going on the biggest date you've ever had... well, the *only* date you've ever had! You need to look amazing." Tiff squealed again, excitedly interrupting my staring contest.

"Sorry. What?" I asked, glancing back at her.

"I said I think we should go to the salon and get our hair and nails done. You're going on the biggest date ever! You need to look amazing."

"It's the *first* date I've ever been on," I laughed, taking another bite of chicken.

"I know! I just said that. It's even more of a reason to do it. Besides, they're fancy at that hotel and you need to fit in," Tiff said. She stuffed a huge fork full of noodles into her mouth and spilt half of it down her chin.

"Okay. We'll go to Angie's after this and ask if they can fit us in. I can't stay too late though - Grandma looked quite unwell this morning so I said I'd be back by two. I don't want to upset her any more than I already have this week." I immediately started worrying about her.

Tiff rolled her eyes exasperatedly. "It's not like you're going out on a normal date though, is it? You're going to be presented with an award and everything. You have to look good..." She broke off, clasping her hand to her mouth. She shook her head.

"What do you mean an award? It's just dinner, isn't it?" I said.

"Oops... I wasn't supposed to say anything about that." Tiff looked down at her noodle box. I couldn't help but take pity on her.

"Don't worry about it, I'll still act surprised," I smiled.

We finished our meals and slowly walked towards Angie's. I hoped they could fit us in. It *was* the only decent hairdressers for miles around.

We stepped through the door to the sound of Katy Perry's, 'I Kissed a Girl', and were immediately greeted by a small woman.

She smiled sweetly at us, her wide grin showing off her brilliantly white teeth. She flicked her long brown curly hair behind her ear and said, "Hi, how may I help you beautiful girls today?"

"Hi," I replied, with a smile of my own. "I need an appointment as soon as possible please."

"Sure. I can fit you in now if you like, my one o'clock just cancelled. It was some older lady wanting highlights," she giggled. "I think she changed her mind."

Tiff settled herself down in a chair to the side and picked up the first magazine to hand. A young blonde girl shampooed my hair and led me towards a chair, chatting the entire time. I nodded and smiled. It was all I could do; she wouldn't let me talk except for when I explained what I wanted.

After an hour - and a lot of ear ache - I finally got to see the results. I blinked at the girl looking back at me in the mirror. She was stunning. Her hair was piled high on the top of her head with tight curls cascading down her face. I blinked again… I couldn't believe that was me and my hair. I looked so different.

"Wow!" Tiff exclaimed, creeping up behind me, "You look amazing."

"Thanks, Tiff." I said, grinning broadly.

I paid the woman, leaving her a generous tip, and left with my arm linked through Tiff's. I couldn't stop messing with my hair and glancing at it in the store fronts.

Tiff laughed at me, "Come on, let's get you home before you or the wind blows your hair down."

She was right. The weather seemed to have changed rapidly; it was darker. A big black cloud was lingering ominously over us. We managed to catch a taxi and began the journey home. I made sure Tiff was safely inside her house before asking the driver to take me home.

The taxi pulled into Grandma's drive and began to follow the path round to the house. As I got closer to home I started to worry. I could see a strange car parked outside. The strangest part was the guy it. He was wearing a black suit with sunglasses covering half his face! He looked very much like one of those Schwarzenegger-wanna-be guys.

I immediately started to panic about Grandma as the image of how she looked before I left barged its way back into my mind. I hoped she was okay. What if she was sick and had needed to call a doctor? Surely not? Doctors don't have drivers, do they?

I threw a twenty at the driver before he could even tell me the fare and jumped out. I didn't bother waiting for my change. I slammed the door behind me and grabbed my bags.

I ran up the path, struggling to find my keys in my handbag, overloaded with all the other bags in my hands. I grasped the door key and pushed it inside the keyhole.

I could hear hushed voices coming from the other side of the door and my heart began to pound. I fumbled, finally managing to turn the key. The door gave a slight creak as I opened it.

I glanced behind me just in time to see the guy in the car speed off recklessly. My heart pounded in my chest. I had a bad feeling about this. I could hear Grandma talking to someone as I walked, shakily, towards the lounge.

A voice replied to hers and I froze in shock. I knew that voice. I took another trembling step forward, pushing open the lounge door and came face to face with... my dad!

REUNITED

KENT

I gazed at her. The apple of my eye, my daughter, Seraphina. A beaming smile spread across my face at her bewildered gaze.

She faltered for a moment then hopped on the spot, clapping her hands and making me laugh.

She looked absolutely delighted to see me, for which I was immensely grateful. I wasn't sure how she would have reacted to me after all this time. It had been so long since I'd seen her.

"Hi sweetheart," I said, grinning a little nervously and opening my arms wide for a hug.

She immediately ran, bolting across the room and leaping into my waiting arms. My mother smiled at me. Clearly she was pleased with Seraphina's reaction. Then out of nowhere, Seraphina startled me by starting to cry, leaning heavily into my shoulder.

"Oh Dad, I can't believe you're actually here," she sobbed.

I hugged her tightly and stroked the back of her hair. I breathed in, deeply remembering her scent, before holding her back at arm's length. I studied every inch of her face before I let her withdraw from me.

She had changed so much. She was looking more and more like her mother, my beloved Talia. This pained me. Tears were falling thick and fast down her perfect cheeks, and for a second she looked very young and vulnerable. Guilt panged in the pit of my stomach. I should have been here for her more, even if it was dangerous.

"I can't remember the last time she's cried this much," my mother chided, an unimpressed look on her face.

Ruby had always been a strong woman and she felt that tears were for the weak. I couldn't agree, having wept quite a few times over the years. Especially after that dreadful day, when I had lost Seraphina's mother. The way my mother had scolded me for crying! I don't think I could ever forgive her for that lack of compassion.

I held Seraphina tightly again and let her cry. It took several minutes for her to control herself and I watched as the fire spiralled and twisted behind us.

"I hear you've become a local hero," I said to her, glancing across the room at my mother. Seraphina blushed with pride as she settled herself on the couch next to me.

I winced slightly at the separation and she smiled noticing my discomfort. She linked her arm through mine and laid her head on my shoulder, wiping her eyes on my sleeve. I smiled back at her and kissed her lightly on the forehead.

"Not really," she said modestly, "I did what anyone else would have done." She shrugged her shoulders.

She glanced at her fingers and intertwined them. I was sure she was starting to feel quite embarrassed by now. I knew I shouldn't start acting the 'proud parent'- after all I hadn't always been there for her. I frowned, feeling guilt flutter around in my stomach.

I looked back at her beautiful face and watched as she pulled at a thin lock of her hair and started to twirl it round her fingers. It was a sweet and endearing motion, one that evidently calmed her down. It was like watching a baby's expression when you give them a pacifier for the first time - the relief and security. Her shoulders slumped and she relaxed instantly.

"Seraphina, stop that!" my mother chided, making us both jump. A sour look spread across her face.

That annoyed me for a moment. It was obviously her way of calming down. My mother should've seen that and left her to it unless no, it couldn't be. It couldn't be because Seraphina's mother used to do that, could it? She had always hated her doing it, almost as much as she hated her. Anger instantly rushed through me as the thought pushed its way into my mind.

"Mother, don't be so hard on her!"

Seraphina took a sharp breath, and my mother scowled at me. I hung my head at her gaze in shame and turmoil. Thinking about Talia too long always made me feel drained and demented with rage. I still couldn't cope with the loss. She was my world.

It just wasn't fair the way she was taken from me, Marina had promised me. She said I would prevail that she would live. I closed my eyes as I thought about that night.

I opened my eyes and saw Seraphina glaring at her grandma in a way I was not happy with.

"Seraphina! Don't let me see you looking at your grandma like that again! Show some respect please," I said.

She instantly looked down at her hands again, the fingers still interlaced in her lap. Maybe that was a little too harsh.

"I'm sorry Dad," she replied sombrely, "I had forgotten how much grandma hated me twirling my hair, but sometimes I just can't help it."

The flames in the hearth behind her flared as she looked to the floor. I caught my mother's eye to see if she too had noticed.

She stared back at me with a knowing expression and nodded in acknowledgement. At that moment I knew it was time to tell Seraphina the truth about who she was and the cruel destiny the Fates had laid on our family.

SERAPHINA BASCO

I could see my Dad and Grandma staring at each other from out the corner of my eye as I stared at my hands. Maybe they were trying to decide how they were going to stop me from twirling my hair. Then Grandma left the room mumbling about tea.

When I was younger, Grandma used to smack the back of my hand every time she saw me doing it. It's maddening, infuriating, most of the time. Plus a lot of the time I'm not aware I'm doing it.

I was so annoyed at Grandma's constant jabs that after a while I had stopped doing it, in front of her at least! I couldn't believe she was reprimanding me about it right now though. Dad *had* just reappeared back into my life with no warning. It was a lot to deal with. In fact *I* didn't know why I had started twirling my hair again.

Maybe it *was* from seeing my dad again – something that reminded me of when I was younger - or maybe it was because I could feel myself losing control again. I often found comfort in it and it did help me calm down. I just hoped they couldn't see that annoying hearth as I knew I'd made it rise from the heat on my back. I couldn't afford to do that right now. Grandma would probably have a stroke, or worse Dad might send me to a 'special hospital' where you're forced to wear straight jackets!

Grandma walked back into the room, clinking and crashing a tray with tea and cookies on it.

"Mom, there's no need to be so hard on Seraphina. She can't help twirling her hair," he said, giving me a wink.

"She's not seven anymore Kent," Grandma shot at him, "I will not have her acting like a child just because you're here. It's a horrid habit that *I* have managed to stamp out of her."

"Her mother used to do that, and I found it very endearing," he said in a small voice. My head shot up to stare at him.

I never knew that my mother used to do it too. I watched as

Grandma looked into my Dad's eyes, anger flitting across her face. I shot up out my seat to help her and we moved over to the cream sofa. My dad followed and sat down next to me, sighing heavily.

I took a huge breath in,capturing his deep, musky scent, and tried to commit it to my memory. Who knew how long he'd stay for this time.

"Sera..." Grandma called, snapping me out of my sulk.

"Err... sorry Gran. What did you say?" I looked back and forth between them. My dad stifled a giggle and my grandma rolled her eyes at me.

"I think you need your ears testing. I asked if you would like some tea." She had her hands on her hips.

"Yes please Gran," I said, sitting up straighter.

She handed me a mug, her hands shaking slightly. My dad stepped forward and took them from Grandma. He frowned slightly, I instantly felt bad - I should have been taking better care of her.

"So, how have you been, mom?" Dad took the pot and poured tea into the white cups which were encrusted with a gold, swirly pattern. I wasn't surprised to see them on the tray because Grandma always used them for special guests. I guess my dad was someone special. She was proud too sometimes! It was only Dad - family, well, when he showed up. He didn't care what mug his tea's in.

"I'm okay... well, coping anyway," she replied.

My heart thudded at these words. *Coping.* Coping with what? Coping with me?

"I had an appointment with Dr. Hardy last week," she said, taking a sip of her tea.

"And?" Dad prompted.

"Well, I'm getting older now and... well, it's getting harder to control," she said, glancing up at me.

What? What was getting harder to control? I wanted to say

something but couldn't. I didn't even know she had seen Dr. Hardy. I hadn't seen him since I was nine and had caught chicken-pox.

"Is there anything he can do?" Dad frowned with worry.

"No. I'll be fine. I'll continue my normal treatment and diet," she said, taking a triple chocolate fudge cookie and smiling at her choice. Dad smiled back at her and also took one.

I was in shock hearing Grandma talk about her health like that. I had had no idea, I mean she hadn't looked well that morning but… It was then that I realised I hadn't paid enough attention to her and that I hadn't taken good enough care of her. I had always moaned and complained instead of being attentive and grateful for her. My stomach flipped over and my chest hurt with the over-whelming guilt I started to feel. I stared at the mug in my hands and thought about how much I had let her down.

"Ahh!" I squealed, dropping my mug and sending it crashing to the wooden floor.

"What's wrong?" My dad asked.

"Nothing! It was just a little hot," I mumbled and went to grab a dish towel. My teacup was red hot and had burnt my lips as I took a sip.

Grandma was mopping up the spilt tea without a word, but was glancing at my dad with a 'see what I have to put up with?' look on her face. This did not help my guilty feelings.

Dad sat back down with a thoughtful look on his face. I knew that look. He was thinking hard and was worried about something. Who was it: me or Grandma?

"There's no need to look so sullen, Kent. I am old and my time will soon be over. It's something you have to accept," Grandma said.

What an odd thing for her to say! She wasn't that old, was she? Oh man, I felt like such a bad granddaughter! I didn't even know how old my gran was! She never answered the question when I was younger and never let me celebrate her birthdays.

"Come now," my dad said laughing, "You talk like you'll be dead tomorrow."

I could see he was trying to lighten the mood, but Gran just arched an eyebrow and poured herself more tea.

"Dr. Hardy is popping in later," she said, surprising me. I told myself I'd be there for that! I was going to find out what was going on.

"Good. I haven't seen him for years. When is he arriving?" Dad asked.

"Oh, not till late about nine," Grandma replied.

"No!" I shouted, making everyone jump.

"What's the matter now, child?" Grandma chided.

"Oh, err... sorry Gran, I just wanted to see him, but I'll be..." I began.

"Well you can't. You'll be off gallivanting around town with *Joseph*," she sneered.

"His name is *Joey* not *Joseph*."

"Oh yes, this guy who's taking you out tonight," Dad said in an interested tone.

Oh man, Gran had already told him her version, then. He surveyed me cautiously over his teacup and I smiled sheepishly.

"I did write to you to tell you, but I guess you wouldn't have got the letter yet," I said, interest rising.

He seemed well informed now though. I thought about it - had Gran already told him everything? I glanced around the room and noticed his cases still in the door-way and his coat on the back of the chair. He couldn't have been around for long before I had turned up.

"I have to get ready," I said, suddenly wanting to be on my own. "Joey will be here in a few hours."

My dad and Grandma exchanged worried glances. Obviously they had been talking about Joey and my date tonight before I came home. Was I about to get a lecture from both of them now?

I squirmed uncomfortably.

"Shoot!" my dad exclaimed as he dropped his chocolate cookie into his tea. I used the diversion to my advantage and ran up the stairs before they could start.

STAY WITH ME

KENT

I looked up after fishing my cookie out from my tea to catch a glimpse of Seraphina's back as she dashed up the stairs. Ha! That girl was quick. Very smart! I chuckled to myself and continued to fish out the remaining cookie that has made its way to the surface.

"She's getting a lot harder to handle these days. She's extremely hot-headed and has no patience at all," Mom said, moving the cookies away from me as I went to take another.

"I can't believe how grown up she is," I said, shaking my head, "It's scary seeing her face to face. It's harder talking to her than writing a letter."

"What you need to do now can't be done in a letter, Kent," Mom said, sympathy and slight annoyance clearly etched on her face.

"I know," I said, trying again to reach for another cookie, "I'm just not sure where to begin."I responded with a pleading look.

I was hoping she would tell me how to do it… and start 'the talk. After all, she had already done it with me. She pulled the cookies further away, sighing. I lolled back into my chair and sulked.

We looked at each other and the silence between us stretched on and on, until I could take it no more. I finally broke it, "It's a hard thing to do."

After a very long pause, I sighed in defeat. I could tell she wasn't going to make it easy for me. I guess I shouldn't have been surprised really; she never had made life comfortable. In her opinion an easy life did not make a strong Defender.

"You need to be tough Kent. The Fates don't take kindly to cowards!" She used to say.

"It's going to change her life and I'm not too sure how to start," I hissed, taking another chocolate cookie from the plate before she had time to react. Wow! I can't believe I was faster than her. That was a first! She flashed a smile that contained a hint of surprise.

"Try at the beginning. It worked for me," she replied, taking the cookies and tea pot back into the kitchen.

I moaned to myself and looked up at the ceiling to Seraphina's room. Something caught my eye and I turned my attention to the corner of the room. A small white cat sat staring at me. It must have been Hiccup. I walked towards him laughing. Her choice for a name made me chuckle. I scooped him up into my arms and carried him across the room to my suitcase.

I rummaged around in it for a few moments and pulled out a small, red velvet box. Inside was a small charm, dangling on a hoop, which I attached to the cat's collar.

"Come Hiccup, I may need your help and protection," I said as he shook his head, adjusting to the new weight on his collar.

He followed me as I climbed the stairs towards Seraphina's room. My difficult task seemed to get more and more taxing with every step I took.

My hands shook slightly as I knocked on the door and Hiccup jumped into my arms. I was grateful for his company as he calmed my rapid breathing.

SERAPHINA BASCO

A small knock sounded at my bedroom door and made me jump. I grabbed my housecoat, hastily tying it securely, and hurried across the room.

My dad was standing there, looking completely out of place with my cat in his arms. I looked from Hic to my dad and had to stifle a giggle. My dad looked extremely odd carrying my fluffy white cat, complete with sparkly collar.

"Can I come in for a moment?" He looked slightly nervous.

"Of course," I replied, opening the door wide and gesturing for him to come in.

I watched as he walked across the room looking around at all my things and finally sitting down on the chair by my desk. I followed him, picking up my newly-shed clothes that were lying around the bedroom floor. I suddenly wished I had cleaned up my room a bit better this morning.

"Last minute cleaning?"

"Yeah, something like that," I said, slumping onto my bed and feeling a little bit ashamed. I definitely wasn't the cleanest person in the world. I grabbed my big, squishy bear and cuddled into it. I always did this when I was feeling nervous or when I was out of my comfort zone.

"You look beautiful," he said, watching me, "Your mom wore her hair like that on our wedding day."

This surprised me, because it was the first time that I knew of that he had ever willingly spoken about my mom. I vaguely remembered seeing an old photo of their wedding, but it was a long time ago and I couldn't remember her hair.

"Seraphina," he began, fiddling with the cat's collar, "We need to talk."

"What about?" I snapped. Clambering up off the bed. My anger rising instantly. "If you're going to try and talk me out of tonight, it won't work," I said, jumping to conclusions.

He stared at me in complete dismay. A crease appeared on his forehead as he knitted his dark eyebrows together in confusion.

"I'm not going to stop you, Seraphina. I just wanted to talk to you." He paused. "It's about your mom," he said in a slightly shaky voice.

What? Great. I suddenly felt guilty for snapping at him, especially when all he wanted to talk about was my mom. Wait… why?

"My mom?" I said, still feeling a tad skeptical. "But you never talk about her," I said, immediately feeling tearful.

How odd. I didn't normally cry over mother anymore. Was it shock?

"Well, you're getting older now and you need to know about her. You also need to learn about our family's history," he said, glancing at the floor.

I had the sinking feeling that Dad *had* been hiding something from me. It was either that or he was about to try and guilt me into staying home. Well I wasn't going to let him change my mind. Why did it feel like I was fighting a battle of wills all the time?

I sat down on the bed next to him and folded my arms across my chest. If he was going to give me the guilt trip I was going to make it as difficult as possible for him.

I knew that, once again, I was sulking, but I couldn't help it. It made me so angry. Why did they hate Joey so much? It just didn't make sense! He had done nothing but be nice to me, even to Grandma.

Hiccup jumped from my dad's arms up onto the bed next to me with a bold stare. I rolled my eyes and scratched his head. It seemed that even he was annoyed with me.

Then I noticed a new charm on his collar. I held it for a moment. It was a small circle with a looped symbol,encased in a diamond shape. There was a strange pattern engraved around the circle, making it feel bumpy.

I looked closer and had the strange feeling that I had seen the symbol somewhere before. I gazed at it for a long time, completely mesmerised. As I watched it started to glow, an extraordinary purple color emanating from it. I blinked rapidly and jumped back from Hiccup in alarm.

"Are you okay?" my dad asked, slightly alarmed at my sudden jumpiness.

"Yes, I just... I thought... I... I thought I could see...." I broke off.

"See what?" he asked, sitting up a little straighter.

"What *is* that?" I said loudly, pointing a shaking finger at the charm.

The cat cocked its head to one side, as if to say, 'what's wrong with you?'

"It's an ancient charm, meaning, 'the one who protects'. It's been made with iridium, one of the rarest metals known to man. I saw it on my travels through Argentina and thought it would make a nice charm for his collar," he said, studying my reactions carefully.

I looked up at him. "*When* were you in Argentina?"

I tried to slow my breathing to control my mood. For some reason I was so angry. Why hadn't I known he was in Argentina? It seemed to be getting more and more difficult lately- the tiniest things were upsetting me.

"Last year, we got a lead on..." He broke off, looking worried and anxious. A lead? A lead on what?

"It isn't important really." He waved his hand dismissively, "just work stuff." He smiled, but I knew something was going on.

He got off the chair and wandered around my room, looking through my books and picking up things to examine them. He eventually stopped beside my shelf, by my bed, where I kept a small, half-torn picture of my mother in a silver frame.

The tear was through the middle, so all you could see was her head and shoulders. It was all I had of her. I watched as he took the photo and looked at it closely. He went as white as chalk. His hands started to shake violently. I was about to get him a chair before he fell when he turned to face me.

"Where did you get this from?"

His expression was tormented, full of pain. Before I could answer he turned his back to me so I couldn't see his face.

"I found it in a box under Grandma's bed in her room when I was nine."

My dad looked at me, tears glistening in his eyes. He placed the photo back on the shelf and walked towards the bedroom door. He stopped and turned back to look at me.

"Have fun tonight sweetheart," he said with a strained smile. He then strolled out of my room.

"Okay!" I called after him.

That was strange. I got off the bed and strode over to the closet. I would worry about Dad's behaviour later. I wondered what it was he wanted to talk about. He seemed down and nervous and I had no idea why!

I dismissed the thought and grabbed my make-up bag. I headed for the bathroom to start getting ready.

KENT BASCO

I watched as my little – well, actually not-so-little - girl marched back and forth beside the fire. She was wringing her hands, mumbling to herself.

"He wouldn't… would he? No… he promised. But where is he? He should be here by now!" She was getting a little hysterical.

She needed to calm down. I glanced over at the big clock. Seven thirty five; he was only five minutes late. She carried on pacing up and down as Hiccup sat next to her on the rug. He was cleaning his paws and watching her intently. His eyes followed her every step.

I folded up my newspaper, placed it on the side table and folded my fingers together underneath my chin. What could I say to calm her down? The flames were rising higher with every pace she took, and forcing them back down was draining my energy.

"He'll be here any minute," I told her. "Calm yourself down, otherwise I won't let you go anywhere."

I knew she wouldn't like that, but she was working herself up. I could see the flames of the fire glowing brighter and brighter the more she paced. It wouldn't take too much longer before she set the place alight or burnt herself out again.

She spun round to face me as sparks flew out the hearth. "I will…" she started, but was interrupted by the shrill ring of the doorbell.

I became ridged and tense as I watched mom stroll towards the front door. I felt extremely nervous and over protective all of a sudden.

I stood up slowly and nonchalantly, trying to act like I was actually fine with the situation. I had to act like I was carefree and happy for her sake. I didn't want her to panic about me being there. I walked over to stand next to her and placed a hand on her shoulder protectively, giving it a reassuring squeeze. I made sure I was standing slightly in front of her so he would see *me* first. He wouldn't be expecting that, and hopefully I would make him stop and think about his plans with my daughter.

I could hear my mom's voice greeting him politely while showing him into the lounge. It was a good job she had answered the door and not me. I wouldn't have been so polite.

They walked through the lounge door together and I was pleased to see him squirm for a moment as his eyes met mine. Mom was right about him; his aura was very hard to read. I couldn't see it clearly defined around him - it kept fluctuating. I stared hard, trying to see it clearly, but it was no use.

"Joey. This is my dad, Kent." Seraphina pushed me slightly, a clear indication that I was starring too hard.

We both walked forward with our hands out-stretched.

"Good evening, Joey," I said, shaking his hand with a firm grasp.

I felt his hand twitch beneath mine. I could also feel a smile spread across my face at his unease.

"Good evening, sir. It's nice to *finally* meet you. Sera's told me a lot about you." He pulled his hand away and glanced at Seraphina. I narrowed my eyes. *Finally?* He better watch his step with that sort of remark.

"You look beautiful," he said, then turned nervously to face me again.

'Yes! I thought to myself. You're right to be worried.'

"Err... I'll be sure to get her home safely,Mr Basco," he said.

"I appreciate that," I replied, I could see my mom pulling a face out the corner of my eye.

"Are you driving her or would you like me to drive?" I asked, not wanting to leave them on their own.

"*Dad!*"Seraphina hissed.

"That's fine Mr Basco, I'm driving tonight. Actually we must get going if we're going to get there on time," he said, smiling at Seraphina.

"Yes, of course," she said, taking his hand, "I'll see you later Dad. Bye, Gran."

I watched miserably as my little girl walked out the door with an excited smile on her face. In some ways she was *still* so young and far too trusting of this guy!

I had tried to keep them talking in the house for as long as I could. I still wasn't entirely sure if this Joey kid was a threat or not. He *was* very careful with me. Those were usually the ones you needed to watch more carefully. Seraphina was far too eager to leave the house and hadn't even noticed any of the signs that he was dangerous. The aura I knew she couldn't see yet, but had she not noticed the red glint in his eyes. She needed training, and fast!

The kid was very good at hiding his aura, whether he had done so purposefully or not. I just couldn't get a real feel for what he was. It *could* also mean he was protected. Every now and then he would slip, and I would see a light pink color surrounding him. He was either protected or a very confused, emotional guy.

I could usually read a person's aura and knew if they were to be trusted or not. The more I concentrated on Joey, the more confused his aura seemed to become.

Yes! He was definitely protected and not yet taken fully, I thought. There was still hope for him! If I had arrived quicker he might not have been too far gone - I could have helped him more, even if I dis-liked the guy for wanting *my* daughter.

Hiccup was meowing at the window urgently, and that's when I knew the situation was as bad as I had initially thought. I didn't like it. I don't trust this Joey guy and instantly knew Seraphina was in immediate danger. Mom was right to worry, and Dana was right to have called me back.

It took three strides to reach the window and I watched through the netting as Joey led Seraphina towards his BMW. More evidence that told me he had almost been taken.

How had he managed to get his hands on a car that flamboyant on his salary? I glared as he opened the car door and watched as Seraphina slid inside, giggling like a child. She was a danger to herself. He knew that he owned her!

Joey shut the door and walked around to the driver's side. He paused, sensing my gaze before looking up at the window, and smiling at me. It sent a shiver down my back. Anger flooded through me.

"Kent, what do you think?" Mom asked, and I turned to see the worried look on her face.

I sighed unhappily and shook my head. "You're right. There's something wrong with him. His aura is tainted. Maura has him - not fully yet, I don't think - but he's nearly there."

For a moment she looked startled, then readjusted her face back into a grim line. I walked back towards my case, which still sat on the table, and opened it.

"Seraphina *is* in danger. I need to protect her," I said.

"She won't like it if she sees you there, Kent. She's too much like you. Her pride and sense of self-importance will be her downfall," she hissed. "You have to stay concealed just in case he isn't what we think he is."

My mom walked over to my side and placed her hand gently on my face. "We need to tell her, now!"

I felt a huge wave of guilt as I looked into her face and saw the hurt and tiredness there.

"Mom," I sighed, closing my eyes and taking a deep breath, "I'm sorry I left you to look after her alone for so long. It hasn't been easy for you, has it?"

"No, it hasn't, but she was safer here with me than with you. I accepted that. You wouldn't have been able to care for her and complete your quest," she replied.

Her pride and sense of duty returned as her face hardened again.

"I should have sent her with…" I trailed off.

"You know that wasn't a possibility for her. Our family, her side of… the two can't live and train there! She wouldn't have been accepted or treated well if she had gone there. She hung her head in dismay. "No. She is *my* granddaughter, and this is the safest place for her to be."

"That doesn't seem to be the case anymore, does it?" I replied, glancing back out the window at the now deserted road.

"No! I am inclined to think that she is in more danger now than ever, and she must begin her journey before it's too late," she said, looking back out the window with a tear in the corner of her eye.

I looked away and peered inside my case. It looked normal to the ordinary eye. I scooped the few clothes out and placed them on the chair. You didn't need a lot when you travelled as much as I did.

I took my keys out of my pocket and found the small circle dangling on a fine silver chain. It was kind of like the ones used on supermarket carts in England.

I placed it into a slot at the bottom of the case which had been covered by my clothes and pushed. A click instantly sounded and a layer popped up to reveal a hidden compartment.

I lifted out a red velvet cloth and placed it carefully upon the dining room table. My mom's attention shifted; she turned from the window to stare down at the cloth, almost as if it was calling out to her.

"I haven't seen that for years," she said, eyeing the cloth with longing and grief in her eyes.

I looked up at her in alarm. I placed my arm around her shoulders and sighed.

"It wasn't your fault. I was the right age. I should have saved him and not have left you to deal with it."

"Your dad always told me my sense of duty would be my downfall. I have no one to blame but myself and I have lost the greatest gift I ever had - your dad." She turned on her heel and walked out the room.

I stared after her for a while, a little stung at the comment. Deep down I just wished I could relieve the guilt she felt, but I knew there was nothing I could do. I was sure *that* was part of the real reason why she insisted on having Seraphina stay with her - to take her mind off my dad.

I turned my attention back to the velvet cloth, which didn't actually look like much, but if I hadn't have had what was inside it over the last eleven years I wouldn't have survived that time. My quests had become increasingly dangerous with each passing year.

The cat jumped onto the table and meowed at me. He pawed the cloth, looking back and forth between the window and me. I studied him for a minute and nodded.

"I know, I know. I'm going now," I told him as I scratched his ears.

I unfolded the cloth, revealing a small, dark, wooden stick. I immediately felt the power emanating from it. It was thicker than a stick, but light, and flexible. I picked it up, raising it to my chin. It began to glow an amber color as I swished it through the air, careful not to release the real weapon concealed within it.

I grabbed my cloak off the back of the chair and flung it around my shoulders, buttoning it tightly. The hood was excellent for hiding your face when needed. I placed the baton in my pocket and turned to face my mom.

"You're a true Defender," she said with a hint of pride as she slipped back into the room.

Her eyes were red and puffy. I knew she'd been weeping silently in the next room. She was strong and disapproved of crying, so it was quite a shock to see the tear stains on her face.

"Now go and protect the next one," she said, giving me a kiss on the cheek and pulling my hood over my head to cover my face.

I stepped out into the warm evening air, Hiccup following me. My mom watched from the window, her face pale, sullen, and pained. I knew by that look that she was wishing she could have done more for the fates of her son and her granddaughter.

"Are you ready, Protector of the Defenders?" I asked Hiccup. "I'm going to need your help."

He stared up at me and meowed indignantly in response. I laughed and bent down to pick him up. Holding him firmly in my arms I spun around swiftly on the spot. Our forms began to evaporate, changing into black, wispy smoke. We whirled up together in a spiral and shot down towards the Hotel of Fortune.

THE SIGNS OF DANGER

SERAPHINA

We were winding down the road towards the town in Joey's new, shiny, black convertible and he was singing along to a song I hadn't heard before.

It surprised me- I didn't know he could sing, and *boy* could he! His voice was amazingly sweet and my heart fluttered with joy listening to him.

I started to giggle at him, out of embarrassment, and he smiled back at me, as he took my hand in his. I felt my face starting to burn red and my heart raced in my chest with excitement.

Joey Parkinson was holding *my* hand! *Get a grip girl*, I told myself. I had to look away from him out the window to calm down.

The road went whizzing past and I noticed just how fast we were going. I knew Grandma would have scolded me for not saying anything had she been there.

Oh well, it wouldn't hurt. What was the point in having a car like this if you didn't drive fast every now and then? I saw the car responded well to Joey, and he handled it well enough. He could stop quickly if he needed to.

I started to day dream, imagining all kinds of wonderful scenarios that might have been about to happen. If I was lucky I might even get my *first* kiss.

Joey interrupted my thoughts. "You really do look beautiful," he said, glancing at my new hair-style before looking down at my new dress appreciatively.

Wow! He was so cute. I couldn't stop myself from grinning like a child as his eyes swept over me once more. My heart was beating so fast I had to take a deep breath to calm down.

"Th… thank you," I stammered. Pull it together! I thought and took another deep breath, "It was just something I had lying around, you know. Nothing special." Cool. Yes that was a *very* cool move.

To my surprise Joey laughed at me! Why was he laughing? Did he know how nervous I was? Could he hear my beating heart through my chest?

He reached across the back of the seat. Oh! This was more than I had expected. I watched as his hand slid down the back of my neck. He started fumbling around with the back of my dress. What was he doing?

My heart practically jumped out of my chest. My body began to tingle. His face was so close to mine I could see the sparkle in his bright blue eyes as he smiled at me. He hadn't been paying careful attention to the road. I was starting to panic slightly now, at our speed.

"I can see that," he chuckled, removing his hand from my back and holding up a tag in front of my face. I blushed even harder and grabbed at the price tag.

How could I have been so stupid and careless! After a moments silence we looked briefly into each other's eyes and burst out laughing.

By the time we reached the hotel we were both in fits of giggles, our eyes streaming with tears. We had been swapping embarrassing stories for the rest of the journey and he told me about the time he left the price tag the bottom on his shoe at a corporate event and how everyone had seen that he had only paid $7.99 for them.

He pulled up outside the entrance and I clambered out as elegantly as I could manage, which unfortunately wasn't that graceful. I wasn't used to dresses as I preferred pants and shorts.

"Wait for me here? I'll just park the car." Joey said, kissing me gently on the back of the hand.

He climbed back into the car and sped off, his engine roaring deafeningly behind him.

KENT BASCO

I stood at the edge of the trees, my hood pulled up to hide my face. I watched the cars pulling up at the hotel entrance and was getting more and more apprehensive with each that arrived.

After a while I heard the roar of a sports car and knew instantly that it was him. He was driving too fast by the sounds of it! His sports car raced round the bend and up the hotel drive.

He was going far too fast. That stupid kid was going to kill them both! If he didn't turn out to be one of Maura's minions then I would kill him anyway for putting my girl in unnecessary danger.

Seraphina was laughing hysterically when they pulled up. That girl needed more than battle training, she needed road safety classes too!

As I watched them laughing I found myself hoping that maybe everything would be fine and that my presence wouldn't be needed.

At least I hoped it wouldn't. I was praying that she had at least another year of happiness left before I had to destroy her world.

I watched as she slid out of the car, not very gracefully, and walked round to him. He kissed her hand and sped off, going even faster than before. I knew one thing was for sure: she was not getting into *his* car again!

I watched her walk up to the hotel entrance, wobbling slightly on her high heels. I couldn't help but marvel at how grown up she was, even at times like this when she tottering on grown up shoes. She was no longer playing dress up.

She looked a lot like me. My chin, hard and angular. My eyes, dark with a hint of green and, from what my mom had told me, she has been blessed with my temper too. That was not good and I definitely didn't want to deal with that.

I edged closer to a tree when my foot snapped a twig. The sound echoed around the now empty entrance and Seraphina glanced up quickly, looking directly at me!

I ducked behind the tree, scraping my arm on the bark, and for a second I feared that she had seen me. It had seemed like she had looked directly at me.

I wasn't about to get caught by her just yet, not before I knew if my presence was necessary. I looked over at the cat, waiting to see if the coast was clear, and he purred softly at me.

I took that as a yes and ducked cautiously back out from behind the trees.

SERAPHINA BASCO

It was a warm night, so I didn't mind having to wait outside. I looked around the grounds of the hotel, watching as elegant-looking couples walked around. It was so beautiful, and a sense of romance hung in the air. The night was definitely one for romance.

As I watched one couple creep off into the trees, giggling madly, I saw a white cat slink off through forest.

No! It couldn't be… I squinted at the cat's back as it headed towards a tall man in a long overcoat. I stared after them in shock. I couldn't see clearly enough for that distance, but he looked like my dad!

I stumbled backwards and bumped straight into Joey, who caught me in his strong arms. He was also staring in the same direction as me.

"Oh, sorry," I said, holding onto his arms. "Did you see that cat?" I pointed at the trees, "and… err…that man." I broke off, still unsure if I *had* seen it.

"I think it was Hiccup and my…" I said nervously, peering out into the trees.

I shook my head. No! I was imagining things. How could it have been Hiccup? How could he have got all the way out here in such a short space of time?

I regarded Joey's puzzled expression and laughed nervously. I was being silly; there was no way that could have been Hiccup!

"My eyes are playing tricks on me," I laughed, trying to break the tension as I pulled him towards the door.

For a split second I could have sworn I saw a flicker of fear in his eyes. Maybe he thought I was crazy and was having second thoughts.

KENT BASCO

Hiccup and I were waiting beside the same tree, watching other couples slipping off into the cover of the trees to steal a kiss or two.

As I sat there I remembered the time I had brought Seraphina's mother, Talia, to the same place on our first date. I was Seraphina's age and I could still remember the butterflies in my stomach.

They got worse when she arrived, her jet black hair billowing in the soft evening breeze. It was long, wavy and curled around itself at the ends. I would run my fingers through it and marvel at how it bounced back into a perfect curl.

I remembered the smell of her perfume, like sweet, crisp apples. I used to trace my finger along her neck up onto her chin and to her nose. I would stare into her deep green eyes for what felt like hours.

I had walked her down the same path leading through the woods that night, just like any of the other couples sneaking away from the hotel, trying to impress her with my somewhat limited knowledge of the town's history.

"Kent, stop," she had giggled. "You're not impressing me." She had a trace of a teasing smile on her face, and that's when I knew I didn't have to try so hard with, just be myself.

"I'm not trying *that* hard to impress you. Not yet, Miss Kahale! When I do, you'll *warm* to me," I replied confidently, with a playful half smile.

I watched her face for a reaction. I saw her mouth twitch and the most dazzling glint appeared in her eye, like she too had a big secret that would without doubt impress me.

"Well, maybe you should give up now, Mr Basco! For *I* have a way of *cooling* people down, plus I fear I am far too clever for the likes of you!" She had stared up into my eyes.

I held her around the waist and pulled her gently into me.

"I promise you. I will impress you!" I said boldly.

I then lent in, kissing her tenderly. It was the sweetest, most mind-blowing kiss I had ever had, and I knew with all my heart that she was the one I was destined to be with, I had been right.

I sighed and placed my head back against the tree trunk. I hated thinking about Seraphina's mother. It was far too painful, but somehow I couldn't stop. Losing the one you love with all your heart, body and soul is devastating. I would never wish that on anyone.

That's why I hadn't been able to visit Seraphina much over the years, she had her mother's smile. It was heart-breaking.

Her sister, on the other hand, was the spitting image of her mother. I hadn't seen Lana for over two years. Thinking about her made a lump of guilt rise in the back of my throat.

Seraphina had no idea she even had a sister as they were separated when she was two. It was for their own safety – together their magical auras would have been too powerful, too easy for Maura to find.

I had spent years debating whether to keep them apart this with myself, but Mom was right - they were both safer apart. At least Lana was safe for now.

Unfortunately this was *my* fatal flaw, I always ran away when things got too hard. In truth I was a complete coward. Talia was the only one who could keep me whole and in one place.

Now she was gone I felt even more useless than before. Don't get me wrong, I could fight just as well. That wasn't the issue. It was more to do with the ones I loved. Lana was a prime example of that.

I had left her alone in England instead of looking after her myself. She was heavily guarded though, with round-the clock-care and the best education money could buy.

She was safe. It was Seraphina I needed to concentrate on now. She was the one in immediate danger.

SERAPHINA BASCO

The ceremony was long and very boring I would have fallen asleep if it was not for the excitement of being with Joey. He was making me laugh. In fact, I was laughing so much that the people next to us were starting to give us funny looks.

Oh man! Come on, even the Chair of Directors was nodding off. In fact he had nearly fallen off his chair at one point, which had made me laugh even harder.

I giggled again at the memory of him slumping in his chair when Joey had to poke me hard in the ribs. My name was being announced by a short, plump woman whose make-up was so over done that she looked strange.

I watched her bright red, shiny lips as she called me up onto the stage for the third time. I managed to gain control over my hysterical laughter, but went bright red in the face at missing my own name twice. All eyes were now on me.

I pushed myself up and out of my chair. I immediately felt self-conscious about *my* shoes. Knowing my luck I would be the first to fall over. I made a mental note not to look at Joey when I got up onto the stage. I would just start giggling again.

I made my way to the woman, wobbling in and out of the chairs, smiling at everyone, as they applauded me.

My face was burning from the embarrassment. Oh man! I also hoped my mascara hadn't run down my cheeks – I had been crying with laughter.

I finally managed to reach the stage's stairs and faltered. I refused to be intimidated by them so, holding my head high, I hitched the bottom of my dress up, raising it above my ankles.

Concentrating hard on the steps I proceeded towards the cheerful-looking woman on stage. She was smiling brightly and half-clapping her hands, a task that had been made awkward by holding my award.

She took me by the hand and turned me round to face the audience. I clung onto the small wooden podium as I stared in horror at the crowd. Oh man, there was so many of them and they were all staring up at me.

"I would now like to announce our very own little damsel in distress - Courtney Morgan," she said, standing to one side so I could see.

I watched as the little girl from the beach, Courtney, made her way up towards the stage holding her mother's hand and beaming.

I looked down at the award, now clutched in my suddenly very sweaty hand. It was a gold pair of hands holding onto a star, mounted on a marble brick, on which was engraved with the words:

"Saver's Star"
Awarded to Seraphina Basco
for Outstanding Bravery.

"Wow!" I breathed. This was an award given to people who were exceptionally kind or have made a huge impact on others' lives. The awards were a token of gratitude from the multi-billionaire Alex Morgan, founder of the world's best and largest electrical products company.

Oh man! *I* had saved a multi-billionaire's daughter. It all made sense now. I watched at Courtney as she approached. She was so cute. Her pretty pink, ballerina-style dress swished round her knees as she bounced along. She had a daisy chain interlaced into her hair which was French braided down her back.

She finally reached me and squealed, throwing herself into my arms. I hugged her tightly as a thousand camera flashes went off.

I wondered if this was just a publicity stunt…The award, and the cute, sweet girl being announced as a damsel in distress! My thoughts faltered as I drew away from the hug.

Courtney's face began to flicker from the camera flashes and my heart pounded in my chest as her features began to change.

Her eyes glowed with an eerie bright light, her nose elongated. Her mouth became full and her chin became rounded and soft. It was the girl from my dream. I stopped as terror overwhelmed me and I started to shake uncontrollably. She watched with worried, anxious eyes.

"Be careful sweetheart. She is close by and you are in grave danger. You must remember me. You must save me," she said.

CONFIRMATION

SERAPHINA

Before I knew what was happening Joey had pulled me off the stage with tremendous force and was walking me towards the door.

"She's fine, she just needs some air. I'll take her out." I heard a muffled response, then Joey's voice clearly as he guided me by the arm, "No, no. It's okay! We're fine on our own. I can take her out."

I couldn't make sense of what was going on. My skin had broken out in a sweat, my head was spinning, my breathing was shallow and my vision blurred.

All I was sure of was Joey's hand on my arm, guiding me out of the hall and along the corridor before the cold night air hit my face and I could finally make sense of things. Finally my sight was beginning to clear, my head stopped spinning and my body had begun to cool down.

Joey was walking me towards the hotel grounds. My feet didn't want to move and my legs were sluggish.

"What happened?" I asked, clutching Joey's arm.

He was steering me towards the surrounding trees, my legs protesting at his speed. We walked into the shroud of the forest until we were out of sight of the hotel. Joey pushed me down quite harshly, forcing me to sit on a fallen tree log. I didn't want to sit down on a dirty log, desperate not to ruin my dress.

"No, I don't…" I broke off.

He took hold of my shoulders and shook me slightly. I stared up into his face, anger now spreading through me. What *was* he doing? What was his problem?!

"Stop shaking me, you're hurting my arm!" I demanded.

He stopped shaking me, but held my shoulders tightly and I stared at him. He looked strange, and his eyes had changed. They were growing darker, with deep purple circles starting to form underneath.

"What did you see? What did she show you? What did she say to you?" His voice was frantic. I winced at his grasp which was really starting to hurt my shoulders.

I blinked at him in bewilderment. "What did *who* show me?" I screamed back, starting to panic. "Let go of me! You're hurting me!"

Tears began to roll down my cheeks and the burning sensation had started to pulse through my body. I couldn't think of what to do. I had to get him off me. I had to get away.

I didn't understand- how did he know what had just happened? Had everyone seen what I had? I was about to scream at the top of my lungs for help when someone jumped out from behind the trees.

"Let go of her!" Their voice boomed.

We both froze in shock. I knew that voice, and I had never been happier to hear it. Joey and I turned our heads to face the newcomer, his vice-like grip still tight on my arm.

Then, as fast as an eagle soaring into the air, he pulled me to my feet and whipped a small blade from his pocket. My arm pulsated from where he had held me as the blood started running back through my veins. It was an intense and painful feeling.

But I couldn't concentrate on that, for a new pain had taken me by surprise. He had forced my head back against his shoulder, locking my arm up behind my back, and he held the sharp blade to my throat.

Oh God. I was going to die!

Tears began to streak down my cheeks and onto my lips. Their salty taste made me shudder as the small blade dug into my throat.

I could feel a warm trickle of blood running down my neck as the blade cut into my flesh. It smelt of rust and made my head spin.

I whimpered slightly in pain and shock as I struggled against him. I tried hard to push him away from me, but my struggling made the pain worse as the blade cut deeper.

During our struggle Joey had somehow managed to grab hold of my hair, twisting it tightly through his fingers and gripping it by its roots. I screamed in pain and he yanked hard again at my hair.

"Shush now Seraphina, or I might lose my concentration and slip. We don't want that, do we? I don't want to kill you if I can help it. She wants you alive." He whispered into my ear in a calm, controlled voice.

Then he laughed - an evil cackle and this frightened me even more than the blade at my throat. This was not Joey, not *my* Joey. It was almost like he was someone else, or that something else was controlling him. The man I knew would never act like that.

How had I not noticed before how evil and unfriendly his laugh was? I tried to think back to the car ride on the way. No. I didn't think it had been.

I trembled with fear and confusion. I was still dazed from what had already happened up on the stage, a few minutes ago.

How could my date have gone from being completely wonderful to something out of a horror movie so fast?

I focused on the silhouette of the tall, hooded figure through my tears. He stood looking calm and muscular, but I could also sense a hint of nerves. He took a couple of cautious steps towards us. Then it hit me: the voice, the shape of the man- *was* it my dad?

I wasn't sure which one scared me more - this muscular man, who may or may not be my dad, or the lunatic boy with a blade to my throat.

All I wanted to do was disappear and get away from them both. The hooded man was holding onto what looked like a small, thick stick. He raised it to his chin like he was about to hit a home run. Seriously, what was he going to do with that?

I focused on the stick and my body began to tingle, heat spreading slowly from my toes and moving up, through to the tips of my fingers. I felt drawn to the thing in the man's hand - my whole body and mind felt connected to it and I felt myself leaning slightly closer.

Joey's fingers pulled tighter on my hair and the blade dug deeper into my throat, causing a new wave of warm blood to trickle down my neck. He pulled me back towards him with a small, sharp tug. I gasped in pain as fresh tears ran down my cheeks.

"Don't be foolish Old Defender, your powers are fading. You can't attack me. I am protected by *Maura*," he sneered. "Besides I have what you need and the other one will soon be ours too," he laughed derisively.

The man took a step closer and lowered his hood. It was my dad. Joey shuffled back, yelling, "One more step and she dies!"

He raised the knife up high and held onto me tighter. I watched it gleam as it moved up past my face. I bit my bottom lip to stop the scream that was building up in the back of my throat.

My dad lowered his stick and placed it carefully on the ground in front of his feet. His eyes flickered from the blade to my eyes and back. *'Be calm I'll save you,'* they seemed to say.

"Good," Joey gloated, "Very good, old man. Now step away from it!" Joey gestured with his head.

I had no idea what was going on. Nothing Joey said was making any sense. What did he mean by 'Old Defender.' and 'other one'? Oh God, was it Gran? Was she in danger?

I did know, however, that dropping his stick was a very bad idea. I also knew that my date was officially, definitely over.

I thought back to the other night at the party and how my grandma had turned up. If she hadn't, I could have been killed that night. A shudder ran through my body at the thought. She was right about him and now she might be in danger, or worse… I couldn't allow myself to think the rest. I had to get out of there and find her.

Joey's grip on my hair was starting to slacken slightly as his attention was directed at my dad and that small, strange stick on the floor. I stared in horror as my dad started to take a few steady and calm steps backwards. What was he doing? Didn't he realize that Grandma was in trouble? He needed to attack or leave me and run to her.

Joey shakily pushed me forward until I was standing directly in front of the stick. I glanced at it beside my feet and felt a strange inclination to pick it up, almost as if it was calling to me again!

I had the bizarre feeling it would save my life someday. As I stared at it intently it began to glow a dull orange and then died back down.

"Pick it up, Seraphina!" Joey demanded, keeping his eyes locked on my dad.

I hesitated for a split second. There was a sense of - I know it sounds insane- magic in the air. I could feel it surrounding this strange stick, and it scared me.

I reluctantly and cautiously bent down and realized I was still clutching my award. I placed it on the ground slowly and stretched my fingers out towards the stick. It was an awkward move to pull off while Joey was still gripping my hair, but at least he had moved the blade from my throat.

I had to do something quickly; I would only have a few seconds at most. Suddenly my dad launched himself forward with amazing speed, slamming into Joey. My head snapped back before I found myself released from Joey's grip.

I saw white fur blur past as Joey regained his footing and snatched at my arm. I screamed as his blade slashed down on it, leaving a deep gash.

I glanced around. Joey was up from the floor and my dad was lying face down in the fallen leaves. Another streak of white fur flew past me from the opposite direction and we both tumbled back to the ground.

Before Joey could straighten himself up I took my chance, picking up the stick. Using all the force I could muster I swung it wildly, and somehow managed to hit Joey's nose. I heard a sickening crunch and shuddered. I dropped the stick, terrified. What had I just done?

"Argh!" He screamed, staggering back and grabbing his now bleeding and swelling nose.

That was all the chance I needed. I ran as fast as I could towards my dad as he also ran forward to join me.

"Run... go!" He screamed as he dove into the air, tucking into a forward roll and managing to pick up the stick thing.

I stood there, my mouth hanging open in shock. A noise then caught my attention and, looking up, saw the girl from the *store* running towards me through the trees.

I glanced at my dad as he charged towards Joey. The girl was closing in on us, waving what looked like a sword! Without thinking I turned and fled into the forest.

As I ran I could hear the two men fighting, then an ear-splitting growl, like a lion's roar, echoed through the trees. I carried on running, too afraid to look back at the scene behind me. I couldn't believe I had just left Dad there with a girl brandishing a sword!

After running for as long as I could I stopped and hid behind a bush, crouching low so it covered me entirely. I felt I should have gone back - my dad might get killed! But which way had I run from?

My heart pounded so hard in my chest it felt like it would burst through my ribs. My entire body was tingling from the adrenaline and fear which I was sure would haunt me for the rest of my life.

What was I going to do? I couldn't run back to the hotel because I didn't know which way it was. I couldn't call my grandma because my cell was in my bag, which was still inside the hotel, on our table.

I knelt down and let out a sob. My dress was torn from the branches in the woods, and a small trickle of blood still ran down my neck and arm, flowing onto the now dirty blue satin of my dress.

Tears flowed freely. My dad, my grandma. What had happened to them? I sat hidden for what seemed like hours –darkness fell and it turned cold. It was hard to see anything.

The rustle of a branch made me jump and I let out a terrified scream. I clamped my hand to my mouth as I heard a light patter of feet on the forest floor. I looked around frantically, trying to see what was coming without giving away my position. I let out another terrified scream as a pure white cat leapt out in front of me. I collapsed to the ground once again in tears, but those of joy.

"Hiccup! You scared me!" I sobbed. "What are you doing here?"

I picked him up and cuddled him into my chest. The warmth from his body seemed to calm me down and made me feel safe. I clambered to my feet and started to walk - I was sure I'd be stuck here all night if I didn't.

I still had no idea what had happened to my dad or Grandma. I was full of fear, panicking that Joey and that girl would find me, alone and defenceless.

Hiccup began to struggle in my arms so much I had to put him down on the floor. Instantly he started to run and I was so terrified of being on my own that I ran after him. It was strange but I followed my cat rather then stay by myself deep in a dark wood.

A MOMENT IN TIME – REVEALED

KENT

I still sat by a tree waiting and watching, Seraphina and Joey were still inside the hotel and I was getting bored. A tiny flame began to dance across my palm. It was really beautiful, beguiling and calming. It took years of training to make even a tiny flame. Still, it seemed that every Defender, no matter what their element, always wishes they could do more.

It was my darling wife who had encouraged me to push my powers and explore my capabilities. I actually had very little power for a Defender. My mom however was *amazing*, she is stronger in mind and body than me, and therefore more powerful than I could ever be.

She put my limited elemental powers down to giving up trying after I lost Talia. Of course, she was right; I knew I had lost the will to fight. I shouldn't have - not when my angel needed me- but still I struggled with my loss.

I did have some useful powers though. I could sustain a small flame on my hand for quite a long time without feeling drained. I had learnt self-control at least, thanks to Dana's coaching. Wood-wives, known to be extremely wise, have decades of patience behind them. If Seraphina was in trouble I would need my strength for combat, my *real* talent. I really hoped she was not going to need it though! So far the night was dull and there are no signs of anything going wrong yet.

My another ability smoke travel was a gift given to me by the wizard Mojo when we were both young and it had saved my life more than once. I remembered when my mom had first taken me to meet him when Mojo… well… was whole and untroubled. He had suffered just as much as I had. A lot more, actually.

I start to remember the day, it felt like it was only yesterday, for it was also the day I had met Talia. Mother and I had travelled to the wizards town in Belgium to seek guidance from the Scrying Font. I hadn't wanted to go and sit for hours with some old, creepy man instead of chilling at the beach with my friends, but my mom made me. Still, I *had* needed to learn the ways of Defenders, and it kept me away from my dad. I closed my eyes and learnt back against the tree…

"We won't be long here, Kent," she had said.

Her eyes kept darting back and forth, as if she were expecting an attack.

"Can't I go home?" I asked, sulkily. "I *really* don't want to be here."

"No! This is more important than a silly beach trip. Now stop sulking and keep your eyes open."

"Fine," I snapped back.

I hadn't seen the need for me to be there. The Font had nothing to do with me. I had acquired my powers only a few weeks before and already resented them. I felt like they were nothing but trouble, cutting into my social life so much that I had already failed my driver's test and I was missing another day out when my friends were mad at me for always dropping out of things.

"Stop sulking, Kent!" She had snapped again, "You will have plenty of time to spend with your friends. We have a gift that's more powerful than anything you can imagine,but we need to learn to use it wisely and safely." She had stopped her fast pace, turning to glare back at me. "Maybe Mojo, the Wizard's son, will teach you a thing or two!"

I hadn't liked the sound of that. From what I had already heard, this Mojo guy was a weirdo! He apparently spent most of his time locked up in his room poring over books and crystals. Hippy rubbish. So uncool! He couldn't have had real powers like I did.

I had tried to imagine what he was going be like as we walked for another mile. Tall, skinny, his glasses falling off his nose, a thick mop like hair. Oh yeah this guy was definitely going to be geeky-looking.

I had followed my mom as she darted in and out of a crowd. She had seemed to be constantly checking her watch and glancing around nervously. I had been watching the small cobbled stones under my feet when she stopped so abruptly I collided into her and fell backwards.

"Kent! Watch those clumsy feet of yours!" She had pulled me to my feet and pushed me forward into a doorway.

I had just glared back in response. The nerve! *She* hadn't warned me she was stopping. It had nothing to do with my feet!

I had rested my hand on the doorway, feeling the rough stone surface that rose up into an arch above. Chiselled into it were strange markings, like ancient runes. I had only known that because mom had a book about them that I had used for spy games.

My mom had taken one last look around before grabbing the huge, brass circle door-knocker and pounding the door. She pushed me behind her, again glancing once more up and down the street. What had she been so scared of?

I heard bangs coming from the other side, as if someone was knocking things over, then the faint shuffle of feet became louder. Finally, with a creak, the door had opened.

I had taken an involuntary step back at the sight before me.

A short, plump man with blue hair, which was sticking up in all directions - stood in the doorway. He looked in permanent shock, like he had stuck his fingers in an electric socket or something. He was wearing some kind of safety goggles that made his blue eyes pop like a chameleon's, and he had the biggest wart I had ever seen on the end of his chin. He had stood there surveying my mom for a moment before smiling.

"Ruby," he had simpered in an uncharacteristic girly voice, "Come in, come in. It's been too long." My mom grabbed my hand, smiling back at the man, as we stepped through the door.

Once over the threshold I had felt a wave of hot air wash over me, making me feel instantly sick and dizzy. I had held my head in my hands and screwed up my eyes, trying not to throw up.

"Relax, Kent," my mom said soothingly, "the feeling will pass in a moment."

"Ahhh, this must be your son, the next Fire Defender! That, my dear boy, was a charm that searches your aura and lets me know if you are a danger or not," he had said, smiling impishly.

I had glanced at my hands, saw an orange glow surrounding them and immediately panicking, tried to wipe it off.

"Don't worry. It's your aura glowing. It will fade in a moment," my mom had said, holding my hand.

I had gasped as she clung to my hand hers was a deep red and I had stared at the two colors as she guided me through to the lounge. I still don't know much about auras really, except everyone's got one - even norms - and everyone's is supposed to mean something different.

The guy had busily asked us if we wanted drinks or food, but hurried off into the kitchen before we could reply. I had stared around me, screwing up my nose at the smell it was like cabbage and dirty socks - and everywhere I looked I saw strange objects. There was a brown, battered couch in the middle of the room, with small tables holding books or magazines, some with small bottles of glowing liquids, silver trinkets and what looked like wooden Scrabble tiles, cluttering the rest of the room.

"I guess you know why I'm here," my mom had called to the wizard.

"Of course! You wish to consult the Font," he replied from the next room.

"Kent, why don't you find Mojo? We have a lot to discuss and it might take a while," she had said squeezing my hand.

"Yes, he'll be in his room - straight up the corridor, second door on the left," the wizard had said as he re-entered the room carrying a heavily-laden black tray.

I've always known when I'm not wanted. Typical isn't it? Your parents drag you along to these things and then push you together with someone you don't know! I had nodded politely and made my way through the maze of tables and up the corridor.

"He has a good aura, Ruby. He'll make a great Defender," I had heard the wizard say as the door to the room closed itself behind me.

I had known I was definitely not wanted! I took a few more steps and looked up at the door. It seemed normal - just a brown wooden door. I reached towards the knob, but hesitated; should I knock or just go in? I had decided to knock first; after all I wouldn't have wanted some weird dude walking into *my* room uninvited. I had knocked loudly, then waited. No answer. I pushed the door open and walked in.

"Hello," I had called, the room seemingly deserted.

I had taken two more steps inside before being hit on the head with something soft. It bounced off me and a white cloth bag landed in my waiting hands. I had looked around to see where it had come from.

A small desk to my right on which stood a computer still switched on. Ha! Definite geek. He had been playing an online game called 'Two Worlds'. I hadn't played it myself, but some of my friends had. SoI knew it was a virtual mythical land where you battled wizards and other mythical creatures.

To my left was a single bed, the sheets pulled back, the same way I had left mine that morning – with an electric guitar lying across it. I had thought that maybe the guy *was* cool, after all. There were clothes spread across the floor and half hanging out of a drawer. Wow! This guy was messier than *me*.

I had turned in a slow circle, taking in the row-upon-row of shelves lining the walls of the room, each littered with books and strange looking objects just like the front room, including a pair of silver handcuffs! Hmmm, I hadn't been sure what to think about that!

Then a movement had caught my eye and, looking up, I saw a boy about my age, suspended upside down high in the air. His long, black, wavy hair hung down an increasingly pink face.

He had been tied to the ceiling, his feet bound by a long rope that ran to a hook on the opposite wall. I had watched, fascinated, as he squirmed around like a fish out of water, and suppressed a laugh when I saw a hole in one of his stripy socks,a small toe peeping out.

His hands had been handcuffed behind his back and I saw a titanium ring with an aquamarine stone glittering on his left hand. His white shirt was threatening to come loose from his black pants, and it was torn on one side from his efforts. I had noticed a long, thin silver chain hanging from his neck, with a variety of keys attached to a silver hoop.

"Dude, what are you doing? Do you need some help?" I had asked,confused.

What *had* this guy been doing? Had his dad got fed up with him and tied him up there? I decided he was either really brave, trying some daring stunt, or really stupid and someone had tricked him into tying himself up on purpose.

"No!" He had shouted, his voice strained with effort and his face turning a dark shade of pink.

"You sure man?" I had asked sniggering. "Your face is like a tomato!"

"No! Don't touch anything," he had said, struggling against his restraints.

I had sat on his bed and watched this strange guy tugging at his handcuffs and swinging himself, wondering if he was trying to get his keys.

He had looked like he was about to pass out - his face was a deepening shade of purple. I eyed the rope tied to the hook and walked over to it.

"No, don't! I'm nearly there," he had wheezed.

I had taken a hold of the rope and untied it. Immediately it came loose and he crashed to the floor. Ouch! That had to have hurt;the floor was made from solid pine boards.

He had sworn loudly, groaned, and turned himself over. Clambering to his feet, swaying slightly, he had panted for a few seconds as his face started to return to a normal shade. He had glared up at me, his fist clenched before his face eventually slackened and, sighing, he sat down on his bed.

"Would you mind?" Turning he held up his cuffed hands.

"Sure man, err... which err... which one?" I stumbled, grabbing at the keys around his neck.

"The smallest one... no, not that... yes, that one," he said.

I had grabbed the smallest key, no bigger than my little finger, and undid the lock. He had rubbed his wrists and began to untie the rope from around his ankles.

"So err... what were you doing?"

"I'm devising a key that will unlock anything." He had smiled, holding up his bunch of keys. "Oh, and training myself to have the stamina to escape any situation, hence being up there." He nodded towards the ceiling. Yeah, this guy was certifiably nuts!

"So, who are you?" He had asked with an interested tone.

"I'm Kent Basco, the 15th Fire Defender," I had said, trying to sound macho but actually coming off as pretty obnoxious.

"Oh, right. Ruby's son," he had said, picking up all his clothes and shoving them into various drawers. "I guess they're consulting the font and shoved you in here out the way."

This guy was observant, or had this just happened a lot to him? "Yes. So…err… well," I began.

"Don't worry about it. Listen, I've got to run some errands in a minute and they…" he had nodded in the direction of the lounge, "won't be finished for hours, so you can come with me if you want." He spoke lazily whilst pulling on a pair of black leather shoes.

"Sounds better than staying on my own," I said following him out the room.

We had gone into the town, delivering potions and trinkets to his dad's customers. Mojo seemed quite cool. We had chatted about the kinds of things he did with his dad, which sounded a lot cooler than what I did with my mom. It turned out that he was developing all kinds of magical keys that could open all kinds of things, from handcuffs to doors leading to other realms.

He had also been developing several magical potions and objects that did strange things, like protecting people or allowing someone to shape-shift and change their form.

"That sounds cool, how does that work?" I had asked, genuinely interested.

"Well, it's simply a matter of physics and magical properties. I'll show you when we get back," he had said, shrugging and putting his hands in his pockets.

"Sounds cool," I had said as I slammed into the back of him.

He moved so swiftly that I had to blink to recover. He had darted behind a bush trying, unsuccessfully, to hide. I looked around for an explanation, then I saw them: two girls. They were around our age, I guessed, and one was breath-taking. Beauty radiated from her like beams of light. Her hair was thick, jet black and fell to her waist. She had pale skin, piercing green eyes and a smile that would weaken the hardest of hearts.

The other girl was the complete opposite, with blonde, curly hair scrapped back into a ponytail that sat so high on her head it looked like a curly pineapple.

"Who are they?" I had whispered to the hidden Mojo.

"The black haired girl is Talia Kahale and the blonde one is *Katherine Gain*." He had said her name like it was his life-line. I smiled as I understood; he *liked* her.

"So… you have it bad for that one?" I had taken a step towards them as I spoke.

"No! Don't…" But his protests had come too late - I had already gone.

"Hello ladies, I'm Kent Basco." I held my hand out to the blonde girl and she smiled.

"I'm Katherine and this is my friend Talia," she said.

I had turned to Talia and held out my hand and as she took it a spark flared between our palms. She had looked up at me and smiled. She was so beautiful!

"Can I get you girls a soda?" I had asked boldly.

"Sure," Katherine said, "as long as Mojo comes along too."

Ha! She obviously knew he was hiding in the bush and we heard him curse as he stumbled out, covered in leaves.

"H-h-hi," he stammered.

The girls had started to giggle and clutched one another, and I couldn't blame them – he had been a funny sight with all those leaves in his hair. We spent the rest of the afternoon walking by the river, just messing around. Mojo had begun to relax and Katherine ended up taking his hand in hers.

I boldly took hold of Talia's and she withdrew. Ouch! The pain of rejection was bitter. She had looked at the floor.

"I'm sorry… I just don't know you that well," she had said shyly.

"That's cool, I understand," I replied, trying not to sound wounded.

After that we had sat on the grass and chatted about schools and friends whilst Mojo and Katherine went for a walk. I was telling Talia about our home by Carlisle Lake when Mojo came bounding up to us.

"You'll see… I can do it," he had shouted back excitedly at Katherine, who was giggling wildly.

"Kent, stand up."

"Why?" I said, bewildered.

"Katherine doesn't believe I have the power to turn you into smoke," he had said, scowling at her.

"Dude! Did you just say smoke?"

Then, before I knew what was happening, Mojo had me in some kind of a strangled hold. His hand was on my head two fingers either side of my nose and he was staring intently into my eyes.

I had tried to protest, but I was stuck still. I could vaguely hear the girls' laughing as I went numb. I felt dizzy. My mind was protesting, screaming, and all I had seen was a cloud of black,with what looked like a river passing by. I had collapsed to the ground, clutching my head and, coming round, I saw to my surprise that I was further down the river than where I was.

Talia, Katherine and Mojo were all running towards me laughing and whooping at what Mojo had just done.

Talia was the first to reach me. "Are you alright?" she asked, frowning with concern. My head was spinning and I felt sick, but the sight of her made me feel a million times better.

Then her face went translucent and she began to glow. She grasped my shoulders tightly and began to shake me.

"Kent… Wake up. Wake up! Seraphina needs you! You must wake up!"

My eyes flew open and I jumped to my feet. I gazed around,

disoriented then heard Seraphina's terrified voice screaming off to my left.

"Let go! You're hurting me!"

I ran towards the sound of her voice and eventually sighted her through a bush. I pulled my hood over my face and watched as *Joey* grabbed her by the arms and started to shake her.

My fists clenched with anger and I leapt out from cover. No one hurts *my* little girl.

"Let go of her!" I shouted.

Joey looked startled for a split second,then grabbed Seraphina's hair, twisting her back to him so that she faced me. Her eyes, wide with fear, streamed with tears. He pulled out a small blade and held it to her throat. I recognized it immediately.

I stood shell-shocked. My daughter was being held hostage at the point of *that* blade. The one that had once belonged to her own mom.

Seraphina screamed in pain and I edged closer whilst Joey hissed into her ear, smiling and leering at me.

He laughed derisively- an evil cackle that made my blood boil with anger. Seraphina's terrified, tear-glazed eyes found mine and I tried to reassure her, that everything was going to be fine. I needed her to be calm enough to think clearly.

I took a couple of cautious steps towards them, watching the blade intently. One false move and he would take my angel away from me. I was not going to lose my daughter and fail my family again. The thought of Talia made me strong - I owed my wife and my daughters. I raised my baton to my chin, poised for a skilled blow. All I needed was the right distraction. I could feel Hiccup by my leg, but couldn't afford to look down at him whilst Joey's attention was on me.

Seraphina noticed the baton and was drawn slightly closer to it. Yes! She was clearly pulled to the power of the ribbon so was definitely ready to take her place. The baton had this effect on all

Defenders of our element as it was given to us as gift, and only we had the power to use it.

I winced as Joey's fingers pulled tighter on Seraphina's hair, wrenching her closer to him. The blade dug deeper into her throat, causing a new trickle of blood to run down her neck. My body shook with rage. I was determined to kill him!

"Don't be foolish. Old Defender, your powers are fading. You can't attack me. I am protected by *Maura*," he sneered.

I knew it! She *was* controlling him. Part of me wanted to cut his arms off, but deep down I knew it wasn't his fault; he wasn't in control of his actions. If only I could read auras like Mojo, then I would have been able to know for certain.

"Besides," he jeered, bringing me back from my thoughts, "I have what you need and the other one will soon be ours too," he laughed mockingly.

I faltered for a moment…*Lana*. No! It couldn't be. I had been so careful! No one knew? How had they found her? She was *supposed* to be protected! Besides, she was too young to show any signs. No, it must have meant something else, someone else.

I took an involuntary step closer, Joey shuffled back yelling, "One more step and she dies!"

He raised the knife higher and held onto my daughter more tightly than before. I watched the knife brush against her face and my heart leapt in terror. I lowered the weapon and placed it carefully onto the ground in front of my feet, making sure it wasn't too far from me. I could make a grab for it in a second, after all I had that skill at least. I swayed slightly as I heard the patter of light pads against the forest floor and knew Hiccup was ready. Joey hadn't paid any attention to him. One of the many wonderful things about his cat form was that he was easily overlooked.

My eyes flickered between the blade and Seraphina's eyes, '*be calm. I'll save you,*' I tried to make them say. The knife moved further from her throat as the power drew him in too, and I watched as he leaned closer to my weapon.

"Good," he gloated not taking his eyes off my baton. "Very good, old man. Now step away from it!"

Joey's grip on Seraphina's hair was starting to slacken slightly as his attention was directed at me. I took a few confident steps backwards, making sure Hiccup had a clear run.

Joey shakily pushed Seraphina forward until she was standing directly in front of the bat. I could see the eagerness in her eyes, and for a second caught a glimpse of how strong her powers were. As she got closer it began to glow orange and crimson, but she evidently couldn't see a change.

"Pick it up, Seraphina!" Joey demanded, pushing her closer and keeping his eyes fixed on me.

I watched as she hesitated slightly, stopping to place a gold trophy on the forest floor. I had to act. Her powers were strong, but she was not ready to hold the baton. She would either disintegrate or blow out everything within a hundred metres of us.

She was just stretching out her fingers to it as I launched myself forward with blinding speed, slamming into Joey as he lost his grip on Seraphina's hair. My head hit the floor knocking, me dizzy as I saw Hiccup's feet bounding past.

I heard Seraphina's terrified scream and glanced around to see Joey scrambling up. I looked back down, disoriented and struggling to see clearly. I heard Hiccup take another leap from the other side of me. He was really fast!

Then time seemed to stand still as I watched Seraphina's fingers clasp themselves around the baton's handle. I gasped as it glowed brightly, then watched in amazement as it died back down. She was more powerful than I had ever thought possible!

I watched as she swung it around wildly. The ribbon didn't extend, but she did manage to hit Joey up the nose. I heard a sickening crunch and the baton hit the ground.

"Argh!" He screamed, staggering back and grabbing his now

bleeding, swelling nose. Ha! She's done some serious damage, *good girl.*

That was all the chance I needed. I got to my feet shakily and ran as fast as I could towards them. I needed to get her out of here!

"Run, go!" I screamed as I dived into the air, landing lightly in a forward roll and scooping up my baton.

I swirled around just in time to see a girl about Seraphina's age running towards us, dressed in a flowing blue gown and brandishing a sword. She too had the red glowing eyes of a dark elf.

I charged towards Joey and saw Seraphina running into the depths of the forest in the wrong direction for home. I watched gratefully as Hiccup bounded to my side, now in his tiger form. There was no way these two were getting past us! He roared loudly. It was deafening.

I knew Hiccup was a good choice of protector because he could morph into a white tiger possessing great speed and agility. The girl stopped and stared, first at Hiccup, then at Joey who I held in a tight headlock. Fear seemed to flash through her eyes as she realized what she was doing.

Hiccup roared loudly and pounced, just as Joey hit me in the stomach with a branch. I fell to the ground holding my stomach, gasping for breath.

The girl dived, evading Hiccup's massive claws and grabbed Joey. She smiled as she then sank into a shadow cast on the floor with Joey, just as Hiccup pounced once more. She was definitely a Dark Elf. Only they could travel through the earth.

I rose to my feet unsteadily and searched the shadows although I knew it was no use- they had returned to Maura.

REVELATION

SERAPHINA

I walked for what seemed like hours and finally emerged from the forest. I gasped in shock as I realized I was on the opposite side of our lake -I could see our house on the other side. I started to run round towards it,with Hiccup at my side. I couldn't believe that my *cat* had led me all the way home and I made a mental note to give him a treat when we got home safely.

Joy ran through me as I got closer and closer to the house Grandma was there standing on the porch with what looked like a huge candle in her hand. I couldn't help sighing with relief as I tried to run – pleased to see her alive and well

The closer I got, the more I could see. She looked very worried and tired. I called out to her and she turned at the sound of my voice, her candle flickering as she ran towards me.

As she got to me she scooped me up in a huge bear hug. I gasped, waiting for the flame to burn my skin, but felt nothing. Where was the candle? It had seemingly disappeared. I couldn't dwell on that fact for too long because she rushed me towards the house.

Once inside I felt a pang of guilt. What had happened to my dad? Had he gotten away? Was he already here? Had he been hurt?

"Where's Dad," I asked as she ushered me into the chair by the fire.

"I don't know," she said, rushing into the kitchen.

I looked down at myself and cried. I looked like I had been dragged through hell, and in some ways I had. My dress was torn and covered in mud and blood. My arms were black from the dirt and mixed with the blood from the gash Joey had left me with. My hair was half out, and spiralling down my chest.

Grandma returned carrying the first aid kit and a blanket. She cleaned up my wounds and scrapes, dressing the cuts on my arm and neck.

I sat beside the fire, wrapped in a blanket and drinking steaming hot cocoa. Hiccup curled into a ball by my feet. All I could think of was my dad.

"I don't know what else to tell you," I said after Grandma had continued to question me about what had happened.

She made me repeat what Joey had said over and over again. All the time I was telling the and retelling the story she was darting back and forth from the window to the door, as if debating whether to go out and look for my dad.

"How did you know I was trouble Grandma?" I asked, confused. "I didn't have my cell with me or anything so how did you know I needed help?" I studied her closely.

Something was not adding up here. Had Dad just decided to follow us? I was about to push Grandma for an answer when the lounge door flew open and in he walked, complete with the cloak. He looked fine until he dropped the hood. A huge purple lump, had swollen on his brow.

"Thank God you're safe," Grandma said, hugging him tightly.

"Dad," I breathed as I ran to hug him.

"Are you okay sweetheart?" he asked, running his thumb over my bandage.

"I'm fine, thanks to you."

We settled near the fire. I sat on the rug with the blanket wrapped tightly round my shoulders, and stared up at my dad, sat in the chair I had vacated.

I hadn't understood most of what he and my grandma had been talking about, but from what I could make out Dad had battled Joey. They had both known Joey was up to no good.

"He was fast and strong but still young. He lacked wisdom," he winked at me. "Not bad for an old man, eh?" He chuckled.

I was bewildered. Was he seriously making a joke about the situation? The guy I had such a big crush on had just held a knife to my throat and fought with my dad, and now he was joking about it!

"Calm down Seraphina," Grandma chided, looking from my dad to me and back, "was he working for... *her*?"

"Yes, there isn't any doubt in my mind now. We need to set out first thing in the morning. I think we're safe enough till then. She won't attack so soon, it's not her style. Beside he needs to recover, but he'll be back." Dad glanced towards the window as he spoke.

"Excuse me! Can someone please explain to *me* what's going on?" I was growing more and more anxious by the minute. Who was *she*? Did he mean the girl from the store?

"Of course. I'm sorry, Seraphina. I'll explain everything." He stood up, walked over to the window and peered out. "It all begins with our family's history."

'You've got to be kidding me', I thought. Our family's history? What was that supposed to mean?

"Long ago there was a place known as Tempest," my dad began. This village was small and not very well known. It's people were kind, loyal and peaceful. They were known as The Ashen Tribe. They were our ancestors," he said looking at me.

"One of the tribe's members was Acquanetta. She was beautiful, calm, kind and desired by many men both within her own village and outside of it. One of those under her spell was Aiden.

He was brave and fierce, a demanding tribal hunter. His hunts had always brought victory and wealth to the village and he was admired almost as much as Acquanetta.

For a long time he felt that she should be his bride. He had been in love with her for many years and believed that they, the most beautiful and strong, could rule over the tribe. After many months he finally asked her to become his bride."

"How romantic," I sighed, interrupting him mid-sentence.

"You and romance! Haven't you learnt your lesson yet?" Grandma chided.

"Mother, enough," my dad said, glaring at her as I hung my head in shame.

"However," my dad continued, "Acquanetta declined. She didn't like Aiden's demanding nature, and she was already secretly in love with another:

Ora, the village's newest hunter. He was handsome and gentle. He, would only ever kill for food and survival,not for wealth and glory. That was why she had fallen in love with him.

Aiden became enraged with jealousy when he found out about them. He wasn't used to refusal: he had always gotten whatever he wanted. One night, in a fit of rage, he took Acquanetta for himself. She would learn to love him! He was certain that if he couldn't have her then no one could."

"Oh no, what happened? Did she get away from him?" I asked before I could stop myself.

My dad smiled at me and Grandma huffed in disgust as she walked towards the window.

"He rode away with her, making sure they were hidden many miles from the tribe. He enslaved her in a cave deep in a cliff face over the ocean. He believed they would be hard to find the cave was high and difficult to climb to.

After a few years of living with Aiden and having given up on escape, she began to understand his ways. Acquanetta soon began to love him."

"What! Why?" My dad chuckled at me and patted my head.

"It wasn't easy for her. It caused a raging storm of confusion inside, for she learnt to love Aiden, but it was not the same type of love she had for Ora. She never forgot him or gave up hope of him finding her.

Ora had searched for many years and finally found the place where she was being held. He set up camp, watching and waiting for the right time to approach. He didn't want to fight Aiden as he knew he was no match for him. When night fell Ora crept into the cave. He freed Acquanetta from her chains, but Aiden woke as he broke the last one."

"What then? Did they make a run for it?" I began and saw disappointment in my dad's face.

"No. Aiden was filled with rage and attacked Ora. Acquanetta feared for her beloved and knew neither man would rest until one was dead.

She knew there was only one way to save them from each other. She took a dagger and plunged it into her own chest. She stumbled and tumbled into the ocean below. Her body was carried away by the waves floating peacefully a few miles from the shore.

Ora, devastated and heartbroken, prayed to the gods for justice and for his young love to be returned to him. Aiden also felt remorse and begged to the gods as Ora had. He descended the cave running along the shore line trying to reach her as he shouted to the gods for his prayers to be answered.

"Their prayers were answered. Ora fell to the ground, writhing in pain. He rose into the air and spun around so fast his form changed and he became a tornado. Moving across the ocean, he flew to Acquanetta and carried her back to the shore. The gods had blessed him and honoured his pleas. As the tornado faded and Ora regained his form he emerged holding a small stone, Lepidolite, a gift from the gods used for protection and healing.

"He looked down at Acquanetta, peaceful in death. He picked up the stone and chanted an ancient healing spell and as soon as he had mumbled the last words her body was bathed in a golden glow. She became stronger and stronger and the wound in her chest magically closed.

"Aiden had watched from the cliff side and had become angry. *He* deserved the gift, not Ora. Smoke rose from his skin as he descended and ran towards them.

Fire shot out of his fingers towards the young couple. Acquanetta feared for the life of her love but couldn't move quickly enough to help. She screamed, and as she did a wall of water rose up in front of Ora, protecting him from Aiden's fire. She too had been blessed by the gods, and Aiden had been cursed. He finally admitted defeat and, realizing he would never gain her true love, fled.

"Over the years Aiden began to learn to control his gift. He had to live with his guilt and never stopped trying to find a way to atone for his actions.

After many years of practice he moved on eventually falling in love with someone new. He never forgot Acquanetta and dedicated his life to saving others using his gift. He became known as Adranus, God of Fire.

"Acquanetta and Ora re-joined the tribe and eventually married. They went on to have many children, all beautiful and gifted. When they reached an age where they were happy to leave this world they were taken by the gods and given a place where they were forever worshipped. They became known as Coventina and Aethe, the Goddess of Water and the God of Air." He finished the story with a sigh of relief, as if keeping it to himself had caused him great pain.

"So who are we descended from?" I asked, although I already knew.

"Think about it Seraphina," my grandma chided.

"Sweetheart, *Aiden* was our ancestor. For years his gift has been passed down our blood-line. We are his descendants and so we have his gift. I'm sure you already knew though," my dad said, staring at the flames in the fire which had started to burn a deep blue color.

I had the feeling that there was something else he hadn't told me. I stared at Dad and Grandma wanting to laugh and say how absurd it all was, when my dad held up his hand and clicked his fingers. A small flame floated on his palm. It grew slightly, getting brighter before diminishing slowly. He closed his fist and extinguished it.

"How did you do that?" I cried, leaping to my feet and walking over to examine his hand. Then I remembered: my grandma's *candle!*

"For years our family have passed these powers to each other, and we have always tried to live peacefully. We have learnt to control the gift and used it for good," he said.

Dad and Grandma exchanged worried looks, then each hastily looked away. It was too late. I had seen it in their eyes. There *was* more to this.

I sat back down. "Why hide what we can do? None of this explains why Joey just tried to kill me!"

"Maybe I can answer that one," a new, higher-pitched voice chimed. I turned stared at the cat, back to Grandma, then back at my dad.

"I'm sorry..." I giggled, "but did my *cat* just speak?"

"Yes! As a matter of fact, I did. Well in a manner, I'm actually talking to you telepathically. You are the only one who can hear me," Hiccup said.

"Just checking," I said before blacking out.

THE PROTECTOR

SERAPHINA

I was running through the forest next to my grandma's house. The ground and trees were shifting, changing as I ran, and ahead of me I could see a flicker of light- a fire, maybe? I found that my feet were drawn in its direction and as I drew nearer I slowed down as my nerves began to kick in. What was a fire doing in the forest? Why was I feeling compelled to run towards it?

I tentatively approached the fire. It looked like a small bonfire sitting in a stone circle. Hiccup was sitting next to it. How crazy! What's he doing out here? What am I doing out here? I clutched at my side then as it burned with exhaustion and although I tried to catch my breath to ease the pain it had very little effect.

I walked over to him and sat myself down beside the fire. I suddenly felt calm and comfortable, as if I was meant to do so. The fire was warm and welcoming, and as I sat down I had realized how cold I had been. As I looked down things made sense - I was wearing my pale blue flannel PJ's.

"Ha!" I chuckled, looking up at the stars. Why am I outside in my PJ's? I laughed out loud at the craziness.

The raw earth beneath me seemed soft and warm for a forest floor, despite the fact that my feet were bare. Hiccup turned his head at my derisive laughter looking at me.

"I'm sorry if I scared you earlier at your grandma's. I have been trying to communicate with you for the last three months, since you turned eighteen. I guess you were a late bloomer," he said.

Ha, sure. A talking cat! Why not? I had no doubt at all now! I was either dreaming or losing my mind completely. Well, I thought I might as well humour the situation, after all, how often do you get to talk to your cat?

"So then, I guess... err..." I was stuck. What do you actually say to a cat? Then all the questions I had been storing up suddenly spilled out.

"What do you mean 'late bloomer'? Where are we? What's happening to me?" I asked in a harsh tone, taking slight offence at his comment.

I wasn't a late bloomer! I was mature for my age and didn't appreciate being told differently by a *cat*, no matter how cool that was!

"You passed out at your grandma's house and right now you're sleeping in your bed," he said, nodding at the fire.

Even though I then knew I was dreaming, the fire still startled me. Images of me asleep, in the same pale blue PJ's, started to appear. I jumped and watched in horror as the sleeping me jumped too. I continued to watch as a hand reached across and dabbed my forehead with a towel. I reached up to my own head and felt it was wet and cool.

I was asleep in my bed with my dad and Grandma fussing over me. I could see everything clearly. My father was dabbing my head and my grandma was holding my hand. Yeah! I was officially losing it.

"Most Defenders inherit their ancestors' gift at the age of eighteen, or when the ancestor possessing the gift dies. You are lucky to have your father and your grandma still alive and therefore will inherit it with age."

I thought about that for a moment. He was right; yes, I had lost my mother but at least I had my dad and my grandma, which was more than some people had.

"I've been keeping a close eye on you and knew you would be receiving the gift fairly soon…" he broke off as I chuckled.

"Sorry, it's just that *my cat* has been keeping an eye on me. It's *so* weird," I said and laughed again.

He scowled at me and continued, "…because of the signs you've been showing. When the Defender starts to receive the gift they can start communicating with their animal guide, if they're lucky enough to have one. I've been trying to speak to you." He spoke solemnly.

I looked at him, completely bewildered. "Animal Guide? What symptoms?" "There have been a lot! When you got angry yesterday you started to get a burning sensation in your chest. Your powers seem to be connecting with your emotions, but I can't be certain of that until the cross-over is complete. I stayed with you while you slept and watched you glow redder and redder before you woke up."

I turned back to the image in the flames and watched. I did indeed begin to glow red! My dad and Grandma shot back from me. Oh man, what was happening to me?

Hiccup brought my attention back to him, "Err…not to mention the little trick you've discovered with the candle."

I immediately felt embarrassed and ashamed that I had been trying to hide it for so long, but I couldn't remember having done that when anyone was around. Then I realized - I was talking to the cat! Oh man, I didn't think I would have to hide what I could do from the cat!

Of course he knew. I had even lit a candle with my mind when he was sitting on my lap.

"Yes, well… I was careful. You would have seen that," I said, feeling defensive.

"Yes, you're right. You don't have to explain yourself to me - I am your loyal protector. And Sera, you also don't have to hide anything from me!"

I thought about what he had said for a moment. Animal guide, loyal protector, and my emotions? Oh man, I really needed to see a shrink!

The dream I'd had the night before – when I was burning on the beach having built a sandcastle and watched that girl drown - was very emotional. I knew, deep down, Hiccup was right. I *was* starting to inherit my ancestors' gift, just like my dad's story. Still, there was so much that didn't make any sense.

"There are some things that I don't understand. Like why did you call my ancestors Defenders? What happened to Joey? Why did the girl from the hotel change into the girl from my dream?" the questions tumbled out in a rush, and I felt relieved to finally get it all off my chest.

Hiccup walked around the fire to the other side and pawed at the ground, almost nervously, and then knew he couldn't tell me everything. But I still wanted answers. I realized there were things I had to learn for myself.

"I can't answer all of those questions, because I don't know all of the answers. I'm not a seer, just a guide and protector, but I can tell you what I do know." He stopped and took a deep breath. "First. I am your Spirit Guide and Protector. I was born to protect and guide you on your quest."

"What quest?" I asked.

"The one you will embark on to discover your destiny. You,Seraphina are a child of Aiden. You are a Defender. A Defender of Fire. You were born with a claim to one of the world's greatest powers. As your dad said, most of your ancestors before you lived peaceful lives. They simply chose to ignore their quests." he said, staring at me.

I stared back, bewildered. I didn't really know what to say or do. The air around me seemed to drop a few degrees. I started to shiver.

"Yes," he nodded, "your life has been tied to a harsh destiny. You first need to learn about it, then decide if you'll take it or not. Your future and quest is not entirely clear to us all yet.

As for the question of Joey. Well to understand and make sense of what happened with him you need to learn the history of the other Defenders first," he finished.

Something pulled me back at these words."Other Defenders?" I asked. "There are others with my powers?"

"Yes and no. You are one of five Defenders. Five were chosen and blessed by the one known, as Mother Nature by your people and Gaia by mine, and each has a different power connected to the world's elements.

"Your dad has already told you the history of three of the Defenders: Aiden, The First Defender of Fire, Acquanetta, The First Defender of Water, Ora, The First Defender of Air. I will now tell you about the other two." He spoke mournfully, as if it was upsetting for him. Did he have some sort of connection to them?

"There was another tribe living on the other side of the globe to the Ashen, known as the Avani Tribe. They were peaceful; pleasant but not familiar with the workings of the world.

"The tribe had a leader known as Maura Lilith. She was the first of the tribe to be born with a rare and precious gift. This was the ability to enter the world of the spirits at will and without being harmed. She could drive away the bad spirits that tormented the living, and had the power to ease the suffering of trapped spirits. Some say her mother had made a deal with the god known as Pluto, ruler of the underworld.

"She ruled over the Avani for many years and kept the evil spirits that tormented them away. The tribe was often attacked by these spirits, and many had lost their lives Maura was born. Her aura alone kept the spirits at bay, even as baby.

"She was loved dearly by her people and was honoured with gifts and power. Yet the one thing she wanted more than any other never came to her – she never found someone who loved her enough to marry her and give her a child. You see, although she was loved and thanked, even worshipped, most of the tribe were scared of her gift.

"It was also said that her powers were given to her by the gods so she could help the children of the earth to control spirits that no longer belonged there. She was meant to help the God of the Underworld keep control of the dead."

I watched myself in the flames, relieved to have not been born with her gift. I was terrified of ghosts and demons and all the stuff that kids are scared of. I had enough ghosts in my life already. I always seemed to have the feeling of being followed or watched. It creeped me out just thinking about it.

I also found myself feeling sorry for Maura. Imagine going the whole of your life with people being scared of you and no one *loving* you. I got so wrapped up in my own thoughts that Hiccup made me jump when his thoughts drifted back into mine.

"Not long after Maura Lilith became the tribe's leader, a new member of the tribe was born. Her name was Hertha and she had a new gift, a different sort of blessing.

"She grew up to be one of the most gentle, caring and loving members of the tribe. When she grew old enough to help her parents on the fields she tended to the crops, and it wasn't long before everyone discovered that hers were bigger and healthier than anyone's.

"The tribe profited from this and became stronger. People started to talk about her gift and proclaimed that she had the gift of the earth. Some of the tribe's people said she was meant as a gift of thanks for all of Maura's goodness.

"Maura was fascinated by the girl's gift and studied her intently. She would soon have someone else at her side to help her to rule. Hertha was to be the daughter she never had and, even more importantly, someone else who knew how hard a gift from the gods was to bear.

"She pushed Hertha's powers to new, ever more dangerous levels to see how extensive they were. She secretly hoped that the girl's gift was weaker than her own so she could still be the best..."

"Wow! She seems full of herself. How greedy!" I interrupted.

"Yes," he replied simply. "Maura soon realized that Hertha's gift had no limits and also discovered that it was becoming stronger the more she used it and the older she got.

"Thanks to Maura's help, however, Hertha soon found that she also had the power to bring precious stones and metals from with the earth up to the surface.

The Avani began to thrive on this new gift, using the metals for tools for farming the fields and weapons for defending the tribe from invaders. Again, the tribe became bigger and more powerful with these two gifts.

"Hertha's precious stones, became a symbol for love and worship. They were soon given to loved ones as gifts and peace offerings, a tradition that continues today! Only now I think someone named 'Tiffany' gets all the glory for that." I smiled sheepishly - I had a Tiffany's locket for my sixteenth birthday.

"Soon most of the tribe's people were gathering around Hertha and giving her gifts of fruit and vegetables in exchange for gifts of precious stones and metals. She was beloved of them, and had a huge amount of suitors. This upset Maura, who began to use Hertha's powers to make weapons that were better and stronger than any other tribes'. Her plan was to take them over and rule as supreme leader. When she found this out, Hertha pleaded with Maura, trying to make her see that what she would ultimately lead to destruction. Yet Maura would not see sense and became tired of Hertha's constant cautions.

She was consumed by jealousy of Hertha's gifts, especially

when she denied using them for her own gain. When she saw that she could no longer persuade Hertha to do her bidding she banished her from the tribe. She warned her never to return, or she would drag her spirit to the underworld, where she would remain forever enslaved in darkness.

"Some of the tribe's people, knowing that Maura had been consumed by darkness within her, followed Hertha into exile. Some stayed loyal to Maura, and some stayed for fear of disobeying her, remembering that she could enter the spirit world. Few even stayed for the promise of power and glory and made deals with her - their loyalty for the return of their lost loved ones. Over the years those unluckily ones souls have been corrupt and have taken forms of the Dark Elves.

"Hertha's tribe travelled far away from Maura's and began a new life. For many years they lived in peace, prospering under her rule. She went on to marry and have children of her own, yet sadly only a three survived. Hertha was certain that Maura was responsible for this and the people of the tribe swore it was Maura's influence, a warning to her to stay away." He bowed his head with these words, and I knew there was more to this story than he was sharing. I wanted to ask but couldn't find courage to.

"The tribe worshipped Hertha for her courage and showered her with gifts of thanks. They knew she was protecting her people ahead of her own children, and they could not make that right.

"They worshipped her like a goddess. She was so pleased and proud of her people that the love she had for them one day overwhelmed her. On that most joyful day the whole tribe gathered in awe as their beloved leader glowed with the golden light of the gods, becoming engulfed in it, and disappeared. All that remained was a white-gold ring. Engraved on the outside was a swirling symbol, with an inscription that read 'to make time stand still' on the inside.

"Her husband and children were devastated and could not explain the event. The tribe erected a temple in her honour leaving the ring, lying on a silk cushion, on reverent display inside. It was under the strongest protection anyone had ever known.

"The tribe's new leader was Cherry, Hertha's first born child, who proclaimed that a celebration would take place on that same day every year. It would be known as The Festival Thesmophoria. The people renamed Hertha as Demeter, the goddess of fruit and vegetables after the gifts she had given to them.

"Maura soon heard of Hertha's disappearance and went to the Underworld searching for her spirit, knowing she had the power to rule over it. Hertha then wouldn't have been able to fight Maura's unchallenged rule, but her spirit was nowhere to be found.

"She searched for years and eventually took her rage out on the people of Hertha's tribe. She enslaved them all, including Hertha's husband, bending them to her evil will. However, thanks to their father Hertha's children *were* able to escape. He sacrificed himself to the hands of the Spirit Slaves giving his children time to escape through a secret underground passageway.

"The children, heartbroken at losing both parents, travelled the world seeking help from other tribes that lived with the same powers they had. Soon they found the descendants of Ora and Acquanetta. They then began to form the first Defenders' army and fought Maura, a battle raging at her castle. But their mission was unsuccessful. The war continues to this day.

"Hertha's village and temple lay abandoned for many years, destined to remain that way until either the day Maura is stopped, her people freed from their spirit prison or a direct descendant of Hertha returns." He finished his story and nudged me once more with his head.

I just sat there, staring into the flames. It was so strange hearing this story and imagining all those who had suffered. I felt an instant hatred towards Maura. She had never been defeated! I had a bad feeling about what my quest might entail. The conversation my dad and Grandma had held moments ago suddenly made sense.

"Was he working for... *her*?" Grandma had asked.

"Yes, there isn't any doubt in my mind now," he had replied.

Oh man. My head had started to ache with all the information and questions the story had thrown up.

"Hiccup," I whispered, "Is she... still alive?" I faltered for a second, already knowing the answer. "I still don't... well, I mean... I don't understand. Why did Joey attack me? Is he another Defender?"

This is what I wanted to understand most of all because it hurt too much to think that he was doing it of his own free will. I wanted to believe that Joey was trying to protect me rather than hurt me. Maybe my dad had made some sort of mistake?

"He wanted to know what the girl had said to me at the awards ceremony," I said, tears welling up in my eyes.

I wiped them away on the back of my pyjama sleeve and shuddered from the cold night air that pressed around me.

"I'm sorry Seraphina. I know he meant a lot to you. I do however believe he isn't working for Maura freely." I let out a small sob at the confirmation. "Most of the time Maura takes the spirit of Defenders' loved ones in order to break them. I believe she offers them anything their heart desires, then takes control of their spirit in return." I glanced at him, stunned and hurt.

"Do you mean Joey sold his soul or something?" Then I remembered: the new shiny car! Anger pulsated through me. "He sold his soul for a car?" I shouted, outraged.

"Sera, be careful," he said, slinking away from the open fire as the flames shot six feet into the air.

"Sorry," I said, trying to calm down.

"I do not believe he willingly sold his soul for a car. Most of the time the people she controls do not realize their soul is the asking price until it is too late. I believe that it's not too late for Joey and that he can still be saved from her grasp."

I sobbed into my sleeve at this news. It was such a relief - I might be able to save him from *her*. The question that remained was how.

"How can I save him?"

"It will be dangerous, and there will only be a very small chance of success. Joey should not be your main concern at the moment; you have a *bigger* destiny," he said in a worried tone.

I looked back at him, confused and dazed. What destiny? How could I have a destiny? I didn't even know who I was. I hadn't found myself, let alone a destiny to chase!

"In answer to your previous question… yes. Maura is still alive and Joey *is* working for her," he said bluntly.

This couldn't be true. How could it? Wouldn't she be hundreds of years old?

"I don't understand… When you say he's working for Maura, you mean the *same* Maura from your story, or one related to her?" I asked for what felt like the second time.

I knew I sounded stupid but I just wanted him to say '*Ha! Just kidding! You're dreaming and you'll wake up soon and find that none of this has happened.*' He just had to.

"Yes, she is the *same* Maura from the story!" He said. Oh man, why was this happening to me?

"She was a gifted soul just like you, but her fatal flaw consumed her. She took a dark path and on the journey and she discovered ways to make her life force strengthen over time. Instead of growing old like normal people her body and spirit remain frozen in time."

I was starting to feel odd. I had a deep-set feeling of doom, almost like I somehow already knew what he was saying. It was kind of like when you forget a song until someone reminds you of it, then you suddenly remember all the words.

I could sense something was still missing from the story

though, and it was being missed out deliberately. I sat in silence, pondering for what seemed like hours.

The night air around me became even cooler and I watched as tiny embers dashed and danced above the crackling fire.

There was one thing that seemed to draw the same response from everyone when I brought it up - the girl in my dream. I knew somehow that she was important and I had to figure out *why*.

These last few days had been one big, bad riddle after the other. Could I actually do it? Was I even smart enough for this quest? I had no fighting skills, unlike my dad, and I wasn't tough, unlike my grandma. I suddenly recalled what Hiccup had said about fatal flaws.

"What do you mean by fatal flaws?" I asked, dreading the answer.

"I wondered how long it would take you to ask that question. It took you longer than the others."

This made me feel inadequate and slow, confirming exactly what I had just thought. I hung my head, my chin touching my chest, making my hair tumble around my shoulders and into my face. Tears had finally arrived, thick and heavy, and I didn't want to share them.

"I'm sorry, that sounded rude. You have other priorities that come first. Every Defender has a fatal flaw this comes with having great power. The earth must remain balanced or it will crumble and fall. You have *great* powers, which you will learn to use once your transition is complete and you have embraced them. With that in mind, your fatal flaw will also be great," he said, nudging me and trying to reassure me.

What *was* my fatal flaw? I was about to ask when he answered before I could.

"*I* do not know your flaw. You must work that out for yourself. Only you will be able to tell what it is and how to overcome it. Once you know and accept it, then you can save yourself from it."

He looked at me sternly, almost as if I had done something wrong.

I stared back and sighed. I thought long and hard about what my fatal flaw could be. My grandma was always saying I was spoilt and selfish, but that couldn't be it. I might have thrown a few hissy fits, but it wasn't like I always got my own way. Did I?

"Joey," I said in shocked surprise. "I got my own way with going on a date with him and that led me into trouble." I felt my neck, absent-mindedly, where he had dug in the knife.

I had a cut where the blade had dug in. I refused to believe that the Joey I knew would have done that. I vowed to myself that I would find out what had happened to him and would save him if I could.

"Maybe now is a good time to reflect on your behaviour. After all, most of the time it's not always obvious," he said and nestled into my lap, purring.

ONE BIG MESS

RUBY

The girl was going to end up with a brain haemorrhage if she kept collapsing. Luckily, Kent caught her quickly, so she didn't hit her head on the floor. I decided to give her a serious talking to when she came round. I had raised her to be stronger than that!

"Mother, can you help me get her to her bed?" Kent asked, looking alarmed.

"Oh calm down Kent, this isn't the first time she's fainted," I said, rolling my eyes.

"Please, mother," he scowled at me whilst he lowered her head softly to the ground.

"Of course," I snapped.

What did he think I was going to do, just leave her there all night? Hiccup would have been able to carry her, we just need him to transform. I turn looking for him and then stopped dead, annoyance filled my head. He was curled in a ball on the couch, as still as a statue.

"Oh," I said, looking at Kent, "we have a problem."

"What?" He blurted, shooting to his feet and darting across to the window.

He lifted the pale blue netting and sighed. "I can't see anything..."

I shook my head in exasperation. "Kent… KENT!" I shouted, making him jump.

"What?" he said nervously, then looked down to where I was pointing.

"Oh! Oh … that's not good. We'll have to carry her," he said.

"We should take Hiccup too. If he has dream travelled with her then they might be in danger." I thought about Maura's ability to intercept and change dreams.

I walked over to the far side of the room and pulled back the third book on the shelf, revealing a hidden button. I pressed it and it lit up a bright red color.

"Ha! You still haven't moved that then?" Kent asked.

"Why should I? You never found it when you were a child, so why would she?" I smiled, remembering Kent's face when I had revealed all the secrets the house held.

He returned the smile as we heard a tiny patter of feet and saw the glow from a lantern spread from behind the book case. The bottom drawer opened from the inside, as if by itself, and out bounced Cubby.

"Mrs Basco!" He looked around the room and saw Kent. "Mr Basco… you're here!" He flung his tiny arms around Kent's knees, like when a toddler sees their favorite uncle.

"Hello Cubby," he said, patting his head.

"Oh, we gnomes have missed you, sir," he almost sang.

"Well, it's nice to see you too, but could you let go of my legs before I fall on you?"

"Of course sir, sorry sir." He smiled broadly and turned back to me.

"We need some help… could you call… " I started.

"Oh no! What has happened to the smallest Basco? Is she dead?" He shrieked, pointing at Seraphina.

"No!" Kent shot back, "I mean… No, she's not. She just fainted. We need help getting her upstairs."

"Oh, that will not be easy Mr Basco, for she is glowing," he said, beginning to back away.

Great. As if we didn't have enough to worry about she was also glowing. Her emotions must have been running wild. What was that cat doing to her? What was he saying?

"Cubby, please go get the Fire Fairies and let Dana know what is happening," I said. "Kent, go get a towel and a bucket of ice water. We need to cool her down. I don't want any more fires in here!" I barked.

Cubby flew off back down the drawer as Kent ran into the kitchen. I pulled Seraphina's hair away from her face and stroked her head. My poor granddaughter,was no longer my little girl and would soon know the hardships the rest of us had carried for centuries.

Kent burst back through the door, tripping over his feet and sloshing most of the water onto the floor. He was just as clumsy as Seraphina. How my house had survived for as long as it had was a mystery.

"Sorry," he mumbled, setting the bowl at my side and running back to clean up his mess.

I dipped the towel into the ice water and wrung it out. I immediately felt drained. Unfortunately ice water had this effect on the more powerful Fire Defenders. It was the one thing I had never understood about Seraphina and the sea.

I placed the towel on her brow and watched as the glow began to dim. She would most definitely have a headache when she woke up, what with all she'd been through.

I turned at a clatter and a thud behind me just in time to see Cubby fall out of the drawer and land on his nose. His hat flew off, revealing flattened, shiny black hair. He clambered to his feet, ran to his hat, and hastily shoved it back onto his head. *Gnomes*, they hated showing their hair! I never knew why or cared enough to ask.

"Dana said she will come in ten minutes and the Fire Fairies are…" he broke off and dived to the ground again.

A swarm of small, burning orange lights, glowing like fire flies burst up and out of the drawer. They headed straight for Cubby's head. They snatched his hat and darted about the room, Cubby swatting at them, desperately trying to retrieve it.

"Enough!" I shouted at the glowing cluster of fairies. Why they liked to tease Cubby was beyond me.

Fire Fairies were often described as cute, charming and lovable. I had no idea why; most of the time they caused nothing but havoc and chaos, the mischievous little creatures! They were always teasing other magical folk, even starting fights. I tried to not call on them for help unless I had no other option.

They dropped Cubby's hat to the ground. He dived upon it, again shoving it onto his head.

"You girls are such trouble," Kent laughed as he re-entered the room with a mop and bucket.

The Fairies immediately flew to him, buzzing around him and their glow brightening. They liked my son a little too much. It was one of the only things Talia and I agreed on.

"Kent!" I snapped, "your daughter…"

He looked back at me with angry eyes, just like he had used to when he was younger.

"Yes, I *do* know, Mom." He turned back to the swarm of fairies. "Girls, would you be so kind as to carry my daughter up-stairs to her bed, carefully?"

The glowing swarm raced towards Seraphina, disappearing underneath her. She then rose slowly and gracefully, hovering across the room to the stairs. I got to my feet and followed, holding the iced water and watching as the rest of the fairies glided towards Hiccup and moved him too. Kent placed the mop in the bucket and followed, looking upset and anxious.

KENT BASCO

How could she think I had forgotten about Seraphina? I was pretty sure she was jealous of the fairies, fire ones in particular. Or maybe she was just jealous of other women, no matter who - or what - they were.

I placed the mop back in the bucket and started to climb the stairs behind her. We needed the fairies help. If Seraphina was beginning to lose what little control she had, she would burn. They had the ability to control it, to a degree.

"Come on, Cubby," I chuckled as he straightened his hat on his child-like head. It reminded me of the time I had brought Seraphina a pointy, purple winter hat from Paris. She had stood in the mirror for hours adjusting it.

Cubby and I proceeded up the red stairs, dimly lit by the distant glow of the fairies, towards Seraphina's room. I wished I could finish the task before my daughters grew up. Talia was always sure we would, that our children would grow free of pain, and would enjoy the life we would have made for them. How wrong she had been. How wrong we both had been.

I entered her room, Cubby still close to my knees, and watched as the fairies lowered her down onto her bed. Mother was carrying the remainder of the ice water, looking extremely drained. It affected her more than me as she was more powerful than I was. I had let my mother down in so many ways!

"Here, let me do that," I said, taking the bowl and towel from her hands.

She smiled and patted me on the back. I watched as she walked towards the chair where Hiccup lay. She lifted him up and sat down, cradling him like a baby.

She whispered, "what are you doing with my granddaughter?"

I felt a pang of guilt deep in my stomach again. It must have been so much harder for her. She, after all, had raised Seraphina single handed, and now she had to leave. I could bear the pain on her face no longer and turned to my daughter. She looked so beautiful, like a sleeping princess. I sat beside her and dabbed at her forehead with the towel. She had begun to glow red again.

I glanced back at my mother and she nodded in encouragement. She had, after all, done this before with me. Even though she had told me what to expect, I was still nervous. The stage of the transition was so dangerous. If Seraphina was strong enough then she would be able to bear the glow of power. If she wasn't then... well, I just had hope that she was.

"Don't worry so much Kent, your daughter is indeed strong," a new voice spoke encouragingly.

I turned to the door and saw my friend, my confidante, my one true ally: Dana. She was standing in the exact same pose of how I had last seen her.

Her dark green, velvet cloak hung round her slender frame, pinned together just under her chin by the trade-mark Woodwife pin. It was gold, shaped like an ivy leaf. She pulled her hood down and her dark brown, curly hair tumbled round her shoulders. Her hazel eyes gleamed in the light, making her brown skin glow with warmth.

"Dana, it's good to see you again."

She nodded at me and moved towards the bed, staring at Seraphina. She looked her up and down and brushed a delicate hand across Seraphina's head. Immediately she stilled and calmed. The glow died down to a faint pink.

"Yes, she is definitely strong enough for this. Although her aura is in a delicate state at the moment; she has been overwhelmed," Dana said, turning to my mother.

"I know... I tried..." She broke off, hanging her head.

"It's not a fault of yours, but she will need strict guidelines if she is to prevail. We can't waste any time - we must start her training immediately," Dana said.

We all stopped as we hear a horn sound in the distance. It blasted clear as a whistle. Dana turned to the window and looked out over the forest below.

"I have to go," she said, dashing to the bedroom door.

"Do you need help?" my mother asked, rising unsteadily to her feet. Dana shook her head.

"No, it's fine Ruby. I have my warriors standing guard - you know Trixie, Tralia, Shellita and Dartanian." She smiled at her and exited the room.

I walked towards the window and looked down just in time to see a streak of light whip across the lake and disappear into the forest. I had forgotten how fast she was. In the distance I could just make out three other figures, which had to be the guards. Something must have been happening on the borders, either that or a troll has stumbled its way through the area again.

We had a lot of them roaming this part of the forest, most of the time because the Light Fairies were teasing them. I guess that's why mom didn't like them much.

"What is it, Kent?"

"I'm not sure, I can't see. It's not close to us - the protection boarder isn't lit," I said, moving towards the chair I had just left.

"A troll more than likely." She scowled at the window. "It'll be those Light Fairies again," she shook her head in disapproval.

"I'm worried," I said, rubbing my wedding ring.

"I know Kent, but Seraphina will be fine. She's strong, and a good kid really."

I smiled and nodded, "I know, but it's not her I'm worried about at the moment. It's…"

"Lana," she finished for me.

I nodded and she sighed, knowing how I felt. The last time I saw Lana she wasn't good - she was suffering badly with nightmares. I was more certain than ever that she has been seeing Maura in her dreams.

"Why don't you send Peanut?" My mom made the suggestion whilst dabbing Seraphina's head with the damp cloth.

I watched her care for Seraphina with a mixture of guilt and worry. I should have kept them together. Lana had not had the loving care that Seraphina had, and it makes me feel awful. Joey's words had made me even more anxious - soon they would have the other, and that had to mean Lana!

"I think I will," I said, rising to my feet, "I'll be back before she wakes."

I descended the stairs with Cubby following quietly behind me. I had forgotten he was there.

"You can go back home now, Cubby. I won't need you to help me now."

He looked up at me with wide eyes, so sorry for himself that I had to hide a laugh.

"Okay, you can stay," I said, and smiled as a look of happiness spread over on his face.

I carried on walking across the hall towards the front door. I opened it and looked around cautiously before I stepped through.

It was quiet and calm outside; nothing seemed to be out of place or dangerous. I lifted my arms high above me and whirled on the spot and immediately my body shifted and changed into wispy tendrils of smoke.

I used my mind to move towards Cubby, picking him up in a tornado of smoke. I could only do this with small creatures and then shot myself towards the clearing where Peanut usually stayed.

It took a few minutes to reach it. I landed lightly on my half-formed feet and watched as Cubby stumbled around in circles, like a drunk.

I laughed out loud at him, holding him steady until his eyes refocused. I watched as he turned green in the face and was violently sick, then I felt bad. He wasn't used to travelling that way and I should have slowed down.

I turned at the sound of whinnying and a gentle nudge in my back. There, standing behind me, was a magnificent, chocolate brown winged horse.

"Hello, Peanut," I said, stroking his mane of soft hair. He whinnied and nudged at my long coat. I laughed again and pulled out a shiny red apple from my pocket that I had taken from the kitchen.

"You want this, boy?" I asked, holding it out.

He lowered his head towards it, stomping a hoof. He looked back at me and cocked his head to one side as if to say, "apple...mine...yes!" I stroked his mane again and gave him it. He crunched down on it happily,then continued to sniff at my coat, making me take a quick step backwards.

"Careful boy, I don't have any more for you," I said. "Listen, I have a job for you. I want you to go to England. Find Lana and check on her. Look after her, please," I said,gently stroking his nose.

He nudged me once more, which I took as confirmation he understood.

"Go now then boy," I said and watched as he stretched his enormous wings out and zipped into the air.

I watched him as he flew away, quickly becoming a tiny speck in the distance. Cubby was sitting in the grass, still green-faced.

"Would you like to go now Cubby?" I asked, squatting by his side.

He just nodded, got to his feet and wobbled towards the forest. He would be alright - he only lived a little way through the trees.

I returned to the house, where the real work was only just beginning. I got back just in time to see Seraphina stop glowing.

Hiccup woke and stretched across her chest. Seraphina mumbled something that sounded like 'Daddy,' and I rushed to her side.

I glanced at Hiccup. He purred, curled up into a ball, and fell straight back to sleep at Seraphina's feet.

"It's over, she'll be fine now. Come on, let's get some rest," my mom said as she rose from the chair.

I took one last look at one of my daughter, safe in her bed, and feared for my other. My mother took my hand, guided me out of the room and down the stairs.

FLIGHT OF THE BASCO'S

KENT

I was sitting at the window, staring outside intently. Dana had already gone to investigate the new danger that had arisen. I knew we were safe at that moment, but still found myself jumping to my feet every time I saw a shadow, or even heard the rustle of a branch.

I was sure there *would* be an attack, after all Maura now knew for sure where to find Seraphina. Bedsides, the Woodwives' protection that surrounded the house was dwindling. The protective barrier stopped our magical aura emanating and kept the house hidden from the evil powers of Maura. The barrier had become paramount since Seraphina and Lana were born because our family's power had become so strong. The Woodwives protection had been wearing thin lately because they had their own problems and couldn't guard us all the time.

I felt like a complete failure, I had promised Talia that I would protect her... protect *both* of them. I had to move Seraphina and begin her training as soon as possible. I had definitely let one of them down and I didn't know for sure how safe the other was.

Peanut would keep her safe until we could get there. I was more sure than ever of one thing: the girls needed to be reunited.

They needed to keep each other safe. Just in case I couldn't.

"There's nothing you can do about it now, Kent. Stop tormenting yourself," my mom said, interrupting my thoughts.

I twisted round to face her as she handed me a huge, fresh cup of strong coffee. My eyes lit up at the smell of its sweetness. It was just what I needed.

"Thanks," I sighed, taking a sip and placing the cup on the table in front of me. Just feeling warmth spread down me was heavenly.

"Seraphina is at the right age now. She is already in danger and they would have come anyway. It wouldn't have made a difference if you had stayed away or not. The gift will pass over regardless, and it's a good job you *were* here, otherwise Maura would already have claimed her. If you weren't here last night... well, I'm not sure I could have protected her by myself," she said, looking very grim.

I studied my mom for a moment. She was looking old; there were deep lines etched across her face and big purple circles under her eyes. Even her skin was looking more opaque, like a ghost's, but to me she would always be my mom and Ruby, Warrior of Flames. Her achievements in the magical world were legendary.

However, I felt even worse than before as I realized that I shouldn't have left her with a burden. She had gotten through it all, but I still shouldn't have left her alone. She was doing my job. She still was. I sighed. My fatal flaws - cowardice and self-doubt – were kicking in again! When was I going to learn?

"I know that, but she might have had another year at the very least. You said she was showing no signs on her birthday and you shouldn't have had this on your shoulders for so long." I was arguing with myself more than anyone else.

"I am not going to argue with you," she snapped.

She might have been old but she was as feisty as ever! She *was* strong and still had courage, way more than me. I always ran when things got difficult.

"You can either accept that she was already in danger and move on with her training, or you can carry on blaming yourself and leave her undefended," my mom said, rising from her seat with her coffee in hand. She walked into the kitchen.

She really was wiser than me and was altogether a better parent than I could ever hope to be! I *had* made the right choice for Seraphina, for if she was anything like her grandma than she would be just fine. I knew, anyway, that it was better not to argue with my mom. You never won, even *if* you were right. The problem was that she, of course, was always the one in the right.

Seraphina needed to start her training immediately if, she was to be ready to face the destiny my mother and I had both failed to fulfil. I often thought when I was younger how unfair it was to have this gift, and for a while I had fought against it.

When I was seventeen, I had gotten into a fight with my dad and accidently set the curtains on fire. I remembered that day well, as if it had only happened yesterday.

I was sitting on the same sofa I sat on last night with Seraphina. I was watching my favorite TV show, *Cheers*, when my dad had come home from work. He was late and his breath stank of stale whisky. He had obviously been to the bar after work, which was never good. Not for me!

"Look at him. All he does is sit around all day," he had moaned as he hung up his jacket and staggered over to hug my mom.

"I was just with Simon and his boy, Dave," he said, glaring at me.

Simon was one of my dad's oldest friends. They usually got together on a Friday afternoon and I always made my way to my friend's for the night.

"Do you know what Dave does now?" he asked me.

"Does he go to college or ... wait... maybe he works in the local bar," I snapped.

I hadn't wanted to have this same conversation again about *Dave*. He was Simon's son and we had grown up being pushed together every weekend when our dads' went on their 'camping and fishing' trips. I hadn't seen him for the last four years because he had found a girlfriend and went to college. He had graduated early, the geek.

"No!" he roared at me, staggering over to the sofa, "he is working for Gates Ltd." He glared at me, like I should be pleased or something.

I had continued to stare at the TV. Why should I have cared what that idiot was doing? What did it matter to me? My dad snatched the remote out of my hands then and turned off the set.

"Get up boy!" he snarled.

"What! Why?" I folded my arms.

"Adonis! That's enough!" my mom snapped.

"He needs to get up and make something of himself," he snapped, rounding on my mom.

"You know why I can't do that," I scowled. "It's not like I haven't tried!" I shouted, jumping to my feet.

It was true. I'd had several job interviews and I had even been accepted into college, but then my powers had started showing up.

"Dave is making something of himself and Simon is always gloating about him. Do you know how it feels to have to lie about what *my* son is doing?" He barked at my mom whilst pointing a finger towards me.

"Your son is going to save the world one of these days. He'll be one of the greatest Defenders ever!" She shouted back.

I winced. Even I knew that was the wrong thing to say to my dad at that moment. He had always been kind, caring and loveable until he saw my mom's powers. He had been totally freaked out ever since.

He just hadn't grasped the fact that there was magic in his

home, and knowing that all the myths and legends were not only true but mostly came from his own wife hadn't helped.

I could understand why he had begun to drink, but I also knew that there were better ways of taking the news. I mean, at least he wasn't the one with the powers and frightening destiny.

"This is getting ridiculous! You baby him. He needs to go out and get a job, not train for this so called magical destiny trash," my dad said, looking at me with disdain.

I had kept my mouth shut as normal, just like my mom had always told me to do. My dad hadn't understood the problems I always seemed to have when I went out. I was a danger magnet - I couldn't even go to the local store without something weird happening. My mom had always told me I was special and that one day I would know just how special I was.

'Yeah, right,' I used to think. It seemed that all I've had was monsters chasing me. Oh yeah, and I'd noticed that my body had been hotter than normal. What powers!

"You're lazy, that's your trouble," my dad said, walking across the room and turning off the television again. My mom turned it back on with the remote and started yelling at my dad. I had become so tired of this every day. I got off the sofa and moved over to the window, getting out of the line of fire.

I had hated it when my parents were fighting. What was worse was it was always about *me* during those days. Then, as my dad was shouting and my mom was ranting, my head had started to spin round and round.

I started to feel like I was going to pass out, then heard a new type of scream – one of pure horror - coming from my mom. I had tried to focus on my parents when I felt a pair of strong hands lifting me up, moving me over to the sofa.

I finally managed to focus on the blurry images and gasped in shock. My mother and dad were putting out a fire that was licking its way up the curtains, where I had just been standing. The carpet next to it was nothing but a pile of ash.

It was that night that my mom had told me the family's history and my great destiny. She had explained how our family had been struggling for years against Maura. That was also the night my dad had stopped drinking.

I turned back to the window, shaking my head clear of these memories, and carried on scouring the horizon for any signs of an impending attack.

One thing was certain: we had to leave soon, that same day, to make my mom safe again. She had the right to live the rest of her life out in peace. She deserved that much at least!

I had been thinking about it a lot. There was no way my mother was strong enough to continue. I had to take responsibility for Seraphina. That alone scared me more than the thought of battling a hundred Dark Elves.

I was hoping to get a least a few hours of simple combat training in before we set out, just in case. The door opened slowly, startling me, and Hiccup walked in. He was looking extremely pleased with himself. Mom was right - he had managed to make contact with Seraphina last night. She followed him into the room and sat herself down in the chair next to me. She stared at me, a quizzical look on her face. She was clearly confused and scared, which made me even more nervous. Where did I start?

"I had the worst night's sleep ever," she said, peering at me with fearful eyes. "I've woken up with a million things flying through my head. I'm not sure what's real and what isn't."

I sat and watched her for a moment. I was trying to decide where I should start and just how I could begin when she burst into tears. I pulled her over to me and stroked her hair while she sobbed into my shoulder.

"I know, it's a lot to take in and in such a short space of time," I said, keeping my voice soft and comforting.

"Dad," she sobbed, "did you know my cat could talk to me?"

She asked in such a squeaky voice that I had to laugh. She sat up and stared at me, livid.

"What are you laughing at?" she snapped, wiping her eyes on her sleeve.

I chuckled at her and replied, "Oh baby, I'm just so pleased. I thought your first question would be directed against me!"

She finally smiled back, then laughed with me. She dried her eyes on her sleeve again and hugged me tightly. I *had* really missed her.

"So you've managed to communicate with your protector then," I smiled, and she nodded back. "Yes. I knew that one day you, and only you, would be able to communicate with him."

She gave me a sulky-faced look. "And it never occurred to you to tell me." She stubbornly folded her arms across her chest. I sighed.

"Would you have believed me, even if I had?" I asked.

She paused, clearly thinking about that, and finally shook her head. The answer was obvious; of course she wouldn't have.

My mom walked into the room and smiled at Seraphina. She placed a glass of orange juice on the table in front of her and put down two plates with eggs, bacon, sausage, tomatoes and toast on the table.

"Thanks Grandma," she said with a beaming smile, "I'm really hungry."

I remembered when I had first found out about my powers and how hungry I used to get. For the first few months your energy felt constantly drained, and it left you very hungry.

"You're going to need a good breakfast. Your journey will begin today sweetheart, and you need your strength," my mom said, ruffling Seraphina's hair.

SERAPHINA BASCO

My dad and I were walking out onto the front lawn after a great breakfast. Well, great except for the fact that Grandma had told me I was meant to be starting some kind of journey today. I hoped it wasn't a mental one, you know, like the type that left you crazy so you couldn't do anything without talking to a shrink first.

I already felt like a complete idiot! I had been made to wear some kind of a hard leather jacket encrusted with studs and metal buckles over my tank top. It was ugly, heavy and smelt *really* bad. The worst part was I was wearing it outside!

It made me look even more clumsy and uncoordinated then I already was: just what I needed! My grandma had already reprimanded me when I started to complain about it.

"This is ridiculous. It doesn't go with my outfit and it does nothing for my figure," I had complained, looking at myself in the large mirror downstairs. I could see my dad in the background, laughing at my expression.

"Grow up girl, it might save your life one day. It doesn't matter if it doesn't go with your outfit! You will wear it and you will tolerate it. Now go and start your training!" She had pushed me towards my dad who slunk off through the front door, sniggering.

I couldn't understand why I had to *train*. I wasn't even sure what it was I was supposed to be training *for*, not to mention what kind of training it was, but grudgingly I headed outside. My dad had stopped when he reached the middle of the lawn. He turned to face me.

"Why do we have to do it out front? Can't we do it inside or in the woods? Someone might see me like this!" I thought of what I would say to Tiff if she had jogged past.

My dad ignored me and began to circle around me, looking me up and down. I watched him in utter amusement. I had to stifle a chuckle - this was so ridiculous!

I went to laugh and ask what he was doing when I was hit sharply in the stomach by something. I was instantly winded. What was that? Before I regained my breath I felt something else tug at my ankle, flipping me backwards and propelling me into the air. I landed painfully on my back.

"Ouch!" I cried between winded breaths, holding the back of my head where it had hit the floor.

"That is how easy it would be for Maura's Dark Elves to kill you or, worse, capture you. Your grandma is right. You are still a child." My dad said coldly. What the hell had happened to my playful, laughing dad?

I gasped for breath, clutching at my stomach and head. Little stars blazed in front of my eyes. Had my dad seriously just attacked me?

I risked glancing up and saw him standing over me, his legs slightly apart. He was breathing hard and was holding that strange bat thing from last night again.

"What *is* that?" I asked.

"This…" he said, holding up the bat, "is the weapon of a Defender. It has been passed down by our ancestors for generations."

I stared at it in wonder. The strange pulling feeling deep in the pit of my stomach was starting to stir again. I didn't know why, but I *wanted* that bat!

"It's called the Ribbon of Fire and it is *extremely* dangerous," he said dramatically.

"Right," I laughed, 'that *stick*!"

I watched my dad as he walked away from me. Oh man, he looked angry and I was only kidding! Now he looks angry. I was about to call after him when he suddenly spun on the spot and a long, thin, red silk ribbon shot out of the end of the bat. It fluttered round him like a whirl-wind of fire.

He stopped abruptly, completely still, breathing hard. The ribbon shot back into the tip of the bat. I stood there mesmerized and shocked by what I had just seen. The grassy area all around my dad was cut down to the earth, as if a mower had made one of those crop circles.

"It can take years to master the art of the ribbons, but in your case you must master them as quickly as possible," he said.

He walked towards me and started to circle around me again. Oh no, not again! My breathing was still ragged from the last attack. I did the only thing I could think of to buy some time - I started to circle around him. I felt very nervous, suddenly afraid of that bat!

"I don't have any weapons. This is not fair," I shouted, fear rising in my voice.

"Life isn't fair. Do you think your enemies will wait until you have a weapon? You need to learn to open your eyes and embrace your surroundings," he said.

I had no idea what he was talking about, but I wasn't about to get hit again by my own dad. I glanced around quickly, looking for any kind of weapon or shield whilst continuing to circle him.

I saw Hiccup sitting on a wall watching me and felt awkward. Why was I worried if my cat saw me? Suddenly I hit the floor again.

"Do not let distractions cut into your concentration," he said.

We continued in the same way for what seemed like hours until I managed to dodge the ribbon. I had somersaulted through the air, landing in a forward roll and followed that with a backwards walk-over so I was on my feet again, facing him. Some of my best gymnastic moves! I stood there panting, staring at him and waiting for another attack. I was secretly beginning to feel quite confident.

"Where did you learn to do that?" he asked, completely stunned.

"She's been taking gymnastics since she was five," my grandma said, striding towards us across the lawn.

She was holding two rucksacks that looked like they were stuffed with supplies. She put them down and looked up at my dad.

"I *have* been trying to prepare her for what she has to face. Now, I have packed your supplies and you're all set to go," she said, pointing to the over-loaded rucksacks. How did she manage to carry those, they looked heavier than she did?

"Thank you," he said giving her a quick hug, "for all you have done for her."

He looked sad, then stared at me utterly bewildered, although I thought I saw a hint of pride twinkling in his eyes.

Then out of nowhere, Hiccup bolted from out of the woods on the other side of the lake shouting to me in my mind. How had he gotten over there? When had he disappeared?

"Seraphina, they're coming! Tell your dad we need to go now!" I froze in horror, what was coming?

I turned to face my dad, but he already understood. He grabbed the bags, throwing one at me. I caught it. It was heavy, and I wondered how I was supposed to carry it and how far would we be going?

"Put it on your back. We need to leave now," he said, trying to give me a reassuring smile.

I grabbed the backpack by the arms and hastily heaved it onto my back, I turned to look over the lake. I could see the distant outline of figures moving, weaving in and out of the trees, and dread filled my heart. They were cloaked and couldn't see their faces, but I could still make out the weapons they were brandishing - axes, swords, huge hammers and borrows notched with flaming arrows.

I glanced at my grandma, terror rising through me. "What about you Grandma? Will you be okay?" I almost cried.

"I'll be fine, child. I have my own methods of protection," she smiled at me and shot an arrow of flames out from her fingertips. Wow! I couldn't believe what I had just seen! She smiled at me.

"Go! Go now, Kent!"

My dad quickly kissed her on the cheek, then grabbed hold of my arm. I glanced back at my grandma, then at the cat. For a reason I couldn't explain I shouted, "Hiccup! Protect my grandma," as I was pulled towards the forest.

The last thing I saw was my cat transforming into a giant white tiger whilst in mid-jump, and landing on the first of the attackers, bringing them down.

WOODWIVES

SERAPHINA

I was hunched over in absolute terror. My heart was thudding in my chest. It hammered in my ears and felt like it was pounding its way out through my ribs. I had to calm down.

I was finding it hard to breathe. My head was completely messed up. If I managed to survive the next few days I was going to need serious therapy. How had my life gotten so complicated and dangerous so quickly?

I sprang to my feet at the sound of a rustling bush. I was panicking! I closed my eyes tight; I was sure I was dreaming. I would surely wake up and realize none of what was happening was real and I hadn't even gone on the date yet!

I opened my eyes and tried to hold back a small sob. I was still in the forest. I was still surrounded by the trees and the damp, the mossy and the green grass. I turned to face my dad, worry spreading across his face, and I lost control. I began to shout frantically at him.

"What's just happened? What did Hiccup do? What are those creatures? What happened to Grandma?" I was gasping as cold, salty tears ran down my face.

My hands were trembling as I felt cold dread rise up my body.

"They were Dark Elves, minions of Maura," he replied calmly, stowing the ribbon of flames in his jacket pocket. I stared at him. How could he be so calm?

"What about Grandma?" I repeated grabbing his arms.

"Your Gran will be fine. She's tougher then she looks, and has had more years of training than either of us have." What? The new information didn't do anything to lift my mood.

My grandma had known all along about the so-called family *gift* and, apparently, had been fighting monsters for years. Why hadn't that dawned on me before? The flames, Hiccup talking about her! It suddenly made sense.

Why had she never thought about telling me? Secrets like that shouldn't just be kept, not from your granddaughter. Not from your family. I was so mad at her and was going to let her know just how much next time I saw her. Then a new wave of anxiety hit me: *would* I ever see her again?

"We must move, Seraphina. We aren't safe yet. We need to seek refuge with the Woodwives," my dad said, completely oblivious to the fact that I was having a complete hysterical melt down.

"The what? What are Woodwives?" I asked, hysteria choking my voice again.

But there was something about the word Woodwife that I recognized. It seemed strangely familiar, and gave me a sense of safety.

I was sure I'd heard the word somewhere else before. My dad was running through the forest, going far too fast. I had to spring to catch up or I would have ended up alone… again… in the forest! The thought of that, with those Dark Elf things running around, made me want to scream.

I swallowed hard and sped after my dad, catching my arm on a branch as I passed. It tore at my skin, leaving a cut on my bare bicep. Glancing quickly at it and guessing it would be fine I carried on running. It was not easy with this leather armor on.

"The Woodwives are our allies Seraphina," he called. "They'll help hide us until we can continue with our journey."

He continued to run, dodging through the trees. "We need to hurry! The gateway will close at twilight and it's still quite a way yet." He sounded just as out of breath as I was.

I could almost hear a note of fear in his voice now. I was astonished and realized I was acting like a baby. I had to be brave. My dad needed me to be strong. I straightened myself up and, lengthening my stride, I managed to catch up to him.

"What are Woodwives?" I asked.

"They have been allies of the Fire Defenders for many years now. It was your great, great, great grandma who found their secret dwelling place.

"She was on a mission to save another Defender and found herself in this very forest. She eventually came across the Defender after many days of searching. He had been bound and tied to a tree. She had run straight across the forest floor jumping over the overgrown roots to reach her companion not considering the danger.

"As she approached the tree however it transformed into a surly, dangerous looking woman. She was beautiful - the most beautiful creature you could ever imagine. She had hair that shimmered, but somehow also looked like tree bark, and pale green skin. Her eyes were a dark green, like an ivy leaf, and her voice sang as sweetly as a humming bird.

"It turned out that she was a Woodwife, a protector of the surrounding forest. Your grandma asked for her companion to be released but the Woodwife wouldn't allow it. It turned out that the Defender had cut down a sacred tree to make a camp fire.

That tree was one of their kin. The Woodwife wanted a sacrifice in exchange for the life that had been taken.

"Your grandma had a hard choice to make: sacrifice either herself or the life of her companion. It was more difficult for her than you could possibly imagine.

She had no children of her own at that time, and both her parents had died a few years previously. Can you understand why the choice was so hard for her, Seraphina?" My dad looked intently into my eyes.

I felt immediately uncomfortable. I knew what I would have done, but I didn't think that was the answer my dad wanted to hear. Instead I shook my head and looked at the floor. My dad's gaze became more intense. He finally sighed and said,

"she was the only Fire Defender left. If she had sacrificed herself the balance of the earth would have tipped in Maura's favour.

It was unbelievably hard for her as she stood there staring at her companion, who in turn had two children who needed him, but eventually she made her choice. She chose to sacrifice herself instead of him," he said.

"But if she did that how come we're here? How can we be her descendants if she sacrificed herself?" I said in confusion. The story didn't make sense.

"Yes, you're asking the right questions. You see, Seraphina by offering herself to save another the Woodwives knew she was pure of heart, making her a protector, just like them.

"She had passed a great test without realizing it and, as a reward, they offered her an everlasting alliance instead of death. They granted her the name 'Saviour of the Defenders' and gave her a magical object that would protect her as best it could." He smiled at my confused face and gave me a quick wink.

"You see, the magical object was made from the remains of their kin that her companion had cut down." He chuckled at the look on my face. I was horrified.

"That's gross. They made a magical object from their dead kin?" I pulled a face.

"They do not allow any waste in their domain. They are recyclers, and when you're a tree you are reincarnated. It's a huge insult to them if they're not reused." He gave a hearty laugh.

"I still think that's gross," I said, wrinkling my nose.

We continued to walk through the forest for what seemed like forever and I was getting really tired. I was covered in scrapes and mud. I had to stop for a moment.

My leather armor and backpack felt like lead. I stopped and flopped onto the floor, shrugging the backpack off. My dad stopped and watched me intently. I took a swig of water from the bottle stashed in the backpack and couldn't help but think of my grandma. I fought back tears.

I stood back up, determined to continue for her sake. I hoped she was okay, and I did have a feeling that she was fine;something deep inside me told me not to worry. I focused on that feeling, drawing strength from it, and immediately felt better.

I quickened my pace and looked up at the darkening sky through a gap in the trees. I was so hungry that my stomach growled loudly. It must have been really late! My dad stopped abruptly in front of me and I collided clumsily into him. I stumbled backwards and nearly fell, but a strong hand grabbed my arm and pulled me upright.

"Sorry, sweetheart," he said.

"Are we nearly there?" I was exhausted.

"Yes," he replied in a whisper. He gave me a reassuring smile. I had been asking the same question every half an hour for the past three hours. He had just shook his head in response.

"What do we do now?" I asked, and was surprised to discover that I was actually excited. I couldn't wait to get there having listened to my dad's stories about the Woodwives. I felt drawn to them, and there was a strange familiarity to the stories. They made me feel hopeful, and intrigued me. I wondered what they actually looked like.

I stopped as we burst through some thick brambles and stumbled into a small clearing. It was a small semi-circle bordered by several taller, older-looking trees. They were spread evenly around the half circle, and I started to feel a little bit nervous. I couldn't understand why, but I knew I would either be accepted or would die there!

I didn't like the big trees - there was definitely something odd about them. I felt like they were watching me somehow, judging my strength. I watched in silent amazement as my dad stepped forward and called out to them.

"I am Kent Michael Basco, the Fifteenth Defender of Fire. I have come to ask for your help and guidance. We are in grave danger and seek refuge." Ashe finished he knelt down on one knee and raised his baton above his head.

I watched it intently and could have sworn it was glowing faintly. I rubbed my eyes, but when I stared again it had gone. Blinking rapidly I took a step towards my dad and followed his lead, scooping down onto one knee and bowing my head.

I stared at the forest floor which was littered with decaying leaves and twigs, and heard the rustling of branches. I glanced across to my dad, who was still bowed low, and gasped as shadows moved across the forest floor. Oh no! Had Dark Elves caught up with us?

Just as I was about to rise to run, a very sweet, magical voice began to speak. I froze in place where I knelt.

"Welcome Defender. Rise and enter. You are granted refuge here."

I was pulled to my feet by my dad and I saw a sight that made my heart stop. In the exact same place that the trees had stood were seven of the most beautiful women I had ever seen.

They were taller than any person and as thin as sticks. Their arms were thin, tapering to elongated fingers with extremely long, sharp-looking fingernails. Their faces were bronzed with a hint of chestnut, like the color of tree bark. Their features were sharp and angular and their eyes shone brightly with knowledge and insight.

I couldn't help,but stare at them. I marvelled at their hair, which wasn't like a human's but was a mossy green, almost leafy, like a tree. I gazed at them each in turn, captivated. Some were wearing long,flowing dresses that looked like they were carved from wood but shimmered and flowed like the finest silk.

Others wore shorter dresses in a lighter, but still woody shade, and had long, green flowing cloaks that sprang straight from their shoulders. These creatures didn't have any kind of weapons, but I somehow could sense that one false move would end up costing me my life.

Yet at the same time I felt drawn to them. A feeling of safety washed over me under their steady gaze.

My dad took my hand and walked straight towards the woman in the middle. I hadn't noticed her before, it was almost like she had appeared from no-where, which was strange as she was taller than the others and a hundred times more beautiful. She wore a long, flowing dress and a cloak that jutted out towards the bottom. It looked a little like a wedding dress, but was made of a different sort of wood, one that seemed to be moving and shifting within its own form.

As we got closer I realized that the gown was actually moving. It was shifting towards the edges, pulling itself open to form a pathway right through the middle of the Woodwife's dress.

My dad crouched down, bending low to squeeze through the hole. He rose back up once he was through and, kneeling so he could see me, gestured for me to follow.

"Quickly now, they're not far behind us," he said, glancing towards the trees where we had just come from.

I squared my shoulders, took a deep breath and stepped through. As I emerged on the other side I gasped in disbelief. The sight around me was absolutely breath-taking.

My dad smiled at me and took my hand, guiding me through

an archway made from branches interwoven with small flowers. Tiny glowing lights were inside, darting in and out, this way and that, looking like they were chasing one another.

"They're the protective Fairies of the Woodwives' domain. They can see everything you stand for and everything you will become," my dad said.

"Wow! They're beautiful." I watched as the fairies darted in and out of the branches and flew within an inch of my nose.

We carried on walking along the pathway. I could sense myself smiling with joy and elation. As the path ended we came to an opening which spread around a stunning waterfall that glistened in the moonlight. There five of the cutest little girls I'd ever seen were dancing together under the waterfall, splashing water at one another and generally having fun. They waved at me as we strolled past. I smiled and waved back.

I turned around to look at my dad when my jaw fell open. He was stroking the mane of a magnificent chocolate-colored winged horse. It was the most beautiful thing I had ever seen, even more beautiful than the Woodwives and the fairies. It was strange, but I felt as if I had seen this marvellous creature before. Yes! A vague memory of me stroking it when I was very young flashed into my mind. A tear glittered in the corner of my eye as my thoughts turned to my mother.

I walked slowly over to my dad, stretching my hand out towards the horse. As I got closer it looked like he was whispering in its ear. Just as I got close enough to touch the horse when it bolted so fast that it became a blur, whinnying as if it was scared, hurt or even offended. I stood there, my hand still outstretched, and felt upset by the horse's manner.

"I see you've met Peanut. Don't worry, he only allows certain warriors to touch him. Don't take it personally!" I twirled around to face the new voice.

A young girl, not much older than myself, stood next to me.

She held a golden-hilted sword in her hand, which she immediately stored in a scabbard at my nervous gaze. Her brown hair tumbled around her face, cut just past her shoulders. A wreath made from poison ivy leaves circled her head, with a silver chain hanging down onto her forehead, almost like some kind of crown.

Her eyes were big and bright, with long thick lashes. She was wearing a dark green corset and skin-tight trousers in the same color. She looked tough.

My dad took a step forward towards her and knelt at her feet, bowing his head low. The girl held out her hand. He took it and kissed it gently. He rose and swept his hair out of his eyes, which twinkled at her.

"It's been a long time since your last visit to our domain Kent," she said in a playful way.

This annoyed me instantly. This girl, who now I looked more closely looked younger than me, was flirting with my dad!

"I've been travelling far and wide, your Highness. It's not been an easy journey," he replied, smiling at her. She returned his smile, then turned to me with disdain.

"This," he said winking, "is my daughter, Seraphina." He held out his hand towards me in an invitation to move forward.

I didn't want to bow to this girl. I shot my dad a look that said, "I don't think so!" He looked back at me sternly.

"No matter, Kent. She is still young and has a lot to learn. I can tell that straight away," she said.

"Seraphina, this is Dana." He said like it was supposed to mean something to me. "She is the Princess of the Woodwives,"

I sighed and moved unwillingly closer to Dana, before kneeling in front of her. She gave me a small nod and I clambered back to my feet.

"Come, you must see the king. He will be pleased to see you both," she said, leading us towards a round building made from white, shiny marble.

We walked up some stone steps that led to two large, wooden doors studded with iron bolts. Huge columns of stone carved with beautiful symbols and pictures stood either side of them. As I got closer I could also see that the doors themselves were carved with all kinds of small pictures and patterns.

Two more young-looking girls stood just outside. They were wearing the same outfit as Dana, the only difference being that she had a red sash around her waist where the others didn't. They nodded to her as she passed and watched me intently as I slid by, following my dad.

We entered a large, hollow room with a raised platform in the middle on top of which sat a red and gold carved chair. As I approached I realized it was a throne and sitting on it, slumped over to one side, was an elderly man.

His skin was papery, thin and full of lines. His hands were elongated, just like the Woodwives' outside the gateway. His black hair was scraped back and tied into a plait which ran down one shoulder and stopped by his knees. I moved closer, studying his eyes. They were dark green and surveyed me with amused interest.

"My lord, my king, my father," Dana said, dropping to her knees. "I have brought you two visitors." She rose and moved round to stand at the side of his chair.

"Ahh! Yes! Kent, Fifteenth Defender of Fire and his daughter, Seraphina," the King of the Woodwives said. His voice surprised me - it was clear and strong considering his obvious age.

I shifted uncomfortably but I couldn't stop staring at him. He looked ancient, like he was a thousand years old but somehow still strong. Maybe even dangerous.

He stood up, his long, dark robe falling around him. It too looked like an old tree and he wore the same sort of circle of leaves and twigs around his head as Dana, only bigger. It wasn't much, but it had a quiet, radiant aura of power.

He was holding a wooden knobbly staff, which had a bright, glowing green orb at the top. He leant on it as if it supported his weight, and although he looked old he still carried an air of strength, power and knowledge. His piercing green eyes studied me, as if he expected more than he could see. I started to feel warm;my face burned with fear. I dabbed it with the back of my hand. Great. I was sweating! How embarrassing.

"Calm down, child. You're surrounded by my family and friends. You're in my homeland and are safe here. You must not lose control or you'll burn us all. Your powers are indeed great… your destiny is even greater." His head bowed and a frown appeared.

I glanced at my dad, who was watching me intently. I really felt like freaking out. Everywhere I looked someone was staring at me. Some even had their mouths hanging open. What were they looking at!

"My Lord, she can't be… she's so young and unprepared. Surely you can see…" Dana started, but the king held up his hand and waved her aside. He leant forward and surveyed me with a thoughtful expression.

"Kent," he said, turning to face my dad, "I accept this one and will train her accordingly. You may seek refuge here, but you must leave by mid-moon tomorrow, otherwise you will be too…" he sat back on his throne, closed his eyes and started to snore lightly. Dana sighed, lightly touched the king's shoulder and then moved away from the throne.

"Come with me - we start your training immediately! You're going to need a lot," she said, aggressively. She turned on her heel and rushed out of the room, my dad following closely.

"Go where?" I snapped,when I'd been about to catch up to them.

"We're going to the training grounds." Dana did not look happy about it, and I just couldn't understand why she had taken such an immediate dislike to me. What had I done?

As we left the throne room I decided I wasn't going to like this girl. We speed across the grounds towards another pathway, one I hadn't noticed before. My dad stopped and turned to look at me. He took my hand, and smiled.

"Go with Dana. She will teach you the basic combat training and will help you control your... err... emotions," he said, slightly sheepishly.

I was about to protest when his eyes locked with mine, and for some reason I forgot what I was about to say.

"Seraphina, it's important for you to control your emotions." He let go of my hand and went back to the throne room.

I stared after him, wondering why they all seemed so intent on me controlling my emotions. What was wrong with them? It wasn't like I was throwing a hissy fit like a two year old or something. Considering everything I'd been through over the last few days I thought I was holding myself together pretty well!

"Come, Seraphina," Dana demanded. I stared at her as she seemed to melt into the background. For a second it was like she was part of the trees, then she ran with such blinding speed my jaw dropped. Okay! I had to admit that was pretty cool.

However, I was not looking forward to spending any length of time with her. Deep down, I was a little afraid. Being alone with her was one thing, but having to follow her instructions, well... that terrified and annoyed me.

THE TRAINING AND DREAMS BEGIN

SERAPHINA

I soon found myself in a kind of arena. It was a large, square room with old wooden floors and marbled walls displaying all kinds of gorgeous tapestries. They were truly beautiful works of art and looked like they were ancient.

Dana was standing by the double oak doors, giving orders to a group of younger Woodwives. I decided to have a closer look at a tapestry, an exquisitely detailed picture of a girl who looked like she was about my age. She was holding a baton, just like my dad's, in one hand and what looked like a ball of flame glowed in the other. I stared intently at her face. She looked familiar. Very familiar. Then I noticed the caption beneath which read, 'Ruby, Warrior of Flames'. It felt like my heart stopped beating. This amazingly stunning girl was my grandma!

"Ahh, I see you're admiring my handy work," Dana said, jolting me from my thoughts. Of *course*! It just had to be the work of *Miss Perfect*!

"Yes, your grandma was one of the greatest of your kind. We had thought maybe she was…well, never mind," Dana said, glancing sideways at me.

What had she been about to say? Thought she was what?

"It's...It's my grandma?" I asked, still not believing what I could see. I ran my finger down the face on the tapestry. I was so stunned at the picture's beauty I almost cried – she was young, strong and powerful, nothing like what she had been that morning.

"Yes, it is," she said, looking up at the tapestry and sighing. "Come, we have a lot to do." She turned her back to the tapestry and walked away.

There were so many questions I wanted to ask, but it didn't seem like I would get any answers. I decided to store them for the one I knew would help - Hiccup.

I began to follow her to the centre of the room, where she stood by some kind of wooden mannequin. I hadn't noticed before, but others like it were dotted around the room along with blue sports mats that looked pretty old.

I began to focus more on what was around me once the distractions of the tapestry was gone. On the main wall opposite the double doors was a display of weapons - all kinds from broadswords and huge battle axes, to small hand held blades. Yeah, that really mad me feel safe!

Dana walked in front of me, obscuring part of my view of the weapon wall. She looked again at the tapestry of my grandma and sighed. I couldn't understand her expression; she looked upset maybe? Or worried? What was up with her?

"This is a basic training dummy. We will start you off with this and move on according to your abilities," she barked, making me jump.

Why had that made me so angry? Did she think I couldn't fight? I thought for a moment and decided she was right: I hadn't had to fight before, neither had I had any kind of combat training. When I thought about how I had reacted when I was held at knife point by Joey and the training my dad gave me that morning self-doubt kicked in. Right on time!

"This is what we start all the Woodlings on, when they come of age, which is usually one hundred and fifty years unless they show amazing skills beforehand." What? Had she just said one hundred and fifty? How old was she?

"They get basic hand-to-hand combat training from it," Dana continued, handing me a baton. It was kind of like my dad's, but somehow felt less powerful, clumsy and wrong in my hand, if that was even possible! The ribbon was green, the handle lighter and with a thin coil protruding around it. I instantly took a dislike to it.

"Stand here." She pointed to a spot on the floor. "Face the dummy and defend yourself," she said, stepping to the side. I watched as she moved, trying not to let fear show on my face. Was that it? Was that all she was going to do?

"This," she said pointing to a thin, glowing, green line circling around me and the dummy, "is the boundary line. If you go outside of it the dummy will shut down and you will have failed your training,"

I watched, my eyes and body, oriented to her as she walked very lightly on the line. She followed it as it went around me walking like a gymnast on a balance beam.

"You may now begin," she said, stepping off the line.

"Wait!" I started. "What do I do?"

Dana stayed silent and just stared at me. Then from behind me came, the sound of whirring and a mechanical clicking. Panic kicked in. I was going to die!

I spun on the spot just in time to see the dummy raising a heavy arm up. It hovered over me for a split second, ready to strike. Instinct kicked in and I tucked into a diving roll, narrowly avoiding the blow. I bounced back to my feet, glancing around for Dana. How was I supposed to fight this thing? She hadn't told me how. I didn't even know how the baton thing worked.

Boom!

Another blow. I wasn't so lucky the second time; the dummy's arm caught my left leg. It pulsated with pain that shot up from my ankle, and I immediately felt sick. I managed to stand, gritting my teeth through the pain. I faced the dummy and gripped the baton in my right hand the same way you would hold a baseball bat ready to hit a pitch.

I was ready to try anything! What happened next took me by complete surprise, and I wasn't even sure how it happened. I felt a surge of power rising from the pit of my stomach, radiating out through the rest of my body. For once I felt strong, and in complete control. I somehow knew what had to be done!

The dummy lunged straight towards me, its arms raised, ready for another strike. I whipped the baton around my head, and a green, shiny ribbon shot out from the end. I wasn't sure how I had made it appear, but it did, and surprisingly, it wrapped itself around the dummy's arm. With one quick tug on the baton, the ribbon brought the dummy crashing to the floor, where it sparked and flailed as it tried to right itself.

My temperature rose so quickly that it felt like I was suffocating, the air burning up in my lungs. It felt like the heat was its own flame eating away at the oxygen and I could feel myself slipping into the blackness. My knees crumpled and my head hit the mat before my eyes fluttered shut.

The next thing I knew I was walking through the forest towards my grandma's house. The day was warm and bright. It was mid-summer - the birds were in full song and the sun was searingly bright.

My heart lurched in my chest as I saw my grandma emerge out from the house the door flew open and she carried a silver tray of lemonade balanced on one hand. She was younger then I had ever seen her, so I knew I was dreaming, or having some kind of vision. I was beginning to get used to them.

I watched as she walked right past me round the back, towards the lake. It was weird seeing her in a bright, flowing summer dress and sandals. Why had she walked straight past me? If it was a dream shouldn't she have been able to see me if I wanted her to? I was about to call out to her when I felt a tug at the bottom of my shirt. I lurched away as I looked down to see the little girl from the beach. She was the last person I wanted in my dream. Trouble always followed when I saw her.

"Don't worry, Seraphina. I won't hurt you." She smiled at me sweetly.

"I'm not worried," I said defensively. And completely untruthfully. "Where did you come from? What are you doing here? You nearly got me killed the last time I saw you!"

"I'm here to guide you. There's something you need to see. To make sense of your future you must first make sense of your past. Don't worry about them seeing you either, you're merely in a dream and are nothing more than a ghost to them," she said, ignoring my questions and twirling a lock of her long hair. I stared at her for a moment. I thought I was the only one who ever did that! Well me and my mother.

I turned away from her to the direction she was facing and realized I was meant to follow my grandma. I walked forward slowly, glancing around me as we moved. Even though I was dreaming I couldn't help feeling nervous after what had happened that morning.

I came around the side of the house and heard several people laughing. My grandma was sitting at the old picnic table, although it looked brand new, as if my granddad had only just made it. Grandma was handing out the lemonade from the tray and laughing.

I looked around and noticed my dad, sitting to the right of my grandma, and my granddad on the left. A twinge plucked at my heartstrings when I saw him. I missed my granddad so much.

Then I spotted her. She was sitting opposite my dad. It was

my mother! She was beautiful, her eyes a brilliant bright green and her hair long, black and curled at the ends, just like mine. I was so shocked I couldn't move! She was laughing at my dad whilst stroking the back of *my* hair in a loving way. The girl from the beach held my hand and squeezed it as tears rolled down my cheeks. Then she dissolved into thin air, leaving me alone.

"Hello Seraphina, I thought I would find you here sooner or later."

I glanced around at the voice as gasped as Hiccup strolled out of the trees and through the long grass, heading straight towards me. As he walked I noticed he was limping very badly. I walked quickly towards him, wiping the tears from my face.

"Hiccup!" I exclaimed, scooping him up and hugging him tightly. "Is my grandma okay? Did you protect her? How did you get here? Are you real or just a dream? What have you done to your leg?"

"Slow down, slow down. One question at a time, please! You're not making much sense. By the way I can't breathe," he said, gasping. I released my too-loving grip, placing him back on the ground.

"Your grandma is fine. She is on her way I should expect. I *am* hurt but I should be fine, as long as I stay here. Well, for now at least. And as long as my charm holds out," he said, turning his head back in the direction of my parents and grandparents.

I had no idea what he was talking about, and found myself drawn back to looking at my mother. I watched her laughing in a carefree way and was suddenly filled with rage. It wasn't fair - why had she been taken from me?

I stared at the dream version of the younger me. I wasn't paying any attention to my mother at all. Oh man, I was so stupid. Then again, dream me had no idea she was about to lose her. I watched as my young self scribbled energetically on a pad of paper using big thick, crayons. How could I have been so oblivious to her? I was, what, three or four... Wait a minute... I couldn't have been! My grandma said my mother had died when I was one, but as I looked I decided I had to be at least four. I shot Hiccup, who sat beside me now, a puzzled look.

"Hiccup, I have a few questions that need answering," I began, feeling a sudden wave of anger float through me. He looked up at me, his eyes bright and anxious.

"I know what it is you're about to ask and I can't answer for you. You need to find that out for yourself," he said.

"But you know, don't you?" Before he could answer a loud ear splitting screech sounded from across the lake, making me scream.

My grandparents and dad jumped up from their seats at the same time. My granddad scooped my young self up out of the chair and ran towards the house. A stream of water shot up from the lake, splashing down on my dad. As I turned to watch him I saw my mother's back as she struggled to run behind my granddad. Something was wrong with her.

The dark water in the lake began to stir and bubble. It was as if the water was being heated, and it stirred and dissipated as a dark, ominous shape rose from the depths. It emerged and flew up into the air and I backed up in a rush, stumbling and falling to the ground.

I stared up into the yellowing, slanted eyes of a water dragon. I had seen pictures of these creatures before in my grandma's study. One she had painted herself, and then I realized how she must have been able to paint such a realistic and terrifying picture.

The dragon had the body of a sea snake - green scales covered it, with a blue, diamond shaped pattern protruding down its back. It was massive; far bigger than the house, and its long, snake-like body kept bobbing in and out of the lake. Its head was long and pointed, with tendrils writhing from its chin.

It rose higher, revealing a yellow, scaly belly. It reared back its head and opened its huge mouth to reveal two rows of sharp pointed teeth, and it made an ear-splitting crack as it snapped its jaw shut. Its arms were short, but strong with talons the size of a small child. It was a terrifying sight.

My brave dad ran forward with his baton in hand. It looked as though it was glowing, a strange orange color. I watched, dumb-founded, as he swiped the ribbon round the creature's mouth and tugged on it. For a second I thought he had managed to control the dragon, but it swung its head from side to side, making a deep rumbling sound. I watched in horror as he was lifted into the air and was swung across the grass by the creature. He crumpled as he hit the ground. He lay motionless. I wanted to run to him, but fear anchored me to the ground. My grandma shouted up at the dreadful creature.

"I'm over here, you big ugly dummy! Leave my son alone!" She shouted frantically, waving her arms trying to distract the creature to buy time for my dad to regain consciousness. It had worked as the creatures attention was drawn to her, and it reared back its fearsome head again, opening its mouth wide.

I heard it before I saw it. I could sense it was coming. I think my grandma could too because she smiled tauntingly, and held up her hand, beckoning the creature forward. It shot a stream of fire out of its mouth directly at her. I screamed so loud that I hurt my throat and instinctively looked away from the scene.

I trembled with fear as I it went quiet. I turned my head back slowly not wanting to see, but needing to know. My grandma was standing, as still as a statue, her hands raised in front of her. She was deflecting the flames, like she had an invisible shield spread across her front, stopping the wall of fire as the flames bounced straight off it. Another scream escaped my lips as the creature's tail swiped at her legs. I watched helplessly as she crashed to the floor. Her face was streaming with sweat, and she was trembling from the effort to repel the dragon's attack. I glanced over to where my dad still lay unconscious.

"Come on! Come on...get up!" I shouted desperately.

I then heard the water from the lake churn and turned, dread again filling my heart. What now? The water was rising high, even higher than the creature hovered. It stared, almost dumbfounded for a second before the wave came crashing down upon it, sinking it back into the lake.

The creature flailed and thrashed against the waves which were relentless, crashing against it and dragging it down until it disappeared beneath the surface. I watched in utter amazement as the lake began to freeze over during the blistering heat of the day.

I turned my head as my heart began to pound in my chest. I saw my mother standing on the house's porch, which faced the lake. Her hands were stretched out wide, her hair flying wildly all around her. She had drowned the dragon and frozen the lake. Her body began to glow with faint white light. I gasped as she turned in my direction, looking directly at me and smiling, she was placed her hands around and on her swollen, pregnant belly.

SECRETS

SERAPHINA

I was wrenched from sleep, screaming terrified and in shock from what I had just seen. It was dark and cool and I could sense someone in the darkness nearby. Sweat was beading across my face and my hair was stuck to the back of my neck.

"It's alright! You're fine, I'm here," my dad said soothingly.

I sat up, feeling confused and exhausted. I was dazed momentarily, then anger rushed through me. I couldn't speak. I knew what I had seen - my mother had been pregnant and the child wasn't me. Was that real? A memory I had suppressed? Or was it all a dream? I faced my dad and I could feel the anger tears filling my eyes, blurring my vision.

"What's the matter sweetheart?" Concern was evident in his lined face.

I couldn't say anything. I was irrationally angry and the I wasn't sure if what I had seen was real. How could I explain that I was angry over something that I wasn't sure was real or not? I just didn't have the strength to think about it, let alone actually talk about it.

"Nothing," I managed to stammer. "Bad dream."

I turned my face away so he couldn't see the hurt in my eyes. I looked around, taking in my surroundings whilst trying to control my rapid breathing.

I was in a brightly lit room with beds lined up against the one side of the wall. There was nothing flashy about it - not like the other amazing places built by the Woodwives that I'd seen; it was very basic. On the other side stood a single desk where a very old, withered looking Woodwife sat. I stared at her and noticed she was reading a book titled Magical Medicine and How to Brew It. It dawned on me that I was in some kind of hospital.

I lay back against the soft pillows and tried hard not to think about my dream. Instead, I tried to concentrate on what had happened before blacking out. This was starting to really annoy me! The more I thought about it, the more I decided that the blackouts were Dana's fault.

"Where's Dana?" I spat through my teeth.

"She's on the training ground," he answered, looking perplexed at my outburst.

"What happened to me?" I stared directly into his eyes.

I was sick of not knowing what was happening. He was going to give me answers if he wanted to or not.

"You're still learning and your powers are draining you quickly," he said, uncertainty evident in his greying eyes.

"I don't have any powers," I sulked, "I can't even beat a dummy."

He looked at me and frowned, and had opened his mouth to reply when the door crashed open. Dana marched through, her sword strung up in a sheath on her back.

"Come, Seraphina. You are not going to prepare by slouching around in the sick bay!" "Oh shut up!" I snapped, "I'm getting sick of you." She stared at me with a 'don't mess with me' look, and I instinctively shrank back into my pillows, immediately regretting losing my cool.

"Oh... I see," she whispered, surprisingly. This scared me

more than her demanding tone. "You think you can survive on your own? You think that you're so powerful you don't need anyone's help?" Her voice suddenly rose. "Well you're not, Seraphina Basco!" She was practically screaming at me as my dad stood up and held up his hand.

"That's enough Dana. She needs to rest for a moment." He looked back at me. "I'm sure she will join you in five minutes and will be ready to try again. She needs your help… we all do." He bowed his head as he finished.

What? Why was he treating her with such respect? She had put me in a hospital bed and now wanted to do it again! Dana turned on her heel, swishing her hair behind her, and marched back through the door.

"I'm not going!" I said defiantly.

"Yes you are, Seraphina. I am not having all our years of hard work and effort wasted because of your stubbornness." He glared at me and my heart constricted. That hurt!

"You will respect the Woodwives, because without them you would not have survived this long."

It took me completely by surprise. I'd only needed their help for a day, haven't I? I took a deep breath to calm myself, inhaling the room's delicious smell of lavender and honeysuckle. It worked.

"What do you mean by that?" I asked.

"The Woodwives have been good to our family for years. They are the reason our blood-line survives. Your grandma's home is under their protection, and they have been fighting Maura's demons for years. They have done all of this to keep you safe." All of a sudden I felt extremely guilty.

"I never asked them to," I said in a quiet voice, bowing my head.

"No, but your gran and I did," he said, taking my hand. "Please try, Sera."

"Okay," I whispered. "I will go say sorry to her. I'm not doing it because I think she's right, but for Grandma. She would be disappointed with me if I let her down," I said lamely.

I then felt really bad for having snapped at Dana - after all she *was* just trying to help me. I suddenly understood that.

After a while my dad and I left the sick bay, walking out under a dull grey sky. It was getting late; close to evening. We walked across the meadow, where we had first entered, and headed over to the training ground. Dana was on the field, swinging a sword around her head and dodging what looked like about forty attackers.

I stood there frozen in shock. I was sure I could never look that cool on the battle-field. I couldn't even win against a dummy, let alone a whole swarm of Woodwives.

Dana stopped, and the other Woodwives stopped too, as if they could sense us watching. Dana looked over in our direction with a stern expression on her beautiful face. Then, amazingly, she smiled at me - a half smirk really - and then nodded to my dad.

"She accepts your apology," he said, then turned and left.

What was that about? How did he know that? Dana strolled towards me and gestured for me to approach.

Although I had decided to make an effort I still wasn't happy about it. I grudgingly went to meet her. Half-way across the battle-field she threw the green baton to me, which I caught, but barely in time before it hit me squarely in the face.

"Try again. This time you face these three..." she waved her hand across the crowd of assembled Woodwives, and three of them stepped forward.

Oh man! So this was her idea of pay-back. How was I supposed to face three of them when I couldn't even defeat a dummy?

I eyed them sceptically. One was taller than me but not very well built. Her arms were not muscular like Dana's, but she obviously had strength as she was holding a spear that was taller than she was. Her hair shone in the late evening sun, giving her a friendly look, until I focused on her eyes. They seemed to glow defiantly with a strange green color from which emanated a sense of defiance, even death.

I couldn't meet her stare for more than a second, and turned my attention to the girl on her right. She was shorter than the first, but her muscles were well defined. Her hair had been cut short like a boy's and her eyes were darker then the night sky. I couldn't decide which one of these two scared me more.

The third girl was even smaller than the other two and had a round, childish face. I turned and looked quizzically at Dana. She could obviously tell what I was thinking.

"You are as arrogant as the rest of your race," she spat. "You think because this one is small and young that you will defeat her easily?"

"No! I didn't mean that," I said defensively, "It's just that she looks so young. She's not a child is she?" I wasn't about to try to fight children; I didn't care how powerful she was.

Dana shook her head. "Even the smallest and youngest can be dangerous," she said, backing away from me.

What did that mean? Was she actually a child? I didn't have time to think about it anyway!

"Begin!" she shouted, raising her hands above her head.

I swooped around just in time to see them all running towards me with murderous looks in their eyes. Oh man, I was going to die for sure this time!

The tall one reached me first and lashed out with her weapon. I instinctively jumped to the side to avoid the spear, which would have impaled me if I had not reacted so quickly. I swirled around, flinging my arm out and managing to hit her nose with the end of the baton.

"Dana! Stop them! That could have killed me!" I screamed. She nodded again and looked behind me, out to the field. I followed her gaze and saw the second girl circling me.

I gripped my baton tightly and tried to think clearly. I watched her moves intently and forced myself to meet her gaze, trying to feel for some kind of weakness. I couldn't find anything but I didn't even really know what I was looking for. Then she stumbled, and I noticed her feet.

Although her arm and leg muscles were clearly defined and strong, her feet weren't. She wore old fashioned sandals that showed her toes and most of the top of her feet. They looked old and deformed, with gross, angry looking boils all over them. I knew that had to be her weak spot, so I waited, just circling, trying to keep the other two in my sight.

She attacked and I dodged, not quite quickly enough though, and she grazed my arm with her weapon, a glinting gold sword. An angry looking gash appeared on my arm, I howled in pain and rage. Before I knew what I was doing I flew at her, flicking my baton, and watched as the ribbon tangled itself around her feet. I pulled sharply and she hit the floor with an almighty thud and an alarming scream. I knew her feet were hurting where the ribbon had slashed around them.

I stood there trying to control my breathing and heard a small crack from behind me. I was turning to face them, but was too late as the smaller girl that I had ignored jumped on my back. I whirled around, frantically trying to throw her off. She hooked a thin chain, like a necklace, around my neck and started to pull it tightly.

I gasped for air, still struggling to get her off my back. The more I struggled, the tighter she held on. I was getting extremely tired and began to fear for my life. What kind of training is this? My eyes started to flicker and my vision began to blur. Not again! I thought to myself.

I hit the ground and started to feel her grip slacken. I managed to take a huge gulp of air and felt a sudden burst of energy coursed through my body. I drew strength from the sensation of the air circling in my lungs and threw my arms out wide in an outburst of rage.

I heard muffled screams in the distance and I opened my eyes wide. There, at my feet were all three Woodwives. Everyone had been knocked out cold.

"Well done," Dana said, with a sideways smirk on her face, "finally we're seeing some of your powers." She held her hands up to the sky in an exasperated gesture.

"What! What powers? What did I do?" I asked, staring at the three girls at my feet. Shock was threatening to tear me apart.

"Come, first we must eat, then we shall talk." She strode off, swinging her sword back onto her back.

"What about these three?" I asked in shock. I looked at the smallest one and a shiver of pity shot through me. "We can't just leave them here like this."

Dana wasn't listening to me. Instead she was speeding her way towards the edge of the meadow, which meant I had to sprint to catch up to her.

I glanced back over my shoulder at the three figures on the floor as I ran and was surprised to see them getting to their feet, brushing the dirt from their knees and helping one another up. The smallest one had to sit back down whilst the other two crouched over her. What had I done?

THE WOODWIVES REALM

SERAPHINA

We walked hurriedly away from the training ground, entering a large, rectangular hall. I gasped in surprise because it didn't look like a hall but more like a forest.

At first I assumed we were still outside and had just walked through a dividing wall because there were tall, dark trees all around.

When you looked up you couldn't even see a ceiling through the mass of dark green leaves and dark brown branches. It was only when I searched the canopy of green carefully that I found a gap directly in the center, through which could a perfect night sky adorned with twinkling silver stars could be seen. It was breath taking.

I stood in the door-way gazing at the beauty of the room and listening to the calls of the birds. In the trees were creatures I had never seen before. They're bodies were small, but they're legs and arms were longer and out of portion. They had squashed, fluffy faces with black, beady eyes. I saw them in all sorts of colors ranging from the brightest pink to the deepest green.

"Please remove your shoes before you enter," Dana said, removing her own and placing them on a shelf.

"Why? Isn't this a dining room?"

"You'll see why in a minute," she smirked before walking away.

I removed my boots, placing them next to Dana's, and rubbed my feet. It was only then that I realized how much they hurt.

I took a step through the doorway onto the main floor. It looked and felt like freshly cut summer grass; the smell was amazing. It reminded me of the long summer days when grandma and me used to have picnics together by the lake.

There was a definite magical, warm feeling to the room. Almost fairy tale and dream like. This was highlighted by the tiny glistening lights that fluttered all around us. They were leaving trails of delicate, sparkling dust behind them as they meandered through the air. I watched several of them chase one another round the trees, and suddenly remembered they were the Fairies from the entrance. Each lights and trail was a different color- even the ones that were blue seemed to be slightly different shades.

I extended my arm, stretching out my hand, and one of them landed on my finger with the lightest of touches. I brought my hand back closer to my face, carefully so I wouldn't startle it. I then saw it more clearly. It was a girl.

She was like a tiny porcelain doll and reminded me of the ones I had had when I was younger. Every inch of her was perfectly proportioned and she was about the size of my index finger. Her skin was pale gold and glowed with warmth, almost magically. Her hair cascaded down her tiny frame to her knees in a wave of dark golden curls. Her ears were tiny and pointed up, protruding through her hair.

Her eyes were the deepest blue I had ever seen and, were big and round, like saucers. She smiled widely at me whilst twirling around on my finger. I returned the smile and she giggled, bringing her hands up to her mouth. She fluttered her beautiful, transparent butterfly wings at me, making glittery dust fly into my face. I felt it flow up my nose, tickling the hairs and making me want to sneeze. I tried hard to suppress the sneeze, squashing my eyes shut and screwing up my nose. It didn't help, I sneezed embarrassingly loud making the closest group of Woodwives laugh loudly. How embarrassing!

Alarmed, she jumped off my finger into a perfect dive. She straightened up into a glide and disappeared, lost amongst the other glowing lights.

"Pretty aren't they?" My dad's voice drifted in from behind me. I turned to see him smiling at the little lights.

"Yes. They're so... magical," I spluttered, rubbing my face as the dust was making my skin itch.

"They are indeed, and very useful when they work together, however most of the time they fight amongst themselves." Just as he said that the gold fairy that had been so friendly and settled on my finger began to fight with a pink one. I watched in horror as they violently hit one another and ended up in a tangled ball flying straight out of the door, leaving a new trail of color behind them.

"I hear you had some success out on the training grounds," he said, his voice jolting me back to the conversation.

I wasn't ready to discuss what had happened. After all I wasn't certain myself what I had done. I did have questions about the baton though, ones that I needed answering.

"Dad, how do the baton's work? Why, is the training one green and yours is red? I'm not sure how I made it work?" I said, in a rush as the thought of the weapons confused me.

"They're very temperamental Sera, that fact that you managed to use the training one at all is a great accomplishment. Although they look nothing more than baseball bats, it's what's inside them that counts," he chuckled. "Don't look so confused, it's actually really simple. Inside each baton is a ribbon. It's not a ribbon you would use for your hair or round a parcel. These have different qualities and strengths."

"Is that why they have different colors?" I asked thinking of the green one I used today.

"Exactly. My ribbon is rare and can be extremely dangerous if you can't control your gift. The ribbon inside mine has the agility of a necklace, but the strength of iron. It's very hard to break, but moves swiftly, lightly like a piece of fluttering silk."

I thought about this for a moment and became confused. Is that all it can do? Why is it temperamental?

"Will I get one?" I asked, thinking about the hidden secrets I could discover with my own.

"When the time is right. You need more training first."

"Oh," I looked down at my bare feet not wanting him to see my disappointment.

"Let's get something to eat you must be hungry," he said laughing. My stomach growled loudly, making my cheeks go pink.

I sighed. Just another embarrassing thing to add to my list today.

He took me by the arm and guided me over to a large, round marble table. I peered down at it not entirely sure what I was looking at. It was heaving with all kinds of dishes, none of which I had never seen before.

I started to feel a tiny bit disappointed. I had been having a rough day and all I really wanted was some of my grandma's homemade cherry pie. I looked up at my dad, not entirely sure if I should ask him what everything was.

He took a plate from the side which looked like it was made from a big dark leaf and handed it to me. I examined it for a moment. It definitely looked like a leaf but it didn't feel like one, it felt like porcelain. I tapped it on the marble table. It even sounded like porcelain.

My dad chuckled, "Don't worry, you'll get used to things. It's hard taking it all in at first. You're doing better than I did anyway. I totally freaked out and set half of the throne room on fire," he said, winking. I didn't know what to say to this, so I just smiled weakly.

"This is potato and cheese mixed together," my dad announced.

He was pointing to a dish that looked nothing like cheesy mash. It was red and sat inside its own little wooden boat dish, complete with a leaf sail. I decided to take one though because it smelt gorgeous.

We walked down the long marble table, my dad pointing out what everything was, and before I knew it my plate was over-flowing with all kinds of wonderful treats.

I had taken some orange pasta, which had been made with peach and blossom flower. I also had several small boiled eggs which were marbled green but smelt like garlic and broccoli.

The one dish that really made me stop was triangle shaped toast with water-cress and soft cheese. It would apparently also make me glow in the dark. I wasn't sure I wanted that to happen.

My favorite had to be the exploding chocolate puddings, served in tiny edible Martini glasses. One Woodwife said they popped when you bite into them. I couldn't wait and shoved a whole one in my mouth. The effect was immediate; I could feel tiny pops on the tips of my tongue and bigger pops as I swallowed. It tickled the inside of my throat and belly, a very enjoyable experience that made me laugh out loud.

There were so many more wonderful dishes, but I couldn't fit anything else on my plate. All I knew for certain was the more I took, the hungrier I somehow became, and my plate was almost overloaded as I finally followed my dad to a toadstool table and sat down. The food tasted even more amazing than it looked, and I smiled at my dad as we both bit into small blue pears that bubbled and fizzed in our mouths.

I shovelled food into my mouth so fast that I knew my grandma would have been disgusted with me if she had been there.

Thinking about my grandma and home made me go very sullen and my eyes welled with tears. I could feel a lump of pain and guilt rising from the pit of my stomach. I felt so bad every time I thought about Grandma and the trouble we had left her to face. I felt cowardly, as if I'd abandoned her. I should have stayed and fought alongside her, even if I didn't know yet how to fight.

I put down my fork and picked up my glass, trying to distract from my now morbid thoughts. The last thing I needed was to cry in front of all these threatening looking warriors. I looked around me a the groups of chatting Woodwives, a table to the left of ours were all wearing sashes round the waist, the same as Dana, so I guessed they were warriors. The table to our right had a mix of women and men all with clipboards and maps. I wondered what they did and what the maps were for. I tried to lean closer to see what was written on the map closest to me, when one of the men pulled it away and gave me a skeptical look. I looked away scared of his intimidating glare. I could still feel his gaze on me so I took a sip of the glowing, foamy, purple liquid in front of me - served in a silver goblet - and it instantly felt warm to touch and made me feel a million times better. Even though it was purple, it tasted like fresh orange juice with a slight hint of caramel and was ice cold. That was a surprise as the goblet was warm.

"It's good isn't it?" my dad said, smiling broadly at me.

I grinned back impishly, feeling so happy and elated I could have sung out loud. I welcomed the feeling with open arms - it made such a change from the dull ache of pain I had felt for so long.

"It's lovely," I replied. "What is it?"

"It's Manjora juice. It's made from a rare flower that can only be found here at the Woodwives homeland. It tastes different to everyone, but it makes you feel elated and courageous," he said, choking back a laugh as he watched me.

"It's not a drug, is it?" I asked, suddenly worried.

I would not tolerate drugs and knew Grandma would throw a huge hissy fit if she ever found out I'd taken them, by accident or not.

"Not at all, Sera! Do you really think I would allow you to drink it if it was?"

"No," I said, feeling instantly relieved and a little stupid.

"It's a tonic that helps revitalize your body's natural energy supplies, making you healthier and happier," he said, taking another sip of his drink.

"What flavour is yours?" I asked.

"It tastes like pink lemonade. It was your mother's favorite drink," his smile soon turned into a frown. "Well, happy on the surface anyway," he sighed.

He was upset again now and I knew how he felt, but at least he had known my mother, which was more than me. This made me feel irritated again as the images from my dream popped back into my head. I shuffled my feet under the table and prodded my potato pie with my fork. I was too scared to ask anything else, so I took the last bite of pie to avoid having to say anything else and watched in surprise as the boat it was served in sailed itself away, back over to the marbled table.

I sat there staring after it, I had no idea what to say and was inwardly grateful when someone approached our table.

"Hi, do you mind?" the tall Woodwife from the battlefield said, gesturing with her hand towards the empty seat next to me.

"Of course not," I said, feeling a tad nervous. Oh why did there have to be an empty seat by me?

I had to say something about earlier. But what? An apology seems like a good place to start, but before I could say anything she spoke.

"Well done today. You showed great improvement with your moves. My name's Trixie."

I just looked at her, perplexed.

"Err... thanks," I mumbled, feeling like a complete idiot. Everyone kept telling me I had improved but I couldn't see how.

"Don't worry so much. You didn't hurt us. We're used to worse than that by now. Dana makes us practice three times a day." She looked a bit annoyed as she glanced over at Dana, who was sitting on a chestnut mushroom table that was raised above everyone else's. She was next to her dad, the King, and was chatting animatedly with him. I watched as she poured more Manjora juice into his glass and placed food from her plate onto his.

She glanced up at me then and gave me a glare that, if looks could have killed, would have made me drop stone dead. I looked away swiftly, feeling like I had intruded on something sacred and private. Or maybe she just didn't like showing her sensitive side? She couldn't hide it from me - I could see it a mile away; she loved her dad.

"Don't worry about that," Trixie said. 'She likes to act tough in front of us but underneath it all she really is lovely. A little hard sometimes, but great."

"She doesn't seem like it to me," I said, self-doubt kicking in again as my dad gave me a stern yet troubled look.

"Excuse me please girls, I have to..." he broke off as he got to his feet and strolled towards the door.

I stared after him. There was something bugging him! I could tell! The question was what? I didn't know if I could take anymore secrets or revelations.

"She has to look tough, otherwise she'll be challenged for the throne," Trixie said, pulling me back to the conversation.

"What... What do you mean?" I replied, a little taken a back.

"If she shows weakness of any kind then anyone of us could challenge her ability to rule. If she's proven to be a weak and poor leader then anyone can challenge her to a battle to the death then take over the kingdom." She shrugged, like such a big change was no big deal. I didn't like the way she had spoken instantly felt a wave of mistrust. I didn't really like Dana, but even I could see she was going to be a strong queen.

"Why would anyone do that? Surely when the king dies Dana will receive the… err… the crown?"

"Of course she will, but our laws are different to your human laws. If we think our ruler isn't strong enough to lead then we challenge them. It's been that way for centuries." She watched Dana with a look of suspicion.

I didn't like the way Trixie spoke about over-throwing Dana as if it was no big deal. That's when I knew without a doubt that I would stand up for Dana if I ever had to. After all, she could have quite easily killed me but she didn't. She was trying to help me.

This thought made me smile over at her. She looked back with a confused expression. I quickly looked away again, back down at my plate. Dana stood up, clapped her hands together once and unfurled them up towards the crowded room.

"Sisters, brothers! The day is drawing to a close. It's time to turn in for the night. Guards, you are to swap your duty shifts with the next in line for the new century shift." As she said this four Woodwives got to their feet, bowed at the king and then at Dana before leaving the room.

"Did she just say a century shift?" I whispered to Trixie.

She nodded her head at me, as if this was perfectly normal.

"We can live for thousands of years. A single century or even two isn't much to us. I've just finished my second century shift," she said smiling.

My jaw dropped and my throat went dry, "So how old are you?"

Trixie laughed shrilly, "I'm only four hundred and twenty seven years old," she finished like this was no big deal.

I couldn't believe what I was hearing! She only looked my age, but I guess in a way it kind of made sense. I turned back to Dana and listened intently as she carried on talking about security and training. She really did push them hard.

"There will be a morning training session tomorrow," Dana continued, after the guards had left. "All seniors are to report to the training ground at five a.m. sharp," she barked, waving her hand to dismiss the room.

MORE MAGICAL CREATURES
SERAPHINA

I watched Dana fussing over her dad and barking several more orders at the younger Woodwives for a while longer. Eventually I rose from my seat and scanned the room for my dad. The group from my right had hurried towards the door with their maps chatting about a cave somewhere. The group from my left were rising from the table discussing the change of guards, and one was complaining loudly about doing another century shift. I couldn't help smile at her, I would complain too. Most off the room were heading for the main doors and yawning. I stood still watching and not entirely sure what to do now.

"Excuse me! Miss! Miss Seraphina!" A squeaky voice came from behind me and I felt a gentle tug on my bare arm.

I turned to see a small girl standing next to me, smiling sweetly. She was adorable –probably only two or three years old, with chubby cheeks and big, brown, instantly loveable eyes.

She wore a pink, pointed hat and matching pointy shoes and a cute pink and a white checked shirt half tucked into a dark green skirt. Everything she wore was embroidered with daisies.

"Hi there," I said, bending down on one knee to see her better. She had adorable dark curls peeking out from beneath the hat, which sat on her head lopsided, and she was beaming, wearing the biggest smile I had ever seen.

"I'm Delphinium, your gnome guide. I'm here to escort you to your sleeping quarters," she said pleasantly.

"You're a gnome?" I blurted out before I could stop myself.

"Yes Miss. We live with the Woodwives, who graciously gave us refuge in their domain." She grinned with pride.

It was all too weird! I rose to my feet and looked around for my dad. I just wanted to see him before I went to sleep, but he was nowhere to be seen.

Delphinium took my hand and started to gently pull me towards the door. Finally, with a sigh I let her lead me from the room.

She led the way to my room, chatting non-stop. She told me all about her life working for the Woodwives who, from what she said, seemed to have the better end of the deal. They had agreed to keep the race of gnomes safe in exchange that they swear an oath to work for them. From what Delphinium had said they seemed to be little more than slaves, working all hours - day and night- in the gardens and nurseries.

"My husband, Filbert, said we are two of the best Gnomes here. Our flowers grow the tallest and our patch of grass is the greenest…" I held up my finger to interrupt her. Something she said had taken me by surprise.

"Wait a moment, did you say… your husband?" I stammered under her baffled gaze.

"Yes, that is what I said. My husband. His name is Filbert." She stood with her hands on her hips, still smiling brightly.

For just a moment she looked like my grandma when she was waiting for an explanation. She had that same look on her face that Grandma had when I had done or said something I shouldn't have.

Oh man… I could have really put my foot in it then, but it was just because she still looked like a small child to me. I decided not to voice my opinion, after all I need friends at that time. It wouldn't be the best idea to go offending a whole race.

"Oh right. Yes, of course. I was just checking," I said, trying to mask my shock.

"Humans," she said with a tinkling laugh and proceeded down the corridor beckoning me to follow.

Evidently she knew exactly what I was thinking. It was just another thing I gotten wrong. Great.

I followed her, feeling like a fool. Seriously, how was I supposed to know that gnomes actually existed? It just hadn't occurred to me. I wondered what else I was to discover to be real, flying pigs. I'd already learnt more than I wished to remember.

We walked for a while down a long, winding corridor lined by tall doors. These seemed evenly spread out, with one appearing every few feet. Each was decorated differently.

One was covered in bright yellow roses which were overrun with tiny purple butterflies. I stopped and stretched out my hand to them. The smell was intoxicating, and I had an overwhelming urge to smell them closely. Delphinium pulled back my other arm sharply.

"Careful Miss! Just because it looks pretty doesn't mean that's all it is," she said, pointing to one of the roses.

I watched in horror as a purple butterfly had landed on it and instantly the rose had snapped its petals tightly shut trapping it inside. I recoiled in sickening fear - what kind of flowers *were* they?

"That room belongs to the Warlords. They develop weapons for the Woodwives army. It's not a nice place," she said, edging away from the door.

I followed her lead, shaking my head to rid myself of the smell.

"Filbert had to clean it last year and every night he would come home with burns or cuts." She glanced over her shoulder at the door again and visibly shuddered.

We carried on, past another door covered with poison ivy and one that had small acorns growing right out of the wooden door. As we made our way further down the corridor the doors themselves became larger and were spaced further apart.

"These belong to the Elders. They are a council of advisors to his Majesty. They help make all the decisions and rule the kingdom," she said, smiling up at the doors.

Suddenly the door next to us swung open and another gnome came running out. He was almost the same size as Delphinium and was wearing a very similar outfit, except his was blue and covered in tulips instead of daisies.

I examined his face as he came closer. His smile was warm, genuine and welcoming. He had a brown, wiry beard that seemed to travel to the floor, covering the top of his feet. I had to stifle a giggle as I wondered how he got around without tripping up.

"Oh hello! I'm just attending to Oakley. He wants his afternoon tea in his room." He shook his head and kissed a blushing Delphinium on the cheek. "He's got so much work to do…" he broke off and looked at me. "Who's this?"

"This is Seraphina, the new…" she trailed off and glanced at me somewhat nervously.

"It's nice to meet you Miss. I'm Filbert," he said. He gave Delphinium a quick, reassuring smile.

I shook his hand, which was surprisingly warm and soft. After another wave of kisses to his wife and a whole lot of blushing we waved goodbye to him.

Delphinium seemed to glow with joy after her husband left, and she wasn't making that much sense anymore. In the brief time I'd spent with the gnomes I'd come to realize how easily distracted they could be.

We came next to a circular opening as big as the dining hall and the doors were bigger here than any of the others.

"This is the Royal Circle, for our Majesties and distinguished guests," she said, bowing low to me and looking so proud, as if she had made them personally. I began to wonder if the Gnomes actually had.

The circular opening consisted of four double doors. The first was the biggest and was made of the oldest looking-wood I had ever seen. It had grape vines intertwining around the outside, with little white flowers dotted between the fruit. There was every grape imaginable from green to purple to bright pink. I eyed them sceptically and made a mental note not to touch anything that looked pretty without checking first.

"This is his Majesty's room. It is decorated with grapes and lemon verbena herbs. These herbs were his wife's favorites. She had them on everything she ate." She giggled with fondness at the memory. "And these grapes are his favorite. Each door is decorated with things that symbolize the occupant," she said.

The next door was slightly smaller than the first and was made from a shiny dark wood that looked hard and sturdy. It was decorated with some kind of leafy plant that sprouted big orange flowers every few inches.

"This is curry leaf. It is used by the humans as a form of medicine. These are marigolds which are the plants of protection," she said, smelling one of the orange flowers.

This room obviously belonged to Dana. Who else would have protective and medicinal symbols? I walked straight past, not waiting for Delphinium to finish smelling the flower; she was obviously besotted with Dana.

I strolled over to another door and stared intently at it. It was blooming, covered with lots of different flowers and herbs, and was by far the most elaborately decorated door of all I had seen. Delphinium noticed me and hurried over. She watched me attentively.

"That there is an orchid. This one in particular is extremely rare and usually dies quickly. It's a symbol of the purest of loves. Your parents shared this room before..." she glanced up at me and hurried on quickly. "This one here is a lotus. It symbolizes fertility. And this is a herb known as garlic - another symbol of protection and healing - and I think you humans like to eat this as a garnish." She giggled, clearly finding the idea extremely funny. "Not us gnomes. We don't like the taste or smell of garlic," she said, holding her nose attempting to stop the smell from entering.

I held back a laugh at the little gnome, who I was now becoming quite fond of. I fingered the door and felt a pang in my gut; my mother used to sleep here. When? Did she come here when she had had me? Had we both stayed in the room beyond the door?

Delphinium spoke, breaking my trail of thought. I fingered the lotus once more and moved over to her. "This is your room, Mistress," she said, pointing to a plain door that looked like it was made from maple wood.

My stomach lurched at her words as disappointment spread through me. It made me sad as I looked at it because it was plain and boring - nothing special at all. Delphinium seemed to sense my disappointment and smiled.

"Do not worry Miss, it will start to bloom in a few days when it's looked inside you. It flowers based on your aura." She seemed very pleased with this advice and gestured towards the door.

That made sense. I stretched out my hand towards the door and stopped half way. There was no handle.

"Err...Delphinium? Where's the door handle?" I looked up and down the door again.

She just laughed at me and said, "Not to worry Miss. You need to use your mind to open it." She turned and walked away.

I stood there debating if I should call her back. I decided on the latter - I could open it myself.

I turned to face the door and spoke to it in a confident voice, "Hello, door... Can I come in?" Okay... so maybe my voice didn't come out as strong as I hoped and instead sounded like a complete nut.

I waited for a few seconds, hoping something, anything, would happen. Nothing. I closed my eyes in exasperation; I was not going to lose my temper over a door!

At the same time, I didn't want to stay out there all night and risk someone seeing that I couldn't even open a door. I took a step back to re-examine it. What had Delphinium said? Use my mind. And...*do what*?! I started to feel a little bit frustrated with myself and tried to imagine what my grandma would say.

"Come now Seraphina, it's obvious. Use your *mind* to open the door." Then it hit me. I focused attentively on the door and tried to picture it in my mind.

I could see myself reaching out with my hand and trying to push it open. It was tough at first, almost like the door was pushing back and stopping me from opening it. I reached out more and pushed even harder with my mind. I could feel the muscles in my face screwing up at the effort.

Then I heard a faint click. I opened my eyes. I blinked several times to rid my eyes of the tiny light spots dancing in front of them and saw, to my surprise, that the door was open by an inch or so, but enough to release the catch and push it open all the way.

I took an uncertain step forward, taking a deep breath, expecting something spectacular. When I entered I got a great shock... *my* room! It was just as if someone had picked up *my own* room from Grandma's house and placed it inside the Woodwives' lair.

A sense of familiarity and safety washed through me, calming me and making me smile. I ran towards my bed and flung myself down on it, feeling exhausted. I took one last look at my all- too -familiar room and closed my eyes. I was secretly hoping that when I opened them everything would have been an *extremely* bad dream!

Next thing I knew I was back in the cold, dark wood. A cruel sense of fear was welling up inside me. I wanted to run, but something told me to stay where I was, as I knew I was waiting for something - or someone - but I didn't know what or who.

Maybe it was my mind playing tricks on me because of what had happened the last time I was there. Tension filled the air, and I could sense grave danger, but couldn't make out exactly what it could be. I looked around, squinting into the dark trees and listening acutely for any signs of danger.

Everything was hazy and blurred, but this did little to help my nerves; I jumped at the sound of rustling branches to the side of me. I readied myself for an attack. There was a nicely sized branch to my other side, and I was preparing to reach for it when Grandma came striding towards me through the bushes.

She was carrying a hunter's knife and a sword that looked far too big and heavy for her. Her dark blue blouse was torn at the shoulder, with an ominously dark stain seeping over the top. Her trousers were wet, from sweat maybe, and her hiking boots were covered in mud. I squealed loudly and wrapped my arms around her. She was safe!

I ran to her and hugged her tightly. She patted me lightly on the back as she pushed me to the side, her eyes darting around the forest.

"Grandma," I whispered, "I'm so glad you're here. You're safe!"

"Well, safe as can be for now. Where's your dad?"

"I don't know. We were in the Woodwives' lair. He left at dinner... and I... I went to bed... I must have fallen asleep," I said, comprehension dawning on me.

"I'm here to warn you and your dad!" She tugged my arm and pulled me towards the edge of the forest.

"What! Why?"

"Hiccup has been badly injured. He needs your help," she said looking grave. We started to run towards the edge of the forest and came into the circular clearing that was the entrance to the

Woodwives' lair.

There, curled up on the mossy green, leaf strewn floor, was Hiccup. His once pure white coat was flecked with blood and mud. He *was* injured, and badly! There was a huge gash in his side and cuts on his legs.

"Hiccup!" I screamed, running over to him. "What happened to him?" I shouted at my grandma.

"We don't have much time, Seraphina. You must wake up and tell your dad. We'll wait here for you. Go! Go now, girl! Dreams are one of the most dangerous places for us to be, so go!"

My eyes flew open. Sweat was dripping from my face and a small sharp pain was swelling in the pit of my stomach. I blinked my eyes a few times and jumped off my bed. I stumbled towards the door, tripping on a pair of shoes that were in the way. I staggered on, shaking my head to focus on what I was doing.

I threw my hands out in front of me willing the door to move and it flew open with such force it banged loudly against the wall. That was so much easier than earlier. Maybe it was because I'd done it before, or maybe because I was more focused.

I burst out of my room, back into the circular shaped corridor. I looked around wildly. Panic started to settle into my chest but I knew I had to be strong: no tears! I need to find my dad.

I looked from left to right and my heart leapt at how easy it was to find him. He was with Dana standing in front of his door. They just stood there watching me, expressions of shock clearly etched on their faces.

"Dad!" I started to run towards him. "Grandma and Hiccup are hurt. They're outside the entrance," I stumbled. Dana stared at me sceptically. I could see she didn't believe me.

"How do you know that?" she said mockingly.

I couldn't believe it. Why should I answer her stupid questions? We needed to go, *immediately*! I turned to my dad, "Please Dad. Grandma told me."

"How did she tell you this?" his tone was quiet, calm.

"In a dream," I replied, getting more and more agitated. Even listening to myself I sounded like a deranged lunatic.

My dad and Dana glanced at each other once, then ran with blinding speed down the corridor. It took me several seconds to realize they had moved then ran after them. My heart was pounding in my chest.

We raced up the corridor, across the training ground and through the meadow towards the tunnel of arches. Dana approached the tunnel's end and held her palm up towards the wall of dark bark, revealing a small tattoo I hadn't noticed before.

It was on her palm, just under her thumb and above the wrist. It was a big W, surrounded by a minuscule list of names. Instantly the bark shimmered and dissolved into a doorway. I went to run through it, but found my path blocked by my dad's arm.

"Caution is wise here, Seraphina," he said, pulling his baton out of his jacket pocket. Dana drew her sword from the holster on her back, held it up in front of her face and took a step forward.

She was gone for what seemed like a long time. I looked at my dad with worry. If he would just let me go I could show Dana where Grandma and Hiccup were. Just as I was about to barge my way past him a shadow darkened the entrance where we stood. My dad pushed me backwards behind him and I watched as my grandma came through, carrying Hiccup in her arms.

WHAT HAPPENED NEXT

KENT

I grabbed Seraphina just in the nick of time. I could sense her unease and seized her by the arm just as she made a dash for the entrance.

I knew I shouldn't get mad, but she still had so much to learn. She's always been very gullible and hadn't a clue about the amount of danger she is in.

She turned to look at me, her eyes wide with panic. My heart leapt with pity - she wasn't used to such danger. She couldn't understand my caution, or what was happening. Dana and I just hadn't had the time to stop and explain everything to her.

She had no idea that Maura was well known for planting visions of our worst fears in our minds as we slept. It was perfect for her and a convenient way to control us. She wasn't known as "The Spirit of the Night" for nothing.

Dana and I knew of this ability, of course. It had happened to me on the night of that dreadful day when I lost Talia. I looked back at Seraphina as her mother popped into my mind. Not that she was ever far from it.

"Keep them safe for me. Love and protect them both always," she had said. A small tear formed in the corner of my eye. I brushed it away hastily.

"Caution is wise here, Seraphina," I said attempting to delay her natural reactions which, of course, were the same as mine, only she had no control over them.

She didn't look very pleased with me, so I pulled the baton from out of my jacket pocket to show her I was taking the situation seriously. Dana mirrored my idea, simultaneously drawing her sword. We had become so used to fighting alongside each other that our movements had become synchronised, almost telepathic.

Dana glanced back at me, pulled herself up a little straighter and disappeared through the entrance. I knew she would be okay, even if there was any kind of danger on the other side of the magical barrier. Still, I couldn't help but worry.

As usual it was me pulling behind, trying to act like I had something occupying me so I didn't have to go out first. I am such a coward! I should have gone through the barrier, not Dana.

We had been standing in silence for a few moments when I saw someone coming back through. I raised my baton and held on even tighter to Seraphina, pushing her slightly behind me. If I had to fight, I could. I would!

Luckily, my mother stumbled over the entrance of the Woodwives' lair, barely holding onto Hiccup. I threw my baton into my pocket and ran forward, Seraphina close on my tail - I took hold of Hiccup whilst my mother stumbled into Seraphina's open arms.

Seraphina was strong and quick to catch her grandma that fast. It was a good sign. Maybe my daughter would survive her terrible fate after all. I tried not to think about that and instead turned and ran for the Healing Quarters carefully cradling Hiccup in my arms.

We soon found ourselves there. Mother had been hit by an arrow, non-poisoned thankfully, and was looking slightly better.

I shuddered at the thought of what could have happened if it had been poisoned. The dark elves arrows were coated in a poison that was lethal; it caused immense pain and fever. The poison works slowly, making its way through the body's blood stream and causing vital organs to shut down one after the other. She wouldn't have been able to make it back unaided. Humans were more affected by Maura's poison then magical creatures. Talia was proof of that.

The Healers, a mixture of some Woodwives, gnomes and fairies cleaned the wound and bandaged it up. Mother was back to looking like her stern old self again, which was both good and bad news.

I was listening intently to her account of what had happened after we left them at the house and was trying to keep calm. I could see Seraphina out of the corner of my eye looking pale and fidgety. She would soon have to deal with the pain of guilt that we Basco's have carried around with us for centuries.

"We were surrounded," my mother said, looking at me with a fierce determination. "Kent... there were thirty or forty of them! More than I have ever seen in one place before."

"Are you sure?" I felt slightly sick and mystified.

If it was true it only meant one thing: Maura's powers were growing stronger. That was *not* a good thing. It would make our fate, and Seraphina's destiny, even harder. We were losing valuable time!

"Yes, of course I'm sure," she snapped, "she's getting stronger and her minions are growing in number."

"What happened? How did you get out of there?" I took a seat next to her bed.

"I was fighting the Elves that were in front, at the side of the lake. There was one that was larger than the others and had a Weapon of Power,"

I gasped. The Weapons of Power were meant to be with the

Defenders who were alive. They're the most powerful weapons in existence and only four were ever made and entrusted to Defenders. As Fire Defenders, we were blessed with the Baton of Flames - forged by the Woodwives - when our ancestors proved our worth.

I also knew the weapon for the Water Defender. I immediately felt even sicker than before as the image of Joey came rushing forward. He had used Talia's knife and had held it to Seraphina's throat. The question remains, how did Maura get Talia's blade?

I couldn't bring myself to think about this anymore and held on tightly to my mother's hand.

"I was concentrating all my efforts on him. At first it seemed as if we were winning the fight until I heard Hiccup roar in pain. I had managed to kick the Elf to the ground, but as I turned my back I was hit in the arm by one of the others' arrows.

"I pulled it out and ran towards Hiccup. I could see he was badly hurt. I used the last of my strength to call Peanut to transport both of us into the forest.

"I must have passed out because when I opened my eyes I heard footsteps and opened my eyes to see Seraphina," she finally said, looking over to where Seraphina stood.

"Mother!" I reprimanded. "It was extremely dangerous to Dream Contact."

"Of course I know that, boy! I am the one who taught you how to do it! I couldn't help it - it's not like I can smoke travel like you, and Peanut had gone," she snapped anger spreading across her face.

"Excuse me," Seraphina interrupted, "but what is smoke travel and, err… who is Peanut?"

"Smoke travelling is my ability." I replied. "It means I can transport myself to another place by turning myself into smoke. I will show you soon. Peanut is the winged horse you saw earlier." I watched the expression of incomprehension and confusion spread across her face.

I turned back to my mother. "Carry on. What happened next?"

"I don't really know. The next thing I remember, I woke up in The Circle of Elm, with Hiccup lying beside me. I knew he was hurt, but I didn't know how badly until I saw him. He was in cat form and unconscious. He would never have fallen asleep like that whilst I was unprotected unless he was…" she broke off, glancing towards the door where the Woodwives had taken Hiccup.

"Did you say cat form?" Seraphina interrupted. "What is that supposed to mean?"

"Seraphina," I began, "Hiccup is not a normal cat. He has a special gift… or two." She stared at me, her arms folded across her chest and her brow furrowed.

"Hiccup is a Protector," my mother snapped, like it was completely obvious.

"I know that! He told me that part," Seraphina replied in exasperation.

"Yes, but what you don't know is that Hiccup is a special Protector and has another…err… ability." I stumbled, trying to find the right way to phrase it.

"He is known as a Spiritual Protector," Dana said as she emerged through the door.

We all stood in alarm, except mother, of course, who was still lying on the bed. Too weak to even sit up.

"He has the ability to morph into your Spiritual Guide, a white tiger, as well as being your Protector, in normal cat form," she said. "Kent, can I speak with you a moment?" she added casually whilst strolling back through the door from which she had come.

THE QUEST

SERAPHINA

I stood opened-mouthed as my dad walked off, trailing after Dana without even glancing back. That was really annoying! Since when did she have such a huge amount of control over him? Seriously! I had questions that needed answering. *I* was the one who had found Grandma and Hiccup. It should have been *me* going into that room, after all it concerned my cat.

"Oh sit down Seraphina! You're going to burn yourself out again!" My grandma's voice, snapping in annoyance, yanked me away from my thoughts.

I glanced at her, taken aback, but dutifully sat back down. I couldn't argue with her whilst she was so fragile. What kind of grandchild would that have made me?

"When are you going to learn that it's not all about you?" She spoke as if she could read my mind. She winced in pain. I made to touch her then shrank back. There was nothing I could do for her. I studied her lined face and the thick bandages on her arms and felt immensely guilty.

"I'm sorry Grandma. I'm just frustrated. I have no idea what everyone's talking about most of the time and it makes me feel useless." Tears of anger started to swell up inside me and I could feel my body's temperature rising with the anger.

"I know it's frustrating," she said in a kinder tone. "Your dad and I have not prepared you well enough for this. It's all happened so fast, and this is not how we would usually explain the situation to a new Defender. Let's talk about a few things." She held out her hand for me to hold.

I took it gently in mine. It was cold and rough, with tiny scratches from the bushes all over it. I stared into her wise old eyes that seemed to gleam with worry, understanding, empathy, and most of all. Love - for my dad, for Hiccup and for me.

"First, Dana is right." She paused. "Hiccup can change form, from Protector to Spirit Guide. Do you know what a Spirit Guide is?"

I sat up a little straighter and thought about the dream where Hiccup had spoken to me for the first time.

"It's someone or something who…err… helps you," I said uncertainly.

"That's right, to an extent. Hiccup has chosen you, and as such will help and guide you throughout your life. He can communicate with *you* and only *you* by connecting his thoughts to yours.

"His Spirit Guide form is the white cat you have grown up with. When you need him to protect you or someone else, like back at the house, he will take on the form of a white tiger." She spoke about it like it was the most obvious and ordinary thing in the world.

I was a little stunned, but also felt relieved. I wasn't going crazy, and the more I thought about it the more I realized that I already knew what she was saying. Maybe I just wanted someone to confirm it, I mean other than my cat talking to me in a dream!

"So… Hiccup *can* transform into a tiger?" I knew I had seen him do that back at Grandma's house when we were being attacked by those Dark Elves. The relief I felt from saying it aloud and not have people laugh at me was heavenly.

"How do I get him to transform?" I asked. Excitement flooded through me at the idea,which of course was a mistake. The candle on Grandma's bedside table flickered and spat tiny flames, making us both jump.

Grandma studied me for a moment and then furrowed her brow at the candle. The flame flickered and died down, then went out altogether. I looked at her awe. Had she just done that or had I?

"Ask him to!" Grandma snapped in exhaustion, rolling her eyes at me.

It became obvious as she said it, which of course made me feel like an idiot. That seemed to be happening a lot!

The door which Dana and my dad had disappeared through opened and they strolled back in. My dad looked concerned and Dana was looking like... well, like an *arrogant jerk really!*

My feelings of hatred towards her welled up inside me and again,and the candle beside my grandma relit itself.

"Sweetheart," my dad said, looking grave and staring at the candle, "we need to talk." I had a bad feeling at those words.

"What's wrong Dad?" I asked, not *actually* wanting to know.

"It's Hiccup," he said, glancing at the door. My heart constricted. "He's not doing so good," he sighed and sat down on the chair next to Grandma's bed.

"Why? What's wrong? What can I do to help? *Can* we help him?" The questions just burst from me and the candle spat a small flame into my dad's lap.

He patted his trousers, glared at the Woodwife at the desk and snapped, "Can we remove these please?"

The Woodwife looked up from the book she was reading, nodded and clapped her hands. I turned to the candle just in time to see it vanish!

"Of course *we* can," Dana sneered, bringing us all back to the conversation.

"What is *that* supposed to mean?" I shouted, jumping to my feet and storming around the bed to face her.

"It's exactly what I said. *We*, as in your dad and me!" She took a step closer to me and reached for the dagger that hung at her waist.

My eyes followed the movement and my face began to burn. *Just try it!* I thought.

"Enough!" Grandma shouted and instantly gasped in pain.

I turned back to her side, "Grandma! Are you alright?" I placed my hand on her forehead to check her temperature. She was burning up! Or was that just me?

"I'll be fine as soon as you two stop this ridiculous fighting! Dana, Seraphina is young but strong-hearted and she needs guidance, not rejection. She is not in control of her powers yet. You have to train her!" She turned to me. "Seraphina, Dana is older and wiser than you. You need her guidance, so stop pushing it away otherwise we are *all* going to fail in this battle." No one offered a word of resistance, not even me.

I watched helplessly as she sank back into her pillows with a sigh. The Woodwife from the desk bustled over and handed my grandma a glass of blood red liquid.

I watched as she took it, crumpled up her nose and downed it in a single gulp. She wiped her mouth on the back of her hand. The color returned to her face immediately and she smiled.

"That's better, thank you," she said, handing the glass back to the Woodwife.

"Yes, we can help him," my dad said, as if nothing had just passed between us all.

"How *do* we do that?" I asked, looking directly at Dana and acting nonchalant, just like my dad.

"Do you remember the new charm on Hiccup's collar?" He asked, drawing my attention back to him.

"The one you brought back with you?" It suddenly seemed like a life-time since that day.

He nodded as an image of the charm pushed its way into my mind. Then I remembered the purple glow surrounding it.

I looked up, suddenly comprehending. "It's not just a pretty charm, is it?"

"No, it isn't." He smiled looking pleased at my response. "It's a charm of protection, like I said, but it's also designed to protect your Protector. I discovered it in Argentina when my quest sent me there. Without that charm Hiccup *would* have died already." He paused and looked at Dana. She considered him for a moment then sighed in defeat.

"Your dad has been on a quest for the last eleven years. A quest we have *both* been on…. and now, it's *your* turn to continue in his place," Dana said.

"What quest? In my dad's place?" I turned to him. "Are you not coming with me?"

"No, I can't," he said. He looked at the floor.

I turned to Dana. "What does this quest have to do with my cat?" I was trying to be polite and not let my tone betray me.

"You'll find out if you listen without interrupting," she snapped. I turned back to my dad, ignoring Dana's sneer.

"We were travelling through Argentina and found ourselves in the Cueva de las Manos," he began.

"In the Cave of the Hands?" I asked in confusion and bewilderment. How did I know that?

"Yes, that's right," he said, looking at me with a worried expression. "They were named after two Spanish thieves who took refuge in them after committing terrible crimes.

"It was said that they hid there after stealing the most precious jewels in Argentina. The Argentinians pursued the thieves to bring them to justice, but unfortunately most of them perished in the caves. Some, however, managed to flee and never went back in fear of what they saw," he said.

"Right... so big scary caves with two bad guys in there. How is this connected to Hiccup?" I complained impatiently.

Why do older people take forever to answer a simple question?

"We soon found ourselves trapped inside the caves as a result of an attack and we stumbled into a magical dwelling place," he said dramatically. I sat up straighter as a spark of interest shot through me.

"What kind of dwelling place? Is it like this one? How many are there in the world?" My day was getting more and more complicated as it went on!

"There are probably many dwellings around the world but there are only a couple that we are sure of and have found.

"Most of them have not been discovered as their borders are protected by magic. *This* is part of your quest Seraphina; you must find these magical dwellings and seek an alliance with their people. Not all are the same as this one," he said, a sparkle glinting in his eye.

I could tell he was fond of this place and deep down I *knew* he was very fond of Dana.

"The new dwelling place is the home of the dwarves," he said. The room went silent. I sat for a moment trying to process this.

"Okay. Dwarves... right... *Okay*," I stumbled, like an idiot.

What else could I possible say? For most of your life people stand there telling you things like Fairies and Dwarves aren't real, then in the space of three days you discover actually they are! I mean, they'll be telling me next that Santa is real and actually lives in a mountain in Switzerland or something!

I felt like I was going to break down any minute. There was just too much to take in. My dad seemed to sense this and took hold of my hand, giving it a reassuring squeeze.

"You need to go to Argentina and find the caves. Ask the Dwarves to help mend the charm," he said softly. "We got it from them and they are the only ones who can fix it."

How was I supposed to go to Argentina? I didn't even own a passport and I hadn't a clue where these caves were!

"Do you remember what I said it was made from?" He stroked the back of my hand, jolting me back from my worries.

"Yes, Iridium," I said in a slightly shaky voice.

"That's right. It can only be found in The Caves of Hands and that is why you have to go there."

"Why me?" I asked in alarm. "Why can't you come with me?" My voice was beginning to shake. Of course, I knew the answer before he gave it.

"You are the next Defender and Hiccup is *your* Protector!" Dana snapped indignantly.

I ignored her and continued to gaze intently at my dad, then at my grandma waiting for an answer.

"*You* have to do it Seraphina, if you don't Hiccup will die. Your dad can't go with you - he is needed elsewhere." My grandma spoke in a faint voice that, I'm sure, shocked even her.

I looked at her and felt a sharp stab of anxiety shoot through me. I was not ready for a quest!

"What about you, Grandma? Are you going to be okay?" I let go of my dad's hand and took hers again.

"My life is nearly at an end Seraphina, I am not going to last forever," she stated bravely.

Tears welled up inside me. I was going to cry. How could she say that so simply, like it was just a matter of fact?

She gazed at my face intently and squeezed my hand, "I will have no tears from you Seraphina. Stay strong. I will stay here until the end comes for me and continue on to the next life."

Then she said with a playful smile, "I think I shall come back as a Healer Fairy, I've always liked them."

Out of the corner of my eye I could see my dad fidgeting in his seat. I wondered how he was feeling about all this.

"Go now. Go and make me proud my angel," she said and

turned her head to face the other direction.

I was sure I could see a tear in her eye. I rose to my feet shakily and tried to walk calmly and confidently out of the medical bay.

Dana and my dad followed me in silence. They watched me carefully as I pushed open the next door to where Hiccup was waiting for me.

REALIZATION

SERAPHINA

The room was noticeably different to the one where my grandma lay. It was bright white. Three Woodwives stood next to a small, oval shaped bed, which was waist high and made from grey marble. On the top of it lay an oval shaped basket stuffed with feathers, like a bird's nest.

In the middle of the downy bed lay Hiccup, sleeping peacefully. He seemed fine from the outside. I couldn't see any evidence of injury like on my grandma.

I turned to stare at my dad. "What's wrong with him?" I asked the question in the most confident voice I could muster. "I can't see anything wrong." I turned back to face Hiccup.

"Typical *human* response," Dana said, tossing her hair to one side and walking over to an illuminated wall. I stared after her. That was the second time she had commented on *humans*, inferring they were beneath her, inferior! Well, maybe we were a little, but still I didn't like her voicing it!

"As you can see from these scans, he is far from well," she said, beckoning me over to the wall.

I stared up at the pictures of Hiccup and squinted. All I could see was a cloud of shapes and graying colored patches. None of it made any sense.

Dana shook her head in exasperation, as if she could sense what I was thinking, and pointed to one of the pictures.

"This... is Hiccup," she said in a slow, patronizing tone, pointing to the outside shape.

"Yesssss," I said in an equally patronizing tone.

"This blue bit here is the venom from the Dark Elf's blade. Hiccup shows no signs of damage on the outside because of his magical ability to heal such superficial wounds. He's able to recover quickly from any scrapes, gashes or cuts in a matter of seconds.

"Unfortunately his powers will not work against Maura's evil, poisoned venom. Once it's inside his body he can't fight against it without help." She spoke in a hush, the kind of low tone you would use at a sick friend's bedside.

I just stood there, not really knowing what to say or do. I wasn't entirely sure what was happening to Hiccup and how he was still alive if he couldn't heal himself.

"The venom from the blade will travel through his body, poisoning him from the inside out. The only reason he isn't already dead is because the charm your dad brought back is still working only to half its strength as the blade hit that too - but it has enough power to last until we get to Argentina."

I couldn't say or do anything. I just stood there, starring at the scans. I understood! My cat, my Protector, my *friend* was dying. And it was entirely my fault.

I shouldn't have left him and Grandma there to fight. I should have stayed with them and tried my best.

"Seraphina, are you okay?" My dad asked tapping my shoulder. I pushed his hand aside and strolled over to Dana.

"What do we need to do and where do we need to go?" I asked, determination suddenly flooding through me. I would save him even if I died trying!

KENT BASCO

I watched in silence as Seraphina powered through the door. I was waiting for her worries to crash down on her, but she showed no signs of losing control. That had to be a first!

I had gifted her with Hiccup when she was *very* young and, whether she knew it or not, he had helped her through tough times.

She would not take the news well. I was sure of it. Hiccup was there for her all the times I wasn't and now he was dying. I was sure she would blame herself, ridiculous as it sounds. I knew it would be true because that's how I felt.

"What's wrong with him?" Not knowing how to answer her I looked at Dana, hoping for support.

"I can't see anything wrong," Seraphina said, looking directly at me.

I inhaled deeply trying to answer when Dana saved me. It was so hard for me to talk about this sort of thing. It just brought back too many painful memories of Talia's death.

I watched as Dana explained it all, pointing - a little harshly and patronizingly, I thought - to the area where the venom was trapped.

Watching her finger trace the line around the cat's limbs to the veins where the venom was slowly spreading took me back to that terrible night when it was Talia's picture on the wall of illumination.

I replayed it all in my head again. It was still crystal clear, the same dream-like state that had been tormenting me for years. The paleness of her skin, the shocked look on her face as the venom spread through her body. The pain. She had screamed in unfathomable torment. And eventually there was nothing but the cold, hard stillness of her body as she drifted away, away from me, away from the girls and away from the living world.

I wiped my eyes on my sleeve and tried to shake the images of Talia from out of my mind. I could not afford to lose control. It was Seraphina who needed me now!

She was staring into space, transfixed on a point I couldn't see. I patted her shoulder lightly trying to bring her attention back to the room.

"Seraphina, are you okay?" I felt useless as I asked the question. A fool.

I should have been hugging her or something. I should have been doing more, much more than just tapping her shoulder. Then she seemed to snap out of it, pushing my hand to one side. In the space of a few seconds – and with just three steps – she was back in front of Dana, strong and ready. Something had happened to her. She has accepted her role and was ready to fight to save her beloved cat and friend.

"What do we need to do and where do we need to go?" She spoke in a voice that was transformed, suddenly booming with determination. Her posture had changed too, from slouching sulky teenager to ready and willing adult.

"First," Dana said, with a glance towards me and a small smile in the corner of her mouth showing she too had noticed the sudden change, "I suggest you talk to your dad."

They both turned to look at me. My heart sank. It was time. Time for the Pass Over. The Pass Over of information, of hurt, of uncontrollable torture. And a mission that may never be complete.

I nodded at Dana. "Come Seraphina, there's a lot to do and not much time to do it," I said, turning on my heel and striding back to the door.

I walked towards the training fields with Seraphina at my side. My chest felt as heavy as lead. However, I knew what had to be done if she was to stand any chance of prevailing.

"First I need to talk to you about our family and the events that led us here," I started.

"You already told me that Dad. We were on our way here, remember."

"No sweetheart, not our ancestors and their history. I mean us as in you, me, your mother… and your sister."

MISSING INFORMATION

SERAPHINA

I stood there in complete shock. Had he just said *sister*? He had. I was sure of it. I knew it! My hands were trembling and my heart was racing.

I felt light-headed and a sense of deception hung in the air around me, which suddenly felt stale. My dad studied me intently, watching me twisting my hands around each other. He observed the expression on my face, which was probably a very confused one.

I knew he was waiting for me to respond but nothing came into my mind. I just didn't know what to say, well nothing *nice* anyway! What *do* you say to news like that?

Images started to flash through my mind. I saw my mother standing on Grandma's front porch holding her stomach, and me, as a small child, whispering to a tiny baby with jet black hair in my dad's arms. Then my dad was crying by the fire, an older woman standing over him and holding the same child.

I had no idea where the memories came from. It was like someone had given me access to these files from my past after so long of being told they were classified.

The dream I'd had about my mother, standing on the decking

by the lake battling that monster, came flooding back into my mind again.

"I have a sister!" I exclaimed and knew deep down it was true. I also suddenly realized I had known for years, somehow.

I was shaking even more than before as I started to pace back and forth in agitation. What did this mean? How was it going to affect what I had to do? I had to see her!

"Yes," my dad said, hanging his head and staring his feet. I could see the years of shame he obviously felt written in lines on his face and I instantly felt bad for having snapped at him.

But *I* was the one who had been kept in the dark for so long. I had a right to be angry! How else was he expecting me to act?

"Please sit down," he said, gesturing to a fallen tree trunk. I felt a sudden urge to cry but fought it back with a hard swallow.

I perched on the edge of the crumbling log, vaguely worrying about the stains that would be left on my trousers despite everything else on my mind.

"Your mother and I were so proud the day you were born," he began, smiling down at me.

I crossed my legs and folded my arms, determined not to say anything. I looked across the empty field, behind which the sun was slowly setting, bathing the vast open space in a soft orange light. It seemed like a life time ago when I had been in the same place with Dana trying to use my powers.

"Are you alright, Seraphina?"

"I'm fine," I said in a faint whisper. "It's just a lot to process." I wished I had had something better to say. We sat in silence, which became more and more unbearable as it stretched on.

"I'm sorry," he blurted out, so loudly and suddenly that it shocked me into looking over at him. His face was streaked with tears. Hurt was clearly taking control of him.

But, *why* was he so upset? It was me who had been lied to all those years. I thought of her and what she would look like.

Where was she? Had she been spending time with my dad when I couldn't? Is that where he'd really been all the time? I don't even know her name, or what she looks like!

Anger pulsed through me at this last thought and I just snapped, looking him straight in the eyes, determined to get a truthful answer.

"Why didn't you tell me I had a sister? Is she even human?"

He looked down at me with a faint smile. "Of course she's human." He smirked, like what I had said was funny.

That made me even worse. How dare he stand there and smile about something so serious!

"*I* don't think it's funny. It's the only explanation I could think of for why you never told me," I shouted, instantly regretting losing my temper.

"Calm down, Seraphina!" He took a step closer to me. "I am still your father!"

That hit me as if I had been slapped around the face. I sat back down on the log, my face in my hands, and felt it shift beneath me as he too sat, then felt his hand sliding across my shoulders to hug me.

"Her name is Lana and she lives in England," he said softly. "She is staying at a place called The Royal Dell Boarding School for Young Ladies," he glanced at me, waiting for my reaction.

I just sat there, my face still buried in my hands. I was stunned. What could I say? Not only did I not know anything about her, but she wasn't even in the same country!

"Why haven't you told me about her before? Does grandma know about her?"

I could tolerate my *dad* not telling me, but I had lived with Grandma for years. Why had she never mentioned her?

"Yes, your grandma knows about her. She visits Lana once a year." I felt sick.

Every year Grandma had sent me to camp. She would insist on

it. And every year I would fight with her to not have to go. Now I understood why she was so insistent. I felt betrayed and, worse, it was at the hands of the people I cared about the most.

"Let me explain," he pleaded, obviously expecting a major tantrum. Little did he know I just felt numb.

"Your mother and I were so happy when we found out we were having you. Everything was perfect. Nothing could have made us any happier. We knew right from the start that you would be like me and not like your mother," he stated.

"How could you possibly have known that?" I had always thought I was like my mother.

"Your mother was a Defender. A Defender of Water, Seraphina," he said gravely. "She was amazing - she could make water balls float in the air. She could control an entire lake and make it do whatever she wanted. When she fell pregnant with you we suspected you were going to inherit my gifts because she struggled with her own powers and was consistently dehydrated," he stopped and looked at me.

I was staring at the floor, mystified. So many thoughts ran through my head, confusing me into silence.

"My mother was a Defender too? Why didn't you tell me this before? Why have you left it so long to tell me about this stupid Defender stuff and my own mother?" Tears rolled down my cheeks. I wiped them away and sat up straighter trying to control myself.

"We couldn't tell you until now for your own safety. If you knew who and what you are and had embraced the powers you were born with then Maura would have known, and you would have been a prime target.

"As your powers grow and strengthen so does your aura which, being a spiritual thing, is something Maura can sense. This is part of her powers - the stronger your aura, the more visible you become to her.

"This is why you and Lana were separated. When you were born we were constantly under attack from Maura's minions…"

I interrupted him. "I had a dream of us by the lake. You were attacked by some kind of snake dragon that came out of it. You and Grandma tried to fight it but it was my mother who…" I broke off remembering the roundness of her belly and how she had stopped the creature.

"Yes, that day was particularly terrible. Your mother saved us all. She was the strongest she had ever been when she was carrying Lana. We knew she would be a Defender of Water. There was no doubt about it. The pregnancy was so different to yours…" As he trailed off my instincts started to tell me that he was holding something back from me.

"Lana was an adorable little girl. You never left her side. We were the perfect family," he smiled, reminiscing to himself.

"So what happened? Why did you break us up?"

His face paled. He swayed slightly and stumbled towards the log, his hand trembling. It was obvious I had asked the question he had been dreading.

"It was seventeen years ago," he whispered. "You were two and Lana was one. Your mother and I had received a letter from a friend of ours in Australia.

"New information had come to light regarding Maura and her fate. There was a Wizard, Mojo, who lived in The Wizard's Town in Belgium. He had a vision, a visit from the Fates who revealed a prophecy to him. He knew it was about Maura, but he was foolish and, in a drunken state, told anyone and everyone about the visit. He was, however, still sober enough not to reveal the actual prophecy to anyone.

"Your mother was eager to go and find him so she could hear this prophecy herself, and also to make sure he was well. She was determined that we would be the ones to defeat Maura, and rid the world of her evil.

"We left you and Lana with your grandparents and set off for Belgium. As our journey began we started to notice that we were attacked less and less the further we got from you and your sister. We knew then more than ever, that whenever we were all together it meant more danger. The combination of all our auras, in one place, were too strong to escape notice.

Your mother was horrified when I suggested breaking up the family. I only did it, to keep you safe. Your mother, told me she would lay down her life rather than have us separated.

"We eventually arrived, late one night, at The Wizard's Town. We had seen it many times, but you never quite get over the beauty of it. After all the time it had been since our last visit it was unbelievable.

"The first thing that catches your eye when arriving is the main building in the middle of the town. It is by far the tallest building there with white stone walls and thin windows made from colored glass. The whole building is illuminated by tall street lamps and wall lights. It's beautiful.

We crossed the cobble-stones and over the white stone bridge that spans a small canal. I remember your mother joking about the polluted water, saying how the buildings are immaculate, yet their waters are more polluted than Maura's own toilet."

"She had a great sense of humour and was always making little jokes about Maura. I think it made her feel less afraid." He shrugged and got up off the log, striding a few meters ahead of me.

I just sat there, staring into the black sky. There were only two things I knew now about my mother. She was funny and didn't want us parted, there was so much more to learn about her. My heart pounded in my chest and my breathing became heavier. Tears fell thick and heavy and I felt as if there was nothing I could do to stop them.

My dad turned, saw me and hurried back. He sat down and

placed his arm around my shoulders again.

"I'm sorry, sweetheart. I don't want to upset you. I'll tell you the rest tomorrow. You need to sleep now," he said, trying to pull me to my feet. But I wanted to hear the rest straight away - sleep could wait!

"No!" I shouted, "I'm not going to sleep. You have to tell me everything." I knew my voice was shrill, almost a shriek, but I just had to know more. It couldn't wait.

He placed his arm back round my shoulders and steered me towards the log. He sat me back down and looked directly into my eyes,

"Okay... Okay! If you're sure. So... your mother and I had made our way through the town, taking in all the wonders of a new place. It really is amazing. There were all sorts of different creatures there too..." He broke off as I looked at him sceptically.

"What do you mean?"

"All kinds of creatures visit The Wizard's Town because it's the only place where you can trade magical items safely. Of course, there are other places you can acquire magical objects, but it's definitely the safest place..."

I interrupted him again,

"So is it another secret lair, like the Woodwives', or is it a normal place?"

He smiled at my question and I thought I could see a trace of humor there... yes he was definitely laughing at me. I couldn't help but laugh back. I guess it was a strange question after everything he had told me.

"Yes," he chuckled, "it is a normal place. Ordinary people live and work there." He held up a finger to stop me interrupting him again. "Only those with magical auras can see the things we do. You will find all sorts of magical beings there, from wizards to Trolls," he finished with a smile.

"Will I get to go there?" I asked, fidgeting like a six year old.

"Someday. Yes, I should think so."

I stood up from the log. My mind was racing with so many questions. My dad also got up and took my hand in his. They felt rough and hard, compared to my soft hands. I stared at them, remembering it was only the other day I was having my nails done with Tiff.

We started to walk back towards the medical bay and I began to wonder what she was doing and if she had tried to call me yet. She would be worried, I must call her somehow.

"Your mother and I eventually found Mojo in the town's tavern. He was wasted." He rolled his eyes. "He wasn't always like that; he took to drink after he... well, we just watched him for a while, to make sure he wasn't being watched. After fifteen minutes, several magical outfit changes, and floating tequila bottles we decided it was safe." He laughed at my expression, which must have been showing the confusion I felt.

"He *is* the world's greatest wizard and with such fame and power comes a heavy price. Drinking was his way of dealing with it, I suppose.

Anyway, we waited for another five minutes, just to be safe, before we approached him. It took us a while to get him home and sober – at first he thought me and your mom were two of Maura's minions in disguise." He chuckled at the memory.

"Where did he live?" I asked, picturing all kinds of magical places and fantastic looking castles.

"Well... err...It was nothing but a run down house! It was full of little trinkets, potion bottles, books and tequila bottles. Completely bizarre! Your mother, of course loved it. I never understood it, but it was his father's house."

I looked at him with amusement, just as I stumped my toe on a rock as we left the log and walked through the vast field.

"Careful," he said, grabbing my arm to steady me.

"Why did mom like it?" I rubbed my throbbing toe.

"She said it brought his character to the surface. I never could understand your mother," he said, shaking his head. A small, painful smile played on his lips.

"Anyway!" He blinked rapidly. "We helped him home and he fell asleep, leaving us to explore his now run down home and find some amazing things.

There was a whole shelf of potions of all different colors, pinks, greens, blues, reds, silvers and even golds - but there was one bottle in particular that was the most intriguing. It was filled - with a deep black liquid,which bubbled inside, and the label read

Extreme caution: use in emergency circumstances only!

To draw or pull energy to or from

Transforming the light or consuming it.

It was really intriguing, and I wanted to see what it did but your mother wouldn't let me. She had a bad feeling about it and if there was one thing I had learnt over the years it was never to argue with a woman.

We also found a small, round table full of magical items - necklaces, pens, rings, cups, crystals and hundreds of keys all shapes and sizes.

We must have been exploring the place for an hour at least when Mojo woke up. He was groggy and confused, really in a bad way, and the first thing he did was grab another bottle of tequila.

Your mother, of course was able to persuade him to leave it alone and tell us the information he had held about Maura. He eventually led us to a stone basin. It looked like a bird bath but was full of silver oil. I hadn't seen it before but it wasn't surprising - you always found new and intriguing things his house.

"He started to explain about the basin, which was actually called a Scrying Font. His dad had found it deep in a cave under the Tasman Sea off the coast of New Zealand. He was very fond of it and bragged of the power it was supposed to possess.

"Your mother had become increasingly nervous the longer

we had stayed and wanted to leave. Her instincts were right, of course. Mojo had started telling us about his dream and the telling of the prophecy by using the basin when his house was attacked by the Dark Elves. Your mother and I ran without looking back, something I now am ashamed of. We should have stayed to help Mojo." He looked up at me as he finished, his face a picture of fierce determination which faded to deep remorse.

"Dad, it's not your fault you left. There was nothing you could have done. What would be the point of staying behind just to die?" I patted his back, trying to comfort him. "What did the prophecy say, anyway?"

He looked at me with a strange expression on his face, one I couldn't understand. Was it regret, anger or deception?

"That prophecy was nothing but trouble! Once your mother heard it she became obsessed. She believed it was about us, but her judgment was impaired from hearing it," anger evident in his features.

"What did it say?"

"I don't know the whole of it just what Mojo was able to tell us before the attack." He stared into the distance and recited

"By the next planetary alignment, a choice shall be made.

United together,

Fire and Water, to determine the one true Defender."

"Your mother was adamant it meant her powers in combination with mine would defeat Maura. She was wrong." A ball of flames shot straight from his hand as he spoke. It hit a tree, setting it on fire.

Before I could do so much as shout several Woodwives emerged from the surrounding woods and doused the tree.

"I'm so sorry," he called over to them, looking sheepish.

"What was that?" I asked, my eyes bright with eagerness. "Could I do that?"

"It's a power you will soon possess," he said, glancing down at his upturned hands. "I lost control there. I'm sorry. Our emotions can be one of our greatest weapons but also our greatest weakness." He glanced over at the tree, which was now magically restored and looked healthy again.

"What's your fatal flaw?" I asked.

He looked directly into my eyes and I felt a shudder run through me.

"I'm afraid," he said simply. He turned his back to me. I thought about that for a moment, walking slowly behind him. What would my dad be afraid of and how could it be his fatal flaw?

"Your mother and I had left you and Lana with your grandparents on the day we set out to defeat Maura. I can still remember it perfectly; the sun was shining brightly, and the sky was blue and clear. The breeze was warm and I remember the sweet smell of honey from the bee-hives by the lake.

"Your mother was beautiful... her hair was pulled up into a high ponytail and her face shone in the summer sun. We were on our way to Veytaux, Switzerland to find Maura's castle.

"I had tried to talk her out of going for nearly two weeks, but she was determined to see it through. When we arrived at the boundary line to Maura's castle and I was still trying to persuade her to turn and go home.

But she was so hard headed and determined to put an end to Maura's reign that she didn't stop to think about what we had heard. It was obvious we didn't know all of the prophecy and I had a bad feeling about acting on it so quickly." He looked at me and sighed.

My instincts immediately flickered; something was wrong with the way he was acting.

"Why do I have the feeling that you've lied to me about more than just Lana?" I put the question to him nervously.

"I'm so sorry, but please try to understand. Your grandma and

I were only trying to protect you and keep the promise we had made to your mother." He shuffled his feet and hung his head. "We had managed to get inside the boundary wall when we stopped, by a dragon shaped rock, to take a rest.

I was still trying to persuade her to go home when the attack began. Maura had sent her Spirit Warriors after us." He stopped and looked up as I gasped.

I wasn't sure what Spirit Warriors were and I most definitely didn't want to find out.

"Yes, Spirit Warriors. They are the tormented, twisted souls of what were once good and loyal people. Maura has power over them more than the power over the living. She can command them to do what she wants them to. She can also physically hurt them with the power of her mind, causing unbearable pain and torture. We had encountered them before when we had first met. Your mother was just as determined then as she was at the end." He squinted out across the field with a faraway look on his face. I knew he didn't like what he was about to say.

"I had grabbed hold of her hand, tightly, and we were running as quickly as we could. I remember looking back and tripping over a dead shrub. It started to grow and a vine strapped itself around my ankle, dragging me to the ground. Talia was still running ahead of me, and I remember being relieved that she was at least safe.

I was trying to grab my baton from my pocket when she stopped to look at me." He paused and looked me straight in the eye, tears streaking down his cheeks. My heart restricted with pain as I watched my dad cry for my mom.

"She shot a stream of water from her hands and the shrub instantly released me and sank back into the ground. Of course, by then it was too late - the Spirit Warriors had caught up to us. We fought with all the strength we had left when…." His tears fell thick and heavy and I just stood there feeling a heavy weight pressing against my chest.

"One of the Spirit Warriors had sunk its hand through your mother's chest and poisoned her heart," he finished, before breaking down sobbing.

My tears over flowed as I could feel a burning, passionate, hatful heat rise through me. I hated the Spirit Warriors and I hated Maura even more. She had made them kill my mother, who hadn't drowned in the lake like my dad and Grandma had said.

I made a silent vow with myself that I would do everything in my power to kill her and rid the world of these evil creatures. Not for me, or even for the force of good, but for my mom.

NIGHTMARE

KENT

I watched as Seraphina balled up her fist slightly in anger. She began to glow brighter and brighter. I knew I had to calm her down before she lost control and set fire to the field. I might have set fire to the tree, but I still had some control. She would end up unintentionally killing someone.

"Seraphina, you must calm down! You're losing control," I chided.

She turned on me quickly, her face distorted with rage. I stumbled backwards a few steps.

"Calm down?" She shouted the question, her voice breaking.

Her aura was changing, shifting into a muddy-red, and her hair began to kick up around her face and head, like a wild wind was stirring up and howling through it. The energy she emanated was so strong that it whipped her hair into a wild frenzy. Her hands began to burn with a bright orange flame, licking its way up her forearms and lighting her face in a golden glow.

I gasped in shock. This was rare for a Defender so young and raw. It had taken me four years to learn to ignite even the smallest flicker of a flame on my hands, yet she was practically setting her whole hand and half her arm alight.

"Seraphina," I started, looking pointedly down at her clenched fists. "Look at your hands."

"I don't care about my hands! How *dare* you stand there and tell me to stay calm! For my entire life Grandma has told me I lost my mom after she drowned in the lake!" Her face was shining red and her eyes burned with anger.

"You and Grandma have lied to me! I have a sister as well!" she shouted, striding over to confront me, her face pushed towards mine.

I glanced down at her burning hands and took a step back. I had no need to fear - fire can't hurt any of us Fire Defenders - but there was so much hurt on her face I just couldn't bear to look at her.

"Please calm down…" I moved my hands up running them down my face in frustration, blocking my view of her eyes. "I know it's hard to understand and accept but it was for your own good." The words stumbled out of me and I quickly realized I had said the wrong thing. It was thunderous and I could tell by her eyes that she was past reasoning.

"How exactly do you figure that? How would these lies help me?" Her breathing was heavy and her hands were still encased in flames.

I couldn't pull my eyes away from them, mesmerised by the flames licking around them. How had she not passed out? Even after thirty seven years I couldn't hold a flame for more than ten minutes without feeling dizzy, but she was showing no signs of tiredness at all.

"You were safer being apart. Your aura is strong and when you were together your auras were too noticeable," I shouted losing my head altogether.

She stared at me. Her breathing started to ease off and was becoming shallower. The flames suddenly extinguished and she crumpled to the floor.

"Seraphina," I sighed. She was crying and her hands had returned to normal.

"I'm so sorry," I whispered into her ear, taking her my arms and holding her tightly. "It was best for you both not to know about each other. If the worst had happened and Maura had discovered either of you then you wouldn't have been able to tell her about the other. It was a plan we had spent days agonising over. It had nothing to do with us not loving you or trying to deceive you." She tried to push me away but I just held on tighter.

We sat there for several minutes, Seraphina crying and me stroking her auburn hair when a loud bang and flash of white light startled us both.

"What was that?" She jumped to her feet. I glanced around us. Our walk had taken us to the very bottom of the training field, with the palace to our left. I squinted back at the Woodwives' Palace and gasped.

"We must go, now!" As I shouted the words, Seraphina was already moving towards the palace.

"Grandma!" she screamed as she ran.

SERAPHINA BASCO

I stood in the main forecourt watching the scene unfold before me. Littered all around, dotted every way I looked, was fire and destruction. Huts and trees were lit up with orange ribbons of flame, and some of the Woodwives were running, screaming as their cloaks were also a-blaze. This made my stomach flip with disgust and panic. What was happening? I watched one run past me holding a hose directed onto another.

Woodwives were running around and screaming – in fear or cry of battle I couldn't be sure – then I noticed Dana, in the center of it all, shouting orders to her warriors. Fairies were tearing about trying to extinguish the flames with their wind, rain or water powers and the gnomes were also running back and forth from the well with little pails full of water, not that it was doing much good. They were so small that their tiny pails weren't helping that much.

Suddenly my breath was knocked out of me, like someone had punched me in the gut. As I stood watching all the commotion, clueless as to what to do I saw Grandma was in the center of it all.

She was wielding a purple flamed baton, battling several Dark Elves. I watched in disbelief as it swirled around her waist and up above her head, instantly taking down everything in its path. The whip of her baton was slicing through the Elves like they were made from paper.

Her hair had fallen loose, from her usually neat French braid and was swishing around her shoulders. Her face was stern and concentrated, betraying no sense of fear or weakness from her injuries, and she looked more like a ribbon dancer than a warrior. She looked deadly, but also had an air of grace and poise.

As she swirled around, like a ballerina once more, I saw what was happening clearly. Arranged in front of my grandma, in a semi-circle, was a line of advancing Dark Elves. There had to be a hundred of them all edging forward but they dared not come too close to Grandma's weapon.

Every few seconds the largest Elf, who must've been the leader, would push another into Grandma's path, making her back up slowly. A few had shields but quickly found out they were useless against her baton as she whipped each one clean from their arms.

I stood transfixed for a few seconds then dashed forward to help, but my dad materialised in front of me, emerging from a whirl of smoke. He pushed me back towards the safety of the meadow.

"Go! Seraphina! Now! I will help your grandma." He held up a finger to stop me interrupting him. "Quickly, follow those two," he pointed to the gnomes, "and get Hiccup to safety. Please!" He begged with big, pleading eyes. For once I couldn't and didn't want to argue.

I turned to see where he was pointing and spotted Filbert and Delphinium a few strides away and cradling Hiccup between them - still in his feather basket.

I ran straight towards them as fast as I could but found my path blocked by the ugliest Elf I had ever seen. It was taller than me and smelt like a week's worth of trash that had been left out in the sun. I clapped my hand over my nose and mouth, trying to control the feeling of sickness that was rising from my stomach.

I took another few steps backwards, still with my hand clamped over my face. He smiled - a crooked,blackened smile - at me and raised his sword, ready to strike. I stared, eyes wide with fear, into the red eyes of the monster that would kill me.

Then out of nowhere the tip of a sword jutted out from the middle of his chest, stopping just short of my face. He fell forwards, his arms still raised but his smile gone, and hit the floor as I jumped out the way. Dana stood in front of me.

"Run," she said simply and raced off behind me, her sword held high. I couldn't believe what had just happened. She had saved my life. I watched as she ran and felt a pang of guilt hit me. I would never doubt her again!

"Miss! Miss! Come…. come quickly please," a little gnome I hadn't seen before had appeared at my feet and tugged at my pants.

I ran after the tiny gnome, fleeing across the battlefield and jumping over the stinking bodies of the dead Elves that littered the ground. I had to sidestep Woodwives as they fought, narrowly missing a sword point a couple of times.

I paused only once on my rush through the battle to pick up a sword that lay abandoned from the floor. We ran through the fields where I had trained with Dana only the day before and where I had walked through moments ago with my dad. We finally stopped in front of a giant thorny bush covered with tiny roses. I stumbled slightly as I realized where we going. I couldn't go in there - it would have cut me to shreds; the thorns had to be two inches long.

"Don't worry, miss. It's not what you think," the tiny gnome said and took hold of my hand.

I squeezed my eyes shut and could smell the sweet scent of the roses as I took a few steps forward. I could feel the thorns on my skin, but was surprised to find they were soft not sharp, purely an illusion. I allowed the tiny Gnome to guide me through and started to relax after a while.

"You can open your eyes now miss, you are safe with Cubby."

I opened my eyes and gasped.

"It is our secret boat, miss." Cubby said.

A magnificent ship sat upon a golden lake. It was as tall as our house and as long as a football field. It was made from what looked like tough iron, but had a strange silver-green metallic shimmer to the outside.

Directly in the middle of the ship stood a single, deep green mast holding a lighter green sail that billowed magnificently. I took in the scale of it and found myself whistling in awe. I could see a golden wheel at the helm of the ship, standing big and bright in the moonlight. I could just imagine how it would look sailing across the ocean. Beautiful!

As Cubby started pulling me forward to board the severity of the situation suddenly came flooding back to me, like a wave crashing over a rock. I could hear the distant bangs, cries for help and the battle cries of the warriors, all coming from the Wood-wives' Lair and flashes of light. I could also smell a revolting mixture of burning flesh and wood, mixed with the chill of the breeze coming from the lake. I stopped abruptly, looking back to the flames and screams. My grandma and dad were still in there. I hesitated. I just couldn't leave them there.

"Miss... help me! Quickly, please... Miss Delphinium needs help with Hiccup," Cubby urged in a squeaky voice.

I looked down at the small gnome and was able to snap into control of the situation. I ran round to the side of the ship where the boarding ramp lay, bobbing up and down slightly with the delicate waves of the lake.

Delphinium and Filbert were struggling to lift Hiccup's basket onto the ramp. I ran forward, throwing the sword to the floor, and scooped up Hiccup into my arms, holding him tightly. No sooner had I touched him than a feeling of ease welled up inside me. Despite the situation I had a feeling he was helping me as much as I was him.

"Let's get him on board," I said taking control.

Delphinium, Filbert and Cubby all followed me up the ramp and onto the ship. They instantly ran across the deck to various points, loosening ropes or lifting up hatches. I watched them as I scanned the deck for a safe place to put Hiccup.

I found a large empty box at the foot of the helm that was secured to the floor with ropes. I placed Hiccup's feather basket in there and ran back to the side of the ship, staring in the direction of the thorny bush from where we had come.

The air around me started to stir. It was cold and the sky somehow began to blacken again even though, it was already the dark, early hours of the morning. I descended down the ramp and walked cautiously towards the rose bush.

I looked at the bush, ahead and my heart pounded with anticipation and anxiety. I felt a slight tugging at the bottom of my pants again and Cubby stood there, looking up at me with fearful eyes. There was a loud scream and he jumped in fear.

"Miss, we must leave now before the bad ones discover our boat!"

"Not yet, Cubby," I said, flashing an encouraging smile at him. "Just wait a few more minutes. My dad and grandma will be coming soon." I spoke in the strongest voice I could muster.

He didn't look very happy, but I didn't care. I wasn't going to go without my family. I couldn't. We waited for ten minutes as the noises from the lair died down and the sky had began to lighten with the dawn. Most of the smoke had started to clear.

I was hoping that the fighting had stopped and we could go back to find my family and my new friends. Then the bush began to stir. I held my breath.

Suddenly it was pushed aside and out ran Trixie and the other two Woodwives I had practiced with yesterday. She ran straight towards the ramp, shouting and waving her hands.

"Pull up the anchor! Pull it up!" She ran up the ramp, bouncing onto the ship's deck. I stared at her as she barked orders at the gnomes and other Woodwives.

"No wait! My dad," I shouted back at her.

"There's no time to wait! We must leave now. Pull up the anchor!"

The others hesitated for a split second, then ran to the windlass preparing to pull up the anchor.

"No!" I shouted. "Not yet!"

"I am in charge right now and our mission is to get you to safety! That means leaving, now! I will not hesitate in knocking you out if it means getting you to safety!" She glared at me with annoyance on her face.

Just then the sound of shouting came from the bush. I spun on the spot, my chest heaving with emotion. The branches move to one side and Dana emerged, blood running down the side of her face. She was hauling someone on her back.

I ran past Trixie and down the ramp to Dana to help and, with a shudder, I realized it she was carrying my dad. He was half conscious - his eyes flickering and rolling backwards. His hands were trembling and he smelled of sweat and blood.

I grabbed his other arm and threw it over my back and shoulders, taking as much of his weight as I could, and started to walk towards the ship with Dana. We had just reached the ramp when the sounds of battle grew and Grandma's voice carried across the wind.

"Give it up! I can do this all day." She laughed wildly.

Then she came bursting through the bush, swinging her baton with unbelievable strength as she whipped it into the advancing rank of Dark Elves.

Dana and I struggled to get my dad up the ramp and onto the boat. We placed him carefully on the floor of the deck and Dana took the wheel. The anchor was raised, the sail billowed in the wind and Dana was at the helm. We were pulling away slowly from the docking. I watched with tears in my eyes as Grandma slashed at the remaining horde, stabbing with her dagger and whipping with her baton.

The Elves lay defeated on the ground and Grandma stood to the side of the dock, her weapon at her side as her hair fluttered in the wind. She waved. I waved back, feeling proud. She was really something. Dana placed a hand on my shoulder. "Your grandma will be fine. She's one of the greatest Defenders we have ever seen," she said quietly.

That's when we saw it. One of the Elves had struggled back up from the ground, grasping a spear. I screamed a warning too late as it was thrust into her back, piercing her body and emerging through her chest. Trixie, who was standing beside Dana, immediately shot an arrow directly into the Elf's head. It crumpled to the floor, finally dead.

"Grandma!"

She smiled back at me and blew a final kiss as her knees buckled. She fell on her side, still and peaceful in death. Tears streamed down my face, rolling off my cheeks onto my out-stretched arms.

"I love you," I whispered. I slide down the side of the ship, my face in my hands.

"Seraphina... Dana!" someone from behind us called softly. We turned around to see the Woodwives and gnomes gathering around my dad. I ran over to him, my feet sliding on the deck's surface, and threw myself down at his side.

He opened his eyes and looked up at me. He held out his trembling hands and took mine in his.

"Seraphina," he said in such a quiet voice I had to crouch closer to hear him.

"It's me, I'm here Dad," I said in a surprisingly calm tone, even though my tears were still rolling off my cheeks.

"You must continue on the quest. You must..." he broke off in a cough. "You must help Hiccup. You need him." He began to breathe at a rapid pace and I noticed for the first time that an arrow was sticking out of his side.

Dana gasped and reached for it. She pulled it out and my dad let out a painful cry.

"Filbert! The medical bag, quickly!" I watched as she rummaged through it and pulled out a bottle of gold-looking liquid. She poured some onto his wound and I watched in amazement as it began to close. Even the blood began to be drawn back into his body.

"Kent, can you hear me?" Dana asked softly stroking the side of his face.

I watched her lovingly caress my dad's face when it hit me: she was in love with him!

"Yes," he said in a cracked voice.

Dana held his hands to her lips and kissed them lightly. I was stunned into silence. For the first time I understood.

He turned his head back to me and smiled. "You need to find Lana and work together. Tell her everything I have told you. Tell her I'm sorry. Please tell her I love her very much and you too Seraphina, my angel. My firebird." His eyes closed and his hand fell limply to the deck.

"Dad? Dad!" I screamed in shock. "Is he...?" I asked Dana my nerves shattering.

"No, he's just sleeping. He'll be fine by morning. We're lucky the arrow was not poisoned," Dana said, standing up and walking towards Trixie.

She ordered her and the others to carry my dad down to his sleeping quarters. I followed dutifully behind. I sat there for what felt like hours holding my dad's hand and thinking about everything I had seen and been told over the last few days.

I didn't cry. If anything all I felt was anger towards Maura, and I knew more than ever that she had to be dealt with. Once and for all.

I kissed my dad lightly on the forehead, stroked Hiccup and left the room to find Dana. My journey was not over. In fact it was only just beginning...